BY KEVIN NGUYEN

Mỹ Documents

New Waves

MỸ DOCUMENTS

MỸ DOCUMENTS

—

A NOVEL

KEVIN NGUYEN

ONE WORLD
NEW YORK

Published in the United States by One World,
an imprint of Random House, a division of
Penguin Random House LLC, 1745 Broadway,
New York, NY 10019.

ONE WORLD and colophon are registered trademarks of
Penguin Random House LLC.

LIBRARY OF CONGRESS CATALOGING-IN-PUBLICATION DATA
Names: Nguyen, Kevin, author.
Title: Mỹ documents: a novel / by Kevin Nguyen.
Description: First edition. | New York, NY: One World, 2025.
Identifiers: LCCN 2024045741 (print) | LCCN 2024045742 (ebook) |
ISBN 9780593731680 (hardcover; acid-free paper) |
ISBN 9780593731697 (ebook)
Subjects: LCGFT: Novels.
Classification: LCC PS3614.G888 M93 2025 (print) |
LCC PS3614.G888 (ebook) | DDC 813/.6—dc23/eng/20241001
LC record available at https://lccn.loc.gov/2024045741
LC ebook record available at https://lccn.loc.gov/2024045742

Printed in the United States of America on acid-free paper

oneworldlit.com
randomhousebooks.com

1st Printing

First Edition

Book design by Edwin A. Vazquez

The authorized representative in the EU for product safety and
compliance is Penguin Random House Ireland, Morrison Chambers,
32 Nassau Street, Dublin D02 YH68, Ireland,
https://eu-contact.penguin.ie.

"I fell in love with my country when I was a prisoner in someone else's."

—John McCain

MỸ DOCUMENTS

EXTENDED FAMILY

—

Bà Nội's story had everything: history, conflict, romance, loss—all the elements of a compelling tragedy.

During the war, she'd been the one who kept the family safe. Whether it was bribing corrupt government officials or dealing with the sudden imposition of U.S. soldiers, Bà Nội paid off whomever and cooked meals for whatever foreigner, as distasteful to her as it was, if it meant not causing any trouble.

Her husband was a different story. He was a poet, a brave soul who never lied and held true to his beliefs. Not exactly ideal during a civil war, Bà Nội used to joke. But she admired his perseverance, even when his convictions put the burden of breadwinning and childrearing on her. Ông Nội made pitiful money teaching at the university. He was invested in the lives of his students, hosting late night "discussion groups" with them at the bar and returning in the early morning, just when Bà Nội was getting their own kids ready for school and herself for work. She loved him anyway.

Ông Nội had been warned by the police, who suspected he was distributing antiwar material. Which, of course, he was, despite Bà Nội's pleading. Bitterly, she explained: a man would rather risk everything, including the livelihood of everyone he cares about, than be told what he shouldn't do.

Saigon fell, and many of Bà Nội's friends and extended family attempted to flee. What was the rush, though? The war was over, and the government she'd lived under had lost. But how much worse could this regime change be? The brunt of the violence had ended, and Bà Nội imagined that it would just be a new set of bureaucrats looking for pay-outs, and soldiers in different uniforms tromping around the streets. They could leave in time, and on their terms, rather than scrambling for the nearest exit. The French occupation of Bà Nội's childhood had left Saigon with a number of cinemas, and with her a love of film. She hoped they could go to Paris.

The North's sweep through the South had been more vindictive than she'd expected. The Communists seized all of her money and converted her savings into a new, worthless currency. Soldiers ransacked the home she had raised her four children in, taking everything of value, except for the small stash of jewels she'd hidden in a statue of Buddha.

Bà Nội felt foolish for not getting her family out sooner. Now it would take months to arrange safe passage out of Vietnam. She tried everything, but most of her attempts were thwarted by logistics or made unfeasible by cost. One arrangement involved purchasing a boat with a close friend. That ended in betrayal, the "friend" taking the vessel to sea without notice. Years later, Bà Nội told this story without a hint of anger in her voice. Maybe the decades since had softened her; maybe she just understood what was at stake. In desperate times, she said, the only thing left was family.

Eventually, Bà Nội recognized that getting everyone out of Vietnam at once was impossible. But vanishing one by one, that was less impos-sible. She schemed ways to migrate her children out of the country in-dividually, so as not to be noticed. Paris was not an option without attendance at a French school, but the United States, perhaps out of American guilt, was easier. Her eldest son was granted a visa after en-rolling in a university in the Midwest; another son she handed off to missionaries, who promised that he would have a rewarding and faith-filled life in the States. The next, a daughter, school age, was gifted as a temporary servant to another family that had been granted transit to New England. Each departure took something of her with them, every missing child reducing the breadth of what she could feel. By the time the third had left, Bà Nội's spectrum of emotion hadn't narrowed but washed out, like photographs faded by the sun. Even at the movie the-ater, where she had most enjoyed laughing and sobbing in the dark, her sensations felt diminished. Bà Nội told herself she would be restored when she saw them all again, safe.

The last of her children was four years old, too young to be sent off on his own. Bà Nội arranged an escape for her young son, herself, and her husband by way of a commercial fishing boat—a journey that she knew would be miserable and treacherous, especially with pirates so eagerly raiding ships now that the U.S. Navy had withdrawn. The hope was that the boat could make it far enough in the South China Sea to end up in a refugee camp in Malaysia, or perhaps Indonesia. This path wouldn't take them to the U.S. directly, but for Bà Nội, it was drifting in the right direction.

The plan was to meet at the dock and leave together, as a family. The departure was late on a Tuesday evening, a getaway made less conspicuous by nightfall. But as the moon rose, Bà Nội still couldn't locate her husband. She assumed that he was already there and took her four-year-old aboard. She scanned the deck, but Ông Nội was nowhere to be found. An hour passed, and he never materialized. Bà Nội pleaded with the captain to delay, but every minute they lingered increased their chances of getting caught. If she wanted to wait for her husband, the captain said, she could do it on land.

After so many failed attempts to flee, Bà Nội knew she couldn't leave opportunities on the table. She hoped that Ông Nội might eventually find his way to the U.S., to reunite with them later, after she'd tracked down their other three children, and they could be a family once again.

Bà Nội spent the journey dizzied by seasickness, thinking furiously about her husband. How could he not have shown up? He was probably still in Saigon, drunk again, involving himself in the petty dramas of his pupils. Maybe that was all he ever actually wanted—to be swept up in the small, frivolous lives of young people, the desires of a coward.

It was months after arriving at the Galang Refugee Camp in Indonesia when Bà Nội received word about her husband. The day they were set to depart, police had seized Ông Nội at his university office. A naïve student had passed on his anti-Communist writing—some bad poems, barely distributed. In prison, he'd gotten sick and, with little medical support, had died of pneumonia.

Ursula teared up every time she heard this part of her grandmother's story. It hit her in the gut: the strong matriarch who sacrificed everything for her family, making the unbearable choice of leaving her husband behind, and having to live with that decision for the rest of her days.

THROUGHOUT HIGH SCHOOL, Ursula wrote and rewrote Bà Nội's journey. She kept getting rewarded for it. As a paper, it was the champion among final projects in an American history class, one teacher so thrilled with it that Ursula was given special merits by the administration at the end of the year. It was the personal statement on her college applications, which got her into several schools she had no business getting into with her middling GPA and average test scores. That same year, she won an essay competition writing about how her grandmother's life made her feel, which came with a two-hundred-dollar reward—an extraordinary amount of money that Ursula immediately spent on a bag.

But Ursula knew she couldn't use her grandmother's story forever. Adulthood meant creating your own narrative, not regurgitating the details of someone else's. Yet, by crafting and refining the tragic arc of her grandmother's story, she learned something about what people liked hearing. Nobody wanted a tale about refugees where an entire family makes it out unscathed. For it to be compelling, to be important, there needed to be a sacrifice. Something had to be lost.

It wasn't until Bà Nội's disheartening prognosis that Ursula had started taking an interest in her grandmother's history. To Ursula it seemed so dumb, so cruel, that a woman could overcome such tremendous obstacles and succumb to the same boring fate as millions of other people. That it was the most common variation, breast cancer, felt like an even greater insult.

The diagnosis had activated something in Bà Nội. Now she wanted to write her story down, from the beginning: growing up impoverished in Vietnam, the American war, fleeing, the long road to immigration. Hers was a life of constant and great escape. And now Ursula felt the burden of both being respectful to her bà nội's wishes and trying to squeeze as much information out of her sick grandmother as she could.

"Why did you ask me?" Ursula asked. Though they hadn't been close, Ursula was flattered that Bà Nội had wanted her help. There were other, older grandchildren, ones who were full Viet and spoke the language and spent more time with her.

"Because you are the writer in the family," Bà Nội had said, as if there could only be one.

They lived far apart—Bà Nội in California and Ursula now at college in New York—so they talked often by phone. The project may have been Bà Nội's idea, but it wasn't easy to get her to open up. So Ursula had to start with small talk: things going on at school, the city, what she observed on the subway. Bà Nội delighted in hearing about the ordinary, no matter how many times Ursula charted her path from the library to the dining hall and back. Even as her days became more precious, Bà Nội had little to say about them. Cancer was vicious, and it was mundane.

Bà Nội had an incredible story, but all she ever wanted to talk about were the things she liked. She listed out her favorite foods, of which there were plenty, mostly soups. (Not knowing Vietnamese, Ursula did her best to jot them down phonetically.) Bà Nội's favorite sport was football. (Omitted by Ursula: her fondness for gambling on the NFL.) Favorite color? Purple. Favorite song? "Stayin' Alive." Favorite city? Paris, or San Jose. Movie? Inexplicably, *Babe: Pig in the City.*

"*Babe . . . Pig in the City?*" Ursula asked, just to be sure.

On that call, instead of hearing about her grandmother's extraordinary life, Ursula was stuck hearing the plot details of a movie about a talking pig. Bà Nội had seen it probably a hundred times. Ursula promised to watch it someday.

When Ursula got her to open up about her childhood in Vietnam, Bà Nội spoke with such remove and finality, like everything that had happened was inevitable and everything was now in its right place—the cold distance of history. When faced with the limits of her mortality, Bà Nội was relaxed about the whole thing. She'd had a long and gratifying life, something that couldn't be said of many of her friends and family. She had four beautiful kids, and they'd had even more beautiful kids of their own.

Ursula found this phrasing, the way her grandmother had crafted it, particularly tricky. "Even more" was an elegant way of glossing over the truth: that Bà Nội could not say how many grandchildren she actually had. It was Ursula's father who was responsible for the uncertainty. He had a tendency to start families and leave them, and it had happened at least twice, as far as Ursula knew. She took some pride in believing that she was the first kid, though in reality, she could never be sure.

Listening to her grandmother talk about her past, Ursula found that one of the things that seemed clearest was that in their family, people were always leaving.

DURING THE WINTER of Ursula's junior year, Bà Nội's condition rapidly worsened. Near the end, she could barely muster the energy for a conversation. But Ursula would never forget one of their last calls.

There had been a stranger on the subway—an unwell man in Chinatown who had chased Ursula out of the car and called her a slur. She was shaken up but otherwise fine. Bà Nội assured her granddaughter that she had done the right thing: never confront, just run away. You must always think of yourself first, Bà Nội said. Survival is a selfish act.

It was New York. Ursula assured her grandmother that the weird interaction on the subway hadn't been a big deal, that here, it happened all the time. But on the phone, Bà Nội was unusually talkative, especially about life in Saigon, about what it took to survive. Ursula listened, unsure what to make of what her grandmother revealed next: it hadn't been a tragedy of timing that had kept her husband in Vietnam. The story of him dying in prison was just something she told people because it made them stop asking questions. In the end, how do you reason with someone whose beliefs outweigh their common sense? What do you do with a person whose principles are so immovable that it leaves them incapable of caring about anyone else? You do what you have to do, of course.

"Bà Nội," Ursula finally asked, "what are you trying to tell me?"

She was telling her granddaughter something that no one else had heard. That Ông Nội never had a place on the fishing boat, that he never even knew about it. Bà Nội *had* made a decision all those years ago. But it wasn't a hard one.

AT THE FUNERAL, Ursula found herself bowing and chanting for nearly two hours, a white ribbon tied around her head, as part of a Buddhist ceremony that was both confusing and hard on her knees.

She felt out of place, as she often did around extended family. Ursula and her younger brother Alvin were the only half Asians. And nearly everyone at the service was speaking Vietnamese, with the exception of Jen and Duncan. They were, technically, younger half-siblings, sharing the same absent dad, but out of kindness, the family referred to them as cousins. Ursula watched Jen and Duncan scan the room, hoping their father would appear. Maybe it was the wisdom that came with being the kids who'd probably been abandoned first, but Ursula and Alvin knew that he wouldn't.

The reception was held at Bà Nội's house, a modest single-level two-bedroom in the sprawl of San Jose. The event was lively for the occasion of someone's death—Ursula's Vietnamese family was always loud, always laughing. They were fun to be around, but today, it sickened her. *Everyone is sad,* Ursula thought. *Why aren't they acting sad?* She eased herself down the hallway, resolved to hide away in her grandmother's bedroom.

"Where are you going?" Jen asked.

"Homework," Ursula lied. She'd been excused from her academic commitments for bereavement. It wasn't lost on Ursula that her grandmother's life had gotten her into college, and now her death was getting her out of class.

Closing the bedroom door, sealing herself off from the rest of the house, Ursula realized she'd spent so much time hearing all her grandmother's magnificent tales about Vietnam, yet she recognized very little of that drama here in the States. The entire time they'd been talking on the phone, Bà Nội had likely been in this bed, watching this old televi-sion. It comforted Ursula to know her grandmother's later life had been uneventful, suburban, easy. She rummaged through the large plastic tub of VHS tapes in the closet and found the copy of *Babe: Pig in the City*. Ursula had still never seen it.

At the funeral service earlier that day, there had been offerings of her grandmother's favorite fruits. Who didn't like peaches and mangos? This seemed like a special way to honor Bà Nội, with her favorite film. Watching it today, alone, Ursula was stunned, moved, and—in the throes of grief—devastated by *Pig in the City*. It was scary for a kids' movie; for an adult, its terrors were existential.

In order to save the farm, an earnest pig journeys from his rural home to an overwhelming urban landscape. Unlike the countryside, the city is cruel. In a climactic scene, this pig, Babe, is pursued around a canal by a bull terrier with no clear motives other than the blood in-stinct to hurt someone, fury in his dopey eyes.

There was a moment that made Ursula burst into tears, choke through ugly sobs. As Babe is being chased, when it appears that there is no escape, he bravely turns around, looks his canine assailant in the eyes, and, in the face of needless violence, has the audacity to ask: "*Why?*"

ADMISSIONS STANDARDS

—

BEFORE SHE SAW HORROR MOVIES, JEN READ WIKIPEDIA FIRST. THE synopses didn't take the terror out of jump scares or gruesome killings, but there was something about the act of research that put her at ease. Jen liked to be ready.

A nightclub like Roundabout wasn't quite a slasher flick. And yet, Jen still found herself looking up the Yelp reviews. She did not understand the appeal of a club. But also, she'd never been to one before, and this, she was told, was the point of going to college, of living in New York City. Another student assured her that Roundabout was fun if you were drunk enough. How much, exactly, was "drunk enough," Jen wondered.

Roundabout had 477 reviews and an average rating of two out of five stars.

Chloé C.
I HATE this place with every ounce of my being. It is the most discriminatory establishment I've ever been to.

Jiayang F.
Lots of pretty girls inside but the process of getting in is very unreasonable even rude

Alison W.
Terrible and horrible! A nightclub with racism can still do business in NYC? They only let the Korean girls in!

A pattern emerged. If you were Korean—or at least Korean looking, meaning fair-skinned Asian, Jen deduced—you would get in for a twenty-dollar cover. Otherwise it would cost you sixty dollars, if they let you in at all.

Jen glimpsed herself in the mirror. Her features were thin and flat, her clothes modest and unmemorable. Back home in Indiana, she was notable just by being one of the few Asians in town. Here, people wanted to know what shade. Jen had spent a great deal of the summer outside, enjoying the sun and the lake, and now she imagined it might cost her an extra forty dollars.

Robyn K.
Rudest staff ever! They claim that they don't have my coat even though I checked the coat earlier.

Brendan K.
Very racist!!!! I would never go back to this club. I was pulled out of the line because I wasn't fashionable (my shoe). Meanwhile, I saw other korean guys getting in with their snicker. Very racist!!!!!

Alex J.
DOORMEN ARE THUGS

Less than encouraged by the reviews, Jen texted Ursula to see if she would want to go clubbing sometime. She stared at her phone, annoyed, waiting for her cousin's reply, and was disappointed when it finally came through:

lol come on

JEN HAD FELT guilty for applying to schools out of state, away from the rest of her family. She'd done it in secret, after her mother assumed she would just go to a school in Indiana. Or better yet, maybe her daughter would have a change of heart and go to a small Christian college. But

Jen had paid the application fees herself with Christmas money—eighty-five dollars for Columbia, seventy dollars for Fordham, eighty dollars for New York University.

She had shown Má the acceptance letter from NYU, which was less of a letter and more of a packet full of information—forms that needed filling out, brochures to be admired.

"But why New York?" she asked. "Why so far away from home?"

Jen knew Má would ask this question. She'd known for days and hadn't come up with a good answer. She had squealed in the privacy of her room when she first got the acceptance email, disbelieving that this could be her future. But Jen had waited for the packet to arrive in the mail to tell her mother, to give her something to hold on to.

So MUCH OF college had been unlike anything she'd imagined—the energy on the street, the buzz in the dorms, the complete isolation she felt in a city so big and overwhelming—and every new experience thrilled her. But the inaugural AAPISA meeting was Jen's first taste of something familiar in New York: a sense of community.

She had been hearing about something called *Uh-pee-suh* from the moment she stepped on campus as part of a multiday orientation program designed to inundate new students with the school's numerous opportunities to get organized, make friends, and do something extra-curricular beyond getting very drunk and letting strange boys touch her.

But it was a strange boy who compelled her to join. He was short and white, a sophomore, on campus early for soccer preseason.

"*Uh-pee-suh* throws the best events," he'd said while trying to feel her up.

She asked what *Uh-pee-suh* was, mid-kiss, not really caring about the answer.

The boy explained that it was AAPISA, though he couldn't quite recall what the acronym stood for past "Asian American" something. *Uh-pee-suh.* Looking around, amid the raggedy wood desk chairs, red Solo cups, and sunken couches, Jen finally noticed that there were a lot of Asians stuffed into this dorm room. The boy was a bit too handsy, but he wasn't wrong. It *was* a pretty good party.

AT THE END of high school, she'd stopped attending church events. She didn't miss lukewarm pizza and half-hearted condolences. But she craved being part of a group. Belonging. A sense of purpose.

Here, among the Asian American Pacific Islander Student Association, everyone looked like her. Sort of. Way more like her than what she was used to seeing in Goshen, where she'd always stood out. Strangely, she'd never thought about how isolating that was until now. And she still felt out of place. Even now, in this room, she was unsure what a Pacific Islander was.

The AAPISA members were gathered in a lecture hall, tiered seating surrounding a lazily erased whiteboard. Most members were upperclassmen already familiar with one another. Jen noticed Irving immediately. He was a Chinese kid from Florida, lean but broad shouldered, the build of a swimmer. She liked picturing him in a pool, shirtless.

While Irving didn't run AAPISA—that honor belonged to a humorless Filipina girl named Grace—he was the heart of it. With Irving in the room, everything became a competition for his attention. Girls giggled at his every joke. The boys invited him to every social function—house parties, improv shows, DJ sets, anything—please, Irving, just show up.

The only person unamused by Irving's charms seemed to be Grace, who ran the meeting and was visibly annoyed by the disruptions caused by Irving's mere presence. She had printed out an agenda and a list of decisions that needed to be made: famous authors to come and give talks, several fundraising goals, and a big celebratory potluck to cap it all off, which evoked a few hollers from back of the room. At the end, Grace ceded the floor to Irving. He'd prepared a speech of sorts.

"What does it mean to be Asian American?" he asked.

The audience, rapt, did not answer.

"We are diverse. Our cultures are vastly different. Our food is different," Irving said. "Our parents are not all Tiger Moms. We are not all quiet nerds, though some of us definitely are."

People laughed.

"But really, what actually unites us?"

Someone said, "Boba," and Irving, with a sudden seriousness in his voice, told him to shut the fuck up.

"That's the shit that gets us nowhere," Irving said.

The tenor of the room changed.

"The truth is, what unites Asian Americans is racism," he continued. "I *wish* we were united by *fucking boba tea*. Nobody takes seriously the way we are neglected and dehumanized. We may not look much alike, but we look alike enough to be called 'chink.' Or 'gook.' We are the same in that people think we're as privileged as white people—in which case, we are job stealers. Otherwise, the assumption is that we are dirty and poor."

A shy but enthusiastic reaction from the crowd. They were getting it. Irving was pulling them along.

"Being Asian means being invisible," Irving said.

The audience cheered.

"We're like ghosts," someone shouted from the back.

"Nah, that's not right," he said. "People believe ghosts lived."

When Irving said this, the raucous energy of the room again shifted and settled. People were actually thinking about what he had said. Irving was a beacon, his words an illumination. Did Jen agree with him? She didn't know, but she couldn't wait to tell Ursula about it.

IN LINE FOR the club, dressed in what she thought was a cute outfit— a T-shirt and plaid skirt she'd borrowed from a girl across the hall who described herself as "classy for an ABG" (another indecipherable acronym)—Jen was freezing, even though she was one of the few women wearing a coat. She had texted Ursula about proper attire the night before, and she'd been frustrated when Ursula said something about showing skin. But she wasn't wrong.

Jen's first instinct was to describe these women's outfits as "slutty." Long, skinny legs for days, propped up by a sea of high heels, which she wondered how anyone danced in. But she knew that was the judgmental Christian upbringing in her, and she'd gotten better at immediately squashing the impulse.

"Everyone looks so cute," Jen said to Irving, who had swapped the artfully slouchy sweatshirt for a traditional collared shirt.

"This is just what the club scene is like."

To which she replied: "Doesn't seem like my crowd."

"But it could be," he said, looking up from his phone with the slyest of nods.

The anticipation was exhilarating, but also Jen was freezing, wedged between people who were already slurring and stumbling, shivering, because no one, her included, seemed prepared to wait outside in fall weather.

Irving was texting people, thinking that they might be standing in another part of the line. Jen studied her fake ID. Tonight, she would be Naomi Yamashita, born on November 13, originally from Hilo, Hawaii. The photo of Naomi was washed out, unflattering in the way most government identification was. Jen still admired her bangs.

"Do you think Naomi Yamashita has a Hawaiian accent?" Jen asked. "Or speaks Japanese?"

"What?" Irving looked up from his texts.

"Do you think we'll get in?" Jen asked. "I read that the bouncers are really strict. Maybe they'll see that I am clearly not Naomi Yamashita."

"They're not going to quiz you on the details of your ID."

"Konnichiwa," Jen said, then raised two fingers to make a peace sign. Irving didn't laugh, but she had his attention now.

"I was reading about how, in Russia, they have this term for clubs that only let you in based on how attractive you are," he said.

"Isn't that how clubs work in America?"

"Look at you. Never been to a club, and yet you talk like you're an expert." Irving smiled at her, and Jen relished that this was the most considerate he'd been to her—or at least not to his phone—since they'd lined up. "Yeah, but the Russians are notoriously harsh about who they let in. They have high admissions standards. So much that they call it 'face control.'"

"Face control?"

"Face control. Like, they look at your face and are like—" Irving put his palm on Jen's anxious smile and declared: "'*Controlled!*'"

They both laughed. But in that crushing moment, Jen realized that it reminded her more of a familial touch, the way someone might treat a sibling.

His phone dinged.

"Oh, Davis says the rest of them are at the front." He grabbed her hand and tugged her out of line.

so what "club" are you going to?

Jen hated that Ursula had put the word "club" in quotation marks. She knew Ursula hadn't meant it as a slight, but Jen couldn't help but be frustrated by the way her cousin continually treated her like a child. She was only six years younger.

it's called roundabout. have you been?

But really, the source of Jen's annoyance was bigger, simpler. She'd been in New York for nearly a month now, and though Ursula only lived a few stops away, they had not hung out in person once. Growing up, they lived in different parts of the country, and during family reunions, were inseparable. In Ursula Jen saw a role model, an aspiration. Now they were in the same city, and their relationship was still entirely over text. It was like Jen could've been anywhere else in the world. She would never admit it to her mother or to anyone, but part of choosing NYU had obviously been to be closer to Urs.

i haven't been. is that the asian only club?
worse: it's korean only
lol have fun!!!

AFTER ALL THAT TEXTING, Irving had finally made contact with Davis, who found them and pulled them to the front of the line.

"This isn't you," declared the bouncer, a gigantic white guy with a shaved head, raising Jen's ID into the light to further examine her photo.

"Come on, bro," Irving said, stepping in. "You're an expert on Asian faces?"

Irving was seemingly one tenth of the size of the bouncer. Still, he leaned in, like they were equals. Because the advantage here wasn't that of proportions but privilege. Irving was a customer.

"It's okay," Jen said, and yanked at Irving's arm. She pulled him back a little. The motion took Irving by surprise. "Sorry about him."

Davis insisted that he knew the owner of Roundabout.

The bouncer remained focused on Jen. "When is your birthday?"

"November 31," Jen said, confidently and incorrectly.

The bouncer looked unsatisfied by her answer, but he motioned her through.

"I'm going to keep this ID," he said. A fair trade.

Jen thanked the bouncer. "Konnichiwa!" She flashed him the peace sign.

THE INTERIOR OF Roundabout was smaller than she had expected. There was a dance floor at the center, flanked by a couple bars and some minimal seating, already staked out by people who had surely been there for hours. Then there was the staircase leading to several VIP sections, each higher level corresponding to a more exclusive, more expensive class.

And it was crowded. Too many bodies. Jen couldn't tell which aroma she detested more, the stink of sweat or the whiffs of cologne and perfume. Oh, and the music. If there was a melody, it was overpowered by the low throb of bass that made the sticky floor tremble.

Irving was in his element, though, even when the gin and tonics he bought for himself and Jen cost forty dollars. He either came from money or simply did not care.

Davis was the one pulling the strings. He'd been able to get them to the front of the line, and then inside without a cover. No part of Jen wanted to pay for entrance, but some part of her was curious if she would have been charged the Korean price or the broadly Asian price.

Davis led Jen, Irving, and a throng of AAPISA girls up a staircase, through several more bouncers and velvet ropes, to the very top. Jen made eye contact as she moved past the various boxes, where beautiful women and stern-looking men ogled her with jealousy. *Who is this bitch?* Jen imagined them thinking, feeling satisfied as she ascended the staircase.

"Our boy hooked it *up*," Davis said gleefully, showing Irving and Jen around the private booth. A bottle of champagne in a bucket of ice, accompanied by a set of glimmering flutes. There were bottles of Hennessy, too, and also, for some reason, platters of fruit. Jen toothpicked a cube of pineapple.

Davis was excitedly chatting up the owner, a bigger Korean guy who actually looked like an older version of Davis—wide face, tall hair. Jen wondered if it was racist to suspect they were related.

"I'm shocked Davis came through," Irving said.

Jen didn't really know what to say, so she said, "Yeah, free drinks. That's pretty cool."

"Who actually gives a shit, though?" Irving was suddenly pissed. It confused Jen. Irving turned to the group. "Time to go *fucking* dance."

Everyone cheered and slowly filed down the staircase behind Irving, their fearless leader. She would need to break open that Hennessy if she was going to dance.

"You're not going with your friends?"

It was Davis's pal, the owner.

"No, I think I'll just stay here."

"It's a good view," he said. Jen thought he might introduce himself, and she was strangely relieved when he didn't. She wouldn't have to tell him her name either, since she wasn't sure if she needed to be Jen Nguyen or Naomi Yamashita.

He reached for the bottle of champagne and poured her a glass. They clinked and looked out over the balcony. From this height, the crowd barely looked like people—just abstractions of bodies, bathed in strobes. It was hypnotic, disgusting in a way that was just occurring to her.

"When I opened this place, I wanted it to be a safe space for Koreans," he said, surveying the club with an expression of recognition, but no longer fondness, like God looking over Eden after it had run amok. "Ten years later, it's a safe space for *all* Asians."

It was unclear what he meant exactly, but he sounded disappointed.

"I don't know if the club scene is for me," Jen said. "I keep hearing this is the best one and all I can think about is how it's too loud."

"Then why did you come?" the owner asked, not offended, but amused.

Jen paused for a moment, and then decided to be honest. "I am trying to figure out what I like, and I end up following people places."

"There's nothing wrong with that. It takes time to know yourself, and you have to go to a lot of places first to know that they're not for you," he said. "Besides, I'm skeptical of anyone who knows what they want from a young age."

It was broad wisdom, but that didn't make it any less convincing. Growing up, her mother only had the platitudes of the Bible; her father hadn't even bothered. Jen had to hear it from strangers, apparently.

"Don't sweat it, because you've got time, is what I'm saying." Then the owner asked, "How old are you, anyway?"

Jen, again, was honest.

"Eighteen."

"Jesus fucking Christ," he said, burying his head in his hands, "I gotta fire the bouncer."

IT WAS 3 A.M. when Jen looked at her phone again, delighted to see that Ursula had checked in on her.

so how was it?
did you suck face with ivan?
it's irving
and nah, it's not like that

After the club, the crew had stumbled into a Korean barbecue joint around the corner, which was open solely to cater to the runoff of Roundabout patrons. The group had dwindled to six as the night went on.

As soon as they'd been seated around the grill, Davis passed out. Irving, of course, took charge, ordering a round of Hites. He settled on several orders of bulgogi and no vegetables, despite the protestations that someone didn't eat meat.

There were three other girls there—older, cuter, skinnier than Jen, all more interested in Irving than she was. Jen wasn't actually that hungry and hoped she wouldn't be sharing the check. But she soon realized her role at this meal was to prop up Davis's big, unconscious head, which had slunk against her shoulder, his mouth open, a stream of drool beginning to drop off his chin. It didn't even bother Jen at this point. Her shirt already smelled like a brilliant stew of other people's stink and spilled drinks. What more could a little saliva do? Jen snuck a selfie of herself and Davis, out cold, and sent it to Ursula.

lolololololol

Ursula returned with a photo of herself, feigning collapse at her computer, to signal that she was up late working. Right, her very important job. How could Jen forget?

By the time the beef had cooked, one of the girls had also passed out. (Amanda, Jen was pretty sure.) The other (Tina?) was looking at her phone. The one sitting to Irving's left, who had never introduced herself to Jen, was especially stunning—high cheekbones and full lips. She quietly and delicately ate her meat, but nearly dropped a piece, her arm jolting a bit before the bulgogi entered her mouth. Maybe she was drunk, Jen thought. Then she noticed Irving looking off in the distance, a little too coolly, and Jen blushed as she realized his hand was making small, circular motions under the table, deep in the girl's skirt.

Jen could feel a thick trail of Davis's slobber making its way down her arm. She laughed, thinking: *We're both getting wet.* She sipped her beer. This was a joke she knew she'd text Ursula later. Maybe this time she'd even get a meaningful reaction.

MOUNTAIN VIEW

—

In the two months leading up to Alvin's move to San Francisco, all anyone did was warn him about the traffic. That and the fact that his Google internship would be located not in the city but southeast, in the suburbs. Forty minutes without traffic. But there was always traffic.

Google shuttle buses transported tech workers to headquarters and back, like day laborers. All the major tech companies had them. If you didn't pay close attention, you might take the wrong nondescript white shuttle. Still, all the talk of crippling congestion on U.S. 101 made him nervous on his first day. So he took the earliest available shuttle at Valencia and Twenty-fourth. It had been nearly a decade since he'd regularly ridden a bus to school, and here he was again, waiting for a bus at the crack of dawn, a backpack cinched tight at the straps. It was a cool and crisp autumn morning. The sun wouldn't be up for another hour, maybe longer.

Because of his final exam schedule the previous semester, Alvin had not been able to visit the Google campus before he'd accepted the job. Not that it would have mattered—among the other engineering students in his class, it was widely agreed that Google was the most prestigious opportunity. A year-long internship in Mountain View basically guaranteed a full-time offer after the fact and, at the very least, an impressive line on the resume if Alvin wanted to work anywhere else.

Alvin's salary worked out to around six thousand dollars a month, which was more than anyone in his family made, and a number that made him nervous and pleased. But rents in San Francisco were high enough that Alvin still needed to share an apartment with three other boys—also engineers, who would take different shuttle buses in the morning. He had imagined getting a place in the city would feel grown-up, but it just felt like more school.

When he told his older sister, Ursula, about the pay, he could sense both pride and envy in her voice as she explained how that was great for him, and it stoked his guilt. Alvin knew he didn't work harder than other people in his family, especially not Ursula, who'd chosen to be a writer, a future that everyone in their family—all of their aunts and uncles, especially—had tried to steer her away from. He hated the way they talked about it, like her pursuit of journalism was somehow a self-ish or irresponsible one.

Ursula had been the first person he'd called when he got the Google offer. Then his mom. Then his father, who he hadn't heard from in a few months, which was normal. Alvin left a voicemail with the good news and had yet to receive a response even weeks later, which was less nor-mal. Dad never reached out, but at least he responded. The disappoint-ment of him not showing up was becoming common enough now that Alvin could try to not take it personally. At least he had his cousins (or half-siblings, or whatever they were).

Orientation was actually scheduled for 11 A.M., and now, combined with how he'd overestimated the traffic, Alvin had four hours to kill. He meandered away from the building to one of the bicycles that were free to use around the campus.

Once you got outside the main cluster of buildings, the rest of the campus was more of a sprawl. There were nicely paved roads and un-imaginatively landscaped trees. It was like any other office park, but it took Alvin half an hour to do a loop of the entire campus, so he pushed farther, invigorated by the chill of morning air.

Alvin pulled up a map of the area on his phone. The only thing that came up nearby was a pin for the Computer History Museum. *Why not?* Alvin thought. He still had hours.

It was only 8 A.M., and the museum was closed. Next door was a municipal history museum for the City of Mountain View. Also closed. But the receptionist, who looked like she was just getting settled at her desk, let Alvin in. They didn't appear to get many visitors.

The exhibitions were modest: mostly archival photographs, some aged blueprints, and a few portraits of austere-looking city leaders of days past. Lots of black and white. "This exhibition about Japanese internment is new." The woman at the desk walked over to him and introduced herself as Lily. She turned out to be not a receptionist but a curator. Well, she worked the front desk, too, she admitted. Lily was cute. *Really* cute. Long black hair, severe bangs.

"My grandfather was a farmer interned at Manzanar."

"'Interned?' What does that mean?"

"Well, 'incarcerated' is the more accurate word."

Though she called Alvin's total unawareness of the mass evacuation of Japanese Americans during World War II "typical," she said it in a way that felt more critical of the history itself and less of Alvin's own ignorance. After the attack on Pearl Harbor, she explained, President Roosevelt signed Executive Order 9066, which authorized the mass removal of people deemed national security threats to concentration camps. Some Germans and Italians, but almost entirely Japanese Americans. It didn't matter what their potential of being an Axis spy was— anyone of Japanese descent was a suspect, apparently, even if they were mostly farmers. As Lily got further into the details, Alvin realized the more she spoke, the less he knew. Incarceration? Camps? How had this entire period of American history stayed unknown to him? He thought back to his AP U.S. History class and realized he'd spent most of it thinking about the girl who sat two desks ahead of him. He didn't remember her name, just her short denim skirts and thick eyeliner. In college, an engineering major had allowed him to gleefully skip past the humanities, but that had been part of the design as well. Now, out in the world, he felt overcome with embarrassment. This was partly his history, was it not? He wondered how much he didn't know, and what he'd missed out on.

"That sounds pretty racist," Alvin said, weakly.

"It was." Lily nodded, acknowledging what was obvious.

"I thought Roosevelt was one of the presidents people liked."

Lily shrugged. "People still like him."

She continued to walk him around the small room, taking him through the exhibit. Before the war, Mountain View had been a farming town. The land hadn't been very fruitful for the white farmers who had worked it for years, so the Japanese farmers—many of them recent immigrants—moved in and made the land arable. They had more sophisticated techniques, but Lily said her grandfather never blamed the land or the weather for a bad harvest. That, he believed, was what made him so successful.

"It's kind of like all the Asians coming to the Bay Area to work in tech," Alvin said.

Lily didn't agree and, in fact, seemed frustrated by his comparison. She guided him toward more photographs. She pointed to a picture of her grandfather's farm, a sturdy two-story wood building. Four women were posed outside of it—from left to right: her grandmother, mother, and two aunts, Lily said. He was not thrilled to have fathered three daughters instead of sons. But they all worked the land, as hard as boys would have.

"It's cool that you're so in touch with your family. And your history," Alvin said. "My grandmother lives in San Jose. Well, lived. I feel like when she was around, I never got to know her. I wasn't sure what to talk to her about."

"I understand that," Lily said. "Don't tell anyone, but I don't think my grandfather would've let me use these photographs for the exhibit if he was still with us. Having to leave the farm was the great shame of his life."

Her attention had returned to the framed image of the homestead, but Alvin was taken aback by such an easy admission. Lily's intentions had been good. Still, Alvin wondered if you could truly honor someone's legacy if it might be against their wishes.

Alvin tried to shift subjects. "Do you know a lot about the Vietnam War, too?"

"I majored in history at Stanford with a focus on twentieth-century American history," she said, a touch of smugness. "So yes."

"I know so little. It's funny, when I took AP History, our unit on the Vietnam War was a day long? Maybe two, tops. And none of it showed up on the exam," he said.

"And yet, we know all these fun facts about George Washington. We know what color his horse was. How he chopped down a cherry tree."

She paused for a beat.

"What kind of lunatic chops down a fruit tree?"

BEFORE DEPARTING THE MUSEUM, Alvin worked up the courage to ask for Lily's number. He'd been good with girls in college, but that was ancient history. Now he was trying to project a new confidence—he had so much to offer, didn't he? She seemed amused, and scrawled something quickly on the back of a receipt. Strangely, he felt victorious. This was his life now. Maybe he'd show Lily the Google campus, they'd bike around it together, have a drink; she could tell him more about her family story and, frankly, probably tell Alvin about his own.

But there would be no date. When he opened the scrap of paper, there was only a simple message in her hand: LEARN YOUR HISTORY.

VIETNAMESE LESSONS

—

URSULA WAS AT DRINKS WITH HER FRIEND SUSIE AND THEY WERE ON their way to a long and hazy night. Susie, who had grown up in a very Korean suburb of Chicago, was finishing a PhD in Asian American Studies at Columbia and needed to vent.

You didn't have to be in academia to recognize Susie's resentment toward her job. The thankless tasks, the low pay, the judgmental superiors who you had to be nice to despite their frequent cruelty because they held your future in their clammy, tenured hands. Every workplace, it seemed, offered the same kind of exploitation.

They often joked that Susie was the "real Asian," insinuating that Ursula, who was only half and often passed for white, was not. Susie was a bit of a one-upper, though. When Ursula mentioned her low reporter salary, Susie complained that academic jobs paid even less. When Ursula talked about the long, grueling hours, Susie asked her to imagine that, but with the added load of grading papers.

Because she got out of work so late, Ursula had picked someplace dingy and cheap near her office, and they were well into a third round.

"I'm going to finish my dissertation, apply to every Asian American Studies program, and lose each opening to a precious Japanese woman who thinks the most interesting thing about her is that she dates white men because her own father was so terrible."

Ursula thought this sounded oddly specific but didn't press— sometimes solidarity just meant leaving it alone.

"That's the only thing that gets rewarded these days," Susie said, her voice loud and slurry. "Shallow preciousness. Racial identity is just a thing to be exploited and explained in a way that makes people feel smart about themselves."

Even just a year into the job, Ursula had seen shades of this in journalism. The desire for a more racially diverse newsroom had been creating "opportunities for different perspectives" and "opportunities for new voices." A co-worker had suggested that Ursula, qualifying under the banner of a "person of color," should lean into it.

She was ready to try anything that might improve her circumstances, but most days, Ursula did not feel like an actual journalist. She had taken the only offer for a writing job she'd received: to blog about beauty products for a website called Top Story. It was a massively popular publication, a sprawl of articles, videos, and podcasts—material that fell under the broad label of "content." (The site's early success came from search engines inadvertently convincing users that what they were clicking was the "top story.")

But Top Story had a prestigious and ambitious News arm, focused on politics, business, and culture. Ursula was already angling for a move. She just couldn't quite figure out how to make the leap. Ursula could barely keep up with her day-to-day assignments, aggregating stories from other outlets, assembling slideshows, listening to other people use the phrase "content creation" without a lick of irony.

"This is all very typical," Susie said.

"What part?"

"Being trapped in the beauty category."

"Because I am so beautiful?" Ursula batted her eyes playfully.

"Ursula, you *know* you're fucking *gorgeous.*" It was a little too aggressive to be flattering, Ursula thought. Susie explained: "You are a genius, and you would make a brilliant investigative journalist. But they're always going to see young Asian women as frivolous. As objects. As things that can be relegated to the unserious parts of the magazine."

Suddenly, her voice had attained a clarity, like someone who, perhaps, spent their entire day thinking and talking about these things.

It was funny. Ursula was half Vietnamese, but she'd grown up in the largely white suburbs of Boston, raised for most of her life by a single white mom after her dad left when she was ten. The closest thing people in her town came to an "identity" was Irish, which basically translated to rooting for the Celtics. There were only two places Ursula really felt Vietnamese. One was in California, among her extended family, and the other place, of course, was when she was at a bar with a very drunk Susie.

As they wrapped up the evening, Ursula remembered what she'd wanted to ask Susie before the drinks kicked in.

"Do you know if your grad program offers Vietnamese language classes? Something I could audit?" She was too embarrassed to tell her friend that her motives had less to do with embracing her ancestry and more to do with setting herself up at work.

"I don't know," Susie said, barely taking interest, waving down the waiter for another round. "Can't you just check the website?"

Later, as they exited the bar, Susie was a bit wobbly. She clutched Ursula's arm outside as she called a car. Ursula checked her phone and must have sighed, because Susie asked what was wrong.

"Oh, my cousin sent me, like, a million texts." It was only four. "She goes to NYU and always wants to hang out."

Ursula felt bad for the way that came out, knowing they'd barely spent any time together since Jen had arrived in the city.

"Is she a cousin on your mom's side or your dad's side?"

"Dad's."

"Ah," Susie said, "a *real* Asian."

Susie was one of the few people who had all the details about Ursula's family: how her father had at least a second wife—a Vietnamese wife—and two other kids, whom he'd also left; how they were all united by being abandoned by the same man. This was the one story Susie couldn't top, having grown up in a very undramatic household, the only child of two stable and loving teachers.

Ursula and Alvin's favorite cousins were not technically cousins at all. They were half-siblings—Jen and Duncan—the offspring that their father had made when he was with his other family. There was probably a word in Vietnamese to describe a half brother or half sister, but either out of kindness or laziness, no one else in their family used it. Cousins. That was simpler. And at least the revelation of a deadbeat dad brought her closer to her half-siblings, closer to her Vietnamese side.

The car Susie had been waiting for finally pulled up. As her friend stepped into the black Camry, Ursula wondered why drinks with Susie always made her feel like shit.

OF THE FOUR COUSINS, Duncan, despite being the youngest, was by far the largest. When the aunts and uncles made fun of Ursula's ass for being too fat, she reminded herself that it was less insulting than the way they talked about Duncan, who just seemed too big to be in the family. By the age of twelve, he was already over 150 pounds. Now, at fifteen, he was not only tall but bulking up because of football. The more he grew, the more Ursula adored him. She knew he was getting stronger, but he stayed a shy and sweet boy who would ask thoughtful questions and was always the first to help with the dishes.

Jen was another story. In many ways, she was Ursula's opposite: needy and unassertive. Jen wasn't quiet, but rarely had anything interesting to say that wasn't approval seeking. Both Jen and Duncan were raised in the Midwest, among extremely devout Catholics, mostly from the influence of their mother. Duncan never seemed that aggressive about it, but Jen, who had been an active member of the youth church group, was. Which made Ursula, an atheist after watching a Richard Dawkins YouTube video in middle school, bristle at her cousin's naïve worldview.

Ursula recalled one overly detailed story Jen told about how her church group was doing yadda yadda yadda about blah blah blah in Africa. When pressed on which specific country this was taking place in, Jen grew flustered. She named Madagascar, only to take that back seconds later to say Morocco, before going back to Madagascar. Or was it Malawi?

To be fair, that was Jen in early high school, and as she neared college age, she seemed to be growing more skeptical of her indoctrination.

Ursula was proud of her cousin and thrilled when Jen called to tell her she was going to enroll at New York University. She'd not only escaped the church but also her Indiana hometown, her devout mother.

But the reality was that Jen in New York was, well, still needy, even if they hadn't spent much time together at all. She texted Ursula constantly—never about anything important. It was all run-of-the-mill college stuff. Classes, boys, weird experiences at parties. Jen wanted attention.

As Ursula waited impatiently for the Q train, regretting yet another long, hazy night with Susie, she looked over her texts.

when are we gonna hang out?
soon!
you keep saying that
i promise

It had only been a few months, but her cousin had yet to learn the number-one lesson of people in New York City: everyone is really busy.

THE ROOM FELT MAKESHIFT: a handful of folding tables, metal chairs at odd angles, positioned toward a whiteboard on wheels. Clearly this wasn't supposed to be a classroom. Also, it smelled sharply of chlorine because of the real reason most people ever came to this building—its proximity to the YMCA's pool.

The pupils could be divided neatly into thirds: there were the full Vietnamese, the half Vietnamese like Ursula, and the white guys. At the beginning of the first class, the teacher, a petite woman with a large gold cross around her neck, asked everyone to introduce themselves and share why they had signed up for Viet 101. With the exception of one woman who was already fluent in the language and was there to learn how to read and write, everyone else's answer had been some form of "I'd like to be able to speak to my grandparents" or "I'd like to be able to speak to my girlfriend's parents."

Ursula wondered if the other Vietnamese in the class could tell she was half, or if they were lumping her in with these white bros to her left. Unlike her brother Alvin, Ursula passed, and after their father left, and with their grandmother now gone, even her last name, Carrington, erased any trace of her heritage. She'd been signing her name that way, introducing herself that way, for most of her life. Rejecting her given surname had felt cathartic; but as her anger toward Dad cooled with time, the change felt more like a technicality. It only started feeling more permanent when it appeared on all her bylines: Ursula Carrington.

HER SENIOR YEAR of college, an editor at Top Story had visited her thesis class, mostly to talk about himself and how he'd found himself in the industry. His name was Rosco Reed, and he was in his early thirties, handsome in his lean build—either a runner or a rock climber, Ursula guessed.

But aside from hearing a hot, smart guy talk for an hour, Ursula loved hearing from somebody who was doing the thing she wanted to do, and with such honesty. Propped coolly against the desk at the front of the class, and to a room of eager, mostly white students, he explained that the current state of the industry was bleak. The internet had overturned everything. In his ten years working professionally in newsrooms, Rosco was on his fifth job. The first couple he'd been swept up in rounds of layoffs; his next two were out of self-preservation, moving on before a place collapsed. Being a Black journalist, he said, made him scrappier, someone who had to learn how to survive in a floundering media landscape.

Rosco talked about advertising. (If you want to know when the sky is falling, make a friend on the sales team, he joked.) The main revenue source for many publications had been ads, and online, the market had been subsumed almost entirely by Google and Facebook. It hadn't been deliberate, but these companies were so massive that, among the many industries that they'd ruined, media was just a bit of collateral damage.

"What is the hardest thing to learn as a journalist?" Ursula asked.

"As an editor, you hear lots and lots of pitches for stories," he said. "Many interesting things in the world happen. But not all of them are stories."

"So, what makes something a story?"

He paused to think about it.

"A good story always tells you something about people—how they live, and how they delude themselves."

After the class was over, a handful of students lined up to talk to Rosco. This happened every time there was a guest, but never had Ursula seen so many people wait around. Finally, Ursula made it to the front.

"Is it really that much harder to make it if you're not white? I'm graduating this spring and honestly super freaked about finding a job. My family already thinks I'm an idiot for not trying to be an engineer."

"I get that. My brother is a doctor—a surgeon. I don't even think he's particularly good at it, but he'll always have job security," Rosco said. "He does take better care of Mom, though."

Ursula wasn't sure where he was going with this.

"But to answer your question . . . I mean, I think it depends on what kind of not-white you are. For example, it's probably tougher for someone that looks like me than for someone that looks like you."

"I'm *not* white."

"I don't think you look white. But you understand my point, right?"

"Can I get your email address, Mr. Reed? In case I have any more questions?"

"It's Rosco. And no, you can't."

Suddenly, Ursula was embarrassed that she'd overstepped. She thought he might respect someone who was a bit more aggressive.

"Any journalist with potential can figure out someone's email address, especially if they have their full name and place of employment," Rosco said. "If you can't do that, then I highly recommend you do what my brother does and cut people open for a living."

URSULA DID FIGURE out his email (it was just rosco.reed@topstory .com), and before graduation, she hit him up, trying to be casual. Rosco saw right through her. No open News positions, but he could refer her to the Entertainment team.

The first editor she talked to seemed less interested in her ability to understand the mercurial nature of what made a story, and more in whether she was interested in beauty products (sure?) and if she felt capable of writing two to five short posts a day (sure???).

The second editor, Amelia, was a bit more straightforward.

"It sounds like you are out to do hard news, and frankly, that's not what this job is," she said.

"No, I am really passionate about a lot of things," Ursula replied, unconvincingly.

"It's okay, Ursula. I'm just letting you know what you're in for if you take this job. It's a lot of writing lists and quizzes and trying to make stuff go viral. The people are great, and fun, and I love working here. But if you're really invested in breaking news stories, I worry that you'll be frustrated."

"Well, no, I—"

"I'll make it easy for you, Ursula. I would love to work with you. Your college clips are strong, and you nailed the edit test. You can be a writer for Top Story Entertainment. I'm going to tell the recruiter to make you an offer. But I think you should really go out for some other jobs. Try and find a local paper, if they're still hiring."

Before she hung up, Amelia wished her luck.

URSULA WAS PICKING up little in her Vietnamese class. There was homework that needed to be handwritten, and she found herself struggling with the precision of scrawling diacritics after a lifetime of typing. Not that anyone was checking her homework.

During class, she usually texted Jen, who always seemed available and responded immediately to everything. Each Monday evening, as class droned on, she came up with stories about a student named Garrett who showed up every week in a well-tailored suit and didn't speak to anyone else.

his hair is gelled to death
like he's in a nu-metal band

Garrett was one of the white guys there to impress his Vietnamese girlfriend. (Ursula wondered what she looked like. Probably hot?)

The tones of Vietnamese were difficult for the untrained ear. Ursula hadn't grown up around it but had heard enough of the language from family reunions and phone calls with her grandmother that she could pick it up. Garrett struggled. It was funny watching him get called on by the teacher, who'd have to correct him several times before moving on, exasperated by his incompetence. He seemed like someone for whom many things came easily. Not this, though. And that was the thing about Garrett—he was really trying.

that's my favorite part of class
watching this dude squirm

BEFORE ACCEPTING, URSULA had taken Amelia's advice to heart and truly hit the pavement trying to find a job as a reporter—a real journalist. But of the small papers that Ursula tried, many were in the process of downsizing, not hiring. She emailed Amelia, saying she would take the role, if it was still available. And that's how she ended up in New York, even without a dad or uncle already in the media, a Harvard or Yale degree, a fact-checking internship at *The New Yorker*. She was starting her career as a journalist, writing five posts a day about beauty, lifestyle, and celebrity.

URSULA WAS THIRTY minutes late to the review session, and was surprised to find only three other people had shown up to prepare for the Viet 101 final—a pretty poor showing considering it was a class of maybe thirty. To her displeasure, Garrett was there.

He spent most of the time looking at his phone. The girl who had organized the study session, Tracy, barely needed to study. She had already memorized all the vocabulary words and spoke with the most convincing accent out of anyone in the class. Still, Garrett seemed uninterested in her help when she tried to correct his pronunciation.

"It's not an oral exam," he argued, and then went back to looking at his phone. Why was he even there?

As the session wrapped, Ursula asked the group if anyone wanted to get a drink. Garrett, suddenly alert, was the only one who said yes. On the way to the bar—Garrett insisted he knew a great spot in the neighborhood—Ursula thought about how badly she had miscalculated. She was hoping to get to know Tracy better; the other student who'd shown up, a very tall half-Vietnamese boy named Cameron, alluded to working "in fashion," which Ursula wanted to hear more about. No part of her wanted to be drinking alone with Garrett.

The bar he picked turned out to be decent. Quiet, if unremarkable. Ursula would have to keep it in the back of her mind, in case she ever managed to go on a date. Garrett talked about his middle-class upbringing in rural-ish Pennsylvania, how he was the first person in his family who went to college, how he vowed to make as much money as he could as fast as he could to bail his parents out of debt. It was so predictable, he explained, to have a Pittsburgh father who'd been laid off by a steel mill. And yet.

She was mostly afraid that he would put a hand on her knee. But round after round of drinks, he remained perfectly polite.

Finally, she asked about Garrett's partner. How did they meet? (Tinder.) What was she like? (Terrific!) Did he have a picture?

Garrett pulled out his phone and summoned a photo. It captured him at what appeared to be a Halloween party, dressed as Super Mario— overalls, red hat, big fake mustache. Next to him was the girlfriend, wearing a very short pink dress and a blond wig.

"This is Kimmy," he explained. "She's Princess Peach."

Ursula nodded, squinting at the photo. Kimmy was wearing a lot of makeup, and her legs looked good in that dress. Honestly, though? She wasn't a knockout. Ursula was disappointed, and she wasn't sure why.

Still, she had unlocked something. Or really, she'd broken something open, because once Garrett started talking about Kimmy, he wouldn't stop. Kimmy was so sweet, so thoughtful, full of energy. He felt like the luckiest guy on earth. He'd do anything to make her happy, even if that meant humiliating himself in class each week.

THE EXAM TURNED out to be barely a test of anything—some basic vocab, some sentence diagramming. Everyone was done within twenty minutes, and as the teacher collected papers, Ursula wondered if she would even bother grading them.

Once pens were up, the teacher escorted the class to a restaurant down the block. The real test, she explained, was seeing if they could order dinner in Vietnamese. It was supposed to be a nice surprise, this group meal, though Ursula felt like nobody really needed ten weeks to learn how to say "phở bò" to a waiter. Extra credit for đặc biệt, she supposed, suddenly realizing maybe she had learned something.

As they walked to the restaurant, Tracy apologized for skipping out on drinks after the study session. "That Garrett guy just gives me the creeps," she said. Tracy explained she was freaked out by white guys who only dated Asian women. Garrett had "those vibes," she said, admitting that she felt guilty leaving Ursula alone with him.

As the food arrived, the teacher finally noticed someone was missing. "Garrett ở đâu?" she asked—where is Garrett? And because in Vietnamese, things were often repeated, she said it again. "Garrett ở đâu? Garrett ở đâu?"

It became a popular refrain at the table. Apparently much of the class, the other white students included, didn't care much for him. It struck Ursula as a bit harsh—he had seemed harmless enough to her the night before—but it was funny, too. Garrett ở đâu? Garrett ở đâu?

AFTER DINNER, SUSIE met up with Ursula to celebrate passing her exam. They'd made plans a week ago, before Ursula realized how easy the test would be. As the story about Garrett spilled out of her mouth, she realized it lacked shape—no clear beginning, middle, and end. It was just a thing that happened. Yet Susie was riveted.

Somewhere between rounds four and five, a loud group of college-age students rolled into the bar. They were young, rowdy, and out of place. This was a wine bar, a scene for drunk and quiet commiserating. Susie pointed out that they were all Asian, but Ursula had hardly noticed. Suddenly, in the dark, moody candlelight of the bar, Ursula thought she could make out the profile of her cousin.

"Where are you going?" Susie asked.

As Ursula approached the bar, she overheard one of the students arguing with the bartender. They did not serve shots here, he explained patiently. They only had wine and a few cans of beer available. The disappointment rippled through the group and only aggravated their unruliness. One of the boys was yelling animatedly at the bartender, as if they were responsible for the drink selection. It was the cross section of many kinds of privilege: of wealth, of youth, of alcohol-enabled entitlement. Ursula disapproved and would certainly scold Jen for hanging out with these idiots.

But the girl who looked like her turned out to be someone else with straight, shoulder-length hair, which came as some relief. Yet the expectation of seeing Jen and then not seeing her had filled Ursula with an emotion she couldn't yet name—a signal of what was to come. She was suddenly tearing up, overwhelmed by regret for not making more effort. Christmas was approaching, and she'd make it up to her then, tell Jen that she'd been such a shitty cousin, had taken her family for granted. Ursula didn't realize it then, but her guilt, her shame, whatever it was, this was a feeling that would grow and grow and grow.

DEADLY DROP

—

THE ATTACKS WERE RUTHLESS. MORE THAN THAT, THEY WERE COOR-
dinated. The scale and brutality was one thing. At last count, nearly fifty
were dead. But it was the choreography, the efficiency of it that drove
Americans into a frenzy. There were six explosives across six different
airports, all detonated in unison—within minutes of each other.

Atlanta, Los Angeles, Chicago, Dallas, Denver, San Francisco. A list
of the country's busiest airports, targeted on one of the busiest travel
days of the year—December 22, right before the holiday. The Federal
Aviation Administration ordered a ground stop across all of United
States airspace, and every plane in the sky was diverted to the nearest
airport. Nonmilitary flights were canceled, and the president was se-
questered in a secure location. Civilian air travel was reinstated in a
limited capacity four days later, though very few people had an interest
in flying.

Beyond the physical horror of it, terror was also a logistical night-
mare. Amtrak trains came to a halt, as did most public commuter rails
and subway systems. Buses kept going, since it was believed that nobody
rode them; ferries were halted, as they were considered easy targets. A
number of buildings and national monuments were closed. The Statue
of Liberty, the World Trade Center, the Washington Monument, the
Lincoln Memorial, and every attraction at the National Mall—the
symbols of national pride being instructed to turn people away.

In the private sector, concerts were postponed, malls closed. Anything that gathered large groups of people together was endangered.
Disney feared for its theme parks. For the first time in decades, this

meant closures for Magic Kingdom, Epcot, Hollywood Studios, and Animal Kingdom, as well as the two smaller water parks, Typhoon Lagoon and Blizzard Beach.

Which was how it first affected Dan's family, who'd arrived in Orlando a day before the attacks, expecting to spend a week enjoying the various parks that constituted Disney World. They'd already been to Disneyland, in Anaheim, California, Dan worrying the entire time about running into someone he knew, since it was not far from San Jose, holder of so much of his past.

Dan Nguyen didn't care much for roller coasters, but he'd always loved water parks. He had done his research ahead of the trip. There was a particularly gnarly slide at Blizzard Beach called Deadly Drop, which had promised, according to the Disney website, "one fearsome freefall." It would plunge its riders twelve stories straight down, then launch them into a massive spray of whitewater. It sounded exhilarating.

But there was no thrilling freefall. Instead, his wife, Celeste, wept openly. The kids, Justin and Jessie, seemed too young to understand what was really happening. *Thank god for that*, Dan thought.

The Nguyens watched the unending reports from their motel room. One cable network had suggested that the perpetrators were Vietnamese, though the news anchor had cited little evidence to confirm.

Dan joked that there's no way it could be. "We're too messy," he said. And, laughing for some reason, he continued, "We're too loud. No Viet could keep his mouth shut about it." Besides, Vietnam was hardly top of mind. There was the entirety of the Middle East, after all. Or Russia. Or China!

A couple days passed, which Dan tried to fill with the lackluster activities that eastern Florida had to offer: mini golf, all-you-can-eat buffets, the beach, more mini golf. But then the last names of the perpetrators came out, one by one: Nguyen, Nguyen, Pham, Tran, Le, another Nguyen. At that point, Dan wasn't laughing anymore.

Then came the seventh attack.

"I hate the gooks. I will hate them as long as I live."

—John McCain

II

THE TAKING

—

THE DEPARTMENT OF HOMELAND SECURITY CAME FOR THE MEN
first, mostly fathers of households. No one in Ursula's case, since her dad
had been gone for over a decade.

She wanted to check in on him. They talked on the phone maybe
once a year, which, for Ursula, was usually plenty. But she worried that
calling him now would raise some kind of suspicion from the government. Maybe that was paranoid. But was it? This was the same government that would make fathers disappear from their homes for days at a
time, interrogate them as if they were terrorists, and return them home
shaken and spooked.

Ursula couldn't help thinking that excluding women was unfair. Not
that she wanted women to be rounded up and questioned by DHS. The
summons were based on the assumption that only men could commit
atrocities or enact violence. To imagine that no woman could? That they
were so harmless as to be left alone? The whole thing was a bit patronizing.

As the news reports would bear out, the perpetrators of the attacks
were men in their late forties and early fifties. In the photos released,
they looked like the most ordinary people in the world. Menaces to
society, and yet they all looked like boring suburban dads. One was a
dead ringer for Ursula's own father.

When a new rumor emerged that DHS was coming for men of all
ages, Ursula's worries quickly shifted to concern for Alvin. It was unclear how wide a net would be cast. But if Alvin was afraid of being
summoned for interrogation, he didn't say it. Thankfully, Alvin received

no notice. And when they expanded the policy to include women, neither did Ursula. She wondered if they were exempt, raised by a white
mother, bearing a white name.

SHE'D BEEN A dedicated employee, even if her beat bored her to tears,
but now keeping pace at work was out of reach. The stress of anticipat-
ing the government's response loomed large, and Ursula's only coping
mechanism was to scroll endlessly on her phone, trying to take in every
report and rumor, as if more information would give her control or
comfort. As she fell behind at work, Ursula's bosses, trying to be accom-
modating, assigned her beauty roundups, since they were easier and
more straightforward, the closest thing she would receive to mercy in
the workplace. 32 Of Our Readers' Holy Grail Skincare Products. 22
Products From Sephora With Such Good Reviews You May Want To
Test Them Yourself. 17 Beauty Products You Might Not Know You've
Been Missing Out On.

Without Ursula raising a complaint, her boss, Amelia, had recom-
mended she take all the days off that she needed. There were mental
health resources available from HR. Ursula appreciated the gesture,
even though the offer of time off just meant hours she wouldn't be paid.

Besides, Ursula liked being close to the Top Story newsroom. She'd
befriended a couple reporters on the News side of the building, and occasionally exchanged friendly emails with Rosco. Ursula could learn
more through her colleagues who were closely tracking the potential of
the American Advanced Protections Initiative than from what the government was admitting publicly. The legislation had been put forward
by Senate Republicans, with hardly any resistance from the Democrats,
and threatened to suspend, only temporarily of course, Vietnamese Americans' rights while the attacks were being investigated. The specifics were
unclear. Dara, one of the reporters on the policy desk, assured her the
odds of it passing were low anyway.

Dara was Top Story News' best reporter on immigration, having
emigrated from Nigeria herself. But more than her lived expertise, Ursula took comfort in how Dara carried herself. She was confident and

self-possessed. Also, she was beautiful—big eyes, perfect skin, an effort-less sense of style that tended toward bright tops and perfectly fitted black jeans. Everybody adored Dara. This was the kind of person who would never need the lifestyle articles that Ursula was publishing.

"I know that you're scared for your family," Dara said, putting an assur-ing hand on Ursula's shoulder, "but it would be literally insane if it passed."

Literally insane if it passed, Ursula kept repeating to herself. *Literally insane.*

JEN HAD SPENT the entire fall moaning about how Ursula never texted her back, and now, she wouldn't respond to a single message. Ursula knew her cousin had decided to stay at school, even with the lingering threat of violence in the city. There'd been widespread harassment, a few beatings—the tension was escalating.

Finally, Ursula got her on the phone.

"Why would I leave New York? *You're* still in New York," Jen said.

"Yeah, but I look . . ." Ursula trailed off. "I'm just not obviously Viet."

Jen scoffed. "People are angry everywhere. I'm just as likely to be yelled at in New York as I am at home. I'm from *Indiana.*"

The way she stretched the syllables out in "Indiana" made it sound like someone stumbling over the name of a foreign country. Ursula re-minded her cousin that she had a mother and a brother who needed her. Jen didn't see what the big deal was. It would pass. She was sure of it.

"You weren't on the East Coast during 9/11," Ursula pleaded.

"Urs, come on. You lived in the suburbs of Boston."

27 Ways To Convince Someone To Stay Home. 18 Pleas You Might Make To A Loved One So They Take Things Seriously. 11 Signs That You Sound Desperate.

Jen remained deeply unconvinced.

"Really?" she said. "You're talking about 9/11? Really??"

HOMELAND SECURITY HAD taken Uncle Minh—he disappeared for an entire week before being returned unharmed but chilled to the bone.

All of this was being relayed by Ursula's cousin Tom via text, giving her a fragmentary, confused picture of what happened.

what did they ask him about?
barely anything
they held him for a week and didn't interrogate him?
i dunno
says they didn't ask him anything serious
just kept confirming details about his life, how he got the US, etc
what do you mean "etc"? it's not obvious what else they asked about

Ursula found, as she tried to check in on her loved ones, that her family was often more of a source of misinformation than fact. There was so much theorizing about what would happen, particularly with the American Advanced Protections Initiative. Much of it was conspiratorial— a surprising number of the conspiracies blaming China, going as far as claiming that the perpetrators of the attack were Chinese men posing as Vietnamese. 19 Ways To Plead With Your Family To Stop Getting News From Facebook.

She instead attempted to supply her family with articles from *The New York Times, The Washington Post,* the *Journal,* a few from Top Story, even. But the pieces were noncommittal, and too unsure of what had happened, or what would happen. This was a group of people that needed to know what their future looked like, and wild speculation was more useful than admitting uncertainty. The family group texts craved answers of any kind—even outlandish ones. And though it was all fiction, Ursula did understand the appeal. If you couldn't understand the truth, you might as well embrace a lie.

actually cau minh is being weird about one thing though
what
apparently homeland security told him to make sure he had identification on him at all times.
so now he sleeps with his documentation under his pillow

A few days later, DHS came for Uncle Minh again. This time, he did not return.

ROSCO PASSED BY Ursula on his way out of a conference room, nearly skimming her shoulder with his stack of notes. He was exiting the daily news meeting—the one that she had desperately wanted to work her way into someday.

"Were you just waiting for me out here?" Rosco asked.

"No, of course not," Ursula said, flustered. She had a meeting with Amelia in the same room and had been waiting for them to finish up. Though Ursula knew the News team was probably tired of her hounding them for information, she would do anything to learn about AAPI sooner, even if it would just be minutes before the news broke. Dara assured her that she would be the first to know, but Ursula stayed on it, and even asked if she could lurk in the private chat channel for the News team. (Rosco said he understood her motives were good but denied the request, claiming it would "set a precedent.")

Now she was here, in front of him by coincidence, and she didn't even have anything to say. Just small talk.

"How have you been?"

"Fine," Rosco said. "And you?"

"Good. You know, considering."

"Yeah, yeah." Rosco's MacBook was tucked under his arm, but Ursula could still hear the computer fan whirring loudly. "*Considering*."

"Okay, well, I have a meeting here now," Ursula declared.

Rosco stepped aside.

"Lunch sometime?" he asked.

Ursula was surprised by the invitation. "Like, together?"

He laughed.

They'd only made passing conversation since Rosco had helped her get the job over a year ago. Maybe now he would see that she would be a great addition to the News team. She could plant those seeds at least, reiterate her desire to be a serious reporter. Wouldn't it make sense to have a Vietnamese American in the newsroom, given everything?

Then it dawned on her: Was this lunch invitation . . . a date? In hypotheticals, Ursula had always considered getting involved with coworkers to be a red flag. But this was media. Journalists dated—or fucked—all the time. There were at least three couples at Top Story that Ursula knew about, and probably many more who were together in secret. She shook the thought away. A date was drinks, or dinner. Lunch was professional.

A WEEK HAD passed and Jen hadn't responded to a single text.

we don't have to talk. just let me know you're alive

A minute later:

yeah i'm alive

Ursula felt both relief that her cousin was okay and the urge to scream.

The rest of the family was starting to freak out. The momentum behind the American Advanced Protections Initiative was beginning to feel insurmountable. Conservative cable media had been pushing hard for it, and though the editorial board at *The New York Times* had published a piece calling the idea of detaining hundreds of thousands of Americans unconstitutional, the paper had still published several opeds in favor of it.

A paranoia that the government was surveilling their communication had brought the family group text to a halt. That fear didn't seem unfounded, nor far-fetched. But it also meant that Ursula was, for the most part, cut off.

—

WITH ALL THAT was going on around her, Ursula was embarrassed by how nervous she felt ahead of lunch with Rosco. She hadn't spent much time choosing her outfit, but she was overly meticulous with her hair that morning, packing it into a neat, tight bun. She felt like the skin was being yanked from her skull, but she looked serious and put together.

Her great fear was that Rosco would forget—or that something more important would come up. But he messaged her first to follow up, making sure they were still on for 1 P.M. and to meet him by the elevator.

Ursula stopped into the ladies' room after leaving her desk. She checked herself in the mirror, not for anything in particular, just self-assessing her overall vibe. It seemed relaxed but assured. She was trying hard to not look like she was trying hard.

The ladies' room at Top Story was large and bustling—especially around lunchtime, when people were always taking sheepish selfies in the full-length mirror by the entrance. Ursula washed her hands so no one would think that she came into the bathroom just to glimpse herself.

Her phone began to vibrate, but she let it ring out because her hands were still soaping under the sink. Ursula could hear other phones ringing and shaking, too, as if in unison. It was jarring. The only time iPhones went off like this was for a storm warning or an Amber Alert.

When she emerged from the ladies' room, looking around, something in the office had changed. It felt like the temperature had dropped ten degrees. People were moving through the elevator corridor with tremendous urgency. No one was talking.

Suddenly rounding the corner was Dara.

"Hey, what's going on?"

Dara, tears in her eyes, mouthed something that Ursula only recognized moments later, when she was able to collect herself, as "I'm so, so sorry." Dara embraced Ursula. The gravity of what had happened wouldn't hit Ursula until later. In that moment, she thought, *Wow, Dara smells incredible.*

NOMENCLATURE

—

There wasn't an agreed-upon term at first. The government insisted it was detention, since it was what the Department of Homeland Security had done aggressively with undocumented immigrants for the better part of two decades. It sounded temporary and fairly gentle, evoking a grade-school punishment.

Some journalistic outlets favored the word "internment," which harkened back to the internment of Japanese citizens during World War II. What was happening to the Viets was similar both in practice and in policy. Looking back at coverage of the American Advanced Protections Initiative, you can see more progressive-leaning publications using "internment" at the beginning, before resorting to the government-mandated term "detention"—a word that spoke to the largest possible audience. Familiarity meant relatability.

Still, even with the connotations associated with the horrific treatment of Japanese Americans (for which the country later arranged reparations—the clearest kind of apology that can exist in a capitalist system), "internment" was still a euphemism masking what it truly was: incarceration.

The strongest proponents of using "incarceration" to describe AAPI were also the most vocal protest groups: Japanese Americans, many of whom had already organized demonstrations against DHS's detention centers. They already understood Homeland Security's massive over-reaches in policy and power, and saw echoes of the way migrant families were treated in the U.S. When AAPI was proposed on the Senate floor, they were the first to warn about the parallels between the incarceration of their parents and grandparents during World War II and what would happen to the Viets. One Japanese American group marched outside the U.S. Capitol, banging taiko drums, hoping to stop elected officials from repeating a past national shame. It was the most impressive anti-AAPI demonstration, and the last one covered by major media outlets.

Every protest movement is powered by momentum, and eventually, even the most spirited showing from these groups dissipated. AAPI passed easily. As the rallies that followed fizzled, so did the words "imprisonment," "incarceration," and "internment." And the only thing that was left was the language of the government, and the language of the media. Both said "detention." There's the saying that history is always written by the victors. But that assumes a winner and a loser. A more accurate saying would be that history is a reflection of who had power, and how they flattered themselves.

SUBJECT LINE

—

It took Alvin nearly an hour to write a three-sentence email.

> Hey, so for obvious reasons, there's a good chance that I won't be
> around for much longer. So if you're a friend or colleague or someone
> that just feels like getting drunk on a weeknight, let's meet at the
> Living Room on 18th St this Wednesday at 5. Hope to see you there.

It was the subject line that he had agonized over most. What do you
call the drinks thing when you're pretty sure you're about to be detained
in a camp for who knows how long? "Going-away drinks" felt too work
related. "Goodbye" was too dramatic. "Last call"—way too dramatic. So
Alvin settled on the subject line he'd used several times before when
he'd been in an uncertain email situation, like a breakup.

> Subject: Hey

The gathering itself, though, felt a bit like a birthday. People would
arrive, say hi to Alvin, and offer to buy him a drink, even when he was
already holding one. Sometimes he'd ask for a whiskey shot, and when
the person returned with it, Alvin would give it to whoever he was talking to and make them throw it back. They couldn't say no. It was his
party.

Google colleagues seemed the most apologetic, like there was more they could've done to prevent AAPI. It was funny how quickly these conversations turned into Alvin comforting engineers and product managers, assuring his soon-to-be-former colleagues that there was nothing to be done. He was familiar with the hubris of tech workers—he could admit that he'd often walked around with that kind of confidence—but it wasn't exactly soothing to hear people who thought they were powerful now realize that they were not.

Close friends were drunker and angrier. That was more fun. Also more helpful. College classmates, more recent friends—and even friends of friends—were asking if there was anything they could do. They would help Alvin store his belongings. Were there plants that needed looking after? A pet? If it was a cat, they would take them in. They were spayed, right? Neutered? Alvin informed many people that he had already put his things in storage and that his plants already had new homes and that, no, he did not have a cat, allergies and all. Some talked about attending protests, though it seemed like they wanted Alvin's approval for participating.

But he appreciated the offers and the night's general energy until one of his friends in finance drank so much that he had to rush to the bathroom to hurl. That guy, Andrew, returned from the men's room ready to drink again.

"Another round?" he offered.

"Don't get me banned from this place," Alvin said.

"I mean, when are you going to be back?"

And that's when it really dawned on Alvin, when this new kind of sadness washed over him. Sure, Alvin knew that being detained would mean leaving his apartment, his job, his friends, his life. But for some reason, the idea of not being able to come to the Living Room again—a bar he didn't even have any particular fondness for—felt insurmountable. This was really happening and there was nothing he could do to stop it.

Andrew covered that round of shots, and immediately after, they did another.

—

ALVIN WOKE UP with a tremendous hangover and without a real memory of how he'd gotten home. Most of his clothes were still on. He'd removed his pants but, somehow, not his shoes. He remembered it had been a good night, though. Everyone from his life had shown up, and it made him realize just how many people were in it.

He suddenly recalled the best part of the evening: a woman, Fernanda, a product manager from Brazil who'd been in town for work. They'd emailed months before, but this past week was the first time they'd met in person. She had long, impossibly curly hair. Alvin had invited her out, not expecting that at the end of the night, they would kiss outside the bar.

Under his pillow, Alvin summoned the sensation: her cool lips, his hands on her soft skin, feeling the hips beneath. But the overriding feeling was new—being intimate with a practical stranger. God, when would he get to do that again?

His phone dinged. Oh good, he hadn't lost it.

WHO WILL SURVIVE IN AMERICA?

It was a text from Duncan. Alvin replied back.

WHO WILL SURVIVE IN AMERICA?

The joke was hard to explain. It was from a Kanye song they both liked, and somehow that morphed into them texting the exact phrase back and forth—and it'd been a running gag for nearly a year, during which they hadn't sent anything but that line back and forth to each other. Who would break first? Maybe this was the moment, with detention looming.

bro, I got so messed up last night—

But before he could hit send, his phone buzzed, a call from a number he didn't recognize. The Department of Homeland Security? Over the past week, he'd received a number of automated messages from them, explaining what he was supposed to do with himself before detention.

"Hello?"

"Is this Alvin Carrington?"

"Speaking."

"This is Nathan Bowden," the man said.

"Okay."

"You know who I am, right?"

Alvin did not.

"I'm the head of people and culture at Google," he said, obviously annoyed.

"Okay."

"I have some good news," Nathan said. "As you know, at Google, we've been working very hard to file a B-284 for our Vietnamese employees."

"Uh."

"That's the exemption form for the American Advanced Protections Initiative."

"Right."

"Well, our proposal went through this morning and—I'll cut to the chase. You don't have to report to an assembly center."

"Wait, what?"

"It's tremendous. You'll of course remain an employee of Google. And we'll continue to support you and your career development at the company as we all work through this difficult time."

"So I'm not going to camp?"

"Excuse me?"

"I was assigned to Camp Tacoma."

"No Camp Tacoma. No Camp *anything*. You're a Googler, and we protect our own."

"Wow, uh, thank you." Alvin was stunned. "Thank you? Thank you."

It took a minute for it all to settle in. Alvin was overcome with relief. He wouldn't be going to camp after all. His life would remain intact. In the end, he was glad he'd gone with "Hey."

SUMMER CAMP

—

The War Hero made similar appeals to his colleagues in the Senate and to the public, defending the order by relating it to his own experience as a prisoner of war in Vietnam. The Senator recounted in detail how he was cruelly beaten and underfed for five-and-a-half years by the Vietcong, resulting in permanent damage to his body that left him incapable of lifting his arms over his head. In front of several nightly news programs, he looked pained as he attempted to raise them.

But here was the cleverness of the War Hero Senator's tactics. After his account of his own torture, he denounced the way he was treated and said he would never wish that upon any other human being, no matter how much they deserved it—insinuating that, perhaps, the Viets living in America did deserve to be tortured. Instead, he argued, the United States should take the high road. We would simply detain Vietnamese Americans until we could better understand the threat to our soil. They would not be imprisoned. They would not be tortured. They would be treated well—evicted and forcibly removed from their homes, sure, but only for a short time. Compared to what he had experienced, the living conditions that we would put the Viets in would be like a vacation. Free lodging, free food, plenty of activities. For some, it would be an improvement to their quality of life.

"Like summer camp," The Senator famously said. It was a line he'd repeat for the better part of the three years to follow.

SPRING BREAK

—

IRVING HAD VOLUNTEERED TO HELP JEN PACK HER THINGS, THOUGH IN hindsight, she didn't know why she'd accepted his offer. He just kind of stood there, occasionally pacing, while Jen put all of her clothes into a suitcase.

"History just repeats itself, you know? This is why our community needs to learn about its past," he said.

Who was he even talking to?

Jen knew why she'd let Irving watch her pack up her dorm room. She would never get it done without someone there. It took the presence of a cute boy to motivate Jen to clean her room. It was also true that no one else wanted to spend time with her anymore. AAPI had created controversy within AAPISA—the similarities in acronym a big point of frustration and debate, to the point where the head of the organization, Grace, proposed renaming the club entirely. Not that anyone thought it was right, nor did anyone think that Jen was some kind of danger just because she was Vietnamese (though if anyone did feel that way, they were smart enough to keep it to themselves). Everyone knew that Jen was headed to an assembly center, whatever that was. She hadn't made close friends that semester, but she was surprised how swiftly any friends became scarce.

When Jen asked Grace why no one would talk to her, she explained that they were all sympathetic to her situation—and that of all the other Vietnamese students at NYU. But it was hard to think about those circumstances without getting too bummed out. Midterms were coming up, and the semester continued for everyone else, and people needed to focus on their studying.

"I'm sorry I asked," Jen said. "Really, so selfish of me."

Irving was trying to organize protests, but some members felt that the goal of the club was social, not to rally students into activism—especially if it could be dangerous. After the seventh attack, there had been over a dozen cases of assaults on Asian Americans around the country. One man in Lowell, Massachusetts, was beaten so badly that he was paralyzed from the waist down. But most of the reported harassment was verbal—the uncreative suggestion that people should go back to where they came from, dotted with the occasional slur.

This, to Irving, was all the more reason to be out in the streets together, denouncing what was a targeted, racist intrusion on the civil rights of people within their own community. But, Jen wondered, did a fifth-generation Japanese American English major or an adopted Filipina studying hospitality or a Korean studying abroad in the U.S. really owe anything to her? Weren't they all just there to live their own lives?

"It's just so fucked," Irving said, leaning against Jen's desk.

She brushed him aside so she could gather the things from the drawer. Would she need pens and paper at the assembly center? What about her phone charger? It seemed unlikely she could bring her phone.

Irving lay down on her bed, which had already been stripped of its linens.

"I went to a protest the other day—the big one, marching down Broadway—and it was great. Hundreds of people showed up. The energy was incredible. But you know what?"

"What?" Jen answered, still focused on emptying her desk.

"There were surprisingly few Asians there. Like, there were some. You would've thought that we might show up in numbers. But no! We did not show up to defend the rights of our own. Can you believe that?"

"I can't," she lied.

She had no idea what the weather would be like at the assembly center, because she had no idea where it was. The secrecy of the location was a security measure, she'd been informed. Should she bring her winter jacket? Probably, just in case, but packing something so bulky would mean leaving behind something else.

"I don't understand why you're not applying for an exemption," Irving said. "You're a student at New York University. It's a prestigious institution. They have to let you stay."

She'd been through this with Irving several times already. Why did he keep asking?

"I told you. Even if I get an exemption, my mom is still going. And I'm not going to let her be detained alone."

"Don't you have a brother?"

"He's fifteen."

"But isn't he, like, really big?"

Jen didn't know why she was trying to make Irving understand. When she finally finished stuffing everything into her ugly, unwieldy suitcase, she figured she could make Irving useful for once.

"Can you carry my stuff downstairs?" Jen said. "It's too heavy for me."

Irving seemed taken aback, but he had the good sense to just say yes. The suitcase was definitely not too heavy for Jen, but she took some amusement in watching him struggle.

RUNNING JOKE

—

LIVING IN THE SUBURBS MEANT IT ALWAYS FELT LIKE THINGS WERE happening somewhere else. That was precisely what Dan liked about them. In a city, you might run into someone you know. They'd call it serendipity—*What are the odds of running into you here?* said with such astonishment, like it was the best possible thing that could happen in a day.

In the suburbs, you did run into your neighbors, but just the same handful of people. People, most importantly, who did not really know Dan. They knew his wife (Celeste), his kids (Justin, Jessie), maybe a little about his job (insurance). Here, these things defined you. Dan was happy to let that be. He was ashamed of what actually defined him, all the people he'd fled or abandoned. So, at Safeway, seeing the neighbors with the yellowish house at the end of the cul-de-sac, it was just: *How's the wife? The kids? The job?* And then a promise to get together soon before Dan was back to fondling avocados for ripeness.

Dan felt safest in his car, a handsome but monstrous Toyota Land Cruiser from the early nineties that he'd picked up on the cheap at a police auction. He was self-aware enough to realize that his comfort in it came from his history of leaving a place and people and responsibilities, and that this big gas hog of a car had enabled that. But he promised himself that it wouldn't happen again. He was just driving around the suburbs, circling from one strip mall to the next, indulging in an endless list of chores that was mundane and also kept Dan grounded. This time, he wasn't going anywhere.

Dan's documents—his birth certificate, Social Security card, those things—were kept in an old blue Trapper Keeper in the trunk, usually under beat-up sporting equipment that his children used when they went to the park or the beach. At times, Dan was worried what might happen if his kids uncovered the folder. They would be too young to know what to even make of it, but they might show it to Celeste, who had no idea about Dan's previous lives.

Maybe there was a part of Dan that wanted to be discovered. He'd been raised in a family that could best be described as shame and guilt based. It was probably what made it so easy to fit into this new life. Christians *loved* shame and guilt. When he met Celeste, it had been so easy to convince her, her friends, and her family that he was also a life-long Christian. Feel bad about yourself and claim Jesus—the church recognizes you as one of their own.

Sometimes Dan had nightmares about Celeste finding the documents and confronting him. She'd be furious, of course, and rightfully so. He imagined the ensuing blowout. He could see everything that Celeste would say, the disappointment, the look of betrayal. Would Dan fess up, try and do everything in his power to make things right with his family? Or would he bolt—*again*?

But as the years went by, weekends of errands, trawling around the suburbs in his gigantic car, had put him at ease. And so, for many years, Dan's real identity was just left beneath a boogie board or baseball bag in the back of his Land Cruiser, waiting to be uncovered.

WHEN THE AMERICAN Advanced Protections Initiative passed, Dan was unstressed, even though all signs pointed to the government coming for people in his exact demographic: Vietnamese, male, middle-aged. But Dan was prepared. Running away wasn't about remembering what to bring, but knowing what you'd leave behind.

Each time Dan left a place, he learned to take less with him. He was only four years old when his family fled Saigon. He was too young to make any decisions then, but his mother had tried to take as much as possible—clothes, books, old photos, family heirlooms, anything they could fit on the boat. Really, instead, they should have brought as much fresh water as possible, since they nearly died of dehydration at sea.

When they beached at a refugee camp in Indonesia, they would lose all their possessions—the meaningful ones, anyway. The camp consisted of long, unremarkable huts and an under-resourced medical center. There was enough to eat, but it was only ever the most basic forms of sustenance: some rice, maybe a little fruit if they were lucky. Dan's mother believed that their time in the refugee camp would be short. And even as the months passed, she remained confident that those days would end. Young Dan felt he would be in that camp for the rest of his life.

But his oldest brother, who'd managed to settle in the U.S., was able to secure a sponsorship application. Dan's mother thanked Buddha, though it was a family of Catholics who'd eventually take them in once they reached California.

He knew his story was not special. A lot of people arrived in the U.S. fucked up by the war, imprisonment, refugee camps, reeducation camps, whatever. For a lot of immigrants, this manifested as anger. As for Dan, he nurtured a cool acceptance that everything could evaporate overnight, and if it did, he could move on.

Survival was just figuring out the next day. When you can only imagine life a day at a time, it's always money you need, never wealth. Decisions are made in the immediate term. After all, you only worry about the consequences if you're thinking ahead.

So when Dan, watching cable news, saw that AAPI was a done deal, he didn't bother to say goodbye to Celeste or peek into the bedroom Jessie and Justin shared, both fast asleep. No final glimpses.

Instead, Dan walked straight to his Land Cruiser in the garage. He checked the trunk and took stock of his belongings. The Trapper Keeper was still there, buried under a pile of beach toys from an outing months ago. Now he had the patience to unpack, putting back the folding chairs, cooler, and big blue umbrella in their proper spots on a metal shelf he had built two summers ago, swapping them for the camping gear that he and Celeste used more frequently before they had the twins: a sleeping bag, the tent, an extra wool blanket, a small stove. Dan turned off his phone, knowing that he could be tracked, and dropped it inside the cooler. Last, he removed the pair of car seats that belonged to Justin and Jessie, and placed them on the floor of the garage.

As Dan pulled out of the driveway, his head turned around so he could see through the back windshield, his eyes grazed the empty spaces the car seats had left. Under them had remained a layer of assorted crumbs and dust, in the shapes of where his son and daughter had been just hours earlier. He could clean the seats off later, maybe with one of those free gas station vacuums, once he was farther down the road.

Dan felt the faintest touch of guilt—not about leaving but the recognition of how easy it was, and how each time it only got easier.

AMAZON

—

Vietnamese detention, in the end, would be a lucrative endeavor for corporations, domestic and abroad. In fact, hundreds of new companies sprang up out of the market opportunity created by the American Advanced Protections Initiative, in line with the country's great history of capitalizing on and exploiting the moments in which people's rights have been stripped away, their humanity and dignity surrendered.

The first recipient of AAPI's market generosity was Amazon—inadvertently, at least—resulting in one of the company's best sales days ever to not fall on a Black Friday or Cyber Monday.

The Viets, notified of their incarceration assignments, had two days to pack their belongings. Each person was allowed to bring two suitcases. With just forty-eight hours to get their belongings in order, Viets flooded Amazon to take advantage of the site's promise of free two-day shipping. Homeland Security was vague about what would be provided in the camps (largely because the organization had no idea itself what it would get together in time). Basics sold out the fastest: blankets, warm clothing, batteries, matches, lighters, flashlights, lanterns, soap, hand sanitizer, gloves, duct tape, zip ties, two-way ham radios, pens and paper.

Because of the increased demand to areas of the country with saturated Vietnamese populations—Houston, Texas, and San Jose, California, in particular—many of these last-minute orders would never arrive at their destinations. Amazon's supply chain was prepared for holiday shopping but was unable to handle the sudden influx of purchases in a crisis. The company was notoriously good about keeping its promise of two-day shipping, thanks to robust logistics systems and a series of predictive algorithms. But tens of thousands of orders missed their forty-eight-hour promise, the most the company had ever failed to deliver on.

In Houston, it didn't rain the day the Viets were ordered to evacuate their homes, but it did the day after. One Texas man recalled witnessing a huge number of packages being delivered across the street too late, after his neighbors, the Trans, had left their home. The stoop of the single-story four-bedroom that they'd lived in for two decades was stacked so high with cardboard boxes that it obscured the front door. Then the rain came and soiled all of the Trans' purchases—most of them extra clothes for camp—though it hardly mattered by that point. They were already gone.

DEPARTURES

—

Since she'd arrived home, Jen had barely said a word. At first, Duncan was relieved to have her around the house for a few days, because it meant there was someone else to share the pressures of Má's anxieties. But Jen was absent—sealed in her room, appearing only for meals, which she ate in silence while their mother raved about how AAPI was a deeply un-Christian policy, yet argued that complying with it would be the Christian thing to do. Duncan didn't understand how agreeing to go along with something that was wrong was doing the right thing, but then again, no one could really understand Má now.

Jen wasn't even trying. Duncan at least listened. Má got furious when she was ignored. That turned into her nitpicking everything about Jen's behavior—what she was packing, what she was wearing, how her hair looked, as if that would matter at all at the assembly center. So Jen just shut herself away.

Duncan would deliver plates of food to Jen's door, and sometimes he would approach quietly, putting his ear to the bedroom door, just to make sure Jen was okay. Oftentimes, she would be speaking softly on the phone, which was a relief to Duncan, knowing that at least she was not totally alone in this. Duncan wasn't sure why he couldn't be that person.

His friends at school, even his football teammates, had all given him the cold shoulder since the attacks. The people he knew from church were mostly older and could only give their sympathies. The only person left to text was Alvin, and even then, they'd been committed to their

Kanye joke for over a year now. Duncan wasn't going to be the one to spoil the streak. He texted:

WHO WILL SURVIVE IN AMERICA?

"WHY ARE WE rushing to be detained?" Jen screamed, as Má pushed her yet again to finish packing. It was the most emotion Jen had expressed in days, and it immediately boiled over into an argument that Duncan had to literally get in the middle of, his body big enough that he could gently nudge them in different directions. A little physicality, he had learned, could go a long way.

The entire Indianapolis airport had been shut down for departure day, even though this part of the Midwest was fairly scarce of Vietnamese people. Still, even arriving hours early for their Homeland Security–assigned flight, they found themselves among a couple hundred other families, all awaiting an intense, multistage security process. The usual batch of well-meaning but disorganized TSA guards had been replaced by austere men decked out in military camouflage and assault rifles. From what he'd read, Duncan had expected there to be nationwide protests at the airports, but there were none, not here at least. He hoped they were happening elsewhere.

Suitcases were scanned, then individually opened and inspected. There had been little guidance as to what would be allowed, and Duncan saw people ahead of them in line arguing with the soldiers who were confiscating computers and phones, discarding them into garbage bins. Má had instructed her kids to pack only clothes and their Bible.

"It's a good thing we got here early," Má said, like it was a general observation and not a pointed barb at Jen, who wasn't paying attention anyway. The security checks were thorough, and invasive, but surprisingly efficient, and they were done in twenty minutes—less time than Duncan was used to waiting at the airport.

If there was a small relief in sight, something that Duncan had been looking forward to, it was getting to the gate early and buying snacks at the newsstand and getting one last meal at the Chili's. He'd already made up his mind: Swedish Fish and sizzlin' steak fajitas. When they arrived at the gate, Duncan saw that everything in the concourse was closed. He felt stupid for expecting anything to be open, for wanting one last moment of normalcy.

THE PLANE THEY boarded was a small one, so Duncan imagined they couldn't be traveling far. He asked a flight attendant how long the trip would be, and she said a few hours, then seemed unsure if she was supposed to reveal that information to a passenger.

Duncan looked over at Jen, who was fidgeting, covertly, with her phone.

"How did you get that by security?"

Jen shushed him. She explained that she'd placed it on the ground, just before going through the body scanner, and kicked it around the machine. Duncan couldn't believe that worked.

The phone began to vibrate. A quick glimpse of the screen revealed that she had nearly four dozen messages.

"Wow, you're blowing up."

Jen shushed him again. "It's probably not going to work when we get to wherever we're going."

He was quieter this time. "Who are you talking to?"

Jen didn't reply.

"Is it Dad?"

She seemed taken aback at the insinuation. "Why would it be Dad?"

"I don't know. I just feel like sometimes you talk to him and you don't tell me."

"Why would he show up now?" Jen's voice was an angry whisper.

She showed him the phone. The messages—nearly all of them—were from Ursula.

He began scrolling through them. Ursula was desperate to get in touch, to hear that Jen was doing okay. It seemed cruel, almost, to leave these messages on read. "Why don't you answer her? She seems really worried."

"I don't know," Jen said. "It just makes everything feel worse, the pity."

"Even now?"

Jen nodded and turned the phone off, assuming correctly that the device would stop working the moment they landed, that it would be a long time before she got to speak to anyone on the outside.

III

—

CAMP, YEAR ONE

ADJUSTMENTS

—

"Sometimes," Jen said, "being here feels like we've landed on an alien planet."

She turned to Duncan, who was picking up rocks and hurling them at other rocks, the kind of fruitless, mindless activity one did to pass the time in the desert.

"Like, we arrived in a new, foreign place—a landscape that is totally unwelcoming and nearly uninhabitable. Unknown. Forgotten. Where are we, even?"

Duncan let out a slight "Uh-huh," made a little nod. Her brother was no longer throwing rocks at rocks but trying to hit the fence about ten yards farther away. Progress, for sure.

"And we just wander this weird place. Except we don't really. We just . . . live here now."

Jen moved closer to Duncan, his sweaty body. He stunk in a way that was familiar, familial.

"Do you feel something about this place—like it's not right?" Jen went on. "Or it's not real?"

"I'll say," Duncan started, "it does look like Tatooine."

Jen didn't know what that was.

"You know, from *Star Wars*."

Jen still didn't know.

"It's the first planet you see in *Star Wars*. It's a desert. The droids crash-land there and find Luke and Obi-Wan."

"Obi-Wan?"

"Kenobi."

Could he even understand what she was saying? Jen had to hand it to him. Deliberately or not, she was no longer fixated on the existential despair of living in camp anymore. For a moment, it no longer bothered her that she had no idea how many weeks they would be there, or even where they were. She wasn't obsessing over the meaning of trying to pretend she had a life in a place that seemed to exist outside of time and space. No, now she was just wondering if her small hands were big enough to strangle Duncan's fat neck. Out here, in the middle of nowhere, not a soul would see her murder her gigantic, dumbshit brother.

"Sorry," Duncan conceded. "I don't think it really matters that we're in the desert."

"What do you mean? We are trapped in a remote and horrible place. That's the whole point."

"I don't know," Duncan said. "Would it matter if the place were nicer? Cleaner, roomier bunks. Better food. Would hot water make a difference?"

"I would kill anyone—even you—for even a lukewarm shower."

"I'm just saying. Does it matter where we are, or what the conditions are, if it's still a prison?"

Duncan chucked another rock at the fence.

From her pocket, Jen withdrew the phone she had snuck into the assembly center, and now to camp. She'd sometimes turn it on, just to look at Ursula's last texts to her. Now the phone was dead, useless. She thought about throwing it. Then she had a better idea.

"Here, you've got a better arm than me."

Duncan obliged, took the phone, and launched it into the air, straight into the sun.

THE FOURTH STRANGEST adjustment to life in the camp was that Jen was only ever doing one thing at a time. In her past life, she spent her evenings at her desk, doing homework, messaging friends, with music or a movie on in the background. She was switching between tabs, between devices, between playlists, and then she might take a break from all that to get a snack. It seemed a little wild, in hindsight, how much time Jen spent looking at her computer or her phone, just reading and texting, fidgeting. But the absence of that kind of constant stimulation made camp feel even more isolating. She'd been scared of detention—and at times, it *was* scary, with the constant uncertainty and the occasional eruptions of brutality. But mostly? It was boring.

One dull thing at a time: When Jen was eating, she was just eating. Even her sleep occurred without the interruption of dreams. But her main activity was waiting. There were lines for the mess hall. The bathroom. Wrapped around the Office of Detention Culture building, where you waited to make requests or complaints, which would likely be denied and ignored.

And when Jen was in line, she just stood there with her thoughts. Maybe if you were lucky, someone conversational would be either in front of you or behind you—or sometimes you were unlucky because they were too talkative—but you were doing one thing, just waiting in line. What she would've given to have her phone back. Even though she knew she'd never be able to call or text or go online, just the thought of having something to tap and swipe would be a welcome distraction from whatever this was.

THE THIRD STRANGEST adjustment was not knowing everything, all the time. It all used to be at her fingertips. The vast, searchable index of all human knowledge just a few moments away—the name of whatshisface in whatsthatmovie, or the specific forgotten lyric to a song that she'd had stuck in her head, only to discover that the cure to an earworm was not learning the words, but listening to it over and over until she simply tired of it, which she could also do because of the internet.

She craved connection. She missed Google. She hated how every loose thought or reference that came up in her day, at random, could no longer be satiated. Not knowing the band who wrote the song she was singing? Not remembering the name of a book she'd loved at one point? An exact quote from that book? These things, frivolous as they were, just ate at her throughout the day. Remembering wasn't the same thing as knowing; she'd taken for granted the ability to summon the culture she craved.

Sometimes she'd hum a song at Duncan.

"You know? It goes duh-de-duh-de-duh."

"That could be any song."

"Duh-de-duh-de-duh!"

"Not helping."

"At the end it's, like, duh-de-duh-de-duh-deeeeeeeeeee-duh!"

"Please stop humming."

DETAINEES WERE ASSIGNED BUNKS, many not actually finished when they arrived. In Jen's bunk, none of the beds had been assembled. Mattresses, still wrapped, were piled in a corner of the room. No linens, of course. There was a lot of loose lumber, screws, and bolts. Not even instructions on how to put it all together.

When Jen complained to the guard posted outside the bunk about it, he just snarled at her.

"Everything is as it should be."

"What do you mean? Nothing is even ready."

"I don't know what to tell you, ma'am," he said, before repeating himself. "Everything is as it should be."

Eventually Duncan came to check on her. He surveyed the room—all the deconstructed living arrangements—and confirmed that his bunk had been in worse shape, if you could imagine it. But he and some boys in the bunk found a few tools—a hammer, a couple screwdrivers—and figured out how to put the beds together. Lucky for him that he was living with a handyman.

The older men, anyone in their forties and up, had been taken to a different location. It had been three months of no adult men at the assembly center; Jen wondered if they would no longer be separated at Camp Tacoma. She held out hope that maybe she would see her father. But no such luck. For once, Dad's absence wasn't his fault.

Jen admired the boys stepping up, filling the roles of their fathers. Duncan went back to his bunk and returned with the handyman, and they got to work. It was nice, Jen thought, building a bed together with her brother. When's the last time they'd worked on a project together? Lego sets as kids? Beating *Donkey Kong Country*?

Once Jen's bed was in good shape, Duncan offered to help the other women with theirs. It was a generosity she'd seen in her brother before, but it seemed to be growing. Jen was overwhelmed with the pride she felt. Or maybe this freshly constructed bed and newly unwrapped mattress that she was now lying on was the best thing she'd experienced in months.

THE SECOND STRANGEST adjustment was not having any privacy. Getting used to having a roommate at NYU was one thing. A bunk of two dozen women was another.

Mostly, this meant there was no place that Jen could cry. She supposed she could cry anywhere and look like an idiot. But she preferred a private sob. A quiet corner where she could really let it out.

She wasn't even a big crier! But here she didn't even have the option. That in itself made her want to cry.

For all of the expanse of the camp, the detainees were still on top of each other. The bunks were overcrowded. The mess halls were raucous with the sound of shouting and open-mouthed chewing. There were no private stalls in the bathrooms, and Jen's new concern wasn't that she didn't have a place to cry but that she had to take a dump in front of strangers, or even worse, not strangers. One time she'd ended up at the bathroom at the same time as Má, and even though she knew, rationally, that her mother had raised her and cleaned up her shit hundreds, maybe thousands, of times, Jen could not bear the idea of her witnessing it now.

"IT STINKS OUT HERE," Duncan said.

The aroma was specific. It reminded Jen of nước mắm—sweet, and fermented, in a good way at first. Then the deeper notes of the smell would reveal themselves: fishy, sweaty, and ultimately, like shit.

Some days, the camp would be awash in the smell of garbage. It was unclear where it was coming from, but it absorbed the entire stretch of desert where everyone was trapped. It was all-consuming, and seemingly inescapable. Everyone held their shirts up to their noses and made do.

The worst, though, was when you were eating. When the waves of stink came through, it was impossible to eat without imagining shoveling literal shit into your mouth.

Thankfully, that night, the smell had come right after dinner and not before. Jen and Duncan were walking back from the mess hall, hands covering their mouths, as if that might help them breathe in a different kind of air.

"Does anyone know where it comes from? The smell?" Duncan asked.

Jen's eyes started to water.

"Are you crying?" Duncan asked.

Jen wasn't sure whether the reaction was emotional or physical or both.

BUT THE ABSOLUTE strangest adjustment? Well, maybe it wasn't strange at all, because it was so obvious. It was not being able to communicate with anyone in the world whenever she wanted. She couldn't call her friends. Jen couldn't DM Drake, not that she would, nor would he respond, but the fact that messaging Drake was no longer on the table devastated her, which was funny because she didn't even like his music.

She missed texting with Ursula the most.

Sure, it had never really been an equal relationship. Ursula was older. But she was smart and charming and clearly going to do amazing things with her career. Jen wasn't even sure she would escape Christianity, the Midwest, her mother. She'd tried to, and for a moment, succeeded. But camp? It was basically like being back home. She could dodge the Christians as much as she wanted, but they were always badgering her.

And as for Má. Well, it was nice to be around her more, depending on the day.

But still, Jen thought about Ursula constantly. She hadn't realized, in her previous life as a free person, how much she'd relied on her cousin. Every stupid, dumb thought about a stupid, dumb thing? Ursula got it first.

JURASSIC PARK

—

FOR THE FIRST FEW MONTHS OF CAMP, THE ONLY ACTIVITY THAT wasn't a scheduled meal shift or Sunday church was movie night. Only four films had been approved by the Office of Detention Culture: *Forrest Gump, Aladdin, The Godfather Part II,* and *Jurassic Park.*

A dim projector was set up near the ODC building, as well as a couple hundred folding chairs, reserved for the elders. Everyone else sat on the ground. There were scant patches of grass, but mostly the ground was dirt, so people brought their rationed blankets. The sound system wasn't powerful, likely not designed for outdoor use. During the film, people were nearly silent. A rare stillness in the week.

Before the movie started, the guards would take a vote on which of the four movies people wanted to watch. Every week, the winner was *Jurassic Park.* It was the movie with the least dialogue, or just the one that the many older Vietnamese who couldn't speak English could still follow. Mostly, it was the scariest movie of the four. Everyone understood the language of fear.

Duncan was so tired of *Jurassic Park,* but he escorted Má every week. She felt an obligation to go, especially because all of the other church-going folk went. Before the movie started, Duncan watched his mother greet the older attendees, seated in their chairs, blankets across their laps, smiling and eager to speak to her. It was a little odd, Duncan's mother blessing people who did not ask to be blessed.

Though Duncan had always found his mom's behavior corny at church, here it made him a little proud. Sometimes Duncan would walk with her, shaking hands and using what little Vietnamese he knew to ask them how they were doing. They'd smile back, comment on how big he was. Some of them recognized Duncan from the mess hall, his work assignment—everyone in camp worked if physically able—and complimented how he made eggs.

"You see, not everything is bad. Look how much people enjoy movie night. Everyone turns up for movie night," she said, gesturing to the thousands of people who'd shown up to barely hear the film.

"That's because there's not a single other thing to do."

"It's like they say in *Jurassic Park:* 'Life keeps on happening.'"

The quote was actually "Life finds a way," but Duncan didn't correct her.

Jen never went, always opting to use the time when her bunk was empty to read. Sometimes Duncan would bail about halfway through the movie—usually right after the T-Rex knocked the Ford Explorer off the cliff—to bring Jen some popcorn.

Growing up, Jen had been the good child. But when she left for college, it felt like she was truly gone. They texted regularly, but her phone call home once a week was an obligation, their conversation stilted. Duncan couldn't help but feel like he'd been abandoned, left alone to take care of their mother, whose neediness became more apparent once he was the only child at home. Má was clingy, always wanting to talk. She started going to more functions, and dragging Duncan along with her, as if that would bring him closer and not make him want to flee Indiana the minute he got his learner's permit.

He didn't begrudge Jen, and he knew that she had escaped to an exciting new life only to have that freedom snatched away just as quickly. Duncan was just bothered by how little she wanted to see him or their mother now that they were all at camp together. The only thing grounding Duncan was the comfort that he was at least around people who knew him, who understood him. Given the circumstances, what else was there to hang on to if not family?

ONE INCREDIBLE EVENING, movie night went a different way. The winning film was not *Jurassic Park* but *Forrest Gump.* It was unclear what happened. Even the ODC guards were blindsided, laughing about it among themselves. Duncan quickly excused himself from Má's usual meet-and-greet, grabbed a thing of popcorn, and rushed to go tell Jen.

Duncan felt ridiculous speeding down a row of bunks, loose kernels spilling behind him, until he finally reached Jen's building.

But Jen was nowhere to be found. He asked one of the other women in the bunk if they'd seen his sister. She just looked back at him, peeking up from her book, to say she didn't know. Where was she?

It was fine and reasonable that Jen might be somewhere else. Duncan knew that. She was getting up to her own things. *Life keeps on happening*, Duncan thought, though he still wondered how it was happening for her.

LAM

—

Two hundred miles into Dan's trip, he found it hard to express how good being on the road felt, the freedom. Survival was the only acceptable excuse for selfishness.

He was navigating his way through the middle of nowhere using an atlas he'd purchased at a gas station. The copyright was nearly twenty years out of date. Dan had no idea how much the highway infrastructure might have changed in two decades, but it seemed the bones of America's roads remained mostly intact. Besides, he wasn't headed anywhere specific. Originally his plan had been to drive north. But he caught a news broadcast at a bar that'd described DHS catching hundreds of runaways at the Canadian border. That was a no-go.

Dan stuck to back roads as much as he could and avoided any highway with a toll, which could possibly have cameras. He only poked his nose out to get gas, and even then, he obscured his face with a scarf and removed the car's license plate before he approached the station. For sustenance, he went all in on bottled water and energy bars. The hardest part, at first, was giving up his morning coffee. The second hardest part, his nightly whiskey. But with no clear idea how long he would be on the lam, there was only a budget for the bare essentials. Just a couple weeks in and Dan realized it was the longest he'd been sober in many, many years. There was something to that.

Most nights, Dan slept in his Land Cruiser. He laid the back seats down, and it was nearly enough for the full length of him to recline. Usually, he cleaned himself weekly, whenever he could find a quiet body of fresh water. Once a month, he allowed himself to stay at a motel, and really, that was just so he could use a shower. The bed was a relief. But often, Dan was unable to sleep, and he just watched TV into the wee hours of the morning.

Without regular access to the internet, Dan's knowledge of recent events was patchwork from what he could bear to listen to on the radio. There were only suspicious reports out of camp, mostly attempts to show that the detention sites for Vietnamese were not really so bad. Some of the Republican leaders had even tried to sell it like it was a vacation—free temporary room and board while matters of national security were sorted out. The backlash to that was swift. Suddenly the people who supported locking up a million innocent Vietnamese people against their will were upset that camp might be too cushy for their tax dollars.

Dan was just so surprised by how many Vietnamese willingly showed up at assembly centers, ready to be sorted and shuffled off to far-flung destinations for who knew how long. What would be the punishment for trying to elude the authorities? They would throw him in camp, probably, so he would be no worse off for trying to hide.

He had vague memories of the refugee camp in Indonesia. He had been young, thankfully, but the sensory memories stayed with him. The salty stench of the ocean; the way the heat dehydrated his frail body. And then there was the hunger. The sensation of his stomach eating itself, the acid slowly eroding him from the inside. Dan recalled his mother trying to open a coconut without any tools, and in her desperation, she'd repeatedly smashed it against a rock, over and over, until the shell finally splintered, spilling warm milk across her now bloodied hands. Nothing had ever tasted as sweet as that overripe coconut.

Maybe it was true that things wouldn't be that bad in detention. But why would Dan even bother to find out?

TESTS

—

Job placement in camp reminded Jen, weirdly, of applying for college. There were interviews—she'd gotten used to it by now, especially after the ones at the assembly center, which asked prying personal questions about her loyalty to the United States, as well as seemingly unnecessary questions about her sexuality and sexual history. The interviews at camp, at least, were fairly benign. *What are your strengths? What are your weaknesses? Tell me about an instance you overcame a challenge.* Generic to the point of condescension, though after invasive questions about how many people she'd slept with, a welcome relief.

But of course, there was also a test. Jen had scored pretty well on her SAT, she felt, without the privilege of a private tutor, like many of her friends in Indiana had. The test in camp was much different. For one, there were two of them. The first seemed like a personality test. *On a scale of 1 to 5, how would you rate your willingness to do manual labor?* (That was a 1.) *On a scale of 1 to 5, how would you rate your ability to work well with others?* (That was a 5, the correct answer, even though there were supposedly no wrong ones.)

The second test—and one that she later learned was not given to everyone—was a timed typing exam. She was seated at a computer and asked to copy down a passage that was on the screen. Jen had never taken a typing test before, and she wished she'd been able to practice. She made a lot of errors, partly because the keyboard was unfamiliar. But she decided that the best approach was to go quickly and not think about the mistakes. Just go as fast as she could and not worry about being wrong. As she typed, Jen fell into a pleasing rhythm. The clacking became a loud, irregular beat that was under her control.

At the end, after five minutes of typing that seemed over as quickly as it started, Jen was given a score.

"One hundred twenty-five words per minute," the ODC guard said, not making eye contact.

"Is that good?"

He didn't answer. But from his nonanswer, Jen knew she'd done well.

SPORTS COMPLEX

—

When the American Advanced Protections Initiative was met with public resistance, congressional leaders attempted to justify the mass detention of the Viets by assuring its critical constituents that the camps weren't camps at all but "campuses," vocabulary that attempted to evoke in the imagination a university or the office space of a large tech company.

Proponents of the bill released architectural renderings of what a camp might look like—brand-new facilities with spacious living quarters and cafeterias—complete with smiling, happy people, blissfully unaware that they had the same rights as prisoners.

In no instance was this effort more obvious than when it was announced that each of the campuses would have a state-of-the-art athletic complex with a football field, an indoor basketball court, a weight room, and an Olympic-size swimming pool. The Department of Homeland Security would even be pulling designers at Nike to ensure these were the best facilities. (Though it was never made clear what exactly Nike's involvement would be, and later, the company would deny it.)

Even despite their vague role, leveraging the brand association of the world's largest sneaker company worked. While the evacuation of the Viets would be mandatory, it was spoken about in nonpunitive ways. How could detention be a form of internment or incarceration when the Viets would be able to freely play basketball on brand-new courts?

The reality was that only one of these athletic complexes would be built, at Camp Tacoma. Its construction was heavily broadcast, but news of its opening never made it to the public because it never completely opened.

In some ways, the attempt to soften the image of detention with a sports complex backfired. New critics found the facilities too nice, a humongous waste of taxpayer dollars. On his incendiary nightly show on Fox News, one pundit asked, "Why is Congress rewarding these potential guerilla warriors? Why are we giving them a place where they can train and become stronger? On our soil!" To him, exercise was the genesis of terrorism. "Detention Should Not Be a Free Vacation" read the headline of an op-ed by a conservative *New York Times* columnist, who wrote at length about how the planned athletic complex seemed nicer than the racquet club to which he belonged.

It is unclear whether it was this criticism that prevented the facilities from being made available to detainees or whether they were never going to be available to the Viets in the first place. After all, the idea was only generated as a means to deny detractors their claims that mass detention would be inhumane or unconstitutional. Plus, there was a large construction contract to hand out, which pleased both sides of the aisle.

The football leagues across the various camps would become a focal point of camp life and culture, but the rest of the sports facilities would never be accessible. The locker rooms did not have hot water. The weight room was never supplied with equipment. The swimming pool, fitting in dimension and scale for an Olympian in training, would never see a drop of water.

THE BOTTOM OF A POOL

—

THE NEWSPAPER TEAM WAS SMALL—JUST A DOZEN DETAINEES, NEARLY all young women, in nebulous roles. There weren't reporters and editors and photographers and designers. Everyone was asked to do everything, interchangeably, which didn't really bother Jen, because, after all, this wasn't a real newspaper. It was a propaganda arm of the Office of Detention Culture. Unimaginatively, it had been named the *Camp Tacoma Loyalty*, as if *Times* or *Tribune* or *Post* might signal that journalism—or any kind of free speech—would be published within its pages. Two thin editions, one in English and the other in Vietnamese, were sent to the printer every Friday afternoon.

All assignments and copy were overseen by Officer Mitch Paulson, who at a real publication would have been the editor in chief but insisted on referring to himself as the president, both relaying his lack of understanding of the editorial process (even if it was propaganda, there was a process) and illustrating just how much he enjoyed exerting power. It didn't take long for Jen and her colleagues to understand exactly how to handle Officer Paulson. He was an idiot who liked to appear dominant, the easiest kind of man to manipulate.

Allegra, the staffer who was closest to Jen in age, was always flirtatious with Paulson. She was the only one who laughed at his jokes, touched his shoulder playfully. Every tease destabilized Paulson, put the short, bald white man on his back foot, unsure of what to do except clumsily make reference to his wife, as if Allegra might actually sleep with him, as if each interaction with her was a series of temptations that Paulson was—as a man of will and discipline—bravely resisting. It wasn't the illusion of control. It was a farce. The whole thing was by turns pathetic and amusing, but almost always useful.

For one, Paulson signed off on all assignments. If Jen wanted to spend more time with her brother, Duncan, she'd propose a profile of one of the cafeteria chefs. Something glowing, of course, about how the menus were conceived and how well-run the mess halls were. That kind of thing.

"How long will it take you to submit?" Paulson would ask.

"You mean to file copy?" Allegra interrupted. Using the journalistic nomenclature that Paulson was unfamiliar with always made him feel stupid. Which meant the next things out of his mouth were attempts to seem smart rather than substantively answer the question.

"Yes, uh, file copy. For editing."

"About a week," Jen would answer, even though in reality a more reasonable timeline would have been an afternoon. She could spend the week doing whatever she wanted, and all she had to do was jam out 750 words of rubbish by Friday.

Allegra covered all the sports for the paper, the most popular section, and she convinced Paulson that she needed to attend every football practice. She'd just hang out on the bleachers and get day drunk sneaking shots of bootleg booze.

It was annoying being around a dolt like Officer Paulson, president of the *Camp Tacoma Loyalty*. It was also the easiest job they could have. Jen sometimes felt bad that her brother was confined to a hot kitchen, or that the other people in her bunk were stitching garments or cleaning the bathrooms. Nearly everyone at Camp Tacoma was forced to do manual labor. In her job placement interview, Jen had said she was part of her college newspaper, knew Photoshop, and could use a camera. None of that was true, but you only got punished for being honest.

ALLEGRA AND JEN departed the ODC building where they worked on the newspaper. Each time they entered and exited, they were forced to swipe an ID badge, to track their comings and goings. You had to keep your badge on you at all times. Last week, ODC guards caught an older man—must've been in his thirties—who explained that he'd forgotten the badge in his bunk. But his English wasn't great, and the guards made an example of him anyway. The man lost a couple teeth and was sent to the infirmary. Unsurprisingly, the *Camp Tacoma Loyalty* did not report on the incident.

In the earlier days, Allegra had pushed to report on the actual living conditions of the camp. She knew that it was an uphill battle, that the paper only existed to keep people feeling optimistic about detention. (Paulson had called the newspaper "a morale booster," which was a funny thing to think about: the morale of prisoners. Jen whispered to Allegra that the easiest way to boost morale was to release everyone.)

Before camp, Allegra had been a journalism student at Northwestern. "One of the best J-schools in the country," she'd explained, several times, to Jen. After she graduated, she would work at a local paper as a beat reporter, then after a few years, find herself in a midsize city paper—Chicago or Houston, maybe. When Jen pointed out she was calling the third- and fourth-largest cities in the U.S. midsize, Allegra ignored her, continuing to lay out her plans: her dream job would be reporting on climate change for *The New York Times*, or at worst, *The Washington Post*.

Yet it only took a few issues of the *Loyalty* to come out before she gave up arguing with Paulson. And now she spent her creative energy strategizing how to figure out assignments that allowed her to slack off as much as possible.

"You're cool, right?" Allegra asked one day, as they were headed toward the sports complex.

"What do you mean?"

"I mean, like, you're *cool*."

The further emphasis on "cool" did not explain what Allegra meant, but Jen felt obliged to nod affirmatively.

"Of course I'm cool," Jen said, which came out unconvincingly even to herself.

From her pocket, Allegra withdrew what appeared to be a joint. The smallest one that Jen had ever seen.

"Oh my god, where did you get that?" Jen didn't even smoke pot. But the sight of the extremely tiny roach made her heart leap.

"Follow me," she said. "Let's go light this somewhere."

As THEY WALKED the long, dusty path toward the football field, Jen attempted to work out what Allegra had meant earlier. Allegra was, by any definition of the word, cool. She was endearing, yet always taken seriously. Her hair was long, naturally textured, effortless. Allegra's self-assurance reminded Jen of Ursula.

Allegra spoke about her commitment to journalism with a familiar combination of swagger and self-importance. It used to drive Jen lightly insane to hear Ursula talk about how serious her work was. When Allegra did it, the arrogance now felt like a comfort. That was how much she missed her cousin, apparently.

Allegra, tall and lanky, took long strides that kicked up dust behind them as they trotted quickly toward the football field.

"Why are we walking so fast?" Jen asked, trying to hide her heaving.

Allegra seemed to not hear, or not care, and continued on with what she had been talking about before. Something about the badges.

"Do you ever think about how everyone here is locked up, but we're, like, the least locked up?" Allegra asked. She held out her ID. "Everyone is confined to their bunk, their assigned mess hall, and the building where they do their job assignment, if they're even lucky enough to have one indoors."

Jen eyed her badge, which was dangling from a lanyard around her neck.

"Our passes, though, let us go pretty much anywhere, because we have to go to so many different buildings across camp to write for"— Allegra broke into an impression of Paulson's tough guy voice—"the *Camp Tacoma Loyalty*."

This was true. Jen had thought of the newspaper job as a cushy one, not one that came with extra access or powers.

"The ODC is still tracking everywhere we go. So it's not like we could try to get away with anything. They would know exactly where we'd been."

"They know where we go," Allegra said, "but not what we do."

Suddenly, a cart pulled up alongside them. Camp Tacoma's vehicles were all electric, which explained why Jen hadn't heard it approaching.

In the driver's seat was a man around their age, matted, tousled black hair and a K-pop swoop across his forehead. He was cute, Jen noticed. Really cute.

"You guys want a ride?" he asked.

Allegra didn't stop walking, so Jen didn't either. The cart slowed down to match their pace.

"You don't even know where we're headed," Allegra said.

"I'll take you wherever you want to go. I just finished delivering ground pork to Mess Hall 12. If you guys are headed north, I can drop you off on my way to the loading area. My whole day is just unloading this pallet of pork at different kitchens."

"You just drive around all day?" Jen asked.

"It's a pretty good job, compared to some of the other assignments. My mom, she's on janitorial duty—spends all day cleaning gunk out of the showers. But you guys have it pretty easy, too."

"What would you know about it?" Jen said.

His focus was back on Allegra. "Wow, Legs, your friend is fun."

"Jen, this is Brandon. Like everyone named Brandon, he's a bit of a fuck boy."

"Nice to meet you, Jen," Brandon said. He leaned across the passenger seat and put his arm out for a handshake.

BENEATH THE FOOTBALL stadium bleachers, Allegra lit the joint and took a quick puff.

"Only short ones," she instructed. "This thing isn't going to last us very long."

Jen didn't know much about smoking, but even she knew that this spliff was not going to get the three of them high.

Allegra passed it to Brandon, who puffed so quickly that it seemed like he took nothing into his lungs at all, and handed the joint to Jen, who did the same. There they were, three teenagers skirting their obligations to smoke pot under some bleachers. Allegra took a longer drag this time.

"Okay, I'm gonna go up top and be the lookout. You two finish that."

Allegra climbed up out of the bleachers, the clanging of her steps fading as she walked out of view.

"Aren't you going to get in trouble if you're not at the loading area?" Jen asked.

"The sooner I get there, the sooner someone has to load up my cart, and the sooner the ODC guards have to get off their asses and pay attention to us," Brandon said. "So, no, I'm not going to get in trouble for being a little late. No one in camp is particularly motivated. Especially not the guards."

Jen must've looked unconvinced.

"Everyone will get their pork," Brandon said, defensively.

Jen could hear the sounds of football practice: pads making contact, the grunts of boys overexerting themselves, the occasional shrill of a whistle. It was soothing as ambient noise, even the way the echoes rattled among the metal bleachers.

"So, your job is pretty easy?" Jen said.

Brandon chuckled. "Yeah, I just drive this electric cart around. Honestly, it's . . . pretty fun? I usually help unload things I deliver to the kitchen, since they're mostly staffed by old ladies. I think they like to watch me carry heavy things."

"Wow, you're such a gift."

"A handsome, polite, slightly-above-average-in-height Vietnamese boy. What's not to love?"

A particularly loud crunch, followed by a pained groan—someone out on the football field.

"I know some people in camp are mad that the football teams get shorter work shifts so they can go to practice. But tackling drills and running suicides sounds way harder than most of the stuff we got assigned to," Brandon said.

Jen felt lucky, grateful, for her slacker job. Which was a ridiculous feeling: gratitude, given everything. But maybe that was the right feeling? Gratitude, given everything.

"So how do you know Allegra?" Jen asked.

"I don't know her that well," he said. "But we were both at Northwestern before all of this."

Brandon gestured vaguely toward their surroundings.

"Yeah, but . . ." Jen could feel herself prying but couldn't help it. "What's the deal with you guys?"

Brandon returned her prying with a smile. It was sly, knowing, betraying nothing. God, he was cute.

"That's probably the last hit, right there," he said, handing her what was left of the pot. Then he asked: "So how did you get involved with El Paquete?"

"El Paquete?" Jen took the last puff, the lit end reaching her fingertips. It didn't hurt, but the surprise made her drop the joint. She stomped it out with her sneaker.

"Oh, uh, never mind, then," Brandon said. "I thought since you knew Legs . . ."

"No, really, what is El Paquete?"

"Sorry, I assumed—"

"What are you guys talking about?" Allegra was back. She was midclimb between bleachers, and gracefully lowering herself to the ground.

"You said this girl was cool."

"She is cool, Brandon," Allegra assured him. "Isn't that right, Jen? You're cool?"

"I know we're not actually high," Jen said, "but I am confused as hell."

THE THREE OF them left the bleachers and headed into the men's locker room. The entire athletic complex was an expanse: a tennis court, a basketball court, a pool. No one was permitted to use them without ODC approval, which meant no one used them.

But there was an upside to all the vacant recreational facilities. Allegra knew no one would ever be there. And the athletic complex was large enough that it would be impossible to track where they were, or where they'd been. All they needed to do was scan their badges at the entrance, but once they were inside, they had free rein.

"What's with all the secrecy?" Jen asked.

Allegra didn't answer. She and Brandon just led her toward the pool, still waterless.

"This is eerie," Jen said. Again, no response.

Brandon climbed down into the empty pool, using a construction ladder that had been propped against the side. Clearly, it wasn't the first time they'd been here.

"Why do we have to go into the pool?"

"Just watch your step," Brandon said.

Jen followed his lead, and Allegra stepped down the ladder, not far behind.

It was an odd experience, being at the bottom of a pool. The walls were oppressively high, and the pool was nearly twelve feet deep—impossible to get out of if that ladder fell.

Allegra's and Brandon's tenor had changed. At first, it seemed like the day would be sneaking around and getting a little high. Now they were both quiet.

"This isn't some hazing thing where you both leave me here, is it?"

Allegra scoffed. "We'd find a much crueler way to haze you if that was the case."

"Everyone stand over here," Brandon said, pointing at a corner of the pool. Jen and Allegra obliged.

Now the three of them were standing very close to each other, close enough that Jen could pick up a whiff of Brandon's hair. It smelled good, better than the harsh soap available in the shower. Was that lavender? Who could say—it'd been so long since Jen had caught the scent of anything that didn't reek of the desert.

"Okay, I think we're out of sight," Brandon said.

"Out of whose sight?"

"Come on, Jen." Allegra rolled her eyes.

"There are cameras all over the place. But they didn't account for the pool being empty, so this is one of the blind spots," Brandon said.

Allegra added: "That and the bleachers."

"Yeah, but the bleachers are too obvious for this."

"Too obvious for what?"

"Are you sure about her?" Brandon was now looking at Allegra.

"Yes, I'm sure."

Brandon's eyes were back on Jen and she could smell his breath now. It wasn't quite as pleasant as his hair.

"We need people. People we can trust. Can we trust you, Jennifer?"

"Nobody calls me Jennifer."

Brandon's eyes snapped back to Allegra, a shot of incredulity.

"Yes, of course you can trust me," Jen said.

"You are very valuable, just like Allegra, because your job assignment gives you access to nearly every building in camp."

"And here I just thought you liked me for me."

"This is serious," Allegra said.

"I do my part," Brandon said. "I'm distributing things on my routes to the kitchens."

"Like pot?"

"No, I'm distributing medicine, food, computers, things that people can't get in camp but need." Brandon paused for a second. "Okay, and yes, also pot."

"There are a lot of places I help Brandon get into," Allegra said. "Because our newspaper assignments give us cover, it makes it easy for us to move around camp, largely undetected."

"This seems risky," Jen said. "Dangerous, even. What will the ODC do if they find out?"

"What are they going to do? Throw us in jail?" Brandon did his gesture-toward-everything motion again. This time it was less cute.

"No, Jen is right. This is dangerous," Allegra said. "But it's important."

Brandon was cagey on specifics—Jen suspected he didn't quite trust her yet. But in broad strokes, this network was much bigger than just

Brandon and Allegra. It was a coordinated effort across what sounded like dozens, perhaps hundreds, of detainees, moving contraband around camp.

"Thanks to us, nearly every bunk has a computer."

Jen had wondered where the laptop in her living quarters had come from, though she'd never had a chance to use it herself, since it was always being hogged by one of the families—the Vus, always watching Korean soaps at night and reacting loudly enough that Jen's one desire from the outside world was a set of soft foam earplugs. Jen had assumed that the Vu family had snuck it in with their belongings, and that the ODC just didn't care about a beat-up old Dell that chugged when it played movie files.

But no, this was the work of El Paquete, Brandon explained. They'd provided the computer, and all the K-dramas, too.

"I thought you just provided essentials," Jen said.

"Art *is* essential," Brandon said.

Allegra laughed involuntarily—a guttural sound that rattled around the high walls of the pool. "Brandon, patron of the contraband arts, is also a poet."

The way Allegra said "poet" had sounded dismissive, and it made Brandon blush.

"We believe that giving people TV and movies and music and books will keep them going. Like, what is the point of living if we don't experience things that tell us about who we are? That's how they're going to kill us in this camp. Deprive us of art and culture for long enough and we'll just be fucking empty inside."

"Sure, Brandon, all these installments of *Paris by Night* are really gonna stop folks from wanting to end their miserable lives."

There were clearly some old arguments, and old wounds, that these two needed to sort out. Not here, though, in front of Jen. It was already too uncomfortable.

"So why are you telling me all this?" Jen interrupted.

Allegra and Brandon turned to Jen, as if for a moment, they'd completely forgotten she was there.

—

THIS, OF COURSE, was a recruitment effort. Cool people only wanted her attention when they needed something in return. But Jen didn't mind. She was flattered to be asked.

Detention had been an unraveling of her life. But if she was honest with herself, there was something liberating about it. Jen's first year of college had been tough. It had also felt selfish—the cost of her loans, she knew, was hard on her mother, who helped pay tuition for a faraway institution that she didn't even want her daughter to attend. As a person attempting to move into the next phase of her life, Jen felt guilty that she hadn't focused on her schoolwork.

She would never say it out loud, but detention was, in some ways, a relief. Now that she'd settled into the rhythms of camp, Jen was free of the pressure she put on herself, the pressure her family put on her; free of expectations.

That said, Jen told herself she was not about to immediately get wrapped up with El Paquete. She might help out here and there, but the commitment Allegra and Brandon were talking about sounded like they were plotting a revolution. Escorting people into buildings she had access to. Distributing banned materials and substances across camp to the people who wanted them. Hiding materials, especially for the more exposed members of El Paquete who knew they were being closely monitored. Allegra mentioned she did some writing, too, though Brandon brushed by that detail.

Every turn was a chance to help their people, to undermine the ODC, to disrupt the rhythm of camp, which they felt was already too ingrained. It made detainees complacent, too willing to accept the harsh conditions under which they were forced to live. Here was an opportunity to make a difference—the promise she had so often been sold in life outside of detention by clubs, recruiters, people only claiming interest in her future. No one ever seemed to reckon with the fact that change could make things worse.

"I'll have to think about it," Jen said. She could tell they were disappointed. A "maybe" always sounds like a "no."

"We're not trying to radicalize you," Brandon said.

"We're not?" Allegra shot back.

She gave Brandon a look, signaling that he should leave. "Let us girls talk for a second." Brandon, his exaggerated body language communicating "hugely annoyed," climbed up the ladder and out of the pool area.

Allegra stepped in, very close to Jen, to the point where they were nearly cheek to cheek.

"I get it. This is scary. I'm scared all the time."

Like Brandon's, her hair smelled amazing.

"There are lots of ways to help. Some of them are less risky than others. We can find something that works for your level of comfort."

She got even closer. Jen could feel Allegra's wet lips against her earlobe.

"But you're going to help us. Because I will make your life hell if you don't."

Allegra withdrew and quickly scrambled up the ladder. As she climbed over the lip of the pool, she pulled the ladder up behind her.

"What are you doing?" Brandon said, confused.

"Showing Jen what the stakes are."

Allegra stood, arms folded, at the top of the pool, looking down at Jen. There was no way up.

"This is a joke, right?" Jen asked, nervously, knowing it wasn't, the tears starting to come.

"This isn't funny, Legs."

"It's not supposed to be, Brandon. Come on, let's get out of here. We'll be back when Jen makes up her mind."

Jen's chest felt tight. Like, really tight. They couldn't possibly leave her here—that would be insane. She had to be back to the bunk by curfew. There were real consequences here. Allegra was her friend, wasn't she? Suddenly, Jen's head was dizzy, too. The walls of the pool felt at once like they were moving farther away and closing in on her.

Jen could hear Allegra and Brandon arguing, but couldn't make out their conversation. And after a moment, she couldn't see them anymore. And then she couldn't hear them. And then she heard the slam of a door. Then silence.

She tried to control her breathing. She slowed it down, then sat, calmly, cross-legged, in the center of the pool. There was nothing she could do now. Eventually, Jen relaxed a bit, and then lay on her back. The cool, clean tile felt nice against her skin. Jen imagined the pool filling with warm water, slowly lifting her up, till she reached the surface.

"This pool thing," Jen said out loud, "do you do this with all your recruits?"

A beat. And then finally:

"No, first time."

Another beat.

"Pretty effective, though, right?"

Allegra sounded pleased with herself.

"Don't you worry about alienating people?"

"It doesn't matter. People need to realize they're already sitting at the bottom of the pool."

Allegra's head appeared over the side. She was smiling, which pissed Jen off to no end. But she was also relieved to see Allegra had never actually left.

"Okay, let me up," Jen said, defeated.

"I really thought we'd have to wait around longer."

Brandon appeared over the pool lip, leaned over, and offered his arm.

Jen eyed it for a moment, then leapt for Brandon's hand. With surprising momentum, he swung her up and out of the pool.

"Wouldn't the ladder have been easier?"

"Yeah, but I just want to show you how strong I am."

"That poet's strength," Allegra teased.

Brandon scoffed. "You're the one using the empty pool as a metaphor."

"*People need to realize they're already sitting at the bottom of the pool,*" Jen mimicked.

Allegra laughed and put her arm around Jen's slightly shaking shoulders as the three of them made their way out of the sports complex, into the heat.

FLOW STATE

—

GOOGLE OFTEN TALKED ABOUT ITS CULTURE, WHICH SEEMED TO CELEbrate the diversity of its workforce while also unifying it under a homogenous vision that everyone was here for the same mission, the specifics of which were vague but seemingly progressive and important and world changing. It was true that Alvin had been enchanted by the company's purpose to build tools and technology that would better people's lives. But the reality: he was here because it was a job, and jobs paid a salary.

Still, nobody really talked about money at Google. Alvin's extended family had always been very open about it. Perhaps it was people who did not have a lot of wealth who were the most honest about income. For his family, money had been a sign of prosperity. But more than anything, it was a means of survival. Having money solved money problems—and those seemed to be the majority of the anxieties in Alvin's household growing up.

Pam had always said it was rude to speak of money. That was the polite New Englander in her. But Alvin could see, even as a child, that raising two kids on her own was not only emotionally draining—it was expensive. She did her best to hide that stress from her kids. But Alvin always thought it was a little funny, Pam being a tax accountant who did not want to talk about money.

So it was with tremendous pride that Alvin sent, for the first time, part of his first paycheck home. Despite everything going on, he was surviving. He was helping. There was a reason he'd been spared. Pam had called him and asked him why a check for $1,000 had been addressed to her.

"You still have student loans," she said on the phone.

"I can afford to pay for both."

"Just trust me: save your money," Pam said. This was the closest that Pam had ever come to openly discussing money, even if it was disguised in vague and practical advice. "When your aunts and uncles and cousins finally get out of detention, that's when they'll need your help."

ENGINEERING WORK TOOK hours of intense focus, but you could fall into the rhythm of it. Alvin's co-workers affectionately referred to this as a "flow state." It was like a runner's high, in that you could work yourself to the point where you were hypnotized into a productive trance. There was something thrilling about reaching this mode. Nothing else in the world mattered except the coding problems at hand. If the Bay Area was a tech bubble, and Google an even smaller bubble within that bubble, the flow state was the final form, so many layers removed from the rest of the world that Alvin could put out of his mind just how much he missed his family and every question he had about their whereabouts, their health, and when he would see them again.

Since AAPI had passed, Alvin found it more difficult to reach a flow state. It wasn't him, he believed, but everyone else. He'd remove his headphones and stand up at his desk to observe the people around him. A sea of engineers, doing their work, minding their own business, like nothing was happening outside of their lives. It infuriated Alvin, and yet he longed for that same ignorance.

He texted Ursula, something he knew she would at least respond to.

google engineers keep going like nothing has happened. super rich people, pretending like the world is the same. could be a good story

Alvin waited for her reply. It came surprisingly fast.

nah, that's not a story

THE TOWER

—

Recently declassified and heavily redacted documents revealed a number of contracts between the Department of Homeland Security's Office of Detention Culture and a defense manufacturer called Paladine. Though it was a relatively new company, Paladine was founded and funded by several traditional weapons manufacturers and Silicon Valley venture capital firms, a collaboration between what could be considered the old-money establishment and new-money technologists.

What Paladine hoped to accomplish was a cozy reputation with government bodies domestically, developing and supplying technologies that could be put to use quickly. Though sourcing on Paladine's motivations is thin, it is widely believed that the company saw Vietnamese detention as an opportunity to test surveillance and population control tools that could eventually be sold and deployed abroad to support the country's many conflicts overseas. Or perhaps used in the States.

The reality is that Paladine was never entirely a company unto itself but a body that accepted government contracts and then contracted out that work. Some experts believe that this was a necessity for Paladine, which had taken on orders that needed to be fulfilled quickly—faster than a new defense contractor, no matter how well funded, could. Other sources close to Paladine believe that the company's intention was always to obfuscate the money.

Paladine's one proprietary piece of technology was a large-scale airwave jammer. To most people, it was simply known as the Tower. In appearance, it was just a tall black pole. One was placed at the center of each camp. Aside from its height, the Tower seemed inoffensive: a skinny obelisk, visible from anywhere in the camp. But its looming presence made it the subject of rumors among the Viets. It didn't help that they were kept in the dark about what exactly the Tower did; even Office of Detention Culture guards weren't told about its purpose.

Among the wilder conspiracies was that the Tower emitted radiation that specifically targeted the young men in the camp, rendering them infertile. More grounded rumors claimed the Tower was a surveillance device—that it tracked detainees' every movement, that it was watching them eat and sleep and shit.

Though it was a panopticon of sorts, the function of the Tower was simpler than most believed. It was built to interfere with wireless signals—anything emitting radio waves, like a cellphone or a laptop with Wi-Fi, but also benign objects like microwaves or a heated blanket malfunctioning at just the right frequency—preventing anyone from communicating outside of camp by casting an "electric fog" over an area. The fog also blocked the transmission of things coming in, such as television transmitters and CB radio signals. The Tower was a tool of isolation.

The technology of the Tower was inspired by areas around the world known as "quiet zones"—designated areas of land cordoned off, usually around observatories, to allow extraordinarily sensitive telescopes to operate without radio interference. These research facilities were often tasked with looking at the deepest reaches of outer space, in search of new celestial bodies. Billions of dollars to fund astrophysicists pointing their concerns to the sky.

Though one might assume that the Tower's height was instrumental to its effectiveness, technical documents reveal that it did not need to be as tall as it was. In fact, early tests showed that a slightly shorter, bulkier version of the device had better range and even drew less energy. But the Tower's imposing, ominous stature was deliberate. It was a reminder to detainees in the camp that they were being watched, monitored, that surveillance was not passive but always active. It was a threat.

At night, the Tower pulsed. The red lights at the top resembled those often found on skyscrapers, used clearly as warnings to prevent aircraft collisions with the buildings. It's likely they were placed on the Tower for the same reason (though the airspaces above the camps were strict no-fly zones). But several detainees recalled that the feature gave the structure a menacing presence when it got dark, the red lights beating in the distance.

WORD PROCESSING

—

ONCE JEN SAW IT, SHE SAW IT EVERYWHERE. THE HUSHED TONES IN which people spoke about El Paquete, like a secret everyone knew but didn't want to invoke too loudly. Every electric cart that whirred by could be making a routine stop, dropping off nonroutine goods at a kitchen. But it was impossible to know who was in on it, and who was just nodding at Jen to be polite.

Some of the material changes were obvious. She knew that there were vital medicines and health-related items being distributed, but the more conspicuous ones were vices. Cigarettes had always been allowed in camp, and had in the past been restricted to one kind of Marlboro. Now there were varieties of brands, brought in from the outside. (Even American Spirits, which Jen only recognized because the yellow pack was Ursula's favorite.) Walking by the back of the mess hall, she occasionally caught a whiff of pot, and sometimes even an ODC guard smoking up with detainees. Alcohol had started showing up in places—particularly at football games, passed around in nonrevealing containers—moonshine so strong it could blind an elephant, the crowd's drunkenness masked by the sloppy enthusiasm and anger that one would come to expect from a bleacher full of sports fans.

And then, even less conspicuous, was the delivery of electronic goods. Each week, an El Paquete delivery boy, usually a tech-savvy teenager named Benjy, would stop by Jen's bunk with a small hard drive of new digital files. He'd update the computer with movies and TV shows on Sunday evenings, and for many people in Jen's bunk, it was the most exciting time of the week. As the files downloaded, the women would casually flirt with Benjy, mussing up his long, thick hair.

Since there were few computers available—all had been deliberately unnetworked, retrofitted so they would be stripped of all internet capabilities, rendering them invisible to the Tower—people carried small, keychain-size USB flash drives with them. Personal and portable files.

El Paquete's influence was growing. As detainees were settling into camp, so did the guards, who, despite being armed to the molars, were becoming more lax. The aggression and hostility the ODC once imposed had de-escalated. In the early months of camp, each command from an ODC guard was punctuated by the threat of an AR-15. But a chest can only be puffed for so long before it needs to take a breath.

In that space, El Paquete's network was spreading and gaining influence. Some groups—mainly the more religious sectors of camp, which included Jen's mother—tried to stay as far away from El Paquete as possible. The Christians claimed to be law-abiding, but mostly, they were afraid of trouble. Being in camp was suffering enough; why introduce the possibility of punishment that would make it worse?

As for everyone else, they were now subscribed to the gifts of El Paquete. A smaller group on the west side of camp had a thoughtfully organized method of taking requests for medication and, more impressively, a way to smuggle and distribute that medication to the detainees who needed it. Insulin shots for diabetics. ACE inhibitors for high blood pressure. Lexapro for the depressed, which there were an increasing number of.

Jen had put a request in for cortisone, for her eczema, but that hadn't arrived yet. Priorities, of course, were for those with serious health problems that weren't being treated by the ODC. Jen thought about the person seeing her request for skin cream and imagined them just rolling their eyes out of disappointment. Her poor, itchy elbows.

"They do the real work," Brandon said, of the medicine smugglers.

Jen nodded affirmatively, not really listening. She was curious about how El Paquete operated, but hearing Brandon ramble on and on about it was exhausting. It was an intricate network of people risking their safety to do selfless things for their community; there were a number of clever fixes that had to be imagined and carefully executed to make these things happen. All of that was interesting. But it became clear immediately to Jen that Brandon was very low in the pecking order, and was desperate to move up. It reminded Jen of the way her cousins would complain about work. Ursula, always frustrated with her bosses, her assignments, her hours, her desk, her company laptop; Alvin, describing some kind of obtuse hierarchy that he both was critical of and had entirely bought into. It didn't matter what the job was, Jen observed. Hearing someone complain about it never meant anything unless you worked there yourself.

Brandon was still rambling. It was amazing how you could want someone—their attention, their affection—and still, at times, find them so tedious.

Though El Paquete operated in secret, it seemed to have the cover of at least a few ODC authorities, who looked the other way for a small fee. Everyone was getting theirs.

"We grease the right pockets," Brandon said, somewhat proudly, like a caricature of *Goodfellas*.

Jen tried to imagine the feeling of a greasy pocket, then realized she was distracted, again, from the task at hand. Brandon had a way of getting things out of camp, which meant that Jen might be able to communicate with the outside. She would attempt to reach Ursula. Surely, whoever was on the other side could find a way to get a message to her half sister, right? Brandon made no promises, and confessed to not really understanding what happened to things after they left camp. He sent out lists of requests and had never thought to contact his friends. Not that they would be able to do anything for him anyway.

But Jen wanted to try. Ursula was a journalist. That came with a kind of power that might make a difference.

Still, that didn't solve Jen's more pressing issue. Before she could get a message to her cousin, she had to figure out what to say. And right now, she didn't know how to start. "Greetings from state-sponsored incarceration" wouldn't quite cut it.

Because of her job at the newspaper, Jen was one of the few people in camp with access to a word processor. Earlier that day, she'd spent the afternoon trying to figure out what to say to Ursula. She wanted to tell her cousin about all the horrors of camp, but couldn't quite summon the language. It was hard to describe. There was the looming threat of violence. But more than that, the daily terrors were existential. How long would they be there? How much worse were things going to get? Jen didn't know how to put that despair into a blinking cursor in Microsoft Word.

There was also Jen's pride. The last thing she wanted was for Ursula to pity her. Even though her entire life had been upended, admitting that pain to Ursula would be showing weakness. Jen was tough. She could survive this. Or at least she needed Ursula to believe that she could.

"Can you do me a favor?" Jen asked Brandon. "Take me for a ride."

IT REMINDED JEN of high school, being driven around the suburbs in overpacked cars with destinations that were never more imaginative than a mall or a movie theater or a Quiznos.

She loved Brandon's little cart, too. It was zippy. Its engine made the most adorable hum when he tried to speed up past twenty miles an hour, the breeze flowing through her hair. Brandon always took turns a little too suddenly—especially given that there was no traffic—and once had even sent Jen flying out of the cart, scuffing up her right knee. She remembered to hold on to her seat from then on. That made it even more thrilling.

They passed by a mess hall.

"Stop the cart!" Jen demanded.

Brandon slammed on the brakes, the cart kicking up a big plume of dust behind them.

Jen snapped a few photos of the cafeteria. Then a couple of the sky.

Brandon seemed confused. "Is this your art project?"

"I can't figure out what to write to my cousin," she said, "so maybe I'll just send her some pictures." The newspaper had issued Jen a camera for work.

"Scenic photos from detention?"

Jen didn't pay him any mind. She worried taking photos of detainees might be too suspicious, or worse, get them in trouble. But if she kept everything innocuous—shots of buildings, the dusty roads, maybe a few candids of people with their faces obscured—that might not raise suspicion with the ODC guards.

There were truths of camp that Jen wouldn't be able to capture. The scores of sick people crowding the medical facilities, unable to get real treatment or see a doctor who gave a shit about whether they lived or died. Or the growing number of suicides—at first, hangings, but increasingly overdoses from stolen painkillers. Or the violence. Even though things had de-escalated since the start, brutality was a present hazard. Submission was the only thing you could do to protect yourself and your family.

But what Jen wouldn't have been able to photograph was the sadness that had washed over the detainees. People here were without hope. Most couldn't say it, let alone express it, and Jen watched as it slowly consumed them. One hundred thousand people at this camp, trapped and just wondering when their lives would return to normal, if ever.

No, there was no way for Jen to capture that on film. She snapped a picture of an American flag, tarnished by dust, blowing in the wind in a pathetic fashion. Maybe Ursula could appreciate an obvious metaphor.

THE PHOTO DETOUR had made Jen and Brandon late for the game. They'd only missed a few minutes of the first quarter, but the trouble was finding a seat on the bleachers after it had started. Football was one of the few forms of entertainment in camp, and people showed up in droves. She'd once overheard a group of guards at the ODC building putting money on the games, and even talking about Duncan. They'd called her brother "the Beast," an upgrade over his high school nickname, "Duncan Donuts."

Despite his being suited up, it was easy to spot Duncan, who seemed like he was always twice the size of the next biggest player on the field. It always took two linemen to block him as he spun and pushed his way toward the quarterback.

Before he began playing football, Jen never considered that her brother might be an athlete. He was always just kind of big, kind of there. Always sweet and thoughtful, considerate of others' feelings.

On the field, Duncan was hurtling through bodies, possessed with a rage she'd never seen before.

It was so crowded that Jen could barely see him. Maybe she and Brandon could get to the roof of the adjacent building and watch from there. Jen's badge would get them into the athletic complex, at least.

She wondered how long her good luck would last before the ODC realized her access was too powerful. Inside the building, they found the staircase up to the roof. Looking down on the game, Jen scanned the field for Duncan, and realized that she was now at a distance where it was hard to identify him. Oh well. As much as she'd wanted to support her brother, she was more excited to be in a secluded place with Brandon.

The lights on the field, the roar of the crowd below. It was the closest that camp came to having a vista. Being on the roof with Brandon—it was almost romantic.

It didn't take long for Jen to feel his hand on her waist. It was too dark to really see his face, but she turned in to him, and suddenly they were kissing, slowly but sloppily. His hands moved up to her ribs. Jen put her hands on Brandon's back, grasping his skinny shoulder blades. In the dark she used her fingers to feel around for his skeleton, the outline of him.

"Good game, bro."

"Good game? We lost."

Jen hadn't really been paying attention to the score, or really any part of the game, since Brandon had spent most of it feeling her up. Brandon hadn't pushed her to do more. It might've been too dark up there anyway, honestly.

"This is Brandon," Jen said.

"Great game," he said, reaching out with a hand.

Duncan shook it, his massive paw gently enveloping Brandon's. "Do either of you understand how football works?"

"Enough to know that you got two sacks," Brandon said.

"Three!" Duncan said, excitedly. "Well, I guess two and a half. I split one with Phúc over there."

He turned and gave the guy supposedly named Phúc a high five. The team seemed in high spirits for having lost. But Jen was happy to see Duncan in a good mood. In fact, she'd rarely seen him smile since they'd gotten to Camp Tacoma. For the past six months, his face had been frozen in a state that betrayed little. Who would've thought this would be the thing that cheered Duncan up, hurting others for sport?

"Okay, I'm gonna hit the shower, sis," Duncan said.

"Please do. You stink."

It didn't take long for Duncan to wash—Jen was almost alarmed by how quickly he'd cleaned up. Duncan shook the water out of his hair, like a wet dog. Jen shrieked and jabbed her brother in the gut. The strike, though playful, had surprised him enough that he dropped his gym bag. It didn't matter how much bigger her younger brother got. She would always be the older bully.

"Your friend seems nice," Duncan said, looking around for Brandon, who had already left.

"Don't even start," Jen warned.

"What? I just said he seems nice." Now he was smiling.

It was dark along their walk to the south side of camp, though there were still people out, wandering after the game. ODC guards were everywhere, but they were less intent on badgering detainees about the quickly approaching curfew. The football game had disarmed everyone.

"Did you see Má at the game?" Duncan asked.

She had not, though she wouldn't have been able to spot her from the roof.

"I saw her briefly at the beginning, but I think she left early," Jen lied. "You know it's hard for her to watch you get hit."

"I did most of the hitting," Duncan said, a little too proudly.

"God, the walk home is so long."

"Where do you have to be? In bed?"

"I am tired of walking and walking forever and getting covered in dust."

"That's weird."

"What? All the lung-eviscerating dust we're inhaling constantly?"

"No." Duncan stopped. "You called this place 'home.'"

ATTACHMENTS

—

HOMELAND SECURITY HAD NEVER EXPLAINED ITS DECISION-MAKING for who qualified for camp and who didn't. There was, predictably, no admission that the process targeted the majority of Vietnamese Americans. Instead, the government had assured its citizens that it had deployed a sophisticated selection process, using a number of secret criteria to determine which citizens were the most likely to be potential domestic terrorists. The word "algorithm" was often evoked in press conferences.

Notices arrived for everyone in Ursula's Vietnamese family except her. She was relieved, and also wondered what, exactly, had excluded her. There could have been a number of reasons. Being half white certainly helped but didn't always guarantee exclusion from AAPI. (After all, her brother was summoned, before his Google-sponsored exemption.) Maybe it was her job. Working at Top Story meant that she was technically a full-time journalist, giving her the fuzzy designation of "public figure" and the legal protections that came with it, even if Ursula most days felt like she was, at best, a third-rate blogger.

It could also have been pure bureaucratic incompetence. If she'd learned anything from following Capitol Hill policymaking these past few months, it was that the government was extremely disorganized. Ursula might've been lucky enough to slip through the cracks.

Ursula felt thankful to not be in camp. But it was also the experience that most Vietnamese Americans now had in common. She'd already felt disconnected from that part of herself. In some of her darkest moments, Ursula could admit to herself that she felt a little left out.

—

WHEN THE EMAIL arrived in Ursula's inbox, it had bewildered her. The subject line had read "FOR YOU" in all caps, while the body of the message had repeated "for you," only less aggressive, this time in lowercase. There were two attachments. One was a Word document named for-ursula.doc and the other was a zip file called photos.zip. It just looked like a virus.

But something compelled Ursula to click it. Though she wasn't religious at all, years later she'd privately think there was some kind of divine intervention—something spiritual, at least—that prevented her from marking the message as spam. Everything in her life would change after opening it.

She started with the Word document. It began with "Dear Ursula"— a letter.

The opening was a lot of pleasantries, an assurance that the writer was "doing okay, all things considered." But it wasn't until the third graf, when there was a mention of Duncan, that Ursula realized what the document was: it was a letter from her cousin Jen, from inside of camp. She scrolled immediately to the bottom to confirm.

All the best,
Jen

No one was allowed to communicate with detainees. How had Jen written this letter? When did Jen write this? And through what illicit channels had this file actually reached her?

She needed to know how Jen was holding up, if she was healthy, what the conditions were like. She needed to know what "doing okay, all things considered" really meant. Ursula scrolled back up to the top.

When she finished reading the second time, the tears were sudden, and her breathing became ragged. And though Ursula had always prided herself as someone who was never emotional at work, she rushed to the bathroom and let out an ugly cry in one of the stalls, loud enough that someone whose voice she couldn't identify eventually knocked on the door to ask if she was okay, to which she aggressively replied, "I'm fine," between ragged breaths.

Ursula cleaned herself up at the sink, carefully dabbing her makeup off with a paper towel, and returned to her desk. The email was still visible on her laptop screen, another file to open.

It wasn't the letter from Jen that would change Ursula's life. It was the attachment.

REAL ESTATE

—

Even before the American Advanced Protections Initiative, the housing market in the Bay Area had ballooned from the high wages of tech workers—some domestic, many from overseas—who wanted to buy homes near their place of work. Or as close as they could be.

Space in San Francisco was already limited, and the inventory of apartments had been strained for nearly a decade. So the surrounding cities of Oakland, Palo Alto, and San Jose saw a surge of homebuyers looking for a little more room outside the city. Besides, for many of the tech workers, the office was actually located farther south, in the suburbs of Mountain View and Cupertino and Menlo Park.

San Jose had always been closer to these cities than San Francisco, but it was the opposite of what many tech workers wanted. San Jose was not a dense yuppie paradise of exciting new restaurants and bars. It was an arid sprawl—mostly populated by Asians and Latinos, scattered across two fault lines. At one point it had been considered a tech hub, but since the crash of 1999, San Jose's reputation as a dull example of suburban development preceded it.

Since the midseventies, after the fall of Saigon, San Jose had also become home to the largest diaspora of Viets in America—and in fact, it was the biggest concentrated population of Viets in the world outside of Vietnam itself. After AAPI passed, a noticeable number of homes went into foreclosure. The banks that acquired them wanted to sell as quickly as possible, both because they were assets that they didn't want to manage and for fear that an influx of newly available real estate would flood the market and drive down prices.

The absence of nearly two hundred thousand Viets meant many tech workers—fed up with their expensive apartments and condos in San Francisco—could finally buy a home with several bedrooms and a yard. And besides, with traffic being so bad on their morning commutes, now they were closer to work, which still meant sitting in traffic, but headed in the other direction, and for far less time. The new money of Silicon Valley had already begun creeping into San Jose, but AAPI had turned it into a full-on land grab.

But as wealthy as many tech workers were, individually they were no match for the greater powers that swooped in on the market opportunity. One Chinese billionaire—his identity obscured by the creation of several shell businesses—had even set up a firm dedicated solely to buying up property in San Jose, leaving most of the homes empty. The company, another shell of sorts, was incorporated under the name Powerful Destiny Management Company. In a year, the vibrant Viet diaspora of San Jose's Little Saigon had become a ghost town of abandoned storefronts and empty homes.

Realtors could easily identify the representatives of the Powerful Destiny Management Company because they were Chinese, but more visibly, because they always paid in cash. Two-million-dollar homes, scooped up with a single check; it barely mattered the condition of the house, what style of architecture, or where it was. These buyers would come in and attempt to close the deal as quickly as possible.

A local NBC affiliate in San Jose did an evening news report on these fast-closing Chinese deals. The segment consisted mainly of interviews with various real estate agents and a PR rep from Wells Fargo, the bank that assumed many of the foreclosed homes, all of whom told stories of Powerful Destiny muscling their way into purchases. One Realtor even claimed that a Chinese rep had showed up to one open house, offered 20 percent above asking so they could close that afternoon, and even insisted that the free cookies that had been set out for interested buyers now belonged to him.

"They don't care what they're getting," the Realtor said. "Honestly, I could list a giant shoe, and if it was in San Jose, someone from Powerful Destiny would put down a cash offer."

The news segment ends with the reporter finally catching up with one of the Powerful Destiny buyers at an open house. He is a boyish man in a suit and with a bowl cut, and remains insistent that he will not answer any questions. The reporter keeps badgering him until he finally relents with a couple sentences.

"We are just making investments," he says, still not identifying himself.

"An investment in what?" the reporter asks.

"What else do you invest in?" he replies with a laugh, as if there could be no other answer: "The future."

INTEGRITY

—

ONCE URSULA'S FIRST REPORT FROM CAMP HAD BEEN PUBLISHED, SHE was whisked over to News. It was almost comical how quickly everything had happened. She'd spent close to two years practically begging her boss to change divisions while churning out posts about beauty and health and lifestyle and anything else that was inoffensive and easily shareable. But one piece about life inside Camp Tacoma, thanks to her cousin, and suddenly Ursula had gotten the thing she'd strived for her whole life: to be taken seriously.

Top Story had an open office plan, meaning her small desk space was always being encroached on the left side by a co-worker, who felt it was important to adorn her work area with a small army of animal plushies, and on the right side by the books editor, who seemed unable to keep up with the pile of galleys that arrived for him each day. Ursula packed up her belongings and moved them to the other side of the office, where she was now seated between a reporter who spent all day shouting with his sources on the phone, usually swearing, and an editor who printed out all the drafts he was supposed to edit so he could mark them up with a pen. Her conditions hadn't gotten better, but she could now endure the annoying habits of her colleagues, because she actually respected their work.

But the best part of the change: Rosco was her new boss. Before, Amelia seemed to like Ursula best when she kept her head down and did her work. Otherwise, she asked very little. With Rosco, she knew that she would be pushed. He would be exacting, demanding. Someone who cared enough about her work that he would be willing to challenge it.

Yet, unlike the Entertainment division, Top Story News had a firm rule about impartiality. Well, the appearance of impartiality. Stemming from a long tradition of what constituted journalistic integrity, writers and editors were not supposed to do any activism or organizing, which meant marches and rallies were out, though most of the protesting had already died out long ago. They were not to publicly express their political opinions, as that would undermine the image of News as a rigorous and unbiased journalistic outlet. Ursula had a wide-reaching, influential platform, and for the first time in her life, she was limited in what she could say.

Writers were told not to post anything political, to "stick to the facts." Rosco asked Ursula to go back through her social media accounts and delete anything from the past year that could appear biased. Ursula scrolled through her old posts, something she'd never really done before. She was seeing a past version of herself, the one that was free to call the president an asshole, or declare this administration an authoritarian regime. Ursula deleted all those. Scrolling down, there were old posts linking to things she'd written: lists of the best eyeliner, great influencer accounts to follow, recipes that could be made in an Instant Pot. With tremendous delight, she deleted those, too.

IN HER FIRST News meeting, Ursula was more intimidated than she had anticipated.

The editors sat at the table, with all the reporters standing in the wings. One by one, the heads of each desk were called on by Richard Earley, the aging editor in chief, who'd won two Pulitzers, been ousted from *The Washington Post* after being accused of sexual harassment, and had landed softly at Top Story. As the boss, he took it all in and asked follow-up questions about what was on the docket that day, and the surest sign of approval he gave was merely a throaty grunt.

Rosco was called on last, and Ursula wondered if that was because he ran the least important desk, or if it was because he was the only Black editor. As expected, Rosco was collected, and read through a list of stories in progress.

A Richard grunt cut Rosco off midway through his detailing of a story about the decline of H-1B visa renewals.

"Sorry, back to the assignment before—the one about the school shooting in Omaha," Richard said, his eyes not making contact with Rosco but remaining down on a steno pad, where he was mostly crossing things off. "Are we hitting the families up for comment?"

Rosco had anticipated this. "Already asked. The way these things go, only a few parents are outspoken at first, but a few weeks pass, the tragedy sets in, and we can get at them then for a follow-up." He winced, admitting, "Sadly, I've overseen enough of these in the newsroom to know that."

If Richard was pleased by Rosco's humanity, he didn't show it. Instead, he held up a printout.

"One thing I never got at the *Post* was a daily traffic report, with recommendations from an SEO department. I'm told that pieces dedicated to victims' families and their grief play well on Facebook."

Richard looked at Rosco, and then made a playful shrug. Rosco laughed, which gave the rest of the room the permission to as well.

"You know I don't care about this shit," Richard said, "but I'm handing you this report, and that means I've done what has been asked of me."

He slid the printout across the table, away from himself. More laughter.

"Okay, anything else out of your desk, Rosco?"

"Yeah, one more quick thing actually," Rosco said. "We have a new reporter on my team—Ursula Carrington. You guys know she had that great piece from inside one of the Vietnamese detention camps. So we've brought her over. Where are you, Urs?"

He began looking around the room. Ursula, sheepishly, stepped forward.

"Honestly, I am just so excited to be here, working with you guys," Ursula said. "I know that I come from the Entertainment side, and that my bylines are all lists and that kind of junk. But I'm really passionate and hardworking and I'm going to do my best here to publish the kinds of stories that will stand up next to yours."

God, what was she saying? Maybe it was the nerves. The reaction was a silence so uncomfortable that she felt her soul leave her body, and wished it well on its departure.

"That's great, Ursula," Rosco said, and turned to the room as if to change the subject.

"So, who is your source in Camp Tacoma? And how did you find them?" It was Richard's question. The boss had a question for her. "No one's been able to reach a single detainee until you."

"I . . ." Ursula's face grew hot. Though she admired this group of journalists, she wasn't sure if she could trust them, nor was she certain that using a family member as her primary account had been totally ethical. She deflected. "I protect my sources. That's my number-one priority."

"Fair enough," Richard said, satisfied. It was a good lesson. Obfuscation made one appear stronger than transparency, and she needed her strength in this room.

URSULA WAS MESSAGING consistently with Jen, who was regularly feeding her tips from inside Camp Tacoma. The turnaround between emails was always a week, but Ursula knew full well that every letter that she received from her cousin could be the last one. She'd published three different reports, exclusive looks inside Vietnamese detention. None of the stories were surprising, but they were nonetheless revelatory. Ursula had the kind of access no competing publication had been able to get—not even *The New York Times*.

The correspondence was a delicate balance for Ursula. She wanted to be sensitive, to show Jen that she cared. At the same time, the demands on a journalist are to constantly produce. Ursula needed things from Jen: details, information, and stories from camp that could actually be published.

The only person who knew about Ursula's source was Alvin, and that disclosure had been an accident on the phone with him after a few too many glasses of wine. Mostly, Ursula wanted to tell someone how things were finally happening for her at work. Her colleagues respected her; her profile among readers was rising. Rosco had just asked her out to drinks—maybe not so professional as a lunch invite—and Ursula was becoming a vital voice in the conversation around Vietnamese detention. She had finally been vindicated in her pursuit of journalism, despite all the doubts her family had loudly expressed. But as soon as the secret was spilled, Alvin really only had questions about Jen.

"How is she holding up?" he asked on the phone. "Does she seem okay?"

She could identify the guilt in Alvin's voice. It was the same guilt she felt day in and day out, like a low hum in the back of her head that constantly reminded her of how lucky she was to be here, and not there.

"From her notes, she seems like she's doing okay. But she keeps a lot from me—I'm not sure how much she can say or who is reading her messages," Ursula said. And then, realizing that Alvin needed reassurance, not the truth, "You know Jen: she's tough, she's going to make it through this."

"Urs, I don't know if I would describe Jen as 'tough.'"

"No, she is. Trust me. I see it in her," Ursula said, trying to convince herself. She wanted Jen to be safe, to be okay. Everything she'd wanted and worked for depended on it.

Rosco could hold his booze. That was clear after the first couple of drinks. But the night had obviously gone on too long. This was number five. Or six? Ursula was a drinker, but the evening was turning into a blur. Still, the vibe was celebratory, even if she was closing down a mediocre Midtown bar with her boss, of all people.

Drinking with most men, there was usually some kind of tipping point, where things would go from fun to weird, and it always happened suddenly. One of her best friends from college, Josh, was really fun until his fourth drink. That was when he got sad. Then there was Scott, another college friend, who around whiskey number six would plead with Ursula to go home with him. (In his defense, they had hooked up a couple times, but that was in school. Now it was inappropriate.) Brady, one of the few colleagues Ursula liked at Top Story Entertainment, was a lightweight—more than two drinks and he might as well be in bed.

But Rosco, she was learning, had one too many and started to get a little personal, and a little petty.

"Listen, I get it. It's the *Times*," Rosco said, beginning to slur. "But will you really feel fulfilled over there? At the *Times*?"

Ursula hadn't looked at her phone in hours, knowing that would be rude. But she would give anything to figure out how to leave gracefully. She'd assumed Rosco had wanted to talk about story ideas—Ursula had come prepared with a handful of assignments, built out around the tips from Jen.

But Rosco was drunk now, and instead he wanted to complain about how Dara had recently been poached. Ursula didn't see Rosco's point: she'd been offered more money for a bigger job at a more prestigious institution. Of course Dara would go.

Earlier, it had been a loud bar. Now it was just Rosco shouting about *The New York Times*. There were a couple other tables of patrons, but mostly, you could hear the sound of clanging glasses, the barback getting ready to close soon. And then Rosco seemed to shake it off, turning again to Ursula.

"A thing I wanted to ask you . . ." he started.

"Yeah?" Ursula worried what he would say next. In that split second, she could imagine a thousand terrible things that would immediately make the career she just stepped into complicated. Or worse, ruin it, on basically day one.

"You pass," he said.

"It depends on the person. But okay, that's not a question."

"You're going to be covering Vietnamese detention—and we want you to be our main reporter on what is probably the most urgent beat on the national desk."

A bit of flattery. Ursula could take that.

"You go by Ursula Carrington but your real birth name is Ursula Nguyen, right? Would you consider changing it back?" Rosco looked uncomfortable but proceeded. "I know it's fucked up to ask, but between us, I really think it would save you a lot of headaches. People are always getting angry about who gets to write what. You know?"

Strangely, Ursula felt the dynamic shift. Another tipping point. It was sudden, like a breeze that swept through the room, like the entire night now depended on how she would respond.

"I hadn't thought of that," she said, finishing her glass. "But I think that's a good idea."

Rosco finished his beer and nodded approvingly.

"It would kind of fuck with your old bylines, though. I went through this once with another writer, and changing your name in the system basically disassociates you from all your old work. But we could put in a request to IT to try and fix that—"

"No, *no!*" That came out a little too strong. But Ursula was just excited by the idea of separating her old identity as a beauty-and-lifestyle writer from what she was building now, the reputation of a serious reporter.

"I'm glad to get that out. The name shit has been on my mind all day, and it took me, like, six drinks to work up the courage to bring that up." Rosco looked genuinely relieved. "Another round?"

ASSIGNMENTS

—

A CAPPELLA

EACH OF THE FOUR HIGH SCHOOLS HAD ITS OWN MUSIC PROGRAM, BUT because there was very little funding from the ODC for instruments, the most common performers were a cappella groups. The North School even had half a dozen different ensembles, and Jen suggested to Officer Paulson that she profile them, knowing it was a sure thing.

So Jen spent a week bopping around after-school a cappella group rehearsals on the north side. All the music they sang had to be approved by the ODC. Generally, they seemed to screen for the obvious things you might expect. Anything deemed too political or too angry was out; it was also a no-go for anything too emotional or too obscure.

The students had no official access to materials outside of camp, so many of the song arrangements had to be written from memory. Often, certain words would be off, or notes would be wrong, or both. Jen heard a version of Lauryn Hill's "Doo Wop" that held true to the melody and featured completely new verses. The Britney Spears' line went from "hit me baby one more time" to "love me baby one more time," which felt deliberate, like something requested by the ODC.

Talking to Carl, the leader of North School group 3, Jen discovered that the head of culture could even assign songs. Because group 3 had a strong beatboxer, they were handed a slate of rap rock songs.

"Yeah, the ODC guy is really into nu metal," Carl told her. "So we asked to do Billy Joel, and instead they made us do Linkin Park."

Jen listened to group 3 rehearse a song called "In the End." The

beatboxing sounded, impressively, like real drums, if not a bit exaggerated. Carl took an angst-filled chorus and softened it, which seemed to
be the unwritten rule of a cappella: smooth the rough edges with ear-
nestness, reinterpret the soul of a song with the enthusiasm of musical
theater. Still, Jen had to admit, it sounded pretty good.

HOT PLATE

HOT PLATES WERE COMING, OFFICER PAULSON EXPLAINED, AND JEN
had the distinct privilege of delivering the good news through her "reporting."

It was true that the hot plates were a big deal. Each bunk would be
getting one, meaning that detainees were now able to boil their own
water for tea or ramen without going to the mess hall. It also meant
warm beverages or small meals outside of one's designated shifts.

"People can cook their own meals again," Allegra said with genuine
enthusiasm. "What's more personal than preparing your own food?"

She had a point. It didn't make the assignment any less boring. Jen
wouldn't be able to explain that to Paulson—nor was it really appropriate to complain that her detention work assignment was not challenging or creatively fulfilling. She asked if she could see the hot plate early.
Paulson said he could arrange that.

She unpackaged the box and studied its specifications. 1,300 watts.
Six adjustable temperature settings, controlled by a single knob. Less than
a square foot of counter space. An indicator light to signal when the heating coil is ready. How would Jen stretch this into seven hundred words?

LOCAL THEATER

AFTER A YEAR OF CONSTRUCTION, AN AUDITORIUM HAD BEEN ERECTED
near the center of camp, just a few rows east of the ODC building, and
its arrival would be celebrated by opening night of a production of *Fiddler on the Roof,* a choice that confounded Jen.

She tried to get an explanation from the director about why he'd gone with this particular play, and the answer was that he hadn't. It had been picked by the ODC.

"The other idea floated was *Miss Saigon*," said Anh, an older woman who was helping with the costumes. She'd been a tailor in Fresno, employed by a Chinese couple for most of her adult life until she could afford to open a shop of her own. She'd missed the work. Anh was old enough—in her seventies—that she wasn't given a job assignment in camp. And she wasn't religious, so there was doubly nothing for her to do during the day.

Jen took to Anh immediately. Talking with her, Jen couldn't help but imagine that this was what she wished her mother was like: maternal, but funny and grounded, and most importantly, not talking about the goings-on of a church group at every possible moment.

"Making these costumes is almost like the opposite of being a tailor," Anh said, as she pushed the inseam of a pair of baggy black trousers through a sewing machine. "I used to make suits look neat and clean. All the *Fiddler* costumes are supposed to be disheveled. Do you know how hard it is to sew fake rips and tears?"

Anh had left Vietnam in the early seventies. She repeatedly called herself lucky, even though Jen would not describe her circumstances that way. Because she got into a graduate program in France, Anh was able to evacuate the country relatively easily. But she left behind her husband and two daughters—both of whom were teenagers—with the plan that they would meet up once Anh had settled in Paris. She lost contact with them, and waited for two years in France, before moving to the U.S., where she suspected that her family had ended up. But even in San Jose, where many Vietnamese had immigrated, she never found them.

"I've spent most of my life just wondering about what happened to them," she said matter-of-factly, the churn of the sewing machine punctuating the end of her story.

There were so many possibilities. The likeliest: that they'd attempted to leave Vietnam and didn't make it. The Communists imprisoned and often killed people who tried to flee. Or maybe they set off on a boat, hoping to be picked up by the U.S. Navy. Or they beached at a refugee camp, and never made it out. It had been forty years. Nearly every possibility Anh could imagine ended with them dead.

"Can I tell you something selfish?" Anh asked. "I hate imagining that my family is alive. That they're happy somewhere, and they simply have no interest in seeing me."

Hearing this, Jen began to cry. It reminded her of the story Bà Nội used to tell, of having to leave her husband to make it out of Vietnam, of how it had been the great regret of her life.

Anh seemed at peace with the idea, which only meant that she'd turned this in her mind so many times that it no longer disturbed her.

"Your family not wanting to see you," Jen said, trying to be reassuring. "I'm sure that isn't true."

"No, you're right. They're probably dead."

FANTASY

—

Every Sunday, seventeen weeks out of the year every year he could remember, Duncan had been glued to the couch—eyes pinned to the big-screen television, attention spanning dozens of games, hundreds of players, thousands of plays—all in the pursuit of something people affectionately referred to as "fantasy."

Football was about points: points for vicious sacks, points for each yard of scrimmage, points for every remarkable catch made by an arm outstretched over a defender. The sport was violent and tactical and thrilling; *fantasy* made it participatory.

The team had originally been Duncan's father's, but as he lost interest in both fantasy football and real-life family, Duncan took over his lineup—the only thing he'd inherited from his father.

Duncan loved the preseason research, where he would pore over stats and analyses of past player performance, their likelihood of improvement or regression. And then there were the rookies, a wildly unpredictable bunch whose collegiate dominance was suddenly no measure of their potential in the pros. It was how Duncan spent most of his time on the internet, letting pages and pages load slowly on his sister's chunky old Mac.

The members of the league were all older, Duncan's dad's age, most of them Viet. A few of them watched the games together on Sundays, but really, the only time they were all gathered in one place was draft day. The other men would tease Duncan about all his printouts. All that fancy legwork, and some seasons, he would still finish at the bottom of the league.

Duncan had only won once, when he was eleven. He had been en-
amored of a quarterback named Michael Vick, who put up a dazzling
series of games in his early seasons. Vick had legs. When Falcons receivers were gobbled up by opposing secondaries, Vick could rush
himself. Each time he did, Duncan watched with amazement and horror, since a quarterback on the move opened himself up to being hit,
and possibly injured. But Vick was tough, and he muscled his way to
much-needed first downs, and the occasional end zone. Plus, he racked
up monster point totals in fantasy. Still, after a brief prison stint, his
return to the league seemed like a bust. Duncan had to beg his father
to draft Vick.

Duncan's father, like the rest of the league, like a lot of America,
never appreciated Michael Vick. There were a lot of excuses. The potential of Vick getting hurt—that was a reasonable one, as to be expected
with any quarterback who trusts their feet. But often the arguments
were about his personality: Vick makes bad judgments, is emotional, a
bad leader. Duncan read enough football punditry and listened to
enough commentary to understand what his father was parroting. They
did not like that Michael Vick was Black and in the most powerful
position on the field.

It disappointed Duncan that his father would think this way, though
he eventually relented and let Vick get added to the bench. Duncan and
his dad scooped up Vick and let the points roll in, week after week, rallying a commanding season and eventually winning the league's $1,200
pool. Though it was Dad who put in the $100 buy-in, he agreed to split
the winnings with his son. For Duncan, at age eleven, $600 felt like an
ungodly sum of money. Dad gave Duncan the cash—a wad of twenties,
stuffed in an old envelope—and told him to keep it somewhere safe.

"Should I save it for college?" Duncan asked.

His dad laughed. "Six hundred dollars is a lot, but it is not nearly
enough for school. Just keep it for a special occasion. One day, I want
you to buy a thing just because you want it."

He went on: "And don't tell your mom."

—

To Duncan's surprise, the football leagues in camp were competitive. Probably because he was used to playing with only people his age, and at Camp Tacoma, the teams combined high school– and college-age kids. In some ways, Duncan enjoyed the construction of the league. Each team played each other team twice, meaning that after getting one crack at breaking an O-line, Duncan would get another.

Requests to El Paquete were a pain in the ass, especially if you weren't asking for something as popular as new episodes of *The Walking Dead*. Duncan wanted to keep up on the NFL season. It made him feel crazy that he couldn't watch any games, or even find out the scores. An entire season passed and he didn't have any idea who had won the Super Bowl.

"You're Duncan, right?"

Duncan was in the mess hall kitchen, just prepping for the dinner rush—he'd picked up an extra shift, in addition to his usual breakfast one—when he'd been approached by a small man, shaved head, maybe early thirties. He wore a beat-up camo jacket.

"Dinner's not till five. Can't feed you early, sorry."

The man laughed. "I am in no rush to eat this garbage."

Duncan looked down at the cabbage he'd been slicing. It was pale, wilting against his knife.

"I just heard that you were looking for NFL games, and El Paquete wasn't getting it for you," the man said.

Duncan put down the dull blade and focused his attention on the little man.

"And you are?"

"Dennis," he said.

From his jacket, Dennis withdrew a small piece of plastic. A flash drive.

"What is this?"

"It's every NFL game from the past season. You could use some tape to study. I've watched a few of your games—you're good, but I think you bite on play action too easily. Study up."

Duncan examined the man's face: high cheekbones, an unwavering, steely expression.

"You've been watching me?"

"Everybody goes to the games." Dennis placed the flash drive on top of Duncan's cabbage bowl, then turned to leave. "Only a few of us pay attention."

EVEN FROM A YOUNG AGE, Duncan knew that enjoying football meant ignoring its obvious problems. That despite decades of research about what repeated helmet-to-helmet contact does to a player's brain, his mind, his sense of self and what he can control of it, this was just a sport. The torn ligaments and crushed skulls the players suffered didn't seem to matter to anyone. The frequent charges of domestic abuse players committed against women didn't either, nor did it matter how infrequently players were punished for those things.

The tragedy of Michael Vick became clear. It wasn't that he got in several different kinds of trouble but that he got into a very specific kind, the kind that was atypical, and therefore, abhorrent. It was the dogs.

When Duncan was in third grade, he watched Vick plead guilty to his involvement with a dog-fighting ring that was located on his fifteen-acre property, the Bad Newz Kennels.

It was illegal because there was unlawful gambling. It was immoral and despicable to the public because animals were hurt. Vick was suspended from football, sentenced to twenty-one months in jail, and suddenly owed millions in debts to creditors once his endorsement deals had to be paid back.

It was the first time the group of his father's friends in his fantasy league had been sympathetic to Vick. Dog fighting? That wasn't a crime. It was a cultural thing, depending where you lived. Where Vick had grown up in Virginia, pit bulls gouging each other for sport had been normal. Owen, an older Black guy—the only one in Duncan's league—had claimed the Bad Newz controversy was just a conspiracy to take down a successful quarterback who was not white.

"America thinks dogs are worth more than Black men," he said, and the room of mostly Vietnamese men, lightly toasted on Hennessy, nodded in agreement.

Another guy, Tuan, didn't see the big deal. They were just dogs, after all. Americans were too precious about their pets. Back in Vietnam, he had, on a couple occasions, eaten dog.

"How'd it taste?"

Tuan shrugged. "Unremarkable."

A third guy, another Viet who went by Joe, disagreed. "They tortured those dogs, though. Did you see the photos of those pit bulls? What happened to them—it was savage." Joe kept arguing. "And they were betting on it. It's one thing to eat a dog. You can kill it humanely and it serves a purpose. But to torture a dog for fun. That's not good."

And all this was said, Duncan observed, moments before they placed their antes for the season.

DENNIS HADN'T BEEN LYING. Every game from the season—256 regular games, plus 15 from the postseason—meant that Duncan now had hundreds of hours of tape to look at. Most people watched the media on their flash drives in the comfort of their own bunks. Since Duncan worked at a mess hall, where there was very little ODC activity, especially at 5 A.M., he just played NFL footage on a tablet while prepping sliced fruit and bread for the breakfast rush.

Duncan kept a notepad of what he saw—of formations, especially when they were designed fakes. The effects were immediate. Duncan could feel himself becoming a sharper, cleverer player in practice, and then in games. His coaches complimented him on the improvement, chalked it up to hard work. But Duncan knew the secret. It was the ability to do research. He was competing with other people who had access to most of the same resources as him—getting to work out at the nice Nike sports facility, doing drills on that newly astroturfed field. As far as Duncan knew, no one else was watching video of actual games and trying to dissect them. It was work. But what else did Duncan have to do? And who was this guy Dennis who had helped him?

—

As a kid, Duncan never felt that Má was controlling his life, but she expressed a very particular disdain toward the idea of him playing football. She could immediately see it was dangerous. Má didn't want to travel to nearby towns on Friday nights to watch her son get repeatedly hit by other kids.

"Any other sport," she said.

She knew that she couldn't stop him, but hoped that withholding the money Duncan needed for pads and cleats would prevent her from being complicit in this bad decision.

Duncan still had the $600, his cut from the winning season of fantasy football, which he had been reluctant to spend in the seasons since and had kept in that same beat-up envelope in his bedside table. But when he counted the twenties, he realized that most of it was missing. His father, when he'd left years before, had done just enough to thin him out: there was $120 left.

Football changed Duncan. A teammate had told him to play from a place of anger, but Duncan had never thought of himself as an angry person. He was quiet, reserved, rarely emotional. He saw himself as rational, self-possessed. But when the opposing quarterback hiked that football, all those things went out the window, and Duncan forced his way forward, through people, his legs summoning strength from the earth, pressing his arms through linemen, trying to reach the ball.

Duncan would remember the first time he sacked a quarterback. He'd somehow been left unguarded—some sloppy play, by a sloppy team—and there was a direct path. Duncan leveled him, and the kid flew backward on impact, limbs flailing like a rag doll as he hit the ground. That play would stay with Duncan, the moment he realized he could really hurt someone.

During the games, with all the bright lights pointed at the field, the crowd going fucking crazy, Duncan was able to put all of that out of his mind. The units of football could be broken down: there were games, which were made up of quarters, which were made up of drives, which were made up of downs. And if you thought of a football game just in terms of downs, and played each one like a lunatic, like the whole thing depended on you, then maybe you could do something astonishing. People always remembered the extraordinary plays. Duncan himself had seen a million forgettable ones, but he would never forget witnessing Vick scramble for forty-six yards, splitting a pair of defenders, and making it to the end zone for a walk-off touchdown in overtime.

And if you didn't make something happen on a play? You would treat the next down the same, as an opportunity, until you did pull off something miraculous—a strip sack of the quarterback, which you could scoop up and run all the way back for a touchdown. A single play that would swing the entire drive, the quarter, the game.

In camp, Duncan's mom didn't come to watch him play; his sister pretended she did, and rarely bothered to stick around after. Usually, Duncan slogged back sore and alone to his bunk to collapse.

But one night, after the game where Duncan and his teammates had celebrated a blowout victory, Dennis was waiting for him. It had been a few weeks since he'd appeared at the mess hall with the USB drive. Same small, weird man in a camo jacket as before.

"Good game, brother," he said.

"Thanks," Duncan said, a slight edge of confusion in his voice. What did he want? "I watched a lot of the NFL games you gave me. They were really helpful."

"The pleasure is all mine," Dennis said, which was a phrase that Duncan had always hated.

"Is there a way I can get you back? Like some extra breakfast?"

"No, no, not at all," he said, beginning to leave. "I just want you to do well."

Which, on Duncan's solo walk back to his bunk, he kept rolling over again and again in his mind. What a weird thing to say to a person you don't know. Why would you say that? Maybe he was tired, or maybe he was cynical, but Duncan knew better than to trust someone who said they wanted you to succeed without asking for anything in return.

—

IT WASN'T LIKE Duncan hadn't seen it coming. His father didn't just leave one day. His departure was a gradual process, which began with a lot of storming out of the house after arguments with Má, and returning after increasingly long intervals—a day, a few days, weeks—until he simply didn't come back at all.

At least he'd had his sister to talk to. Then Jen went off to college, and it was just Duncan and Má in the house. It hadn't felt acute until Duncan wandered in on fantasy draft day, for the first time without his father. No one said anything, but he could tell they were all thinking it, pitying him. Duncan, with his usual ceremonious stack of printouts, and no one even had the dignity to crack a joke about it. That had hurt the most.

PRINTED MATTER

—

ALLEGRA SEEMED TO HAVE AN UNENDING SUPPLY OF THOSE LITTLE joints, and each time Jen hung out with her, she revealed an even smaller, less satisfying one. "How tiny could they get?" Jen joked. Allegra laughed, and said she was doing her best. Detention was not the easiest place to score pot, even if Brandon did have the inside track on deliveries. Besides, if Jen had complaints, she could, you know, get her *own* drugs.

It turned out that if you adore someone enough, you could forgive them for threatening to abandon you at the bottom of an empty pool. You could get recruited into helping out with an underground network that allowed people to smuggle all manner of contraband into camp, at great risk. You could definitely pretend to enjoy smoking a wee blunt.

They were under the bleachers, as they often were. Jen would hang from the seats, arms fully extended, showing off the length of her skinny self.

"So do you have a thing for Brandon?" Allegra asked.

The question caught her off guard. Instead of responding, Jen pretended to cough, stalling while she thought of an answer that would be a convincing punt.

"It's okay if you do," Allegra assured her. "He's a solid lay. Like, eight out of ten, most days."

Now Jen was out of her depth. She'd suspected something had gone on between them. Her two most attractive friends at camp—of course they'd been involved. More than envy, Jen felt the sting of exclusion.

"I didn't know you were together. I would never, ever try to interfere with that." As Jen spoke, she realized she was coming on too strong.

Allegra seemed, as always, unbothered. "No, that was a long time ago. Freshman year. Please, have at it. He's one of the few people I've dated that didn't turn out to be a complete piece of shit."

"Why did you guys break up?"

"He's still a partial piece of shit."

Jen handed the joint back to Allegra.

"No, it was me, actually." She took a small hit. "I cheated on him."

Allegra said it with no regret. Jen even detected a hint of pride in her voice. The government had locked them up in a detention center in the middle of nowhere, and here was a girl—smart, sly, beautiful—who still didn't miss a beat.

"Do you want to know if Brandon likes you, too?"

"Come on, what is this, high school?"

"You were in high school, like, a year ago."

"*Two* years ago." Correcting Allegra did not help Jen's point.

"Do you want me to tell you what he says about you?"

"I don't even care." Even less convincing.

Allegra rolled her eyes. She dropped the blunt and snuffed it out with her boot.

Jen followed Allegra as they walked the dusty route back to the ODC building. They'd told Officer Paulson they were checking out the laundry building for a story. The two of them were getting gutsier with their lies. If Paulson wanted to, he could check where they had badged in—and where they hadn't. Jen suggested stopping by the laundry on the way home, just so they had some evidence in case they got caught.

"Paulson could see when we badged in, and he'd still know we weren't there when we said we'd be." Allegra was walking quickly, as usual. "Good thing he is lazy as fuck."

She seemed to know everything: all the important people in camp, how to play them, how to get away with whatever she wanted. But if Allegra already knew about Jen and Brandon, she didn't let on. They'd already hooked up twice. The second time, they'd run into each other at movie night and wandered off together. Brandon had fingered her slowly, till she finished, and asked nothing in return. Had he told Allegra?

As if on cue, Brandon's electric cart appeared in the distance.

"You know, let's duck in here for a second," Allegra said. She pulled Jen through the entrance to the nearest building, which was some kind of maintenance facility. Was she avoiding Brandon now?

The interior of the building was dark, windowless, lit only by a few dim fluorescents. Jen wasn't sure what the building's purpose was. But it was damp and smelled musty.

"What is this place?"

"Does it matter?" Allegra snapped.

Jen steeled herself. Maybe Allegra knew about everything with Brandon and was going to chew her out. In some ways, Jen would welcome it. A sign of weakness. A signal that Allegra, perhaps, was not always unflappable, that she, too, could be provoked by someone as insignificant as Jen.

"I need to tell you a secret," she said. "But you can't tell anyone. Not even Brandon."

"Why would I tell Brandon—"

"Shut up. Just listen to me."

She took a moment. Though they were alone, the building made itself very much present. A series of things—unidentifiable to Jen—were humming. A loud mechanical drone that was constant, eerie.

"Do you read *Korematsu*?"

There were a handful of underground publications being distributed by El Paquete. In reality, they were just text files that you could get alongside your regular order of *The Big Bang Theory* episodes. Jen had signed up for them all but had never been curious enough to open one.

"Okay, so very few people know this but . . . I write *Korematsu*."

Jen nodded, unsure what the appropriate response was.

"You've never read it, huh?"

"Not even once."

Allegra laughed. She seemed relieved, for some reason.

"Okay, well, you *should* read it. I put a lot of time into it."

"How was I supposed to know?"

"You weren't. But you should read it from now on. Because I want you to help me."

Allegra explained the aims of *Korematsu*. It was a dissenting publication, an antidote to the propaganda that the Office of Detention Culture had them writing during the day. She covered real things that were happening in camp: the mood of detainees, the conditions, the violence. People needed the truth, especially the ones who were trapped there, living it. Writing *Korematsu* was Allegra's form of resistance, she said with a bit of self-importance.

"I thought our form of resistance was just dicking around."

"I'm dicking around a lot less than you are."

This didn't feel unlike being at the bottom of the pool—Allegra pressuring Jen into doing something risky, but assuring her it was for a greater good.

"What do you want me to do?"

"All the stuff you cut out of your stories for the *Loyalty*—turn those into real stories for *Korematsu*," Allegra said. "We are harming our own by working on the detention newspaper. Bullshit propaganda. This is how we atone for that."

Atone. Jen really hated anything that reminded her of her former evangelical life. But if she was honest, the desire to do good never left her. Though if she was really honest, it was the desire for people to think she was doing good, to see her as worthy.

Allegra assured her that this wouldn't be precarious. All the ODC guards were like Officer Paulson—either dumb or ignorant, or both. She put together each issue in secret, on a laptop that no one else had access to. An operation a lot more careful than smoking pot under the bleachers, she promised.

"And we've never been caught with weed."

"Can I think about it?"

"No, you're with me, or you aren't." Allegra was now serious, aggressive. The shift was sudden.

Jen hadn't seen her like this, not since the pool so many months ago. Where was it coming from? She met Allegra's eyes, and it was there that she understood the truth. There was fear. Allegra needed someone to do this with her because she was scared to keep doing it alone.

"What does *Korematsu* mean?"

"You don't really know anything about Japanese internment, huh?"

"Was it the name of a camp?"

"Do you think they would name a Japanese internment camp after a Japanese man?"

I LIVE IN FEAR

—

THE NEXT TIME FERNANDA WAS IN TOWN, SHE INSISTED ON GOING TO the arthouse theater each night for an Akira Kurosawa retrospective.

"Why are you in San Francisco?" Alvin asked playfully as they got in line for the ticket counter.

"I'm here for work," Fernanda said. "We're shipping that update I told you about, the one that will generate descriptions of restaurants."

Fernanda worked on Google Earth—one of the bigger, more prestigious teams at the company. Alvin would've killed to be moved over to Earth.

She reached the front of the line and purchased two tickets for the Kurosawa film before Alvin could offer.

"Yeah, but what are you *really* in town for?" Alvin pressed again, hoping she'd admit that she had flown sixteen hours on the company dime to see him. It had been nearly a year since they'd made out at Alvin's not-going-away party, but they'd talked almost every day since, even going as far as scheduling fake meetings so they could video chat during work hours. Since she'd arrived three days ago, they'd hung out every night after work.

"What am I in town for? This Kurosawa series, of course."

The first night, they saw *Yojimbo*, about a ronin who plays both sides of a poor farm town overrun by bandits. The second night was *Seven Samurai*, the only Kurosawa movie that Alvin had seen before, though he had forgotten just how long it was. Tonight was *I Live in Fear*. Alvin had never heard of it, but it was Fernanda's favorite. She loved it because it was indirectly about Brazil.

"Why do you like Kurosawa so much?" Alvin asked. This evening's screening was much less popular than *Seven Samurai*, so they'd found seats in Fernanda's favorite spot: the back row, right in the middle.

"I grew up in São Paulo," Fernanda said, though Alvin didn't understand. She explained: "There's a big Japanese population there. So they screened a lot of Kurosawa's films when I was a kid."

"I didn't know that."

"Didn't know what?"

"That there were Japanese people in Brazil."

"Americans have this wonderful ability to never conceive of a world outside of their own."

She wasn't wrong.

"So, your big presentation is tomorrow?" Alvin asked.

"Yes, and I can't be out too late," Fernanda said, leaning in and kissing Alvin softly on the mouth. "After the movie, let's go to my hotel and fuck, so I can send you home."

She reached over the seat and quietly groped Alvin's crotch. The forwardness had, at first, jolted him upright in his seat. But he was hard immediately, and had trouble concentrating through the previews.

THE MOVIE WAS not at all what Alvin had expected. The film is set in the late forties, just after Japan had surrendered to the Allies. The aftermath of the bombings of Hiroshima and Nagasaki is not the deadly radiation that lingers, but the constant terror that annihilation could come again. The patriarch of a wealthy factory-owning family is possessed by this fear, so much so that he wants to move his children, and their children, to Brazil.

The kids—most of whom are grown and married and have families of their own, settled in Tokyo—feel that the father's worries about another bombing are just that: worries. The war is over, after all. And they are ready to move on with their lives. But the father insists. His children don't understand what it was like. The terror consumes him. Eventually, the kids have their father committed to an institution. That's where the movie ends: with the father locked in a cell, raving about the threat of the bomb, having been betrayed by his own kin. Alvin emerged from the dark of the theater disoriented, unnerved. He should have been thinking about Fernanda. Instead, he couldn't stop thinking about his own father.

The Living Room was around the corner, the same bar where Alvin had had his fake goodbye party, and where he and Fernanda had kissed for the first time. They came here each night after the movie. But Alvin realized he'd only ever spent time talking with Fernanda here, or at her hotel, or over instant message. A relationship isolated to specific spaces. Inside, they each ordered a drink.

"So, was the father really being unreasonable?" Alvin asked.

"I mean, he put his fears before the needs of his children. He refused to listen to his family. His paranoia was more important than anything else," Fernanda said. "So yeah, I would say unreasonable."

"But he wasn't being selfish. He really believed that the only way to keep his loved ones safe was to move them somewhere else."

"Believing that everyone needs to listen to you—that's kind of selfish, isn't it?"

The bar was mostly empty. It was late, and a Wednesday.

"Should we get another drink?"

"I thought you had that big presentation tomorrow," Alvin said.

Fernanda took a big gulp of her wine and laughed. "It's Google. I could be hungover and still coast through a set of slides. We're doing another movie tomorrow, right?"

Alvin was sure they would, but he hoped it would be a samurai movie next time.

AFTER THEY'D BOTH FINISHED, Alvin dozed off for a bit, and woke up in Fernanda's bed, disoriented by where he was. The lights were off, but he could see the silhouette of Fernanda lit by the glow of her laptop at the other end of the bed. She was still naked, typing loudly. There was the smell of dry sweat, his own and hers.

"Do you always work this late?" Alvin said, groggily, pawing at her bare leg.

"Oh, look who's awake." Fernanda didn't turn around, even as Alvin massaged her calf. She kept typing. "You always fall asleep immediately."

Alvin couldn't tell if she was being playful, or just annoyed.

"Sorry, should I go?"

"No, stay here. I'll need a break soon." More keyboard clacking. "Actually, can you get me some water?"

Alvin turned on the light and lifted himself out of bed. He went to the bathroom to fill a glass from the tap. From the bed, he could hear Fernanda.

"No, from the minibar. They have bottled water in the fridge."

"Isn't that gonna be, like, twelve dollars?"

"This is a business trip. I'm not paying for it."

Business travel, imagine that. Alvin opened a package of fancy gummy bears.

Alvin observed Fernanda working. She didn't seem bothered that he was still there, though she was so focused on her laptop that he might as well have been anywhere else. The words "privileged and confidential" flashed across each of Fernanda's slides as she toggled.

"What is this presentation about again?" Alvin asked.

"I wasn't totally honest with you earlier," she admitted. "But now that you're looking at it, just promise to be quiet about it."

He handed her the candy and watched her fish around the bag in search of a red one.

"Google Earth has satellite imagery of nearly every place on the planet—at least, as much as various governments allow us to," she said. "Lately, we've been getting pressure from the U.S. government to block users from seeing certain locations within the country. I've spent a lot of time talking to your Department of Homeland Security recently . . ."

Alvin popped another gummy. She flipped through some of the slides, and as Alvin looked on, it became clear that her presentation was about how Google would execute demands from DHS to block access to new areas of the country.

"This is just one small part of the negotiation," she said. "I have no idea what all the other things in play are."

"And there are new locations they're asking Google to black out, right?"

Fernanda finally turned around and made apologetic eye contact. There was a moment when it seemed like Alvin would get it, but when it became clear he wouldn't, she explained:

"The camps. They want us to black out the detention sites."

Alvin sat back and pressed himself against the pillows and head-board. "That's dark. Kind of fucked up" was all he could really come up with.

Alvin felt stupid for not understanding what Fernanda meant more quickly. She must've thought he was an idiot. Just dense and unaware of his surroundings, like all the other developers she worked with. She'd joked about this before, how engineers were so bright and yet so fixated that they could never really grasp anything larger than the task at hand. But even if she thought Alvin was an idiot, now she was at least climbing on top of this idiot, kissing this idiot's chest, his neck, working her way up to his lips. She pressed her hips against his until he was inside of her, and continued to press, slowly. His eyes were trained over her shoulder, gazing at the laptop screen on the other side of the bed, as she gripped tightly at the hair on the back of his head, moaning softly into his ear.

SKILLED LABOR

—

WHEN THEY WERE AMONG THEMSELVES, JEN OFTEN HEARD THE ODC guards speaking Spanish—too quickly for her four years of high school classes to keep up with. But you didn't have to be fluent to tell they were laughing and joking. In some ways, Jen felt for them. Sure, detainees were being held in camp against their will, stripped of all their freedoms. That was an existential experience. But she acknowledged that the guards were out here, too, breathing in the same dust, sweating under an oppressive sun.

Maybe Jen just had an easy time making friends. One time she got chatted up by Officer Perez, who had said, please, call him Hugo.

Husky? Stocky? Whatever the polite word, Hugo was clearly a big guy, constantly wiping the sweat from his face with a bandanna. He'd reach around for his back pocket to withdraw the rag, which he had to do with one hand, since the other was usually holding his assault rifle.

With Hugo, it was easy. He was funny, and they soon had an easy rapport. He often saw her with the camera she used for *Loyalty* reporting, and he joked that he would need to go back to hair and makeup before she could take his portrait.

"You're gonna get my good side, right?" he said.

"You're an ODC guard," Jen snapped back. "You don't have a good side."

Hugo held his hands against his heart, like he'd been hurt, critically wounded.

Another time, Hugo stopped Jen on her way back from smoking

with Allegra under the bleachers. It was one of the few times she actually felt kind of high.

"You!" Hugo shouted. "Over here."

There's no way he knows that I'm blazed, Jen thought to herself as she approached him.

"Yes, Officer Perez?"

"I told you. It's Hugo."

"What can I do for you, Hugo?"

"You're . . . you're a woman."

"That's true."

"What would you like to get for your first anniversary?"

"Excuse me?"

"Sorry, if you were married—are you married?"

"I'm nineteen."

"You could be married. I wouldn't judge."

"I am not married."

"Okay, imagine that you are. Imagine you've been married for one year. What kind of gift would you want from your husband, who you love very much?"

Was he fucking with her? Jen eyed him for a moment. Nope, he was dead serious.

"I don't know your wife—"

"It's a hypothetical. No one is saying it's my wife."

"Okay, well, I don't believe you're married anyway."

"That's cold."

"But if I were married and it was my first-year anniversary, I would want something simple. A small gesture. Like flowers."

Hugo nodded for a moment, acknowledging the suggestion. "Flowers . . . I see," he said, staring down at his feet. Then he looked back up at Jen. "You think I am so uncreative that I could not come up with 'flowers' on my own?"

"Listen—"

"Flowers! You must truly think I'm an idiot."

"I don't know you."

"I should shoot you for that insulting suggestion." Hugo motioned to his AR-15.

Jen froze.

"Shit, I'm—sorry, that's fucked up. I really didn't—" Hugo put his hands up, letting the rifle go slack on the strap and fall to his side. "I really was playing around."

"You know some guards do shoot detainees."

"Not me. I swear. God, I—"

"Can I go?"

"What?"

"Can I leave?"

"Yeah, yeah. I'm really sorry. I didn't mean it."

Jen thundered off, long strides, unsure where she was headed, just eager to get away.

THE NEXT TIME Jen saw Hugo, he motioned her over. Reluctantly, she obliged.

"What do you want?"

"I wanted to apologize," Hugo said. "I want you to know that I've never fired this gun."

"So you just use it to scare young women."

Hugo exhaled. "I deserved that."

"Anything else?"

"I also wanted to say thank you."

"What?"

"You were right. About the gift suggestion."

"You really needed me to tell you about buying someone flowers?"

"No, no, I mean"—Hugo took a step back—"obviously I have heard of buying a woman flowers. But you said to keep it simple. Small gesture. Originally, I was planning on getting Elly a piece of jewelry. Maybe a necklace, or earrings. But I'm all thumbs about that stuff—that's why I was asking you."

"That's a nice name," Jen said. "Elly."

"She's an incredible lady," Hugo said. He went to his pocket. Jen assumed he was pulling out his sweat handkerchief again, but he took out his phone. He showed her his background: a photo of Hugo with a cute petite woman, blond highlights, also appeared to be Latina. "My best friend," Hugo added.

"Well, she's much prettier than you are."

"Don't I know it."

"So, what did you get her?"

"Ah, I can't tell you. It's too corny."

"Officer Perez, you pulled me over here so you could tell me. So just tell me."

"Right, okay. So, she's a big *Doctor Who* fan."

"I don't know what that is."

"I made her a cake in the shape of a Tardis."

"I don't know what that is either."

"It's a blue phone booth. I made a sheet cake and cut it in the right shape and covered it in blue frosting."

"So, you can bake?"

"Hell yeah I can bake," he said excitedly. Hugo was tapping on his phone. "Do you want to see a picture of the cake?"

You know what? Jen thought to herself, *I really do.*

AFTER THAT, JEN ran into Hugo most days. She hadn't realized, but most of the ODC guards lived at camp. Since Camp Tacoma was so remote, they had their own accommodations a few miles away, stayed there for five days at a time, and were shuttled in bright and early every morning. It was partly why Hugo wanted to talk to Jen. He missed Elly. Talking about her out loud made him miss her a little less.

"Couldn't you talk about her with your co-workers?"

"They would make fun of me," he said. "I'm some fat Latin dude who's totally whipped by his wife. No way."

This was the story of Hugo. Perpetually an outsider, but never strong enough to actually get out. It reminded Jen of high school, when she felt the pressure of the church. Something about the way he described people—lovingly, yet feeling isolated from them. When a community is full of individuals you like and get along with, but at the end of the day, they are not for you.

"The guys here, they're not all bad. I don't mind them. But, man, when I get back to my bunk, we don't hang out, you know? These are not my people."

It wasn't clear to Jen what he meant by "my people."

Hugo admitted that he hated working for the ODC. Could there be a job he was less suited for? (The man loathed guns.) And in conditions he hated less? (Obviously, there was the heat, and being kept away from his beloved Elly.) Worst of all, he didn't even believe in Vietnamese detention.

"I'm here because the government forced me," Jen said. "Why are you here?"

"A job's a job," he replied. Hugo must've seen how disappointed Jen was in her expression, because he kept on. "Before this, I worked as a TSA agent. You know, doing the scanners. Yelling at old people about taking off their belt. But then, after the attacks—most of them being in airports and all—the Department of Homeland Security decided to re-vamp the whole thing. Hire real thugs to actually protect the airports."

He'd dropped out of high school to help his father as a day laborer. The work was inconsistent, and honestly, too difficult for him, as a self-described "fat ass." He'd arrive early at the Local 79, and when there wasn't enough work to go around, Hugo would be secretly relieved while his father would not-so-secretly express his frustration.

"My dad bailed when I was pretty little," Jen said.

"Ah," Hugo said, nodding, "you were one of the lucky ones, then."

The Department of Homeland Security had received federal funding to militarize the TSA. There were now two checkpoints at the airport—not only at the entrance to the terminal, but at the gate as well. Armed guards were stationed at each, mostly army vets, which played well with conservative constituents, and probably liberal ones, too, Hugo said. "It meant guys like me were out of a job."

Many TSA agents were given the option of working in detention centers—transfer from one division of DHS to another. But it often involved relocating. The airport that Hugo had been at before all this? Boise.

"It was kind of funny being the only Latin dude in Idaho," he joked.

Newly fired TSA agents weren't given an option of where they'd go. So Hugo was shipped here.

"Where is 'here'?"

"What do you mean?"

"Like . . . where are we? What state are we in?"

"You really don't know?"

"We were flown in and then driven to the assembly center, and then there was a long drive to get here. I have no idea where here is."

"Fuck . . ." Like it was dawning on Hugo.

"Hugo, just fucking tell me."

"You're in California."

"Thanks. The biggest state."

"Alaska's the biggest state. Followed by Texas. But you're in central California. The town's called Independence."

She liked Hugo, but the fact that now she knew Hugo liked her— that could be useful in the future.

"So you keep working these jobs that you don't believe in," Jen reiterated.

"I mean, what is a job you can believe in? This whole country is so whack. It'll drive you crazy trying to do the right thing here."

Again with "here." Did he mean camp? California? America? Earth?

"I'll tell you something," Hugo said, which was what he said when he got serious, as if he wasn't already always telling her things. "When I started that job at the TSA, my family had two minds about it. My mother thought it was immoral. You know, the Department of Homeland Security also operates ICE—Immigration and Customs Enforcement."

As if she didn't know.

"My parents are both undocumented. So they live in constant fear of ICE. I have citizenship because I was born here. But my mom, she told me that I was an idiot, working for the government agency that was actively trying to deport her. I tried to explain that I worked for the Transportation Security Administration. Part of DHS, but it was a totally separate body. She wouldn't have any of that. It didn't matter that I struggled to find work. It didn't matter that her son was stuck living at home, and that he might want something else, that he might one day want to move out and live with the girl he loves and intends to marry."

Jen could see that he was starting to tear up a little. Her chest tightened.

"Anyway, my dad, that piece of shit. You know what he says about all this?"

"I don't know. Didn't have a real dad."

"He says, 'Son, you have a job. A steady job.'" The tears were really coming for Hugo now, and he dabbed his eyes. "It was the first time he'd ever been supportive of me. He understood what it means to provide, you know?"

EACH WEEK, JEN and Allegra met up late on a Tuesday at the laundromat to finish *Korematsu*. This week, Jen removed the USB stick hanging from her neck and handed it to Allegra, who plugged it into the laptop that she had hidden in one of the dryers. ("It's broken—no one will ever look in there," Allegra said.)

Each week Jen endured this stress, watching Allegra read her writing. Even though Allegra had assured her that they were now equal partners in the endeavor of *Korematsu*, it was still Allegra's baby. She had approval over everything. A couple times, she'd said a piece wasn't ready, that Jen needed to go back and do a bit more work. Other times, she'd called the language sloppy and gone into the Word doc to rewrite huge portions of a piece. Jen had to witness this in person. Today, she was more blunt.

"What the fuck is this?"

"What do you mean?"

"I meant what I said. *What the fuck?*"

To Jen, that did not clarify, in any way, what Allegra meant.

"This is a sympathetic story of an ODC guard?"

Jen had taken her interactions with Hugo and turned them into a profile. It was a good piece—a guard who felt ambivalent about his role at camp, who questioned the morality of what he'd been assigned to, just another person who was trying to make ends meet.

"We've been at this for two months now and I still need to remind you what we're doing here."

"Okay, yeah, *remind* me."

"Don't take that tone with me. You're annoying enough as it is."

This wasn't like her. Sarcastic, sure. But actively nasty? This was new.

"Are you fucking this dude or something?"

"No way," Jen said, defensively. "He's gigantic."

As that came out of her mouth, Jen realized that phrasing was both unconvincing and deeply gross. But also: Why did Allegra always suggest that Jen was being promiscuous?

"We publish *Korematsu* because we are trying to empower our people. *Our* people. Not some Mexican dude who feels sorta bad about his job, but still collects a paycheck for brutalizing our friends and families."

"I just thought that it was a wrinkle. The reality is not so obvious. Like, maybe most guards are bad. But some are complicated."

"He gets paid to hurt us."

"A job is a job," Jen said. Another regretful thing, out loud, in the world now.

"I'm so angry with you that it's taking every part of me to not hurl this laptop at you." Allegra approached Jen, loomed over her. She was thin, beautiful, but at this moment, all Jen could think about was how much taller Allegra was. Still, Jen caught a whiff of her delicious shampoo.

Jen was unsure of what Allegra would do. They were face-to-face. There were equal odds that Allegra might kiss her or punch her in the face. Either seemed reasonable.

Instead, Allegra backed up and returned to her laptop, resuming her work.

"We're not running this," she said.

And Jen understood. They weren't running this.

INTERNS

—

URSULA WAS FURIOUS WHEN SHE CAUGHT A GLIMPSE OF THE HEAD-
line: "These People Are Review-Bombing Detention Camps on Google
Maps—And It's Giving Us Life."

There was a feature on Maps that allowed users to leave reviews,
meant largely for restaurants, stores, that kind of thing. But oddly, Google
allowed you to review nearly anything it had deemed a "location."

On Google Maps, Camp Oswego, a Vietnamese detention center,
was reviewable. A handful of users had left sarcastic ones.

Poor food & hospitality, rooms are small. Price is cheap. 1 star

The article was composed of review screenshots, followed by: a GIF of
Steve Carell in *The Office* making a pained expression.

Crap food crap rooms no freedom

RuPaul saying, "yasss qweeeeeen."

The detention of Vietnamese Americans is unconstitutional!

A Minion going, "banana!"

The roundup had come, of course, from the Entertainment side.

Ordinarily, if an employee saw something objectionable posted on
the site, there were a couple processes by which they were encouraged to

bring it up. First, they could send a note to the author privately on the company's internal messaging system, outlining their concerns politely and discreetly. If that was uncomfortable, it could be escalated through a human resources funnel, which meant filling out a form that asked for specifics about what aspects of the post were problematic, and what communities it might harm.

Ursula chose neither option and, instead, marched over to the other side of the building. As she was walking, she noticed how the anger had made her entire body tense, to the point that it had affected her gait. She was tromping around, arms akimbo, like a cartoon character.

Through the cafeteria area with the snacks, she emerged on the other side, and realized that since she'd been promoted to News months ago, she had not returned to her old haunt. Some of the desks and tables had been rearranged.

She did not know Piper Pierson, which made her feel extremely stupid when she asked if the small white woman sitting at the desk labeled "Piper Pierson" was, in fact, Piper Pierson.

The woman—girl, really—removed her chunky cat-ear headphones to reply.

"Can I help you?"

Ursula read the headline from a piece of paper.

"'These People Are Review-Bombing Detention Camps on Google Maps—And It's Giving Us Life.' Did you write this shit?"

Piper was bewildered, and alarmed. "Yeah. What's the problem?"

"The problem," Ursula clarified, "is that you don't see that there's a problem."

"Is that supposed to be helpful feedback?"

"Ursula! We don't see you on this side much anymore." Amelia was coming down the row of desks to greet her. "What can we do for the reporter who writes our extraordinary coverage of Vietnamese detention?"

A bit of flattery. Ursula hated that it worked. But she had to admit, it was nice to see Amelia again. Suddenly she felt bad that she'd let the new job drag them apart.

"This article." Ursula handed Amelia the piece of paper. "It's a problem. It's gross."

"Did you print out my article?" Piper asked, impatient, wondering when she could put her headphones back on. "I didn't even know we had a printer here."

Amelia examined the article. "Okay, I can see why this might be in bad taste," she conceded, before joking, "though maybe something got lost when you tried to print an animated GIF."

"This kind of insensitive bullshit makes it harder for me to do my job. How are people supposed to take my coverage of detention seriously if you have idiots like this publishing clickbait?"

It was a crowded office, and people were starting to notice the argument. Ursula could see the headphones were slowly slipping off people's ears.

"Okay, Ursula, I understand your concerns. But you're going to have to bring it down a level. Piper is just a fellow."

"What is that?"

"It's like an intern, but we can't say intern anymore."

"Because of internment?"

"Oh, no. Because 'fellow' just sounds more elevated. But they are basically interns."

Amelia flashed a disarming smile. Ursula knew that Amelia was a good operator in the workplace. She could de-escalate confrontations, settle arguments in a way where both parties left feeling good. There was a right joke for every situation.

But Ursula was undeterred.

"You don't get it. When I call people up and tell them I work for Top Story, they don't know that there's an Entertainment side and a News side. They just think of rubbish like this, even while I am busting my ass trying to publish serious journalism about atrocities happening in America. So you'll have to excuse me if I am bothered when your 'fellows' make what is already an extremely difficult job even harder, for the sake of . . . whatever it is you're trying to accomplish over here."

Now people weren't even pretending to not listen. All eyes were on Ursula. Amelia had shifted herself so that she was standing directly between Ursula and Piper.

"You've made your point. But as she is asked to do, Piper identified something funny happening on the internet, and wrote about it."

"Besides, deploying GIFs like this, with gay slang—it's appropriative of queer culture."

Piper poked her head around Amelia. "Uh, I *am* queer."

"*Black* queer culture."

Piper scoffed.

Amelia had tried to be diplomatic. Now she was pissed.

"Listen, Ursula, I am so happy for you that you got to move to the News side. I know it's what you wanted. I didn't object when you asked for the transfer." Amelia, a woman of infinite patience in the workplace, was done with this. "We get it. You're important."

"That's not what I mean," Ursula said.

"Then what do you mean?"

But Ursula was already leaving the room. She didn't have time to answer stupid questions.

THERE WERE CONSEQUENCES, of course. The next day, Rosco asked Ursula if she could meet with him quickly, in the conference room.

"I was asked to talk to you about this, and I am doing it because that's also part of the job. You're not in trouble," he clarified. "I just need you to be nice. Nice enough that people don't ask me to scold you."

The lights finally turned on. The skittish glow of fluorescence as a punch line.

"Anyway, you got what you wanted. They let that girl go. Pepper."

"Piper," Ursula corrected, then realized that this was not at all what she wanted.

"Whatever. Another entitled white girl gone." Rosco laughed. "Outcomes could be worse."

Rosco was offering solidarity, the kind that made her feel like she was on the inside. So far, in this place, it was the clearest sign that she had any power.

U + 1 E F 9

—

ALMOST EVERYONE IN CAMP WALKED AROUND WITH INCRIMINATING evidence on their person. Jen wore hers around her neck. She'd tied her flash drive to some string so that she could don it like a necklace, but really, it was less that it resembled jewelry and more that it would always be on her. Jen's greatest fear was the thumb drive slipping out of her pocket.

Most of the detainees just stored movies and music and whatever digital files they'd acquired through El Paquete. Jen's held her body of work. Everything she'd written for *Korematsu,* every photo she'd taken, each communication between her and Ursula—and all of her articles for the *Loyalty,* even if she wasn't proud of them. In a way, her work was who she was. It was the closest thing she had to proving she was a person while in camp.

The guards knew each bunk had a contraband computer, and that detainees were carrying around plastic sticks with smuggled digital goods. But they were largely harmless, and so the guards left it alone. Still, it didn't stop Jen from endlessly worrying about being caught.

Her notes to Ursula went in a folder titled "Little Mermaid," since her cousin had shared a name with the villain from that Disney movie. The photos were in a folder called "Pics." She left the handful of shows in a folder named "TV" since there was really no point in hiding those. (And in fact, having run-of-the-mill entertainment would probably throw any curious ODC guard off the scent of the dissident files that were hiding on the thumb drive.)

But for her *Korematsu* writing Jen couldn't help but be a little clever.

The Vietnamese word for America was Mỹ. So the folder for all of that work was "Mỹ Documents."

JEN HAD JUST ejected her thumb drive when she heard it: gunfire.

This was the third time in as many weeks. All three times, she'd been working at the ODC building late, past curfew, which she'd received special permission to do on nights before the newspaper went to print. All three times, the surprise of the gunshots had startled Jen into a shriek, and all three times, her immediate reaction was to drop below her desk for cover. But this third occasion was also a first: there was no ambiguity about what had just happened.

Camp Tacoma was unlit at night, but the central ODC building continued to be heavily guarded and basked in spotlights. No one was supposed to come or go from the complex.

Jen was an exception. When she did leave, she was closely escorted back to her bunk by not one but two armed guards, who, unlike the ODC people she talked to during the daytime, had neither a sense of humor nor the polite instinct to engage Jen in even the simplest of pleasantries. Sometimes she'd just ask how their day was going so she could hear them snarl back.

The ODC building was heavily fortified—anyone approaching the building was visible a few hundred feet away from the manned towers—but at night, those posts relied on a series of searchlights that scanned the ground in a regular, predictable pattern, as if the only way to establish security was to follow a routine. But it wasn't hard to sneak between the floodlights and get within a hundred feet of the ODC building.

That distance was still too far for any malicious actor to meaningfully harm the building or anyone in it. And there were always a half dozen armed guards at its entrance—the intense squad that Jen interacted with at night. With their decked-out assault rifles, they could cut down any suspicious interloper far before they reached the building.

The first one had confused the ODC guards. After that man was gunned down, an ODC agent had come into the newspaper room and found Jen clutching herself under a desk. She asked what was going on and the guard could only tell her that there was some kind of threat, and to sit tight.

A week later, it happened again.

By the third time, it was becoming clear. Jen knew suicides had been rising steadily since camp began. It was unclear why they were escalating now. Maybe it was the cold weather, or that detention had now lasted nearly a year. Regardless, Jen had attempted to keep accurate documentation in her personal files to both distribute in *Korematsu* and, eventually, hand off to Ursula the next time she could get a letter out. The deaths she could track easily; it was the details that were harder. Who were they?

The trends Jen did uncover were disturbing. Almost all men, usually in their early thirties. When she saw photographs of their faces, they didn't look that much older than Duncan.

So on the third night Jen heard a gunshot, she knew exactly what had happened. A man had come to the ODC building acting like a brazen threat. It wasn't hard. You could say you had a bomb—and though there hadn't been a single instance of a person with an explosive since detention had begun, the ODC wasn't going to take that chance.

People lined up at the building during the day with requests: for plumbing to be fixed, for medical requests, for job reassignments, for bunk changes, for a softer bed because their eighty-year-old mother had back problems—for any kind of thing that would usually just be rejected by the ODC's cruel bureaucracy, which existed only to give detainees a process, which only gave them something to hope for, which only crushed them more when it was all for naught.

But at night, you could come to that same building hoping to be killed, and the ODC wouldn't let you down. A few quick shots and you could be done with it. You didn't even have to wait in line.

It was barbaric, but Jen understood. This was the easiest, perhaps the only, way to leave camp of your own free will.

BLOWING UP

—

THE SUICIDES WOULD BE A BIG STORY. URSULA WAS SURE OF IT. A HORror that would render the suffering legible. A truth so violent that people could not look away.

Ursula was impressed with how much info Jen sent along in her last communication. She'd detailed the circumstances of the suicides—that detainees were approaching the Office of Detention Culture building at the center of Camp Tacoma, knowing that they would be shot. Jen confirmed the identities of three of them—Alex Hoang, Huy Vu, Đức Nguyen—and even went as far as to speak to the people they left behind.

Still, Ursula had to shape it all into a story. Jen's on-the-ground reporting had been good, but she really could not put together a coherent sentence for the life of her. She muddied everything up with unnecessary descriptors, a classic symptom of a college student trying to sound smart (and proof that camp had a thesaurus available). Ursula could fix that.

After, she would need to go to the Department of Homeland Security for comment. They would give a vague statement about looking into it, as usual, but they wouldn't be able to deny it.

Rosco recognized what they had as soon as Ursula had filed. He was usually slow on edits—waited a day or two, sometimes a week, unless something was clearly urgent.

"This comes from your same source at Camp Tacoma?" he asked, flipping through the printed draft.

She nodded.

"How did you find him again?"

"I never told you how I found them," Ursula said.

Rosco chuckled. "I was hoping you'd slip and let me in on your secret."

He handed the draft back to Ursula.

"This is exactly the kind of story we hoped you would break when we brought you onto News," he said. Ursula knew he'd meant it as a compliment, but she couldn't help but also read it as a slight, an insinuation that the six previous months she'd been working for him so far had not yielded this kind of result. "Let's get this up tomorrow."

IT WAS HARD to describe the cold feeling of hitting the publish button. Suddenly, the work no longer belonged to you. Maybe it never had, Ursula thought.

The feedback was nearly immediate, and the reception was rapturous. First it was rage. After the initial anger, there was acknowledgment—of Ursula's reporting, of how brave it had been for her to bring this story to light.

The office had a wall-mounted screen that was viewable from most desks. It was a leaderboard showing the top ten stories each day by number of page views. News writers were told to ignore it, since the goal of the hard-hitting journalistic sector of the company was to produce impactful stories, not traffic monsters. But because of the TV's placement, reporters in News were always ambiently aware of it, as the numbers were ever present in their peripheral vision.

Ursula, having come from the Entertainment side where the leaderboard was a stronger indicator of performance, had spent months training herself not to look at it as closely. In fact, it was seen as somewhat gauche among the News reporters to even talk about traffic.

But today, she couldn't ignore the board, and she watched her article quickly climb the chart, surpassing a quiz about different subcategories of millennials and a piece titled "Americans, Here Are 50 Unforgettable Things from 50 Different Countries." Co-workers, some of whom had been strangers, stopped by to congratulate Ursula, especially as the piece took on traffic velocity and hitting the number-one spot felt all but inevitable. Eventually, it happened—Ursula's byline surpassed a viral recipe for an extra-cheesy grilled cheese sandwich—and Rosco emerged from a conference room to shake her hand.

"Your first number-one story," he said.

"I thought we didn't care about page views," Ursula joked.

"We do when they make us look good."

The ascension had felt vindicating. Ursula's extended family may not have understood why she wanted to be a journalist, but that didn't matter now. She was doing it for them, she thought. In the next week, Ursula would be asked to do the press tour for her reporting, appearing on several major NPR programs and a handful of short cable news segments. Other outlets would aggregate what Ursula had broken, the admission of her success with the repeated clause "as first reported by Top Story." Ursula may have never written for *The New York Times*, but now it was acknowledging her, even if indirectly. Legitimacy and validation were coming.

But first, Rosco had a more immediate idea.

"Get your coat. It's time for us to celebrate," he said, rallying the rest of the News team.

It felt at once ghoulish to toast to the suffering of others and at the same time immensely satisfying to be recognized. This was the noble work of journalism, as Ursula had always believed it to be: difficult and thankless on most days, and on a few occasions, urgent and important. Those exceptional moments should be rewarded, right?

NETWORK EFFECTS

—

URSULA TOOK UMBRAGE EVERY TIME ALVIN REFERRED TO HER AS A bad texter. But it was true. How many times had he sent her a message, just to check in, and been left hanging without a reply? It was telling, and slightly disappointing, when Alvin knew he could get his older sister's immediate attention by making it about her work.

Partly, he wanted to tell her about what he'd discovered at Google: that one of the largest tech companies in America, one that was founded with the motto "don't be evil," was working closely with the government to enforce Vietnamese detention, that it was leveraging its massive dragnet of surveillance technologies to help the Department of Homeland Security seek out and capture people like they were criminals. Alvin also wanted to tell his sister about Fernanda.

how've you been?

Ursula didn't respond. Ten minutes went by. So he called.

She picked up immediately. "Is everything okay?"

"Yeah. Why would things not be okay?"

"I don't know. You never call."

"You don't answer your texts. I've got a story for you."

Alvin could imagine Ursula's expression on the other end of the phone with total clarity. She had a journalist's curiosity, but also a journalist's excitement, which meant a kind of smirk she often tried to hide unsuccessfully.

"Check your email, Urs. I sent you something. I think it's big."

—

IT BEING HIS first real job, Alvin wondered how much of the boring day-to-day things he experienced were specific to Google and how much of the tedium was just simply how all workplaces were. For example: everything was organized into "decks," which was corporate slang for the slideshows they prepared for meetings. Everyone was presenting decks, emailing decks, putting all of their hopes and dreams and feelings and fears into decks.

A few nights with Fernanda had proved to Alvin that she was an extraordinarily heavy sleeper, and a bit of a snorer, though in a way that was gentle and kind of cute. Maybe it was the jet lag from her half-day flight from Rio de Janiero to San Francisco. Maybe she was just one of those people who, when she was out, she was really out.

He'd had no concerns that she would awaken when he took her work laptop and her phone to the bathroom. Alvin had seen her type her password a couple of times and had memorized it. Logging on would trigger a separate request for a six-digit code, sent to her phone, which Alvin also had in his hand. He'd glimpsed her password earlier. To break into someone's secure account, you just needed to have another of their devices. The whole thing was stupidly easy, even at the biggest tech company in the world.

It took some rooting around, but eventually Alvin located the deck she'd been working on earlier. Originally that was his only plan: to find that and download it. But in the same folder he discovered a trove of documents—more slideshows, of course—that she and other people on her team at Google had made. Each deck had a dramatic watermark across each slide labeled "PRIVILEGED AND CONFIDENTIAL." He wouldn't have time to read them all, so he compressed them into a zip file and copied it to a flash drive. The whole thing took maybe five minutes. When he was done, Alvin washed his hands.

Fernanda would never suspect a thing. Alvin would return the laptop to her backpack, the phone to the bedside table, and his skinny body back under the covers. Fernanda rustled, but didn't wake, and Alvin easily fell back asleep. They'd fuck again one more time in the morning, though neither of them would finish.

DAYS AFTER THEIR initial call, Ursula wouldn't stop texting. She had a lot of questions, and they were arriving a dozen at a time, phrased vaguely, so as not to incriminate Alvin in case Google could somehow trace the leaked files back to him.

It was nice to finally have his sister's attention, but now it was too much.

Alvin answered the call. "Ursula, can you chill out?"

She was all business, though. "Are you *sure* these files are authentic?"

"You think I made these up? All of them? I sent you, like, two dozen decks."

"Decks?"

"Slideshows. It's what we call them here. Or maybe that's what everyone calls them."

"And they can't be traced back to you?"

Alvin hadn't really thought too hard about that.

"To be on the safe side, don't put any of this in writing," Ursula commanded. "No emails, no texts. Let's only talk about it over the phone."

"I feel like if they were reading our texts, they could also listen in on our calls," Alvin said. He thought he was making an argument that his sister was being too cautious, but he just gave her another reason to be paranoid.

"That's a really good point," Ursula said before hanging up.

So, for the next two weeks, they were cut off. No messages or communications of any kind, at least until the article went live. Ursula couldn't risk Google getting ahead of the story before she could corroborate it. In the end, Alvin's attempts to get his sister's attention ended up disconnecting them further.

But if he'd spent more time reading through the slideshows he'd emailed, Alvin might have recognized what he had actually sent her. This was much bigger than a project to block out satellite imagery over a few hundred square miles of land where detention sites were. That was just one of the smaller features in an expansive and lucrative contract that Google had with the Department of Homeland Security.

Laid out in big bullet points were far more dangerous invasions of privacy—revelations that would take over the news cycle and cement Ursula's career as an investigative journalist.

Alvin saw none of this coming. He barely paid attention to the decks in front of him in meetings. Why would he have bothered to read these?

LOSING IT

—

Jen had never imagined her first time would be at the bottom of an empty pool. Though once things were set in motion, she knew exactly that this was where she would have sex. Besides, she was fed up with Brandon's dillydallying. They'd been doing Everything But for weeks now, until finally, mid–fooling around, Jen asked Brandon when he was going to finally have sex with her. Instead of it being a turn-on, as she'd hoped, Brandon stopped fingering her, withdrew his hand from her pants, and said that he was aware she had never done it and wanted to be respectful of her desires. The opposite of a turn-on: an excuse.

Jen had declared she was ready, but Brandon wanted to make sure it was special, even though they both agreed that was an outdated notion. For Jen, she just wanted Brandon to take charge—to be in control, take what he wanted, hurt her if he had to. But he seemed more daunted by the whole thing than Jen was, all this talk of wanting to "do things right."

Department of Homeland Security detention sites were not exactly set up for young people to get laid, given all the crowding, lack of private space, and government surveillance. There were some ways it could happen: Jen knew people were doing it during off-hours in laundry rooms, in storage closets, in bathrooms. Some bunks had clever systems to give people just the slightest nod to privacy, which reminded her of negotiations she would make with her college roommate. Even so, it occurred to Jen that it would be impossible for her first time to be in a bed unless she wanted ten other people to be in the room. That made her a little sad.

The most privacy they could get would be at the sports complex.

Brandon suggested during a football game, when most of the detainees would be distracted.

"Like, in the empty pool?" Jen asked, mostly joking.

"I'll make it nice," Brandon said. "I promise." Jen didn't know what that could mean, but at least there would be some mystery. In camp, you held on to every good moment, even if you weren't sure what it meant.

WHEN JEN ARRIVED that night, she was shocked to see what Brandon had been able to put together. She found him at the bottom of the pool, where he'd arranged an assortment of blankets and pillows. Surrounding the makeshift bed was an array of candles of assorted sizes and scents.

As Jen descended the ladder, Brandon gestured toward the setup and said, "Welcome."

"Welcome?" Jen laughed. "To your sex palace?"

Brandon was taken aback. "Sorry, it's the best I could do."

Jen felt bad. She was just teasing. She was nervous, of course.

"No no no, it's nice. I mean that. Where did you get the candles?"

"Ordered special from El Paquete, of course. I wouldn't sniff them, though. They're really just here to look nice."

Brandon kissed Jen, gripped her waist, more confidently than usual. *Fucking finally,* she thought, comforted that she might be able to let go, unclenching her muscles, realizing how tightly she'd been holding her body.

They could hear the crowd from the football stadium. Jen wondered if they were cheering for her brother and felt a swell of pride that she immediately tried to shake off. Brandon revealed a pair of earphones, hooked into an old MP3 player, the kind of chunky thing that existed before people had iPods. Brandon inserted one of the buds into her ear. It played music that was soothing—an old R & B song, one that Jen recognized from the radio. Laid-back and dulcet. Predictable but sweet.

"What is this?"

"I actually don't know. You ask El Paquete for music, and they just give you whatever. But I thought this one sounded nice."

"You really thought of everything, huh?"

Brandon took a step back. "Sorry, this is so weird. Everything in camp is so awful. And sometimes when I'm with you, I just . . . forget all that."

Jen closed the gap between them and pressed her forehead against his. "I refuse to believe that camp is to blame for you becoming a huge cornball."

The whole thing was a strange give-and-take. Jen understood what this was: two anxious, excited people. They were each just figuring out where the other was, how they felt, what they wanted. Jen knew they were going to go further than they ever had tonight. But she was familiar with his form. The way he smelled, the way he felt. Like the way she approached anything else, she would start with the stuff she knew.

OVER THE YEARS, Ursula had given her a lot of warnings about sex, reluctantly, over text. Jen couldn't ask Má, unless she thought advice from the Lord would be helpful if she ever wanted to get it in. Sometimes, it was easier to believe that she and Duncan were immaculately conceived than to imagine that her mother had ever had sex.

On the other hand, it was hard to think of Ursula ever getting laid, given how much she complained about men.

"They're dogs," she would say, as if it would dissuade Jen from ever getting close to one.

Her cousin mostly complained about how gross men were in New York. She had plenty of horror stories, though the way she told them was with a confusing combination of shame and pride. Like, was she actually embarrassed to have fucked a guy who asked her to pay for dinner, drinks, the movie, and then later ask for cab fare home? If she was, why would she tell that story to anyone?

At the same time, it seemed impossible to Jen that Ursula would ever lower her standards. She was smart and successful and self-possessed.

will it hurt?
the first time, yeah
maybe a lot. depends on the person

my first time hurt like hell
and there was a lot of blood

This, not surprisingly, did not comfort Jen as much as Ursula had hoped. Every time Ursula tried to be helpful made Jen feel this way.

So Jen kept waiting for it to hurt. But it never did. And honestly, it felt good—great, and didn't stop feeling great. However, it was a little weird at first. Jen was used to the warmth of Brandon's body, but his penis wrapped in a condom was sticky and cold. (Another thing he had managed to be prepared and thoughtful about, thanks, again, to El Paquete.) Still, the rest of him was a comfort. His scent, the frame of his shoulders, the way he held her.

"Is this okay?"

"Is what okay?"

". . . This?"

"Please shut up."

As Jen had imagined, it started slow, and then escalated, both in speed and intensity. Brandon started gripping her more tightly around her hips; she was pulling on his hair, then moving her hands down to his smooth back. They both began to sweat, and she didn't even feel self-conscious about it. She loved the way he smelled.

When they were done, Brandon rolled off to the side of her and reached for a box of tissues, also probably procured from El Paquete. Jen imagined what it would be like, asking the illegal contraband network to acquire some Kleenex so you could clean off after having sex with a virgin in a pool. Brandon handed her a tissue. Such a gentleman. (After wiping herself, Jen turned over to check her tissue for blood. To her relief, nothing.)

They each lay on their back, suddenly apart, staring at the ceiling, which in the dark felt like a million miles away.

Jen felt around for another condom and eagerly unwrapped it. Soon, she was on top of Brandon, pressing all of herself into him. This time felt even better than the first.

And that was when they heard it. The sound of a door opening—the big heavy double doors that reminded her of a school.

As her years of being a Christian had trained her to do, Jen imagined the worst possible outcomes: that ODC guards were going to catch them in the wrong place and strip them of all their privileges, or worse, put them in solitary; or it would be her mother, discovering that she had sexual relations out of wedlock, a sin that God would never forgive her for.

Brandon stood up straight. So did Jen. They scrambled to put on their clothes, a useless attempt to hide what they'd done, considering they were on some hilariously dumb hippie fuck bed, surrounded by candles. Brandon must've thought of this, because he began blowing out the flames, as if that might disguise their location.

The darkness around them only made it more terrifying. They could make out the shape of a figure, moving strangely, heaving. Neither could see over the lip of the pool. An ambiguous groan and then—the sound of a body collapsing, the hard slap of skin on concrete.

"What the fuck was that?"

"I don't fucking know."

"Shouldn't you go look?" Jen said.

"*You* can go look," Brandon said.

Jen was scared, but now also furious with Brandon's cowardice.

Climbing the ladder, she realized how her body had gone from its most relaxed state in months to a full-on tension. She pressed her fingers against the cold metal bars, ascending carefully. Each step was deliberate—as purposeful as any motion she'd ever made.

As she breached the top of the pool, Jen saw the shape of someone laid out, barely moving. They didn't seem like a threat, but as Jen made out the figure in the dark, it became clear it was someone who was hurt and was breathing with difficulty. She rushed over.

Jen realized who it was before she even turned the body over. Even with the thick smell of blood, she recognized the scent of her hair. But her face was nearly unrecognizable—a visage bruised, bloodied.

"What happened?"

Allegra moaned.

"Jesus, what the fuck?"

It was Brandon. Jen had not heard him follow behind her.

Allegra's voice was weak. "They found out."

Brandon shook her. "Found out what?"

Jen shoved him off Allegra. "Back off. Let her talk. She needs to tell us what they know!"

"Who is 'they,' even?"

In the dark, through the violence, Jen could see Allegra's beauty. That long hair, those high cheekbones. This was her gorgeous friend. Jen began wiping the blood and snot and tears from her face. Jen embraced Allegra like she'd never embraced anyone, the way a person does when they know they are about to lose someone forever.

"IS IT RAINING?"

It was obviously raining, but Jen hadn't even noticed. As long as they'd been in camp—nearly a year now—there had never been a drop of precipitation. No time to think about that. They had a lot farther to drag Allegra, though they had no idea where they would hide her.

Jen would only piece it together later, after Allegra had disappeared for good: the ODC had caught wind of *Korematsu,* tracked it down to Allegra, and punished her for it. Perhaps she'd gotten too confident— cocky, even. Maybe this was what she deserved for trying to do the right thing. But don't worry, Allegra assured her, she hadn't given Jen up. She never would, she said, before coughing up blood.

Jen pleaded for her to shut up, and just focus on moving her feet. Allegra had presented as a thin, tiny person, but now she weighed a ton, draped across Jen's and Brandon's shoulders.

The drizzle turned into rain, which turned into a downpour. It was weather they'd never seen here before. The environment was changing. Jen had worked hard to adapt to life in camp, and it had allowed her to ignore the obvious truth: that in accepting these conditions, she was just waiting for things to get worse.

IV

—

CAMP, YEAR TWO

SEARCH HISTORY

—

ALVIN AWOKE TO MISSED CALLS, VOICEMAILS, TEXTS, AND EMAILS FROM his boss. He scanned them and found that they all said the same thing, "Be at the office at 10 A.M. for a meeting," with no other information. The volume of contact made it sound serious. But also: If it was urgent, why couldn't his boss just say what it was about?

The rest of the morning, he decided, would go unchanged. He went for a quick run around the Mission, taking in the cool air of the bay, and washed off all the sweat with a hot shower once he returned to his apartment. Though he still shared a single bathroom with three other people, it was never a problem. His roommates kept more traditional engineers' hours—late to rise, late to bed, never trying to beat the traffic but always complaining about it. Which meant, for him, long, steamy showers in the morning. A bathroom mirror that would have to be wiped down so he could see his reflection while he shaved.

Hopefully, Alvin would get to the climbing gym after work. The beauty of arriving at the office early was that it afforded him the ability to leave early—around 4 P.M., when he'd board a shuttle that would often dodge the worst parts of rush hour. Alvin made a plan for it. He would pack his climbing gear in a duffel and take it to work with him, and after, hop the Google bus that would drop him off closest to the gym. It would be a perfect day: fulfilling cerebral work bookended by the physical relief of sweat and sore limbs.

Alvin arrived at the office, as usual, by 8:30 A.M. He started on his tasks but found that he no longer had access to certain tools and parts of the intranet. He filed a ticket with IT and just made do with what he had.

More permissions errors arose. Right before ten, Alvin sent a follow-up to IT saying he'd be out of pocket for the next half hour or so, and that he hoped the issues would be resolved by the time he got back.

This meeting was in a recently built room—Ho Chi Minh City—which Alvin had never been to. Each building on the Google campus had a theme. The theme didn't manifest itself visually in any way but was instead a name scheme for the various conference rooms. Alvin's building had rooms named after various cities around the world. Daily stand-ups were in Shanghai. Code review check-ins were in Riga. Last week, Alvin sat through a four-hour presentation in Benghazi.

Counterintuitively, they were ordered not by geography but alpha-betically. When Alvin asked someone about it on his first day, the an-swer he got was "Well, what would be easier to understand, the order of *A* through *Z* or where each African capital is located relative to the others?" He conceded that was a fair point. Geography was easier to understand when it was not organized by geography.

Even with an alphabetic system, he got a little lost, passing from Guadalajara to Houston before finding Ho Chi Minh, a small three-person conference room, tucked away in a corner by the bathroom. When Alvin arrived, he was confused to find that his boss was not there. Instead, it was a white woman with short blond hair and an intense gaze. She told him to sit down.

"You know, it's kind of funny. My family doesn't really recognize Ho Chi Minh City? Like, they still refer to it as Saigon," Alvin said, trying to make small talk.

The woman didn't say anything to that. She began typing on her laptop.

"I've never actually been to Vietnam, but I hear that a lot of people still refer to Ho Chi Minh City as Saigon there, too. I guess they can't rename the room, though, right? It would mess up the alphabetization."

Alvin knew he was nervous because he was trying to be cute. Still, nothing from the woman. Barely a reaction, or an acknowledgment. Just more typing. What was this?

"My name is Michelle, and I'm part of Google's security team," the woman announced, finally. "Before we start, is there anything you would like to tell me?"

"Why would I have anything to tell you? I don't even know what we're doing here."

Michelle was typing again, noting his response. "Have you been in contact with Ursula Nguyen?" she asked.

"Yeah, that's my sister. I'm sorry. Who are you?"

"I told you. I'm Michelle, on behalf of the security team here at Google."

"Okay, but what do you need from me?"

"I need to know if you've been in contact with Ursula Nguyen."

"I already told you I have. Because she's my sister. Listen, I think I know what this is about, and if you'll let me explain, I assure you that you'll understand this is all a big . . . misunderstanding."

"I will understand this is a misunderstanding?"

Oh, she thought she was funny? At least it was proof that Michelle, here on behalf of the security team at Google, was a tiny bit human.

"I have some questions about your sister. You are aware that she is a reporter."

"Yeah, she and I are close enough that I know what she does for a living."

"Alvin, your sarcasm will not help you here."

"Help me with what?"

"We have reason to believe that you are leaking confidential information to your sister, a journalist."

"Because I talk to my sister?"

"Alvin, Google does not take issue with people talking to their family members. It's what they tell family members, especially when they are members of the press."

"What do you think I told my sister?"

Michelle, if that was really her name, started typing again. She was the kind of person who typed like they were trying to damage the keys, or their fingers. Hard clacks against plastic. Alvin wondered if this was some kind of intimidation tactic.

"As I said, we have reason to suspect that proprietary and confidential information about the company has been given to your sister, Ursula Nguyen."

"And what makes you say that?"

"Late last night, your sister published a story alleging that Google was working with the Department of Homeland Security."

"I mean, is the story true?"

"It doesn't matter if it is true or not. What matters is whether or not you leaked private and confidential materials to a journalistic outlet."

"I feel like the truth matters."

Michelle's expression was stern, but it softened just a touch. She closed her laptop.

"You need to understand the nature of my job. It is not to evaluate whether things we do at this company should be public knowledge or not. I do not decide on whether the things Google pursues are ethical or unethical. I work on the security team."

"You mentioned that."

"And part of keeping Google secure is understanding how and why private and confidential information was given to a journalist. The truth I am interested in is if you supplied evidence to your sister that this company was working with DHS."

When he'd leaked the decks to Ursula, Alvin hadn't really thought about the actual consequences. He'd been a little surreptitious, and covered some of his tracks. But how mad could Google really get? In his mind, people didn't get punished for doing what was, objectively, the right thing. This was a company that lauded its morals. But as his meeting with Michelle proceeded, Alvin was slowly realizing what kind of trouble he was in.

"So to be clear: you're denying that you told your sister anything about the company."

"The only things I talk about to her are how good the food is."

"And you never sent her any confidential material related to Google."

"Never ever."

"And you definitely did not email her a confidential presentation that was meant to propose certain product changes and features that would adhere to the requests of the Department of Homeland Security?"

"Uh—"

"And you certainly did not write, in the body of an email, 'have at it, sis,' before attaching that PowerPoint to the message?"

"Wait, hold on—"

"And there is absolutely no way that you answered a series of text messages she sent you afterward, about the veracity of those documents, and how you acquired them?"

Alvin knew, rationally, that Google was a massive and complex surveillance apparatus. He just never imagined it would be turned inward on its own employees.

Michelle stood up and knocked on the door of the conference room. A security guard entered. He was a large man—more paunch than muscle, but still intimidating, even while wearing a pool-blue polo shirt with the colorful company logo emblazoned on the left breast.

"Here's what I believe, Alvin. You applied for this internship knowing that you would have access to the inner workings of Google. You did this so you could supply your sister, a journalist, with confidential and potentially damaging information. You thought you could get away with this by communicating those materials with her through your non-work accounts. And your assumption about this last part was very, *very* wrong."

"You don't understand," Alvin said.

Michelle instructed him to leave his laptop, his badge, his phone.

"But this is my phone," Alvin pleaded.

It didn't matter, she said. There was company property on it.

"Earlier in this conversation, I found your tone to be extraordinarily condescending, perhaps a little sexist," Michelle said, gathering his identification. "I find it hypocritical that you were judging me for doing my job when you seemed to think yourself too good to do yours."

THE BIG MAN in the blue polo escorted Alvin out of the building, and followed him until he was clear of the campus premises. Google would contact him in the next few days about whether his suspension would be permanent, though Alvin already knew that it would be.

It wasn't until they'd reached one of the parking lots that the guard allowed Alvin to be on his own. Of course, Alvin did not have a car parked here. He'd always taken the Google shuttle to and from work. And now he couldn't call a car, because he didn't have his phone. Alvin would have to head to downtown Mountain View and find public transportation back into the city.

When the security guard was out of view, Alvin picked up his duffel and marched over to the bike-share station. There was only one left, a yellow bike, and the seat was a little broken and kept moving under Alvin's butt. It would have to do.

The ride was good for clearing his head. The breeze seemed to push many of the anxieties out, at least for the time being. Alvin thought about the things he would say to Ursula next—how she'd totally fucked him over by publishing that story. Of course, that was exactly why he'd sent her those materials. Alvin knew he was really just furious at himself, but he would try to take it out on her anyway. He imagined the embarrassment of telling his mom about losing the job, and the chance at the prestigious and fulfilling career he'd always dreamed of.

Alvin biked past the municipal museum. He hadn't been back there since his first day, when Lily, the curator, had faked slipping him her number. But maybe she would take pity on him this time around. He parked his bike and walked to the front desk, but Lily was not working that day, and the older man at the counter politely declined to tell Alvin, a stranger, her whereabouts. Alvin would leave the museum disappointed, and still have to figure out how exactly he was going to make it home.

BREAKING STORIES

—

Rosco had an office now.

He'd bought a print of a Rothko painting, which had been nicely framed and was leaning against the wall, unhung. Rosco had seen it as a good sign that he'd been too busy to put it up yet. Ursula wondered how deliberate that was, the appearance of being busy, as if any person couldn't take two minutes to put a nail into a wall. Or maybe it was just funny he'd picked a Rothko, a choice that felt like a slightly elevated version of finding a poster of Edward Hopper's *Nighthawks* in a college dorm. Or maybe she was just amused by the phonetic harmony of "Rosco's Rothko." Regardless, she found herself staring at the painting—a smear of reds and gray—not really listening as Rosco went on and on about . . . something to do with a Pulitzer? She refocused. What was he talking about?

Ursula's scoop, revealing the connection between Google and the Department of Homeland Security, had netted them both big promotions—Ursula to senior reporter, Rosco to deputy editor. The changes to their lives had been concrete. Ursula was now up late every night working, trying to satisfy the demand for bigger stories. They didn't just want news hits. They wanted full-fledged features, with dozens of sources, thousands of words, cobbling together a narrative that would tell Top Story readers about Vietnamese detention, but also, America.

Ursula was exhausted from a lack of sleep. Rosco was still talking.

"So the next story has to feel rich, *deep*. Something that isn't just about how awful detention camps are. We've done those stories over and over and over."

"I mean, things are really bad there," Ursula said. "I don't know if I can just ask my source for their sunniest experiences?"

"We're not looking for sunshine. We need something complicated. Nuanced."

Rosco gave vague pronouncements about what would fly with the Pulitzers. Every story had a shape. He—they, the Pulitzer committee—wanted one that felt full, complete. A narrative that was specifically human, and vivid. Told without sentimentality, yet still emotional. You know?

Ursula would leave this meeting with homework. What was the story she could deliver with Pulitzer-minded ambition? Suddenly everything annoying about this conversation was fading to the back of her mind. The Pulitzer. The fucking Pulitzer!

"We're at a severe disadvantage in many ways. We compete with *The New York Times, The Washington Post, The New Yorker,* all these places that have larger, seasoned newsrooms and editorial staffs. Full-time researchers and fact-checkers. Dozens of people on the same beat. A legacy of doing this shit. But you know what we have that they don't?" Rosco said.

Ursula knew the answer: Jen.

"You," Rosco said.

He had demands, which was a thing bosses were allowed to have. He wanted her to come up with a list of new story ideas. No more incremental articles, or small reports about conditions in camp. Find him something that would win them—and Top Story News—their first major reporting award. He believed in Ursula. Together, they would go up against the most venerable and well-resourced journalistic institutions in the world. They might not win, but Rosco knew they could get close. He believed it more than anything.

With all of that encouragement, Ursula got up to leave Rosco's office, and just before she closed the sliding glass door behind her, remembered the reason she had come in in the first place. She'd filed her latest piece, some three thousand words, all written late last night. When might Rosco have a chance to look at it?

"I'll look at it this afternoon, hopefully. I have to head uptown after lunch to talk to a J-school class at Columbia. Diversity in newsrooms and whatnot," Rosco said, deadpan.

WITH ROSCO OUT for the afternoon, Ursula decided she could do the rest of the day from home. She didn't have a desk in her apartment, so she often worked from her bed. Sure, she could've sat on the couch, especially since it was the middle of the day, one of the few times her roommate was asleep. Genevieve was a friend from college who had never quite found her footing after school. Her parents were floating her while she figured it out, which Ursula tried not to be judgmental about. They lived in a cute four-unit brownstone in Park Slope. The building was "prewar," which always struck Ursula as funny, as if there would ever be such a time as postwar.

Genevieve tended to get home around 2 A.M. most nights, never describing her whereabouts with any more detail than "being out." It wasn't too disruptive, since Ursula was often awake, still working. The promotion to senior reporter gave her a slight bump in pay—enough that she could afford her own place, a studio at least, a one bedroom if she was lucky. But living with Genevieve was going just fine, and when would Ursula have time to pack and move?

Ursula sat in her bed with every intention of writing down all of her most ambitious story ideas. But instead, exhausted from several all-nighters in a row trying to file a feature about the poor food quality at Camp Tacoma, she immediately fell asleep.

It was dark when she awoke. Her MacBook had not moved from her lap. Ursula discovered that napping for what had apparently been six hours in the middle of the day did not miraculously summon a list of Pulitzer Prize–winning ideas. But the sleep had done wonders. After an hour of going through her notes, Ursula now had a Google doc full of pitches for Rosco. It felt good to step back and take stock of what she'd learned from Jen.

Ursula went to the kitchen to get some wine. Inside the fridge, a sticky note from Genevieve was on a takeout bag: "Help yourself! Forgot if you eat pork, but the vindaloo rips!" Later, after finishing all of the leftovers, Ursula dabbed the remnants of brown sauce from her cheeks and planted herself on the couch with her computer and her fifth glass of white.

THE NEXT MORNING, Ursula had risen feeling so good about herself that she decided to pick up an Americano and an almond croissant on the way to work. One upside of working crazy hours and not sleeping enough and scavenging Luna Bars at the office was that she was losing weight. Who needed exercise when you could work yourself to the bone?

Rosco was, of course, not at the office when Ursula arrived at 9 A.M. And he didn't show at his usual 10 A.M., or even at his actual 10:30 A.M. Ursula waited. She printed out her two pages of story ideas.

Just before noon, she caught Rosco coming in. Before he could close the sliding glass door behind him, Ursula was there.

"Hey, boss, ready to talk?"

"Oh, hi, Ursula. I had an early coffee meeting. Want to give me a second to grab a snack?"

"Wait here."

She darted back to her desk and returned with the almond croissant, which she had not yet eaten.

Rosco placed himself in his chair and gestured, with some annoyance, yes, he was ready to talk story ideas. Ursula handed him her sheet of pitches.

He looked amused. There wasn't another chair in his office yet, so Ursula sat on the floor, feeling like an excitable preschooler, watching Rosco read through her pitches. She eyed the Rothko print while she waited. Maybe it was her unusually good mood and the fact that, for the first time in a long time, she'd had a full night of sleep and then some, but something about the Rothko made sense to her now. Somewhere between these blocks of color, where pretentious categorizations like "abstract expressionism" broke down, was the revelation. It wasn't a piece of art trying to say something; it was a painting that told you all about the kind of person who would buy it. Ursula just had to figure out what the Roscos of the world were in the market for.

DOUBLE DUTY

—

JEN VISITED MÁ MOSTLY OUT OF OBLIGATION. SHE LIKED SPENDING time with her mother, but even in camp, she found ways to be overbearing, judgmental. But the quarters for the older detainees tended to be nicer: more space; consistent heating; a few seating options that might even pass as armchairs, if you didn't look closely enough; no bunk beds, of course, since even the Office of Detention Culture wasn't cruel enough to make seniors climb a ladder to lie down.

"What are you wearing?"

"What? This?"

Jen was being coy as she threw herself onto the shabby chair by her mother's bed. She knew the T-shirt she had worn, with bold letters that read "FBI," would provoke her mom.

"It stands for Federal Boob Inspector," Jen said, spinning around to reveal the back of the T-shirt, which spelled out the acronym.

Má scoffed loudly. Jen laughed.

Among some of the younger people at Camp Tacoma, there was a competition to see who could wear the most obnoxious shirt. If it had started as a joke, it had quickly become the fashion.

Six months in camp proved that two suitcases could not hold enough clothing to live on. So the ODC had supplied an array of apparel, in an array of sizes, that all seemed to come from a warehouse full of surplus clothing from a decade ago.

Very prevalent around camp was a brand called Big Dog Sportswear, which trafficked exclusively in novelty graphic T-shirts with phrases like I AM THE BIG DOG and DON'T LIKE MY ATTITUDE? TAKE A NUMBER and featured a cartoon Newfoundland folding its arms. But the real gems, if you could find them, were the Big Dog shirts that were canine puns on movies: THE DOGFATHER, AUSTIN BOW-WOW-ERS, DOG WARS: THE EMPIRE BITES BACK, SOUTH BARK ("OH MY GOD, THEY FIXED KENNY!"). The pride of Jen's wardrobe was a sweatshirt with the Big Dog that read EXHAUSTIPATED: TOO TIRED TO GIVE A S#!T, which Má commented on with "at least they had the good sense to censor it."

There was a shortage of smalls and mediums, too, so petite detainees had to settle for baggy, oversized XL and XXL shirts, which they would tie up or crop.

Jen had written up the trend in the *Camp Tacoma Loyalty*. It had been one of the few things that had actually been fun to work on, and that she was proud of. So much so that she copied the entire clip into her last exchange with Ursula. Even in detention, a culture could emerge.

Jen's check-ins with Má had lately gotten shorter and shorter. In the early days at the assembly center, they would spend as much time as they could together, with Duncan, huddling together, trying to make sense of things. But as days rolled on, and they settled into the new normal of camp, the three of them saw each other less. For Jen, gaining independence from family was just as much a form of survival as staying close.

"Your brother still visits me every morning," Má said, scolding. "He brings me something to eat. Usually a sandwich."

"He works in the kitchen!"

"All you bring me is . . . Federal Boob Inspector."

Jen couldn't explain to her mother what was keeping her so busy. At first, her correspondence with Ursula was a tightly kept secret out of fear that speaking too loudly might jeopardize her only line of communication out of camp. But as the months went on and their messages went undisturbed, Jen realized that she had just wanted to keep something to herself. It was hard to have secrets when you were always sleeping mere feet from another person; when so much of your movement was surveilled; when every hour of your day had to be accounted for.

"You're up to something," Má accused.

"What could I possibly be up to?" Jen said.

"I don't know, but don't cause trouble."

Throughout camp, Má had begged her kids to keep their heads down. Camp was a sad fact of life, and there was nothing anyone could do about it. They would serve out their time—no matter how long it was—quietly and cooperatively. They could make the best of it. "Look at Duncan," she'd say. Her son had struggled in high school, but now he had the rhythms of a working life and the excitement of his football team to keep him occupied. Jen was sure that Duncan, like everyone else in camp, was still depressed. But he was hiding it better than most.

Má would've flipped if she knew the truth, that Jen was sticking her neck out trying to report things for Ursula. Or even worse, distributing dissident materials under the banner of *Korematsu*.

And her mother would be right to be scared. Since the incident, Jen had no idea what happened to Allegra. That rainy day, ODC guards had discovered them and forced Brandon and Jen to release their friend so she could be taken to the infirmary. After that, neither Jen nor Brandon had seen her again. That was nearly six months ago.

There was rarely a moment when Jen was not thinking of Allegra. The image of her battered face, her left eye swollen, blood caked around her nose and mouth. It was the smile that she'd cracked—a crazed, desperate smile—when trying to assure Jen that she was fine. That would never leave her.

"You have become so rebellious. And for what?" Má scoffed.

Jen was sick of her mother's patronizing tone. "I think there's no place on earth where it makes more sense to cause trouble than camp."

Now she was just picking a fight. It was bound to happen without Duncan to intervene. Má asked why Jen couldn't just be more like her brother and make the best out of their situation. Maybe there wasn't happiness to find, but one could find contentment in doing what was asked.

Nothing sets off a person more than being compared to their sibling. So Jen asked her mother what kind of god would allow an entire population to be locked up like this. Má could only meekly explain that this was a test.

Jen laughed. More of a cackle, really, loud and mean, before she strode off, resolved to leave her mother alone with her pathetic beliefs.

Even though she was terrified of meeting the same fate as Allegra, whatever that might have been, it did not discourage her from continuing her work on *Korematsu*. It only strengthened her resolve, and proved its urgency. The stakes were clear now. Her mother was wrong. Existing day-to-day was not enough; surviving wasn't living.

DOCUMENT DUMP

—

BEFORE SHE'D SENT THE RECORDS REQUEST—AN IDEA OF ROSCO'S—
Ursula had been against it. She'd imagined herself as the kind of journalist who was out in the field, talking to people. But Ursula's early days
in the newsroom were marked by a lot of nodding along with things,
even when she didn't really know what she was approving of. One word
that came up often was *FOY-uh*. Writers FOY-uhed government agen-
cies for this and that and Ursula pretended to understand.

Later, she'd put together that it was FOIA—the Freedom of Information Act. It allowed journalists to hit up various bodies under the
executive branch for documents on anything subject to disclosure—an
act of transparency. But she liked the way it sounded. *FOY-uh*.

In Ursula's case, the Department of Homeland Security sent an
overwhelming number of documents to fulfill her request. Usually, they
arrived digitally. But perhaps as a means of sending a message, boxes
and boxes of physical files showed up at the office one day. This was
DHS's way of cooperating while also telling Ursula she could go fuck
herself. It took three separate Uber trips to transfer the documents to
her apartment.

So Ursula had enlisted Alvin, who was hiding out after getting fired,
to help her pore through the files.

"'Come to New York,' you said. 'We'll eat at cool restaurants, go see
a play,' you promised." Alvin heaved a stack of papers from one pile to
another. "I would've thought twice if I knew I was visiting to become
your assistant."

Alvin, of course, hadn't really had a choice. He had no money in his

savings—what twenty-two-year-old did?—and so when he was termi-
nated, he needed to move out of his apartment almost immediately. The
timing was good. Her roommate, Genevieve, was looking for a subletter
anyway, after chasing a German boy she'd met at a house show in Bush-
wick and following him all the way back to Berlin. Ursula also felt guilty
about Alvin's firing.

"Are you hungry?" she asked, her attention not really leaving the
pages she was looking at.

"There's never any food in your fridge anyway."

"There's wine."

Alvin took the page he was looking at, crumpled it up into a ball,
and threw it at Ursula.

"Hey! There could be something useful on that!"

Ursula flattened out the paper. It was almost entirely redacted, a
sheet of black bars.

She got up and went to the kitchen to fetch the merlot. "I really do
appreciate you helping me with this," she said, pouring two large glasses.
"It's important, you know?"

She handed one to Alvin.

Alvin took a sip. He winced, not much of a wine drinker. Ursula took
a sip, too, and wondered how long it had been open in the fridge.

"It's cool that I get to help you with your research," Alvin said. "Even
if it means I'm visiting the greatest city on earth, and on a Saturday
night, I am rifling through stacks of paper."

"What do you want to eat? We can order out. My treat."

She handed Alvin her phone.

"Can we do Thai?" Alvin asked.

"Nah," Ursula said, "I'm sick of Thai."

WITHOUT THE EXEMPTION from Google, Alvin was also at risk of being
sent to detention. Even two years into AAPI, the rules weren't clear. But
the safest thing Alvin could do, he knew, was get a job.

It didn't take long for Alvin to start interviewing. That helped allevi-
ate some of Ursula's guilt. Living with a sibling—especially a younger

brother—was starting to get irritating. Alvin had started bringing girls home, and some of these nights were really testing the limits of the noise-canceling features of Ursula's headphones.

Even though he'd only been at Google in an entry-level position for under a year, it was enough to make him an appealing engineering prospect. Or maybe that was just how hungry the job market was for young tech workers. Ursula was happy for her brother as his fourth interview request came in, but she couldn't help recalling how difficult, by contrast, it had been for her to break into journalism.

Still, this was the closest Ursula and Alvin had ever been. They'd spent their childhoods together, sure. But it was different now that they were both adults—autonomous, more honest. Ursula took breaks from her work to help Alvin with his résumé and cover letters, and even helped him prep for interviews by playing the part of a recruiter.

"You know, none of this stuff matters when you're an engineer," Alvin assured her. "They only care about my technical skills. At Google, they made me write code on a whiteboard."

Alvin, to his credit, was a pretty good roommate, aside from his overnight guests. He volunteered to clean the bathroom and always made sure that Ursula had dinner—Cheez-Its and red wine were not a real meal, in his mind.

Each night, Ursula and Alvin spent an hour or so with the FOIA'd documents, which became an evening ritual. Ursula poured some wine, and Alvin put *Parks and Recreation* on the TV. The two of them, highlighters in hand, rummaged through the stacks. Ursula was thrilled that her brother continued to be so committed to helping her. (She guessed it didn't hurt that she was floating his rent.) This was a parent's dream, right? Their kids taking care of each other, building something together.

DARA WENT ON about work—they were shooting the shit at drinks, since Dara was one of the few journalists she could actually have a conversation with. They texted sometimes since Dara had left for the *Times*. At her request, she said, her bosses were moving her around various desks. She was trying to move off of the immigration beat, which she believed was thankless and, perhaps, a career killer.

"You know how it is. You report on this stuff and nobody cares," Dara said, though Ursula didn't feel that way.

Dara was considering a move to D.C., where she could get sourced up on "the Hill." She joked that racism was the best thing going for her among politicians. Liberals wanted to be nice to her so they appeared progressive; conservatives were also nice, as to not appear overly racist.

"Weirdly, I think I prefer dealing with the latter," she admitted.

But Dara did leave Ursula that night with a good rumor. She'd heard mumblings that some Democrats were working on legislation to end detention camps, or at least start the process of gradually removing people, letting them get back to their lives. The slowing economy and job growth had put the president on his back foot among his base.

Ursula didn't want to let herself hope. It had been close to two years since she had seen Jen and Duncan and the rest of her family. One of her great regrets was not spending more time with her cousin when she could, when they were just a subway ride apart, and she wouldn't make that mistake a second time. Maybe Jen would even want to move into Ursula's place. The apartment wasn't so far away from the NYU campus. And Ursula could help Jen get acclimated to real life again. She would make up for all the times she had let Jen down before.

ELECTRIC FOG

—

AFTER ALLEGRA WAS BROUGHT TO THE INFIRMARY, SWOLLEN AND bruised, she was shipped off somewhere else—likely another camp, but there was no way to know—and everything between Jen and Brandon had evaporated in her absence. His charms, the ones that Jen had found so attractive that first day when he rolled up in his electric cart, had been overtaken by fear.

She still saw him weekly. He was now in charge of El Paquete's distribution, organizing how digital goods were disseminated throughout camp. Brandon had architected a complex system that could be run entirely out of a pantry in one of the kitchens—a handful of computers surrounded by pallets of vegetables and dry goods. He'd copy the week's packet onto several hard drives, which were then sent to other locations around camp to be copied again, this time on memory sticks that could be more easily and secretly distributed. Under Brandon, the process had been streamlined and made more efficient, and more efficiency meant raising less suspicion.

The material had not changed much. It was still mostly entertainment—TV and movie files, compressed and converted to download more quickly to people's flash drives. There was even a small group that reencoded episodes of *Game of Thrones* with Vietnamese subtitles.

And of course, there was the underground material. Every Thursday night, Jen visited him to hand off her latest issue of *Korematsu*. Where Brandon had put his new energies toward the packet, Jen stepped in to fill Allegra's role.

She'd hand Brandon her USB stick, double check that he was grab-

bing the right file name, and take it back from him. This was their interaction for months. In, out, with barely a hi or goodbye.

"THIS NEW ISSUE is a good one," Jen said to Brandon. She was proud of
her twentieth solo issue of *Korematsu,* though each week, as it came
together, she thought of Allegra.

"I believe it," he replied, not making eye contact, still fidgeting with
something on the laptop. His operation seemed to be getting more
complicated, and though, from her angle, Jen couldn't see what he was
doing on the screen, he seemed to be typing an awful lot for a person
who was just copying a Word document off a thumb drive.

"I reported on the Tower."

This seemed to pique Brandon's interest.

"What do you mean you reported *on the Tower?*"

"I dedicated the whole issue to it."

Though the Tower had been an imposing presence since the detainees' arrival, it was only recently that people had begun to talk about it.
There were rumors circulating about the sinister features of the tall black
obelisk situated at the center of camp.

Life in the second year of camp had settled into a rhythm. The violence had been more pronounced in the first year in Camp Tacoma—
the aggression, the beatings. Now you witnessed it less often. Even the
suicides seemed to have dissipated. Maybe everyone who was going to
kill themselves already did. Or maybe the ODC was getting better at
covering it up. Either way, things were calmer. Work shifts had been
relaxed, especially as the days got shorter, which meant more time relax-
ing in bunks, playing cards, socializing.

But growing in that new calm was space for people's imagination.
And for some, that imagination morphed into paranoia, and that paranoia was directed at the Tower. You could see it from anywhere in camp.

The most obvious rumors were that the Tower was a surveillance
device. *Big whoop,* Jen thought. To be surveilled while incarcerated was
probably lower on the list of other violations happening on a daily basis.
Some of the other ideas were more far-fetched: that it could see into any

building at any time, using echolocation. That it was emitting a ray that manipulated people's emotions to make them more passive. That it was sending out a radio wave at a specific frequency that brainwashed detainees.

The misinformation wasn't without its more entertaining ideas. Jen's favorite rumor was that the Tower was giving detainees nosebleeds, as if the explanation must be a conspiratorial one and not just a side effect of the dry meteorological conditions.

This issue of *Korematsu* ran at these rumors directly. She had reported out, to the best of her ability, what the Tower was. She'd gotten close enough to the structure itself—which was ordinarily heavily fortified by ODC guards and AR-15s—to see a crew of technicians servicing it. Several boxes of equipment they'd had with them were labeled "Paladine," which Jen assumed was the manufacturer that built the Tower. Another writer had found a detainee in camp who was a telecommunications researcher, and asked him what he believed the Tower was. He couldn't guess the purpose but could identify the range, which, as one might expect, covered nearly the entirety of camp.

Jen herself had gotten the most useful information just from casually asking the ODC people she was friendly with what the tall black thing was. There were some conflicting answers: radio tower, satellite communication, explanations to that effect. But the most convincing one came from one of the guards who serviced the computer lab, Jared. He said the Tower wasn't sending out signals or communicating with anything. Quite the opposite. It was designed to eliminate signals and waves. To prove a point, Jared pulled out his iPhone and handed it to Jen. She looked at the iPhone. It'd been so long since she held one.

The screen was brighter than she remembered. No signal.

The Tower, Jared believed, blocked cellphone signals and Wi-Fi. It blanketed camp in what he called an "electric fog." In fact, the Tower might even be able to detect where those signals were coming from. Jared quickly shut the phone off, suddenly a little paranoid.

All of that information was in the fiftieth issue of *Korematsu,* Jen explained. Brandon seemed amused, maybe impressed. It was the strongest reaction she'd gotten out of him in a long time.

"You know, I'll give it a read right now."

Jen tried to hide her delight. As she waited for Brandon to finish, she picked a head of lettuce from off the pantry shelf and started tossing it to herself like it was a small basketball. Every once in a while, Brandon would nod approvingly—not at Jen but at the screen.

"This is good. A lot more convincing than the wild shit I've heard," he said.

Jen told Brandon to think fast and tossed the lettuce at him. It shed a few leaves midflight and Brandon caught the vegetable, a little surprised.

"Yeah, I heard this one crazy rumor about the Tower making men impotent," Jen said.

"That's probably a good thing," Brandon said. "El Paquete will never be able to distribute enough condoms."

He tossed the lettuce back at her.

"Where are people getting these ideas, anyway?"

"You know Viets love to gossip. Loudest people on earth, and all."

"You don't need to tell me."

"And a lot of it is coming from *Nhật Báo*."

Jen had heard of it before, mostly in passing. But she wasn't sure what it was. She pressed Brandon on it.

"Oh, you haven't read *Nhật Báo*? Here."

Brandon picked his laptop up and handed it to Jen, who exchanged her lettuce for the computer.

He had another document open on his laptop. It was entirely in Vietnamese, and though Jen's grasp of the written language wasn't nearly good enough to read it, she understood what it was.

"There are other underground papers?"

"Oh yeah. At one point there were a dozen, but most people don't keep them up. Yours is the most consistent. Every Thursday night, you're here with a new one. But also *Nhật Báo*. They show up on Sunday nights."

"My Vietnamese isn't good enough to read this."

"Mine neither," Brandon admitted.

"So you have no idea what this says?"

"Not really. But it's popular. A lot of people ask for it. I know from hearing about it that it's a lot of theories about the Tower."

"You distribute this, even though you don't know what it says?"

"That's not my job."

"Not your job to what?"

"To judge," Brandon said.

So Jen asked to start receiving *Nhật Báo*. In fact, could Brandon put all the past issues on her memory stick right now?

Before she left, Jen had chastised him about his responsibilities. He could be spreading harmful information. As the central distributor of actual news around camp, it was his duty to make sure it was accurate.

Brandon had gotten defensive, raised his voice. He distributed anything that detainees wanted—it wasn't his job to be a gatekeeper, or a censor, or whatever. Besides, it wasn't like he was fact-checking Jen's work. At that point, she chucked the head of lettuce at Brandon, missed, and watched it explode on the wall behind him.

Jen had real concerns about the potential of *Nhật Báo* spreading potentially harmful things around camp. But if she was honest with herself, she was more frustrated to learn she had competition.

MOVING THE CHAINS

—

1ST AND 10.

THE BALL IS SNAPPED, and the quarterback tosses it out left to the running back. They've been calling these pitches most of the second half—with a lot of success—since they discovered that keeping the ball in the quarterback's hands too long means being terrorized by Duncan.

The defensive linemen see the play develop quickly, but the motion gets most of them jammed up at the line of scrimmage. The back is small, but squirrelly, and a quick cut to the right gives him just enough space to eke out seven yards before getting tackled.

EVEN AFTER PRACTICE, the locker rooms of the sports complex still had that new-car smell, fresh and clean, not yet having taken on decades of sweat and grime and stink. The rewards of playing football were tangible to Duncan. You got to spend time in the only nice building in all of camp, even if large parts of the building were unfinished and closed off. The steam from the hot showers with great water pressure seemed to clear the dust that would settle and seep into his skin throughout the day, and he'd emerge feeling crisp, at least for a moment, before he had to step back outside again.

It had been impressed on him repeatedly that Nike had designed the athletic center that he was enjoying. Duncan wasn't sure why that mattered, though the ODC guards always seemed to bring it up. But it just made the contrast starker with the things that had not been provided.

Jerseys and helmets, all emblazoned with bright Nike logos, were new, but pads and the rest of the gear had come second-, maybe even third- or fourth-hand, stained and deformed after repeated use. The equipment was always offered to players in a large pile before games, and it was up to each individual to sort through shoulder pads, face masks, neck rolls, cups, and mouth guards on their own. No one in the stands would notice their junkyard gear beneath the new uniforms.

But Duncan understood the reality. The protective gear—the armor, one might call it—didn't really make anyone safer. Sure, impact might not be as rough; protecting the head seemed obvious. But all this equipment did was enable players to hit each other harder. It allowed coaches to ask their players to be more punishing, more violent. Pads allowed bodies to absorb the blows. The helmet turned a player into a spear, ready to be hurled at an opponent, anything to stop the ball from progressing.

Coaches moved Duncan around, from defensive end to outside linebacker. These were position players who casual football viewers took for granted, but Duncan knew they were among the most sought-after in the NFL draft.

Duncan liked it most when he was assigned to be a pass rusher, because it simplified what he had to think about. His job was to bull-rush the line and hit the quarterback as hard as he could. It didn't matter if he got double-covered—or even triple-covered, at times. Success meant possibly stalling out a whole offensive drive. Stalling out enough drives would win you the game. With each play, Duncan understood the opportunity to turn the tide. He always felt that opportunity.

2ND AND 3.

THE OFFENSE HAS two tight ends on the field, which means, most likely, another run. The ball is snapped, and the same running back takes the ball out to the left again. They've run exactly the same play—so arrogant, after picking up seven yards on the attempt last time.

Duncan, though, had anticipated it and set himself at the line of scrimmage. Off the snap, he spins to the right and around a lineman who has been slanted to protect the running back. No luck for them, as Duncan bursts through them and catches the runner by the waist, twisting him to the ground. A loss of a yard.

AFTER THE GAME—a complete drubbing of the opponent—the team celebrated in the locker room, as they did after every win, by blasting a Papa Roach song and howling like wolves. A loss drained you. A victory? It just gave you the energy to do the whole thing over again.

"Duncan, fucking killer game, man."

It was Phúc, one of the other linemen. He'd split two sacks with Duncan.

"Dude, you, too," Duncan said. "You really kicked it into a different gear tonight."

"I've been studying. Come check this out." Phúc motioned Duncan over to his locker. He looked around, to make sure none of the other teammates were paying close attention. They'd all hit the shower.

From a gym bag, Phúc revealed an iPad. He played a video—footage from an NFL game, an all-twenty-two view, the kind professional coaches used to dissect plays when they revisited film. The stuff that Duncan had been watching hadn't even been this useful.

"I got hooked up with a whole season's worth of this stuff. It's basically changed the way I see the field. I've been watching NFL tape every night."

He seemed proud.

"This random dude just gifted me an entire drive of these files. Have you met him?" Phúc asked.

Before he could even say the man's name, Duncan, displeased, nodded. "Yeah, I've met that guy."

3RD AND 4.

WITH THE LAST run going for a loss, the offense will likely be throwing. Duncan could drop into coverage, but instead, he decides it would be more fun to blitz the quarterback, hopefully applying enough pressure to force an errant pass.

The offense lines up in the shotgun formation, two receivers out on each side. After the snap, Duncan heaves himself forward, only to be picked up by two linemen, clearly assigned to double him. The force of two men won't be enough to stop Duncan, and then he sees a third player—the fullback—come to help contain him. Duncan feels that he will be able to break through them all, but the triple effort buys the offense enough time for the quarterback to throw a short pass to a slant route on his left. Duncan sees this just in time and catches the ankle of the receiver trying to squeeze behind him, taking the player down just shy of the first-down marker.

DUNCAN WAS HEADED for the shower when the coach called for him. He had someone who wanted to speak with him in his office. As Duncan entered, he saw a small, much older white man, dressed in a baggy purple athletic jacket and a purple cap. He introduced himself as a scout from LSU.

The man—Alan, he said—explained that he'd been hearing stories of Duncan's performance and had to come down to Camp Tacoma to see it himself.

"You visited a detention site to see a football player?" Duncan asked.

"Good scouts visit all manner of desolate locales in search of someone with your talent." He put a hand on Duncan's shoulder. "And son, you have the kind of potential that made me feel that driving five hours into the middle of the desert was worth it."

Was he really being recruited to LSU? An SEC defense? Out of Camp Tacoma? It was unbelievable. Even less believable: Alan said that if he was interested in playing for the Tigers, he would be able to go back to a normal life.

"What do you mean 'normal'?"

"There are certain things I can do to get you out of here. It would be a real waste of American talent to keep you here. Also, probably better to get you away from these poor offensive linemen you've been victimizing all season."

Alan gave Duncan a business card. *Hilarious,* Duncan thought, because how would he even reach out? Still, he thanked Alan and said he would get back to him. Alan said it was a pleasure to meet and got up to leave.

"Would the rest of my family get to leave, too?" Duncan asked. "My mother and my sister?"

Alan turned around. "I don't think that would be possible. But how happy it would make them to know you were out there, doing what you love."

4TH AND *1.*

DUNCAN'S TEAM HAS been tricked several times this season by a fake punt, but the offense doesn't even pretend that they aren't going for it. They line up in a bunch formation—three receivers to the right, another one to the left. It could be a pass, or just a feint for a pass, with the receivers trying to spread the defense out. Either way, Duncan knows he is going to rush the quarterback. A blitz would stop a run. A blitz might destabilize the quarterback. If the offense is able to get off a quick pass, so be it.

The ball is snapped. The running back moves in to help block again, signaling immediately to Duncan that they're throwing. Downfield, nobody must be open, because the quarterback would've let the ball loose by now. Duncan bursts forward, knocking a lineman into the dirt. The running back comes at him, but Duncan, predicting the movement, spins, dodging the oncoming body. Now it's just him and the quarterback—who sees Duncan and starts running for his life.

The quarterback should probably just toss the ball out of bounds. But instead, he hangs on to it, which gives Duncan full permission to hit him. That's the thing to remember about QBs. They think they're leaders. Which means they try to do heroic feats—make a great play, force the ball downfield. Usually, it just means making selfish mistakes. The quarterback tries a couple jukes to fake Duncan out. Duncan is not fooled. And suddenly, the quarterback is in a full-on sprint in the wrong direction.

Duncan is big, but even scarier, he is fast. And it's clear that even as the quarterback runs toward his own end zone—ten yards back from the line of scrimmage, now twenty, heading to thirty—that he will not escape Duncan. That here, no one can protect him.

SHE MIGHT NOT have watched many of the games, but Duncan appreciated that Jen often hung around after to wait for him.

As he emerged from the sports complex, he was excited to tell Jen the news—that he was being recruited by one of the most prestigious football programs in the country. That someone had come out to camp just to see him play and was impressed enough to offer him a way out.

But he found Jen crying, her head buried in her shirt, mopping up the tears with the bottom of her oversized Big Dog tee.

"What happened?"

She didn't want to say. It was stupid, she argued. Obviously it wasn't stupid. Duncan never knew his sister as one to cry readily.

"Come on, just tell me."

And she let it all out. How she'd been working on a dissident publication with her friend Allegra and how the ODC had found out and beat the living shit out of Allegra and she'd been keeping it from him for months and now she didn't know where Allegra was or what to do. In her life, Jen had never been so exhausted, so alone.

Searching for something comforting to say, Duncan could only muster advice. "It's like Coach says: you gotta have a short-term memory."

Jen looked up, wiping her face. "What does that even mean?"

"Bad things happen," Duncan said. "You miss a tackle. You fumble the ball. You throw a pick. You gotta forget it. Look forward. You forget about the mistakes, the bad things, and you look forward and think about the rest of the game. No use dwelling."

"You . . . really think that way?"

"All the bad stuff I'm feeling, I just leave it on the field. And then I'm okay the moment I step off the grass."

"I think they call that 'compartmentalizing.'"

"That sounds right."

"It's not supposed to be a good thing," Jen scolded.

"Whatever, it works for me," Duncan said, annoyed. "In the end, everything will work out."

"And now you sound like Má."

He knew she meant this as an insult. His mother and sister hadn't spoken in over two months, and had refused to reconcile, despite Duncan's best efforts to mediate.

Jen stormed off, disappointed that she had finally opened up and her brother couldn't understand what she was going through. And it was true: all Duncan could do was listen, and do his best to make her feel better. It wasn't enough. The way he looked at camp, at life, was so different from Jen. At what point, Duncan wondered, had they grown apart so much?

It didn't matter, though. Duncan knew what he needed to believe to survive. Did Jen?

THE FLOP, THE TURN, THE RIVER

—

THE NAME HOLD'EM HAD ALWAYS BEEN FUNNY TO JEN, AS IF A PLAYER might just let go of their hands if not instructed, cards spilling all over the table. These kinds of stupid thoughts were how Jen amused herself when the reporting was tedious, apparently.

The poker games had begun as the ODC seemed to relax. Now they were flagrant—noisy after hours in the mess halls, with guards turning a blind eye, as long as it kept detainees happy and harmless. Though it was an activity that seemed to cater to those slightly older than her in camp, Jen couldn't help but see the poker games as a sign of calm.

She knew the rules of the game, though couldn't recall much of the strategy. Her father had taught her at some point when she was young. She'd been bored by it then, and she was bored by it now. But Jen felt a duty to chronicle it in *Korematsu* as a cultural phenomenon emerging at Camp Tacoma. She hoped maybe there would be an interesting character to profile.

Jen was walking around one of the tables, trying to catch a glimpse of players' cards. But they kept them too closely guarded—holding 'em.

"You know, it's suspicious to take notes during a poker game."

Jen turned around. It was a smaller man, with a round, shaved head, an air of self-satisfaction. He wore a heavy army jacket. She couldn't tell his age—twenties? Thirties? He seemed amused by Jen's presence as an interloper.

"I'm just here to report a story," Jen said, holding her notepad, revealing a blank page with no writing. "It's going really well."

The man pulled a steno pad out of his pocket, too, except his proved more fruitful: pages and pages of notes.

"I don't mean to brag, but I think it's going better for me."

"I think you mean to brag."

"I'm Dennis." He put a hand out.

"Jen."

The formality was strange.

"Are you doing this for the *Loyalty?*" he asked.

"How do you know I write for the *Loyalty?*"

"I put it together: there's a frequent byline for Jennifer Nguyen, and you're the weirdo creeping around, jotting things down during a poker game," Dennis said. "You should be careful: people don't look all that kindly on an ODC collaborator."

"I'm not writing about this for the *Loyalty,*" Jen said, defensive. "It's for *Korematsu.* And I see you keeping notes, too. What makes me so much more conspicuous than you?"

Dennis's expression contorted and pinched—a moment of alarm—before he settled back into his smarmy grin.

"So you're the one that's keeping *Korematsu* going. That makes sense." He motioned to the ODC access card Jen received from the *Loyalty,* clipped to her belt loop.

She felt uneasy that this stranger seemed to know more about her than she did about him. She felt exposed. But at the same time, she relished that someone recognized *Korematsu.* At least someone was paying attention to her work.

"Want to step outside for a second?" Dennis asked. From his pocket he withdrew a carton of cigarettes and offered one. They were American Spirits—the yellow pack, Ursula's favorite.

IT WAS ONE of those nights that emitted a low drone. In the early days of camp, Jen believed it was the sound of crickets, before Allegra explained there were no crickets in the desert. Besides, that hum—it was too constant, too guttural.

"That sound—I think it's the Tower," Dennis said, taking a drag.

"Why would it make a sound?"

"I'm not sure. To remind us where we are? That we're being watched?"

Jen had accepted a cigarette, not because she wanted to smoke, but so it might keep her warm on a chilly evening.

"So, what are you writing?" she asked.

"Poker tips, mostly. It's really basic stuff, but it's what readers are hungry for. How to do x, when to do y." Dennis fished another cigarette from the carton. "People want to be told what to do, and how to feel."

"When they play poker?"

Dennis didn't answer, and handed the carton to Jen, who declined another. She wasn't that interested in what he was writing, but just sought the relief of learning he wasn't actually her competition. Poker instructions? That couldn't be further from the stories Jen wanted to tell.

"So, who reads it?"

"A lot of people," Dennis said, smugly. "I write *Nhật Báo*."

After her last encounter with Brandon, when Jen had him fill her flash drive with back issues of *Nhật Báo,* she'd had a friend in her bunk translate. Each one opened with a section of service and lifestyle articles. But mostly, it was full of half-truths and inflammatory stories. It seemed to exist just to provoke people: unfounded theories about tranquilizing chemicals in the food, to keep the detainees passive; misinformed—and sometimes racist—ideas of who ODC guards were, and where they came from; and of course, as she suspected, each issue had a new and wilder theory about the Tower. *Nhật Báo*'s tabloid-like nature infuriated and worried Jen, and yet she was oddly compelled by it. She'd read every issue.

"So you write the conspiracy-theory rag?"

"That's not a fair characterization of what I do," Dennis said. "Like I said: we have poker tips."

To his credit, Dennis appeared to take the insult on the chin. Her obvious disdain didn't affect him at all.

"I knew your predecessor," he said. "She gave me a hard time, but I think we both respected each other. We were good at different things."

"Allegra?" Jen said, her voice suddenly raised. "Do you know what happened to her?"

He shrugged. "You're the 'real' reporter. I think you're more equipped to find out than I am."

Jen couldn't help it. She found Dennis fascinating. He was unlike anyone she'd ever met. Clearly unflappable, perhaps too self-assured to worry about morals. The kind of confidence anyone would find enviable.

"So, what was your life like," she asked, "before this?"

"Honestly, not great." Dennis looked up at the sky. "Have you ever been so deep in a hole that you can't see a way out? Like, you keep doing all the things people tell you, the stuff you're supposed to, and still, the shit just keeps piling on?"

"I mean, I have a lot of student debt."

Jen smiled at Dennis. Maybe a joke would crack him.

"School, work, it's all bullshit. You look like you were a good student." Dennis never lit his second cigarette, and instead returned it to the carton. "And you're still in camp with the rest of us."

PLAYERS WERE STARTING to clear out, but the remaining participants were focused and seemed to pay no mind as Jen and Dennis observed the game. He was whispering in her ear, telling her what to look for on the table. He was familiar with the probabilities, which meant he knew the risks, and laid them out for Jen. Certain moves were a sure thing. Others you did for pride. If you were stupid, you acted on emotion. There was nothing colder than the hard mathematical realities of poker. And yet, players always wanted to make it a game about skill and confidence and manipulation.

The stakes of these games were entirely reputational—there was no currency in camp, after all. But there was respect, and notoriety. The winners of each night's games were marked on a leaderboard. Every pot won pushed a player's name farther up it. This was counterintuitive to Jen. Wasn't the point of gambling to make money?

"I have a hard time believing that you only value money," he said.

The game was winding down. One player—midthirties, long hair, thin-framed glasses—stood up from the table and walked off in a huff. Another man had a diminished stack of chips and wasn't long for this world either.

Dennis pointed out one of the remaining players, a woman, thin and stern with a short, graying pixie cut.

"That's Thuy. But they call her the Widow."

Dennis went on about the mythology of the Widow, how she'd been married to a white man who had come out in support of detention. He'd feared that Vietnamese people were violent and dangerous, and she'd decided to prove him right—stabbing him in the hand, and claiming that he was dead to her.

None of it sounded believable to Jen, but she was mesmerized. Another tall tale, ripped from the pages of *Nhật Báo*.

"I still don't understand why you publish stories like that. What compels you to make things up? You're misleading people."

"Don't moralize with me. It's like this poker game. The stakes are low. It's entertainment, a distraction from camp."

"It's dishonest."

"Poker is a liar's game."

"You're dishonest."

"You're a subscriber."

She was. But how could she not be?

Thuy was slowly cleaning out her remaining competition, a foregone conclusion that would drag itself out. Jen decided she'd had enough. But before she left, she had a final question: "What are you getting from this?"

Dennis had been patient, but now he seemed fed up.

"I read *Korematsu* every week, and my problem with it is that it reads like someone writing for themselves. My publication is for other people that are here. It's what they actually want to read, and that's why it has the influence that it does."

Jen was sick of this guy, his high opinion of himself, the lies he was telling to keep people entertained but unsettled—why did it matter to him?

Dennis gestured toward the leaderboard. "I think I'm winning?"

PLAYING HOUSE

—

The nights were filled with long stretches of insufferable boredom. Sometimes Dan would read a book. But truth be told, he wasn't much of a reader—even with all the time in the world, the dog-ears in his copy of *Cujo* were inching along only a few pages at a time. So he listened to the radio. Dan had never been a baseball fan. But at least the games were long. If only he had something to do with his hands.

Usually, he was good at turning the radio off before he fell asleep. One night, he forgot, and he woke to find that somehow the small energy draw of an FM station had been enough to kill the car battery. Dan had been lucky—this particular night, he'd chosen a parking lot, which was more public than the dead ends and dirt paths he usually picked. Dan didn't have trouble finding someone to give the Land Cruiser a start the next morning. A nice gentleman in an F-150 who, of course, had jumper cables handy and appeared thrilled at the opportunity to use them. Before he drove off, the stranger asked Dan, "You're not Vietnamese, are you?" Dan had encountered this enough times to know how to handle it. "Don't worry: Chinese."

Later that day, Dan wandered into a pawn shop in search of a battery-powered radio. Lots of stereo systems, but no radios, unfortunately. On the way out, he spotted a computer—an old laptop, a clamshell of white and bright orange plastic. Dan talked down the price to a hundred dollars.

He'd expected that the laptop would be capable of playing DVDs. Earlier in his travels, Dan had collected a strange assortment of movies at a yard sale, where he spent so much time attempting to bargain that the seller grew frustrated and told him to just take the whole bin. But when he tried putting a copy of *Full Metal Jacket* into the computer, it wouldn't recognize the disc. Same for *The Devil Wears Prada, Hulk,* something called *Monkeybone*. The DVD drive was busted.

Having a computer would probably come in handy, though. It at least came with some software on it. The laptop had previously belonged to somebody who went by the name Nell (at least that was the profile name), and all of her old files were still on the hard drive. Dan snooped around. That's how he found *The Sims*.

It quickly became his new obsession—way better than baseball on the radio. The laptop battery only had a couple hours of life each night, and Dan would play *The Sims* until the computer died. The next morning, he'd try to find an outlet where he could charge the laptop, only so he could drain it again playing house with his stupid little characters.

If Dan had been a more self-aware person, he might've recognized what his love of *The Sims* said about him. About how he wished the people he'd been surrounded by might reveal themselves more readily, rather than Dan doing the work to understand them better. About how, when he was exhausted by them, he could just start over again. About how, in his strange, nomadic existence, his overwhelming emotion was not loneliness but total boredom. About how, in his fifty years on earth, while others had blamed his inability to stay connected to family and friends on a past full of pain, Dan's desires were simpler than that: to be able to sever relationships when they no longer suited him, as easy as turning them off.

HOME MOVIES

—

At the beginning of detention, Jen had made it a point to check in on her cousin Tom. He was an actual cousin, not a half-sibling like Ursula and Alvin. And, like the other real cousins, Jen was never that close with Tom or his immediate family. But in the early days of Camp Tacoma, they'd stuck together, when things felt less certain and the only thing you could rely on were the people connected to you by blood.

But the months passed, and it seemed less important for Jen to drop by Tom's bunk to say hi. Plus, Tom and his mother and siblings were situated in the northwest corner of camp, a section that Jen never really needed to be in. Her newspaper assignments rarely brought her out there.

Still, she was delighted to run into Tom on her side of camp one day, setting something up in front of one of the cafeterias.

"Tom?"

"Jen!"

Tom embraced her, squeezing her tightly against his bony frame. "What are you doing over here?" Jen asked.

"I scouted the entirety of camp looking for the mess hall that looked the least like a mess hall," he said, and then pointed at the building behind him. "And this is it."

"Aren't they all the same?"

"They have subtle differences. You really have to look."

"And why are you looking for subtle differences between mess halls?"

"For my shoot!"

Jen now noticed the video camera behind Tom, mounted on a tripod. There was the usual traffic of people moving in and out of the cafeteria, but now Jen realized there were at least three people here with Tom, talking and planning something elaborate.

"Where did you get a camera?"

"You can get nearly anything through El Paquete," Tom said, like getting contraband devices smuggled into camp was as easy as signing up for an Amazon account.

Tom returned his attention to his shoot. He was ordering people around—stand here, move over there—like it was a movie set. Wait, was it a movie set?

"Yeah," Tom said, satisfied, "I'm trying to make something."

Jen had always thought of Tom as a bit pretentious for a teenager, but she appreciated his commitment to it. She asked what the project was, and he gave her what appeared to be a shooting script—maybe ten pages, written by hand.

"I only have one copy, so please be careful with that," Tom pleaded.

The shoot continued, Tom barking orders at his teenage crew as Jen flipped through the script. The title page: "A MILLION FIRST DATES," and in just as large a script, "BY TOM NGUYEN." The plot: two high schoolers go on a date. They're both nervous, but into each other. "Charmingly sheepish" was how Tom described it. Or at least that was what Jen thought it said, the handwriting hurried and difficult to read.

The date hit a lot of the notes you would expect from a romantic comedy. Awkward physical interactions, some playful flirtation.

"Do you like the script?" he asked.

Jen felt like she could be partially honest. "It's great. Very funny."

"Okay, come on. It's not perfect. What are your notes?"

"I only just read it very quickly, and it's hard to read your handwriting, and I'd love to know a little bit more about what your intention—"

"Jen, just tell me what you want to say."

"The ending was a little confusing to me? Like, the date just starts all over?" Jen wasn't sure if she'd followed it correctly, or if she'd read the pages in the wrong order, because after the date is over, the boy and girl run into each other again and act like their first date never happened.

"That's the point."

"Okay . . ."

"These two characters are just going through the motions, again and again, to give themselves a sense of normalcy. They repeatedly pretend to have a nice time and are going as far as replicating that exact nice time."

"But—"

"It plays on viewers' expectations of romantic comedy conventions, and then subverts them in the end, because we learn that the couple we've been watching isn't really on a date. They're just pretending, because that is what gets them through a day. It makes them feel safe."

"This might be too brainy for me."

"Yeah," Tom said, "it might be."

He could be a snot, but she admired his honesty.

JEN HUNG AROUND while they did a couple takes of the scene—a short one, just a few lines of dialogue. It was cute watching Tom become very serious and orderly about his directing. Such confidence. It was like he'd forgotten where he was.

"This directing stuff," he said, turning back to Jen, "it's just like babysitting."

Jen remembered that once, she'd had to watch over a throng of her younger cousins at a theme park in California called Great America. The really little kids, toddlers and babies, sat in the shade with the adults, while the hyperactive elementary- through middle-school-age cousins ran around the park, being chased by Jen and Ursula to make sure they didn't cause too much trouble, or spend too much money.

Tom was the worst of them, but they were all so entitled and demanding. If someone was hungry and wanted chicken fingers, *everyone* had to get chicken fingers. If they passed a gift shop and saw wearable Shrek ears, *everybody* needed to have their own set of Shrek ears, because it was only fair that they all be treated equally—the notion of equality extending largely to what items were available at a Great America gift shop. Maybe Jen would've liked those long, scorching days at the theme park more if she hadn't always been in pursuit of her young cousins. Or if she'd enjoyed rollercoasters at all.

At least Ursula didn't like the rides either. In many ways, those afternoons at Great America were the closest they'd ever been. They made a good team, switching off who would guide leaky cousins to the bathroom and who would order another sleeve of french fries. Ursula always reminded the young ones that they would be going home to Vietnamese food—bún bò, or maybe pork chops. It was the kind of meal that Ursula never got to eat unless she visited San Jose, because her white mom didn't know how to cook that. She joked, sometimes, that it was the only reason she came to the family reunions.

"You know, I've been talking to Ursula," Jen said, realizing she was trying to impress Tom.

"Oh my god, really? How? And how is she?" Tom had always adored Ursula, as did all the young cousins.

"El Paquete, actually. They pass along messages I write to her, and she writes me back."

"Dear Ursula, I am wasting away in a literal hell. How is New York? Did you meet any cute boys? How is the fashion-blogging world dealing with the mass detention of Vietnamese Americans?" Tom said, slightly imitating Jen's voice.

"She's actually reporting on detention. Like, serious journalism now," Jen said, suddenly defensive. "I've been giving her stories about what's going on in camp."

"She can't just visit us herself?" Obviously a joke, but Jen wasn't sure how to respond.

"Anyway, I know she'd love to hear from you," Jen said. "Plus, I am sure she would publish any footage you took in camp."

"That's not really what I'm doing here."

"I'm just saying, I could probably send a lot of footage of camp out to Ursula. She'd put that into the world. People would pay attention if we had video of what's going on here. You could be doing something important."

Jen immediately regretted her word choice.

He took it in stride. Tom said he would think about it, which was what people said when they were absolutely not going to think about it. His actress had finally returned from the mess hall with a glass of water. Tom explained that it had been good to see Jen, that they should hang out again soon, but that he really should get back to his shoot, since he wanted to wrap before they lost the light.

REPORTING TRIP

—

URSULA HAD ONE LEAD: THE EMAIL ADDRESS OF WHOEVER WAS PASS-
ing along Jen's messages.

Unfortunately, he (why did Ursula assume he?) used a different one
each time. A series of burners—usually a first name, followed by a random string of numbers. She'd spent the last year of her life receiving and
replying to messages from jake12508123@gmail.com, paulie948398452
@gmail.com, eduardo7839452@gmail.com. Waiting for each new email,
she was terrified it would never arrive. But then it would. This week:
jeff75612932@gmail.com. She realized this was the most consistent relationship she'd had with anyone since college.

It had actually been Rosco's idea to do a story about El Paquete, the
real person (people?) behind these email addresses. Ursula raised concerns that by reporting on their only means of communication with
someone inside a camp, they risked losing their best source. Rosco
brushed the concerns aside, conveying that the risk would be worth it.
He knew Ursula's real fear: reporting a story out without relying on that
source.

Ursula had been offended by the insinuation, and made a big show
of it, only because it was true. She had become entirely dependent on
Jen.

She figured it would be a quick dead-end on reporting if she
sent jeff75612932 a note and he did not reply. But he answered
immediately—within five minutes, saying he would talk, but only in
person. Could she meet him in California? More specifically, in a town
called, of all things, Independence?

In his office, Rosco, humming with excitement, went over what he thought would be the best reporting plan, rattling off details about keeping receipts and finding the cheapest places to stay. It was not lost on Ursula that Rosco was micromanaging the costs of her story, when he so freely expensed lunches and drinks. But the important part was that she was heading to Independence, California. She was meeting up with an anonymous source, a stranger. There was a sense of adventure to the whole thing, even if she knew that it could lead to nothing.

THOUGH INDEPENDENCE WAS in California, a flight into Las Vegas made more sense. Ursula had underestimated how exhausting it would be to get off a six-hour flight, pick up a car, and then commit to another four hours of driving.

The other thing she'd underestimated: the weather. Because Ursula's impression of California had always been from trips to the Bay Area, she more or less assumed that July would be a little hot, but totally manageable. She was now driving through a scorched desert, and she watched the thermometer on the dashboard creep up past ninety-seven degrees as she drove closer and closer to her destination.

Independence turned out to be less of a town and more of a loose collection of homes. There couldn't be more than a few hundred people living here, and Ursula wondered how a place so small even survived. What did people even do here?

Ursula rolled into her motel. The manager, an older white guy, showed her to her room and asked if she was in town to do some hiking.

"No, I'm a journalist," Ursula said.

"Do journalists not hike?" he said, handing her the key.

Ursula rolled her suitcase into the room and flopped down on the bed. It was only 6 P.M., and the sun looked like it would be in the sky for another six hours, but she passed out hard, in her clothes. When she came to, in the middle of the night, she finally removed her shoes, set an alarm, and fell back to sleep again.

With over twelve hours of rest behind her, Ursula expected to feel better. But her gentle coma had only made her drowsier. She'd woken up dehydrated and immediately hunched over the bathroom faucet to drink.

The motel room had been nicer than she'd expected. The bathroom, less so. The shower sputtered well water at her, covering her in the rotten scent of sulfur. Ursula chose not to wash her hair.

The plan was to meet her source—who she'd still been calling "Jeff" in her mind—at a restaurant in Independence, the only one, Still Life Café, and Ursula wondered if it was meant to have a double meaning.

The place was quaint: lots of framed photos on the wall, dark-red vinyl seating. Ursula planted herself at a table and waited for "Jeff" to show. She ordered a coffee, and the waitress asked if she was here to hike.

The first cup of coffee Ursula drained. The next, she realized, she might have to sip more slowly, as "Jeff" went from ten minutes late to twenty to nearly an hour. Ursula wasn't sure what to do. She'd brought a steno pad that she could doodle on, and she was avoiding her phone, since the last notification she had on it was a text from Rosco asking how things were going.

Another hour passed. Rosco followed up, asking if everything was okay.

it's fine. just waiting for my source
gonna spend the rest of my life waiting, apparently

Ursula had ordered a sandwich, not because she was hungry but because she felt bad about sitting around the café all day. She'd given "Jeff" her number but hadn't gotten one in return, so there was no way to follow up.

Ursula's phone buzzed. She scrambled for it.

Keep your head up. Great journalism comes from persistence and patience. If it was easy, everyone wou—

Ugh, just Rosco again.

—

URSULA GAVE HERSELF until noon—four hours of waiting—before she would leave the Still Life Café. What a disappointment. And the worst part was that she'd booked three days in Independence, meaning she had two more to look forward to in this bumfuck town.

She returned to the motel and spent the rest of the day watching TV. She fell asleep halfway through a movie, even though it was the middle of the afternoon.

The next morning, Ursula awoke with a new resolve.

"Where can I go hiking?" she asked the manager.

He eyed her up and down, trying to hide his disapproval. She was clearly not dressed for the outdoors—flats, jeans, a pristine white T-shirt.

"You're hiking in that?"

"Just tell me where to go."

He indulged her, laying a map on the counter and circling a few different trailheads with a Sharpie. He told Ursula she could take the map. She thanked him.

"Do you have a hat? It's really all sun out there."

"I look kind of dumb in hats," Ursula said.

"Are you bringing any water?"

Truthfully, Ursula had thought about it. But the idea of drinking the stinky sulfur water was just too unappealing. The manager put his hands up—his palms signaling *wait* or *please don't*—and went into the back room, returning a minute later with an old baseball cap and a couple bottles of Poland Spring.

THE HAT WAS HELPING, but her arms were getting a wicked sunburn after only thirty minutes of exposure. Within an hour the water was gone. Ursula had always wanted to be an outdoorsy person, and blamed Pam for not taking her and Alvin camping. She was getting worked up thinking about it. Like, her father could've chosen to be around. He could've been responsible for taking them hiking, camping, climbing, canoeing, whatever. Instead, here was Ursula, just imagining that all those gaps were somehow the fault of her mother.

Okay, it was starting to get real hot. Ursula's existential gripe with hiking was, when you were on a trail that was not a loop—which was most trails—the farther you went, the farther you'd have to go to return. Each inch she pushed herself in the central California desert was an inch that the trail would ask for back. Every part of this was unappealing, but Ursula felt she needed to punish herself some for somehow fucking up this trip.

URSULA HAD PICKED up a pizza from the Still Life Café on the way back to the motel and was eating each piece slowly as she watched cable news. She was barely paying attention to what was on the TV, just appreciating the noise. She felt, for the first time in a long time, that she deserved each bite of this extra-cheesy slice. When she finally finished eating—six slices, a majority of the pizza—the aroma had suddenly started to turn her stomach. There was no refrigerator in the room, so she stuck the pizza box in the bathroom. She could still smell it from the bed.

She woke the next morning, the TV still going, and all the pride she'd felt from making something of the day before had mutated into a strange guilt. Maybe it was dawning on Ursula that she was a hack journalist who relied on sources within her family, her cousin—really, half sister—to risk her neck to do all the meaningful reporting that Ursula would eventually take credit for. Maybe she was feeling bad for putting Alvin—who didn't know any better, having never been in a workplace before—in a position where he could lose the job that he'd dreamed of, and was supposed to have forever. Maybe it was the fact that she was out here in the middle of nowhere, by choice, when so much of her family had disappeared, and no one had any idea where they were.

It was the pizza, probably, that caused her to retch.

ASSIGNMENTS

—

HOW TO MAKE SOUP

JEN WAS THRILLED WHEN SHE HEARD THAT SOMEWHERE IN CAMP, A young woman was making video games. They were being distributed through El Paquete, of course, and though Jen had never really been someone who picked up a controller outside of the occasional *Mario Kart* race, the idea that someone could *make* a video game seemed impossible to her. All she had to go on was a name: Mona Pham.

Jen heard she lived on the northeast side of camp, which wasn't an area she visited very often. But after she asked around for "Mona," it didn't take long to track her down. Jen just wondered about the skeptical looks she was getting every time she asked.

Jen found Mona in her bunk, hunched over a small laptop.

"Mona?"

She turned around. Mona was wrapped in a blanket, which Jen found strange, since it wasn't cold at all. In fact, it was quite hot, and uncharacteristically humid. Then again, creative people were weirdos.

"Can I help you?" Mona asked, her voice delicate.

Jen explained who she was, what *Korematsu* was, in case she hadn't heard of it. She had, actually, which flattered Jen to no end.

"I hear you make video games. Can I talk to you about that?"

"Sure," Mona said. "That's what I'm doing right now. I'm writing a game."

On the screen, it didn't appear much like a video game to Jen. It didn't even really look like code. Mona just had a word processor open.

She explained. These were text games, where the player made choose-your-own-adventure-like decisions. Jen recalled those books, each chapter ending with a page you could jump to depending on your choice. She had no particular affinity for them; she just recalled that they were shorter to get through, and that sometimes she'd knock out a few of those in a row in elementary school if she wanted to goose her reading stats when the reward was a pizza party.

Most of the work Mona did was writing. She strung together the logic of the paths on paper, and then coded it all together later.

"People don't really like my games," Mona admitted. "I think they just put up with it because I'm the only one making them, and everyone here is bored as shit."

Jen laughed. They talked for a while. Finally, it got hot enough that Mona let the blanket slide down her shoulders, revealing her body. That was when Jen realized that this was a men's bunk, a detail that had eluded her when she arrived.

Mona could see Jen putting the pieces together. She seemed unbothered and, in fact, was a little amused.

"You're a little slow on the pickup, huh?" Mona said, chuckling to herself. "It's okay. Everyone in this bunk has been nice to me. Maybe some of the older Viets around are a little weirded out, but it's not so bad."

"Has camp been hard for you?"

"Naturally, the ODC did not okay any of my hormones. So I am diligently shaving this mustache. But I try to focus on the good stuff. At least my dad isn't here. He's obviously in some other camp, but life is easier without him around."

"My dad left a long time ago, way before camp. What brand of awful was yours?"

"Despite everything, he insists on calling me Matt."

"Oh no. I'm sorry."

"Yeah. He's okay with whoever I want to be, whatever I want to be. Or at least that's what he says."

"Then why can't he call you Mona?"

"Because Matt was the name that he gave me."

Jen didn't have a response, other than to nod, to acknowledge.

The game was called *How to Make Soup*. Mona explained that it was a bit different from her other work—most of her games were about "fighting or fucking werewolves," which Jen wasn't sure was a joke. It started to make sense when Mona reiterated that her games were "deeply unpopular" in camp.

How to Make Soup, she said, was her response to that. The text of the game instructed Jen that she must cook a traditional phở bò, and gave her a list of options of what to do first.

Jen had watched Má make phở before, so she picked "Char onion and ginger."

The game approved.

Next up, Jen chose "Parboil bones."

Again, she received an affirmative response that she had made the right decision. She was better at this than she was at *Mario Kart*, that was for sure.

What was next? Jen picked "Put onion and ginger in water."

Wrong! One needed to bring the broth to a simmer first.

The game went on like this. Jen made decisions, and they were either right or wrong.

As an experience, Jen found it largely painful. There was little guidance as to how to make the phở, and the game scolded her at every turn when she made a mistake. It did seem odd: to make a game about cooking when the joys of being in the kitchen—the smells, sights, sounds—were absent. Mona's game did little to evoke any senses. There was barely any voice or color in the language. Plus, there was no flexibility for taste, or improvisation. The game followed a rigid idea that one must stick to some imaginary recipe completely, with zero deviations. The entire thing was mechanical, about putting together a specific dish in as traditional of a manner as possible.

"The unpleasantness . . . is the point?"

Looking a little smug, Mona replied, "Oh yeah. Absolutely."

THE BEE GEES

THE CHOREOGRAPHY ITSELF WAS PRETTY IMPRESSIVE—A NOVEL HY-brid of hip-hop and modern dance, as far as Jen could tell. The hard adherence to a beat, crossed with the fluidity of something resembling ballet. As hard as she tried, Jen could not track down the origins of this routine, nor could she nail it herself, though she'd practiced a few times in the fleeting moments when she was alone in her bunk.

What was funny, though, were the resulting videos produced with this dance. It was only a few steps. Fifteen seconds of precise, distinct movement, recorded on film and set to, of all things, "Stayin' Alive" by the Bee Gees.

Performers, mostly the teenagers in camp, had memorized the routine, perfected it. But when it came time to film, they had to do it without music, because playing "Stayin' Alive" too loudly would alert ODC guards. (Usually during the day, detainees could do what they pleased, but blasting music forced the ODC's hand for discipline because it was so conspicuous.) Every time a dancer did their thing on camera, it had to be in total silence, earbuds in, with the music overlaid later. The result was often a video where the moves looked good, and were just off by a microsecond long enough for the whole thing to feel uncanny.

Jen couldn't understand why, but the younger kids in camp were making these videos like wildfire. She'd see them surreptitiously filming in riskier and riskier locations, as if that was part of the joke, figuring out how dangerously you could dance the same dance that everyone was doing, and have proof of it.

Walking around camp, Jen would catch glimpses of teenagers showing each other their videos, huddled around smartphones that had been reduced to dedicated dance camcorders. It was always the same routine, set to the same song, the only moving variables being the dancer and location. Didn't they get bored watching this over and over? What was the point?

She would have to understand if she was going to write this up for

Korematsu. Jen went as far as asking Duncan, who said he recognized why people were doing this, even if he couldn't articulate it.

"Explain it to me!" Jen pleaded.

Duncan just shrugged, his body becoming a very large and physical expression of nonchalance.

The whole thing made Jen question what the threshold was: Did a writer need to understand something to publish it? Or could they just report what they saw, with vague admiration and obvious confusion?

It seemed like a stupid question. Jen never wrote about the dance.

A MILLION FIRST DATES

TOM HAD FINALLY FINISHED HIS SHORT FILM. JEN HAD ONLY HEARD secondhand. But there would be a screening of it at Mess Hall 4 on a Friday night—exactly at the same time as a football game. Tom must have been challenging people to choose his movie over sport.

Attendance was low. Jen was among maybe a dozen people, most of whom appeared to be close with her cousin already. She wondered where Tom was able to procure a projector.

The story had not changed much since the day Jen had bumped into Tom filming it: a couple going through the motions of a date, asking basic questions of one another. Every once in a while, something would feel out of place, like an armed guard walking by. And then, of course, the reveal that the couple is in a camp, and feigning this experience, as they start it all over again.

It was the same script that Jen had not cared much for when she'd read it. Yet, on-screen, it did capture something else: the mundanity of camp; its repetitive rhythms. The film wasn't moving so much as it was unsettling. When the lights came up, the others in the audience clapped. It was hard to say if everyone else was just being polite, but Jen knew her applause was entirely sincere.

CRYSTAL PALM

—

DAN HAD HOPED SOBRIETY WOULD BRING HIM SOME KIND OF NEW clarity. It had now been over a year since he'd had a drink, a smoke, anything fun. But it hadn't actually been that hard to quit. He did it cold turkey, all his lifelong suspicions that he was an alcoholic now disproven.

It should have been good news. Instead, Dan felt disappointment. For so long, a part of him had been able to rationalize his own behavior—all his bad choices, his issues—as symptoms of a disease. Realizing he didn't have it, Dan could only blame himself. What if he was just a shitty person?

Two years of careful spending and finally the money had run out. Dan scrambled to find a new situation. He spent a few weeks doing under-the-table jobs as a barback or light construction work, but felt exposed. The whole point of hiding was to not be seen by anyone. Eventually, he met an older couple—very Christian—who took him in, asking only that he come with them to the church every Sunday. Dan was never going to believe in God, but it seemed like an extremely reasonable deal for a warm twin bed and three underseasoned meals a day. Besides, he'd faked it before.

The couple—they had names: Bart and Bette, hilariously—were nothing but generous to Dan. And yet he resented them for it. He couldn't stand the way they talked slowly about their tedious days, how their home smelled faintly of mildew, the endless boredom of being there all the time in hiding.

Dan had concealed the Land Cruiser. He'd parked it about a mile away, tucked in some woods, and went to check on the car every few days. He didn't expect anything to happen to it; he just needed to remember it was possible to leave.

Bette asked Dan to speak to the pastor, who asked him if this was a challenge that God had put in his path; if He might have brought Dan to him so Dan could be saved. Dan impressed upon the pastor what his last two years had been like. If this was a test, then Dan had certainly been proving to a higher power that he was resourceful and clever. The pastor was unimpressed. Every problem should be met with solutions that don't involve lying or stealing. Never stray from the path, always remain righteous.

That was the breaking point for Dan. Surely being detained would be more pleasant than listening to this patronizing man for another second.

Leaving Bette and Bart, he realized he hadn't felt this good since he first fled, that first kiss of freedom, and he had a burning need to sit down at a bar. He'd spend what little money he'd stored in the glove box and just get shit-faced, see if it was as comforting as he remembered. Dan drove two towns over and found the local dive, the Crystal Palm. It was perfect because nothing about it was remarkable at all.

The bartender was an older woman with a big hairdo and fake breasts. Before Dan could sit, she asked him if he had an ID.

"You don't think I look twenty-one?" he asked.

"I gotta card everybody," she said. But Dan knew what she really wanted to know: his last name.

Instead of taking out his driver's license, Dan placed some loose bills on the counter and asked for a double. "My plan was to quit drinking for good."

She paused for a moment, like she was considering not serving him.

"Quitting drinking for good would probably be healthy for you," she said, "but bad for business."

She poured it.

THE REALLY BIG ONE

—

URSULA THOUGHT THE LONG DRIVE MIGHT BE GOOD FOR CLEARING her head, but the open road only made space for her to beat herself up over her failure. She knew, rationally, that sources flaked all the time, that it wasn't under her control. Still, this was supposed to be her big shot—her first reporting trip, a promising lead, those lofty dreams of publishing prizewinning work—and she couldn't help but feel like she'd blown it. Even the radio blaring Top 40 at a high volume couldn't drown out her self-doubt.

She was headed to San Jose, to pay respect to Bà Nội's grave. It had been years since she'd visited. At the cemetery, she would light some incense and leave an offering of mangos and peaches (Bà Nội's favorites). But around the second hour on the road, Ursula received a phone call from an unknown number. She'd been getting spam calls at an escalating clip for the past three months, but something about this particular one encouraged Ursula to pick up. It was Jeff. Well, "Jeff."

"Hey, I'm at the Still Life Café. Are you planning on coming?" The voice was younger sounding than Ursula had expected, and clearly anxious.

"I was there two days ago for our meeting and you didn't show."

"No, I said the eighth. Today's the eighth."

"It was supposed to be the sixth."

"Wait, really? Miss, I'm so sorry. Are you still in the area?"

"Jeff" explained that he was waiting alone, like an idiot, at the Still Life Café. A part of Ursula was satisfied that he was feeling the embarrassment she'd experienced two days ago. (Ursula couldn't check her phone while driving, but later, when she was alone, would skim through her email and realize that "Jeff" had been right—she had gotten the date wrong and showed up two days early.)

Realizing the legitimacy of this call, Ursula spun the car around and headed back to Independence, flooring the gas pedal, pushing the teeny silver Nissan to its limits. But by the time she arrived, the source was gone. He'd left a note for her, leaving his number and telling her to call him.

Ursula felt a tinge of pride and excitement. Things were moving slowly, but getting closer.

AFTER A BUNCH of convoluted coordination attempts, Ursula's source decided to pick her up from the motel. He arrived in a beat-up pickup, which was appealing to Ursula for a number of reasons.

"Hi, I'm Tyler," said the man—really, a boy. He was wiry, hiding a lot of long, unkempt dark hair beneath an Oakland A's cap. Ursula had imagined that she'd be meeting someone more rugged, someone closely resembling a farm boy. But Tyler could've passed for any one of her co-workers—handsome, if a bit bashful. He was half Asian, though she couldn't tell if he was Vietnamese.

Ursula introduced herself, shook his hand.

"So you want me to show you El Paquete," Tyler said.

She nodded.

"Okay, it's a little bit of a drive."

Ursula hopped in, and they set off. She was getting into a car with a strange man, going to an unknown destination. Everything in her body told her this was a bad idea; still, she couldn't escape thinking that maybe this was how great journalism got made.

Tyler put on the radio. The truck was in good condition—remarkably clean, really—but it creaked and chugged the way an older vehicle did. They rode with the windows down, even on the highway, the air whipping loudly through the cabin.

"I like your ride," Ursula said, attempting to make small talk.

"Thanks. It's a Datsun. They don't make them anymore."

"What?"

Louder this time: "A Datsun!"

THE JOURNEY WAS longer than Ursula had expected. Eventually, the Datsun pulled into a massive stretch of farmland. Ursula had never seen agriculture at this scale up close: organic beauty, neatly divided, organized and tended to such a degree that its roots in nature were unrecognizable.

"What do they grow here?" Again with the small talk.

"Almonds!" Tyler answered excitedly.

"How big is this farm?"

Even more enthusiastically: "Two hundred acres!"

Tyler pulled the truck beside a large structure that resembled a warehouse. Ursula was unsure what she was looking at. She pulled out her recording device—a cheap little plastic gadget—and put it in the pocket of her shirt.

"What is that?" Tyler asked.

"Just so I don't have to take notes," she answered, truthfully and ready to turn it off.

But Tyler seemed unbothered. That answer had satisfied him, and he led her into the building, where it appeared they were processing actual almonds. If it was a front, the front seemed legitimate.

Their destination was a back room, which was exactly what Ursula would've imagined if someone said "a back room." It was poorly lit, no windows, just lots of shelves and tables.

"Everything happens here," Tyler said. "We try to package things as discreetly as we can. This farm provides the fresh produce for Camp Tacoma. We sneak all the other stuff—medicine, blankets, snacks, whatever—in on the pallets of lettuce and tomatoes or whatever."

He led her out of the back room and into a shipping area, a sea of vegetables being sorted into crates and heaved onto trucks.

"Before they get loaded, we hide all the cargo among the food," he said, motioning toward a handful of workers doing just that: finding enough space in a plastic crate of apples to tuck in a saran-wrapped laptop.

It sounded so simple. Too simple. She had a million questions. And for the next hour, while she watched men pack various wares beneath heads of lettuce and under bags of rice, Ursula pressed the various laborers of El Paquete about logistics.

There was a casualness to what was happening that confounded Ursula. Surely, an operation like this must be more involved, or at least, more secretive. She'd just asked to see the thing, and here she was, witnessing the thing, and now wondering if there was more to the thing.

"So, why do you help the Vietnamese detainees?" she asked Tyler.

"What do you mean?"

"Like, this is obviously illegal. What makes you stick your neck out?"

"I don't know if it's really like that."

"It happens in a secret location. You go to extreme lengths to hide contraband. There's clearly great risk involved."

"I think you have it all wrong," Tyler said. "I do this because it's a job that pays me."

ON THE DRIVE back to Independence, Ursula remained stunned by how much access she'd had. People talked to her, though they didn't have particularly inspired answers to her questions. It still wasn't clear who was funding the whole thing, but people were being paid. If the workers had questions about who was in charge, it seemed to Ursula like they kept it to themselves. No one minded being recorded. She almost got away with taking some photos before Tyler said that it would be better if she didn't.

But Ursula had more than enough for a story.

The ride back was more pleasant than the one out. The recorder was off. Tyler talked about his childhood, moving away at a young age, getting into a fancy prestigious private school in the Bay Area, and quickly dropping out. It was a boarding school, and he was so embarrassed and ashamed that instead of returning home, he ran away and lived on his own for a while.

Ursula did have one last question, about something odd she noticed when they were at the farm.

"So, the messages you pass along from camp, do you read them?"

Tyler didn't acknowledge the question, and instead turned up the radio.

The Datsun rolled into the motel.

"Again," Ursula said, "I really appreciate everything you did for me today. For driving me out there, for showing me how it all works."

"No problem at all. I hope it's good stuff for your story." Tyler tipped his baseball cap as she turned to the door.

She wished him a good night and went to her room. It was only when she was alone that she realized how exhausted she was, and how much she reeked of BO. She tossed herself onto the bed. It didn't even matter how rank the comforter smelled; Ursula just felt relieved to be done with the day—a good day, potentially a career-making day.

Just as Ursula began taking off her pants, there was a knock on her door. The sound startled her, and she quickly tugged her jeans back on.

She opened the door. It was Tyler.

"Oh, hey. Did you forget something?"

"What would I have forgotten? You're the one who left."

"Right, right," Ursula said, realizing what she'd asked was idiotic. So . . . why was he here, then?

"I was just thinking," he said, somewhat sheepishly, "that maybe you and I could keep talking."

Ursula had barely cracked the door. Thankfully, she had not un-latched the chain.

"Listen, I'm really beat after today." Ursula faked a yawn. "But maybe we could have coffee in the morning? Before I head to the airport?"

Tyler pushed—*hard*—against the door, which put the chain at a tension. "Come on. I gave you everything you wanted today. I've been risk-ing my neck for you for months, passing along your sister's messages." Through the crack in the door, Ursula could see that Tyler's expression had turned into something else.

"I should get to bed, you know? Long flight tomorrow."

He pushed again, this time with even more force. Suddenly, Ursula was scared that he would break the chain. The only thing keeping her safe was a small link of metal, and it was about to snap.

Still, Ursula continued to be polite. She was afraid that taking a serious tone would escalate things.

"Good night, Tyler."

This made him angrier anyway. Another shove on the door, and Ursula immediately pushed back. She could feel Tyler resisting on the other side. He put his hand in the space between the door and the frame, and Ursula, with all of her strength, put her shoulder against the door, slamming it hard against Tyler's misplaced fingers.

"Fuck!" he screamed before withdrawing his hand. He pulled back, giving Ursula just enough space to close the door completely closed and seal it with the dead bolt.

She took a step back. Tyler was swearing under his breath outside, but after a few rounds of cursing, Ursula heard his footsteps heading back to his car. The engine turned, and that shitty Datsun peeled away.

She took the deepest breath she'd ever taken and cracked the door again to make sure he was gone.

And then Ursula collapsed on the floor and began to sob.

AWAY GAMES

—

AFTER A SLOW START TO THE SEASON, DUNCAN'S TEAM HAD COME IN first in the league. It was fulfilling to win, to excel. But there was even more exciting news, as this success produced another reward: he would be traveling to play against teams in other camps.

Camp Tacoma's best players would be formed into a separate team of their own, one that would fly around the country to compete against the top talent from other camps. Though Duncan found the Office of Detention Culture's priorities lopsided, he wasn't complaining. The next season would be a tremendous opportunity. That LSU recruiter who he had spoken to never materialized again after their first conversation. But maybe there would be more interest now.

IT FINALLY HAPPENED. Dennis, who had stayed in touch with Duncan— coming by to say hi a couple of times after games, dropping into the mess hall before meals, always making eager small talk whenever they passed each other, like they were close friends—found his moment to collect what he felt he was owed. Duncan had always suspected an ulterior motive, and though he took no pleasure in having to confront Dennis about it, there was some satisfaction in knowing he'd been right all along.

Dennis had found him just as he was leaving the sports complex— the moment right when Duncan, fresh out of the locker room, feeling cleaner than he ever would again, was about to step out into the night, and into the dust.

"I can do so much more for you than NFL tape," Dennis said.

"I don't want anything else from you," Duncan said, suddenly uncomfortable.

"People who don't want things just aren't using their imagination."

The news of next season's traveling football league had reached Dennis. (Hell, he probably knew before Duncan.) The small man had a proposition: if Duncan could make deliveries to the other camps, Dennis would reward him for the effort.

There were assurances. That the work would be easy; that it would be impossible to get caught; that the benefits would greatly outweigh the risks. Dennis would make sure of it. The privilege of being able to travel between detention sites was something special. Dennis could make a lot of things happen, but even he could not communicate with the other camps.

"The ODC is going to be watching us closely," Duncan said. "I'm not going to be able to get much by them. I don't even know what I'll be able to bring to away games besides my pads."

"I just need you to deliver this." Dennis pulled out a thumb drive.

"What's on it?"

"Does it matter to you?"

"You're asking me to risk my neck for it, so yes."

The question appeared fair to Dennis. "It's called *Nhật Báo*. It's a small publication I run. I have people in other camps that are eagerly awaiting this."

"That's you? Jen says *Nhật Báo* is a bunch of conspiracy garbage."

"Does she, now?"

Duncan stepped forward, closer to Dennis, to emphasize his size, his power, before giving his answer.

"I'm not interested."

Dennis appeared unfazed, neither by Duncan's answer, nor by his physical presence. He turned around and began to walk away. Duncan had expected more pushback. Perhaps he'd been clear enough; maybe Dennis was actually reasonable, or understanding. But then:

"You know, I met your sister," Dennis said, still moving in the other direction. "Jen, she's a smart kid."

A threat. But Duncan wasn't sure what kind.

MESSAGE IN A BOTTLE

—

THE IRONY WAS NOT LOST ON JEN THAT THE LAST COMMUNICATION she would receive from Ursula through El Paquete was about El Paquete. Her cousin had taken it upon herself to forward along some of the articles she'd published about Vietnamese detention. It was fun to read, in a way, because it gave Jen a distance from what she was living through. She would look for herself in these articles: the small stories that Jen had told her about camp would often surface; sometimes whole pieces were based on what Jen had told her. Those moments were a bit jarring, her experiences stolen—though she supposed getting the truth out mattered more than who got credit. If she couldn't see what was going on in real life, at least there was comfort in knowing that real life was looking back in on them.

Another fun game: identifying the errors. They usually weren't big, but Jen would often catch Ursula misunderstanding something or, more often, getting the name of a person or place wrong. Like, her cousin kept referring to them as cafeterias instead of mess halls, or overstating how tightly surveilled detainees were, or confusing the different hierarchies of ODC guards—though Jen wasn't sure if she had wrapped her head around that either. It was mostly small stuff, the kinds of details you forgive when someone isn't there, seeing it for themselves.

What Jen really wanted, though, was more news from the outside. Jen didn't need to know what was going on in camp—she was experiencing it firsthand, after all—but how life was moving on without her. Ursula was either reluctant to send it, or maybe she had forgotten, because in only a couple of instances did she forward along some articles.

So all Jen received was fluff: stories about the royal wedding (when had she ever expressed an interest in the monarchy?) or the Patriots losing the Super Bowl (maybe Jen could pass that along to Duncan, at least). Surely something serious was happening beyond the walls of camp. There could be a cure for cancer, or the U.S. could've gone to war with the EU, and Jen wouldn't hear a thing about it.

But what she really wanted to know about was the Tower. She'd asked Ursula repeatedly about it; Ursula confessed she hadn't a clue what "the Tower" was, nor could she find any other reporting on it. And in a way, Jen took comfort in that: there were some questions shared by people in camp with people outside of it.

Still, their last communication was a long one and a short one. Ursula's article about El Paquete—what it was, how it worked, the questions surrounding who was running it and why—was the most thorough and sophisticated piece of reporting she had done.

It also came prefaced by Ursula's shortest personal message ever.

THIS IS A BIG ONE!! HOPE I GOT IT RIGHT:)

JEN HAD BEEN detained at Camp Tacoma for two years now, and life felt strangely settled. She wouldn't say that people seemed happier; just less unhappy, now that some things were more relaxed. The contraband that flowed into camp through El Paquete was out in the open. Guards seemed unperturbed by detainees waving their flash drives, occasionally munching on illegal Doritos. Music was often blasting out of different bunks—a welcome relief, probably, to the guards as well, who were tired of the silence of the desert.

The number of deaths had plummeted, too. El Paquete had provided many with access to medication that had saved lives; Jen had once scoffed at Brandon's assertion that art saved lives, too, though two years in she was convinced that he was probably right. Movies, books, music, games—these provided an escape for some, and a release for others.

Everyone who was left was a survivor, and survival, it seemed, was just the ability of people to let their hair down a little. The amount of breathing room was getting greater and greater, and the Vietnamese detainees were filling it with small celebrations—dance parties with trace amounts of liquor, underscored by low-fidelity music blasted from tinny speakers. The guards no longer cared.

The parties emerged in the absence of Friday night football games. The season was over, a void of activity that needed to be filled. Days passed in camp as if it was a place disconnected from the world. Sports became the only marker of time.

Duncan, despite being half a decade younger than some of the other players on the field, had carried his team to a dominant season victory by menacing the opposing quarterback on every play for three straight months. He mentioned to Jen that college recruiters had come out to watch him. Still, this was how Duncan dragged his sister out on a Friday, even though she would've preferred to read quietly in her bunk.

The celebration was happening outside Mess Hall 8. The music was always the same: a lot of the Police and the Bee Gees. High-pitched falsettos seemed to bridge the gap between the older and younger people in camp.

As Jen watched Duncan bro out with his football teammates, hopping around on the hard ground, kicking up dust and putting back drinks, she felt a number of things. For one, there was relief. Camp had fucked up her life; maybe it would not fuck up Duncan, who, despite being one of the quietest and gentlest humans she'd ever known, seemed in this moment to be thriving. It was probably too much to read into from watching Duncan drunkenly singing the lyrics to "Roxanne" with a bunch of other sweaty boys around a bonfire. But here he was, growing into a version of himself that seemed confident and comfortable.

"Your brother goes hard, huh?"

It was Brandon.

"He deserves it," Jen said. "Football season is long."

"Do you want a drink?"

Jen looked over at Brandon. He was already holding two plastic cups. In the light of the fire flickering across his face, she caught the faintest hint of a grin.

"Sure, I'm out. Why not actually be out?"

Jen slowly loosened up as the alcohol burned across her chest. She resolved not to think about their past, but in a year, she and Brandon had not talked outside of her deliveries of *Korematsu*. They'd both been too guarded after what had happened to Allegra. But Jen saw something in Brandon that she'd been waiting for: permission. A signal that maybe it was okay to relax for a minute.

They slid into their old conversational cadence easily. There were a number of things that Jen had learned from Ursula's piece on El Paquete that she wanted to ask Brandon about. He was just a small part of an intricate network, but she wondered how much he had seen for himself. Ursula had cast El Paquete almost as conspiratorial—many secret identities, money that moved between shadowy figures, an underground enterprise that needed to operate in broad daylight. She couldn't prove it in her article, but the piece suggested that things could only move in and out of camp at that scale with a lot of collusion and help from ODC guards. Was it possible that so many of them were broke enough to be so easily paid off? Or was the phenomenon so widespread that they didn't have a choice? Could it even be covertly sanctioned by the ODC?

Perhaps that was too far, and now Jen was feeling conspiratorial herself. But everything felt like it was in the realm of possibility. Maybe the drinks were having an effect.

She'd ask Brandon later. Tonight things were going so well it felt like they could've been anywhere else.

As the party was dying down, they would head to Brandon's bunk and have sex, unsure, but mostly uncaring, about whether anyone could hear them. And later, Jen would sneak out and make it back to her own bed so she could actually fall asleep.

The next morning, she would wake up, hangover pulsing. Jen would think about how she indulged herself, and remember it fondly later. Because after reading Ursula's latest message, she knew everything was about to change. The delicate rhythm of camp that they had settled into would soon be ruined. Consequences would arrive. Jen would be glad she enjoyed the stability one last time before it was gone.

EL PAQUETE

—

Because of the control of the Communist regime, internet access in Cuba has been deliberately limited, a policy that stems from the financial and information embargo imposed on the Caribbean island state in 1959 by United States President John F. Kennedy. For decades, the government controlled the flow of information by restricting the availability of outside materials as much as it could. And, for decades, it succeeded.

Still, Cuba has a rich history of piracy. Books, in particular, were often smuggled in and reproduced for students, dissident publications distributed through quiet and illicit channels. While the Cuban government had a tight grip on what aired on television and radio, many citizens were reading materials that had been passed from person to person through secret networks.

It's why, even as internet access became readily available to the global south by the early 2000s, Cuba's infrastructure for wired and cellular internet was still in its nascent stages. But even as the government suppressed the presence of modern technology, piracy took its steps forward as well. And so, El Paquete Semanal was born.

There weren't many computers in Havana—maybe one per block. But what emerged out of El Paquete Semanal, which translates to "the weekly packet," was a subscription that Cuban locals could pay for that would supply them with new digital files that came from outside of the country's borders: books, movies, music, video games, all manner of pop culture. Subscribers would get access to the weekly packet, delivered on small

USB drives, or if you wanted, you could bring a hard drive and have the files uploaded. This service cost one Cuban convertible peso (CUC), a substantial amount, considering the average monthly wage in Cuba was between fifteen and twenty CUC.

Because of its informal nature, little reliable sourcing exists on how El Paquete was constructed or organized, but we do know that much of the material was trafficked between Miami and Havana, likely between recent Cuban American immigrants and family still living in Cuba.

El Paquete had emerged as a class movement, meant to empower everyday citizens. The only places in Cuba that had internet access were embassies, consulates, and buildings of foreign companies—institutions of the elite that had special permission to install satellite antennae.

What fascinates me the most is how El Paquete created a disconnected internet within Cuba. Nothing was moving through the air; instead, it was handed off from person to person. Files moving physically, an internet more tangible than the virtual one we know.

But most importantly: El Paquete enabled a community, united by how far it would go to access culture.

When I asked sources if they were familiar with El Paquete, Cuba's internet access, or anything else that could have inspired the infrastructure of the detention site's digital distribution network, I mostly received blank looks. Camp Tacoma had a system modeled almost exactly after El Paquete—so much so that it was even called that. But its origins were unfamiliar to the people who made it run day-to-day.

Though I have struggled to corroborate how El Paquete came into existence, I have cobbled together its origins from rumor and hearsay. It started with a single individual, who was raised in Cuba. The country does not boast a particularly robust Vietnamese population, but there is a small community that emigrated through a Communist exchange program.

Other camps did not have El Paquete specifically, but they did have similar programs known by other names. There has been other great reporting done by outlets like *The New Yorker* and the *San Francisco Chronicle* about those systems. Still, I am never short of amazed thinking about

how versions of the same idea manifested at nearly all of the nine detention sites.

El Paquete is also the reason I was able to report out stories from Vietnamese detention. Thanks to a source in Camp Tacoma, and the transmission made possible by El Paquete, I had a constant—but slow—way to
communicate with someone in detention. And they made it possible for
many of the abuses and atrocities of camp to reach a reading public. It
may sound like a stretch, but I believe El Paquete was the key to the Viets'
survival in camp: both as a way to make it through day-to-day, and also as
a way to finally make it out.

THE GUEST

—

EVENTUALLY ALVIN FOUND HIS OWN PLACE—A SMALL ONE-BEDROOM in Carroll Gardens, not too far from Ursula. If he'd learned anything, it was the importance of being close to family. But maybe not too close.

He had found a job as a midlevel engineer at a startup, a disorganized assemblage of young men crammed into one big room in the Flatiron District, willing to be exploited for extraordinary hours of labor for the chance that the company might one day go public, or get acquired.

He kept waiting for his old Google colleagues to reach out, but no one ever did. Well, Fernanda had texted him.

you asshole

Apparently she'd been fired, too. Alvin felt bad, but not bad enough to reply.

There were some second- and thirdhand murmurings that Ursula's reporting about the company's connection to Vietnamese detention was being discussed internally. He learned this from an article in *Bloomberg* that contained leaked screenshots of email threads where Google employees were fighting about the ethics of the company's relationship with the Department of Homeland Security. There'd been some precedent for this—while Alvin was employed, he caught wind of some arguments about the ethics of Google's presence in China, where it would have to appease an authoritarian government that demanded suppression of certain search results and allowed Chinese Communist Party leaders to view private user data. It was a debate that hadn't been resolved, even if the critics were clearly a vocal minority within a largely apathetic workforce.

Unsurprisingly, Ursula's story played out much the same way. It was a heated discussion among Google workers that burned bright for a minute, only to fizzle as the news cycle passed. After that *Bloomberg* story, nothing else leaked. Alvin was disappointed. He'd lost his job— and perhaps the chance at a more lucrative career—for what? Does a sacrifice matter if no one notices it?

"That *Bloomberg* reporter is such a hack," Ursula said one night. "It's really my piece that's holding Google accountable for its DHS contract. Like, *Bloomberg* can follow my reporting, but it's never going to break the big story, you know?"

Alvin wasn't surprised to see she was taking all the credit.

AFTER THE AMERICAN Advanced Protections Initiative passed, the calls from his dad came even less frequently. Not that they were frequent before.

It had never been clear where his father was, though he wasn't in camp. He'd been moving from place to place. One call came from Louisiana. A couple months later, Montana. There was a six-month gap before his father resurfaced in Maine. Then back to Montana.

The conversations were always short.

"So, your customers are mainly other startups?"

"Yeah, it's B2B."

"What does that mean?"

"Business to business."

"Why can't you just say that instead?"

Dad knew Jen and Duncan were in detention, so he never asked about them. Only sometimes, he would inquire about Ursula, though he always avoided using her name.

"How's your sister?"

"Which sister?"

"Your *sister* sister."

"She's good. But you can call her and ask yourself," Alvin insisted.

"I will, I will," he'd say, the repetition sounding more like a hesitation than a commitment. Whenever the scope of a conversation was pushed, he understood that this phone call would quickly be coming to an end.

"It's beautiful out there. Perfect weather. You should come visit."

"Visit where, Dad?"

"I gotta get going, Alvin. Give your sister my best."

ONCE HE MOVED out on his own, Alvin missed digging around in the piles of documents at Ursula's place. So he took up reading. He'd barely ever cracked a book in his life that wasn't a school requirement (and even then, he did very few of those), but now he'd discovered he liked reading, the peace of it, the focus.

It was a short subway ride from Alvin's apartment to the Brooklyn Public Library, where he'd put a number of books on hold and would, weekly, drop by to return expired hardcovers and exchange them for new ones. He was mostly reading history, and it never ceased to amuse Alvin how the thickness of each book could vary so much. It seemed that a requirement of writing about any part of World War II was making sure you hit the five-hundred-page mark; yet each book about Japanese internment was slim, often published by smaller university presses and bearing academic titles. Vietnam War books tended to carry aggressive, authoritative names. They were on the bigger side, especially the ones that were political or tactical or both.

Upon seeing the stacks of library books in his new apartment, Ursula teased Alvin that he had somehow jumped ahead thirty years in life—to the phase where middle-aged men spent their days in a lounge chair, thinking about manly things, like war. But for Alvin, it was an extension of his work as an engineer. Every war story was a systems story, usually one of a breakdown. Intentions were always good, decisions made at scale. A lot of stuff about how each violent act perpetrated by the country was a battle for the soul of a nation. In the long arc of time, and according to history, America could lose its innocence as many times as it desired.

—

ALVIN EMERGED FROM the Carroll Street subway station, a fresh stack of old books cradled in his arms. But as he approached his apartment building, he saw a cop car parked in front, the red-and-blue lights spinning.

One of Alvin's neighbors, Sheila, was perched at the top of the stoop.

"What's going on?" Alvin asked, shouting in her direction.

"This weird guy was pacing around outside the building."

"So you called the cops?"

"No, I did not *call the fucking cops*," Sheila said, slighted by the accusation. She was a Black woman in her midthirties. She would never call the police. "They saw me yelling at the guy and decided to interfere with business that is not theirs."

The police car had pulled onto the curb, obscuring Alvin's view of what was happening.

"Ma'am," one of the officers started, pointing at Sheila. "You can go back inside."

"No, I am bearing witness, to make sure you guys don't do anything awful to this helpless man."

The officer rolled his eyes and turned his attention to Alvin.

"Do you live here?" he asked.

"Yeah," Alvin said. "Second floor," he added, as if that specificity would be, in any way, helpful.

The officer gestured that Alvin should go inside. He went around the car and began ascending the steps of the brownstone. Sheila stayed on the sidewalk, committed to observing the entire ordeal, recording the officers' interactions on her phone.

"Look at what they're doing to him," Sheila said.

It was hard to see, but the other officer had handcuffed a man and pinned him to the trunk of the car. From his vantage point on the stairs, Alvin couldn't make out the man's face. But his clothes were dirty, his hair long. Alvin just assumed it was a homeless person who had wandered into his bougie neighborhood.

"Was he bothering you?" Alvin asked.

"He looked sketchy as hell, and I was trying to get him off the block. But I did not ask these bums to interfere." Sheila couldn't make eye contact with Alvin as she spoke, and only kept her phone camera trained steadily on the police officers. It was one of the few times Alvin had ever seen her not dressed for work—she was some kind of high-powered lawyer—and was in shorts and a tank top, running shoes.

The man looked uncomfortable but did not struggle. The cops were not gentle, but Alvin imagined that Sheila's footage would reveal nothing egregious. Then the police opened the passenger door and turned the man around to place him in the backseat as Alvin watched.

"Wait," Alvin said. "Wait!"

He dropped his library books and rushed down the steps.

"Officer, stop!"

"Do you know this man?" the first officer asked.

"Not really," Alvin said, "but he's my dad."

A BIG WIN

—

UNLIKE THE LAST TIME URSULA HAD A SUREFIRE HIT, ROSCO DID NOT wait for happy hour to celebrate. He'd opened a bottle of champagne the moment they'd published her story about El Paquete—at 10 A.M.

He poured servings in small Dixie cups for the daily story meeting, though this one didn't really operate like a meeting. Richard Earley said some inspiring, if vague, words about "the work we do here" and how great journalism was "rare" and what we were witnessing today was that kind of rarity that he woke up, every day, hoping to experience.

He ceded the floor to Rosco, who was raring to go. He talked about how this reporting was urgent and enduring—language that had reminded Ursula of the first time she saw him speak when she was in college. And then, a toast.

There'd been a whole PR push for Ursula's article that morning. She was set to do a number of interviews on cable news channels, a show on NPR's national desk as well as phoning in for a number of regional affiliates, plus maybe a dozen outstanding interview requests that the comms person hadn't even had time to respond to. Oh, and a spot was being held for her on *Good Morning America* the next day, depending on how viral the piece went. In a way, Ursula hoped it would travel far enough to be big, but far enough under the radar that she wouldn't be asked to do a morning show, since it would require getting up at 5 A.M. to get to Midtown for makeup.

Everything felt surreal, distant. Some people would describe it as an out-of-body experience. But for her, it felt as if her body had never belonged to her. Everything in her life had led to this achievement, and now Ursula had never felt less herself.

THERE WERE PARTS of the story that Ursula was proud of. And other parts, not so much. But to break it down:

GOOD THINGS

THE RECEPTION. As soon as it was published, the piece immediately took off, which had not been the case with a lot of Ursula's reporting on Vietnamese detention, especially lately. It seemed like people had forgotten, or worse, moved on. Her story proved that to be untrue.

THE SCOPE. After Ursula had returned from Independence, she'd been able to follow up with a few sources who corroborated most of what she'd witnessed with Tyler, that piece of shit. Ursula had risked her ass. At least it had paid off.

THE FRAME. Ursula had worried for months that the stories that took off were often similar. Or more than that: they were always articles about how awful DHS was, which, while true, seemed to somehow distract from the idea that actual people were suffering. Did shining a light on the oppressor really do anything for the oppressed? She'd drunkenly expressed this anxiety to Alvin once. Her brother explained that it was like readers focusing on the Death Star, instead of the people of Alderaan. Ursula had no idea what the fuck he was talking about.

THE POTENTIAL. The career of Ursula Nguyen had been on a fast upward trajectory—but now she had to compete with the highest echelons of journalism talent. If she could break these kinds of stories, what would be next? Finally, Ursula felt that she wasn't struggling to make this thing happen. This thing was happening to her.

NOT-SO-GOOD THINGS

THE FALLOUT. It had been a latent anxiety of Ursula's that reporting on the network delivering goods into camp might draw undue attention to it. The purpose of journalism was to bring awareness to something important, to make the truth known more broadly, right? (God, she was sounding like Rosco now.) But was her work actually making anyone in camp safer?

When she had asked the Department of Homeland Security for comment on the story, they had declined to provide a response. But almost immediately after she had emailed the bureau's press secretary, Ursula received a phone call from her, which was prefaced with the request that their conversation be off the record. Ursula agreed.

"We had no idea. At least at this level, not a single clue."

It occurred to Ursula that this might make things tougher for detainees, that telling this truth, and making it widely known, could hurt the people she sought to help. That fear resurfaced the moment the piece went live, and suffocated Ursula all morning.

Maybe this was just the kind of thinking that happened when you'd been drinking, the worry of someone who was dealing with an acute sparkling-wine headache at 3 P.M.

As the workday ended, and Ursula had wrapped up her celebration tour of PR commitments, Rosco swung by her cube to ask if she wanted to go to the bar. It'd been a long day, she explained, and Rosco put up his hands to show that he understood. But the reality was that he didn't understand. Today was Ursula's day. This was everything she'd been working toward.

CONSEQUENCES

—

ANOTHER THURSDAY, ANOTHER ISSUE OF *KOREMATSU* TO GET TO BRANdon for distribution. Jen had begun to look forward to seeing him. Things between them had started to get less weird, but only by degrees.

Jen slipped the flash drive necklace over her head and handed it to Brandon. He'd had his headphones on when Jen entered his office—the weird pantry of Mess Hall 8—and he had been so absorbed by whatever he was doing that he didn't even notice her come in.

"New issue?" Brandon said, like it could be anything else.

"What are you doing back here?"

"Come look at this." He gestured that she should sit next to him. He unplugged the headphones, and the sound returned to the computer. The music was familiar. "Look!"

He was playing video games.

"I'm just glad I got *Mario Bros. 3* before we got cut off."

Cut off from what? He didn't seem intent on explaining himself further. She thought something might be rekindled between them, but Brandon looked like he just wanted to play his game. Jen tried to not act hurt. It hadn't been serious, after all.

"Can we move this along so I can get out of here?"

He finally paused the game and looked at her.

"Do you really not know?"

Clearly, she didn't.

"El Paquete is done. Nothing's coming in. Nothing's going out."

"Wait, what happened?" She waved the memory stick at him.

"The ODC cracked down and now the entire network is gone."

"Then why are you still here?"

Brandon closed the laptop and placed it gently on the chair beside him.

"It's just familiar, I guess. And I needed to talk to you. This is not how I wanted things to turn out."

Ugh, the self-pity. But Jen couldn't help but fall for it.

"Don't apologize. What happened to Allegra wasn't your fault."

"No. I mean . . ." Brandon was apologizing for something else. "That's not it. They put pressure on me. And I caved. I didn't mean to let it out."

"What are you talking about?"

"I understand why they're so mad, though. You really fucked this whole thing up."

"What are you talking about?"

"Your sister. She's the reason the ODC investigated El Paquete. It was going fine before." He was breaking down now. "I'm sorry but I told him about your messages to your sister. They said they would go after my mom."

Jen was scared now. "Who threatened you, Brandon?"

"Dennis. You need to stay away from Dennis."

The little guy? Who ran the conspiracy rag? Jen didn't believe it.

"Trust me. He's dangerous. And he has influence. Just promise me you'll stay away."

"Why would I promise you anything?"

As she walked off, she realized that that hadn't really made any sense. But at least she'd gotten the last word.

JEN'S FIRST INSTINCT was to check on Má. It had been months since they last spoke, both of them still feeling raw about their last fight. They were both too proud, and Jen knew that not overcoming that stubbornness just made her even more like her mother.

It was getting close to sundown—curfew—and her bunk was on the south side of camp. Jen took off in a sprint and was reminded just how out of shape she was. She thought about how she'd spent her time in camp wasting away, while her brother was getting stronger.

Finally, Jen arrived at Má's bunk, panting.

"Are you okay?" her mother asked. "What's wrong?"

She was perfectly fine. In fact, she was probably better before her daughter showed up looking like a total wreck.

"Noth. Ing. Sorry. I ran. Here." Each pant was so pathetic.

"Why?"

"I just. Wanted to check. On you."

"Well, I'm okay."

Jen finally caught her breath and stood up straight. "Why do you look so disappointed to see me?"

"I'm not." Má rolled her eyes. "I have just been waiting for that young man who puts all the TV shows on the computer. He hasn't come by this week."

Maybe Brandon had been telling the truth. Or maybe El Paquete was just running behind. It wasn't that unusual.

"You should get back before curfew, Jen. It's getting dark." Apparently Má was still cold.

The conversation had drawn the attention of some of the other older detainees in the bunk. Now Jen realized that she was embarrassing her mother. The whole thing felt off. Why had she taken Brandon at his word? Jen had never believed Dennis was the mastermind of anything. How could he possibly be threatening? And if it was true that El Paquete was done, wouldn't that make Dennis even less powerful? Jen felt stupid for not thinking this through before running across camp to look like an idiot in front of her mother.

"I'm sorry," Jen said, unclear what she was apologizing for.

Má finally softened. "Do you want some water? Do you need to stay here?"

"No, no. Sorry to alarm you. I was . . . misinformed." Jen had finally caught her breath, and there was still time to rush back to her bunk to beat the sun.

"I worry you're not taking care of yourself."

"Okay, Má, we can have this conversation another time."

"Wait, I want to say something to you."

They clearly had the full attention of the bunk, but everyone turned away, pushed their faces into their books, to pretend like they weren't listening. Normally, Má would wait until they were alone. But this seemed important enough that she had to say it now.

"I don't know what you've been up to, or where you've been. But I want you to know that I'm . . ."

"Proud?" Jen said, facetiously.

Má didn't like her tone but remained undeterred.

"I want you to know that I trust that you know what you're doing. I have lived my life very afraid of things. I don't know where you get it from—certainly not from your father—but you are brave. Sometimes fearless."

"I don't know," Jen said. "Maybe I'm just reckless."

Má shrugged. She even flashed the suggestion of a smile.

"But thanks for saying that, Má."

Jen turned to leave.

"Is it a boy?"

She had to admire her mother. Má was often more astute than Jen gave her credit for. She was currently preoccupied with a boy, but it wasn't a romantic interest so much as a rival.

"Just someone who thinks they're better than me."

Má chuckled softly. "I know that kind of man."

Jen said goodbye and trotted off to sweat through her T-shirt in the jog across the camp. She wanted to dwell on how annoying Brandon had been.

It was getting dark fast—and the temperature was dropping. Jen kept eyeing the sun on the horizon, like it was a countdown timer, as she made her way back in the direction of her bunk. But she didn't make it very far.

"You know, curfew is almost here." A voice from behind.

Jen turned around.

"Dennis."

She could only make out his silhouette. But more alarming was the unknown figure next to him—a much larger man, whose scowl came into view as he stepped into the light. They both approached Jen, who stood, frozen.

"You won't get to your bunk in time," Dennis said. "Which bunk is it, again?"

"Bunk 18-D," the big man said. She recognized him, but couldn't place his face.

"Right. Bunk 18-D. You won't make it back there."

"What do you idiots want?"

"I want to do you a favor, Jen. We've got a place nearby. We'd like to take you there before the guards catch you out past curfew."

DAN

—

IT WAS HIM, ALL RIGHT. HIS HAIR WAS LONG AND UNRULY; THE FACIAL hair had developed not so much into a beard, but into two disparate entities, a stringy mustache hanging above the lip and a scraggly goatee clinging to the chin. When he finally emerged from the bathroom, after Alvin had demanded he clean up, his father almost resembled Ho Chi Minh.

"Why didn't you tell me you were coming?" Alvin asked.

Dan seated himself on the couch, pushing aside the short stack of library books that Alvin had just brought home. One of the hardcovers tumbled to the floor. Dan quickly reached for it and set it back on the couch.

"Can I have some water?"

Alvin rolled his eyes, but also gestured a "sure" and went to the kitchen to fill a glass from the tap. He returned with the water and asked again. "Why didn't you tell me you were coming?"

Instead of answering immediately, Dan took giant slugs from the cup. Water dribbled down his chin. He finished it and handed it back to Alvin, signaling that he wanted a refill.

Annoyed but obedient, Alvin filled the glass again and placed it in front of his father. He wasn't going to repeat himself a third time.

"Well?"

This time, Dan just sipped from it, slowly, like an actual person, like he was learning to be one again. "It's complicated."

Alvin had always thought of himself as someone slow to anger. He was an even-tempered guy, able to let things roll along. But now he felt his chest get warm, his scalp tingling. His fists were clenched.

"You show up unannounced, after months of radio silence, and expect me to accept 'It's complicated?'" Alvin was standing now. "Where have you been? How have you avoided being in a camp? Why are you here now?"

"Why aren't *you* in a camp?" Dan asked.

"Okay, well, that's all—"

"Complicated?"

"A long story," Alvin said.

Dan looked around the apartment, taking it in. Alvin had arrived in New York with very little. The environment was sparse. Dan nodded, though, with approval.

"It's a nice place." He began sipping his water again.

Alvin realized that this was pointless. "Are you hungry? I could make you an egg."

Dan didn't seem enthused about that option.

"Or we could order something?"

"Yeah, let's order something!"

ALVIN FOUND HIS irritation subsiding once he'd had his fill of chicken lo mein and fried rice and dumplings.

When he'd seen his father in cuffs, Alvin had been worried that the cops would take him in, and that he would be detained. But the officers were surprisingly frank about the bureaucracy. It would be "a shitload of paperwork," they'd said. And besides, detention was the jurisdiction of Homeland Security. They just wanted this guy not bothering anyone. *What a relief,* Alvin thought, *the laziness of New York cops.*

"Are you sure they didn't have orange chicken?" Dan asked.

"What is orange chicken?"

"Sometimes it's called General Tso's."

"Oh, right. Sorry, I didn't look."

Dan didn't seem too disappointed as he shoveled a piece of broccoli, doused in soy sauce, into his mouth. Between bites, he revealed where he'd been for the past two years: basically, everywhere, driving through the back roads of America, trying to remain undetected by DHS.

"You've been living out of your car?"

"Yeah, but it's a nice car," Dan said. "It's a Land Cruiser."

Alvin could not picture the vehicle. "How are you living like this? How do you even make money? Pay for food?"

"When detention started, I took out all my savings and fled. And I've been able to live cheaply. I even had a couple jobs for a while, pretended that I was Chinese, but then it started getting too dangerous. You know?" Dan pointed his disposable chopsticks at Alvin. "I guess you wouldn't know, actually," he said, before returning to his food, having moved on from his plate to now eating straight out of the takeout carton.

Alvin was annoyed by his father's condescending tone, but also felt some pride that he'd been able to elude the surveillance state for so long. It was impressive. His deadbeat dad had spent the past two years fighting the dragnet, and seemingly winning. It probably helped that he'd never had an online footprint, the Luddite in him always paranoid of being traced or identified.

"So, why are you here?" The way Alvin asked—it just sounded exhausted. He hadn't meant it to come out like that, but there was defeat in his voice, a final effort after now having spent hours with his father, asking the same thing in as many different ways as he could imagine.

"I was doing well on the road. Just living. And . . ."

Dan put down the chopsticks, resting them across the lo mein carton.

"I'd like to keep doing well."

Alvin understood. He might've understood the entire time, or at least suspected it. But he wondered if his father would actually have the courage to just ask. Instead, Alvin had to pry it out of him.

"You want money?"

"Yes, but . . . I want you to know it's for survival."

"Survival money?" Alvin said. "Sure."

"You didn't get sent to a camp. I am someone trying to stay out of camp, so maybe don't be so judgmental that I just want to have something that you didn't even have to work for." His father would keep saying hurtful things, but at least Alvin had the power to stop the conversation. It made him sad, knowing exactly what he had to say.

"Okay, Dad, I can give you some money."

The tenor changed, like something had been lifted. Now Dan was defensive. "That's not asking too much, right? You have that great job at Google."

"I told you, I'm not there anymore."

"Of course. The startup. It could IPO any day now."

"Dad, just stop. I already told you I would give you money."

THAT NIGHT, ALVIN and his father watched a couple movies. He didn't have a TV yet, so they watched *Superbad* on his laptop. Alvin fell asleep partway through the second film, and he awoke, briefly, as his father carried him to the bed. It was infantilizing, but by that point, Alvin was too tired to care. Strange timing, for his father to act like a father.

Alvin awoke to the smell of frying eggs. Dan was making toast and a scramble—the only thing Alvin had ever seen his dad cook.

"So, I think I'm going to head out today," Dan said as he served Alvin his plate.

"Already? Are you sure you don't want to stick around a little longer?"

"I do, I do." An unconvincing repetition. "But the longer I am here, the more danger you are in." That was a little more convincing.

Alvin had read about the people who had been caught harboring Vietnamese who had been designated for detention. The Department of Homeland Security had charged hundreds of people with illegally housing runaways, and those well-meaning individuals were arrested, punished. In the TV segment, one woman who'd been caught, in explaining to the reporter why she had broken the law, evoked the Underground Railroad.

"The Underground Railroad had a path, though," the reporter said. "Those people were headed somewhere. Where were your people going?"

It was unclear from the segment if she had an answer, or if they had simply cut her off.

As Alvin ate his breakfast, he listened to his dad explain why he'd been out of touch, why he had to leave. Dan was worried that the government could track his communications, and he didn't want his son to get in trouble.

Dan packed his stuff, and Alvin went to the bedroom to write a check. He'd wiped himself out moving to New York and being jobless for a few months, and had only started rebuilding his savings account. Alvin supposed he would just have to begin again.

He handed his father the check.

"Alvin, I don't have a bank account anymore."

Around the corner from the apartment was a Bank of America that always had a miserably long line. Today was no different. But he waited, checking his phone every so often out of boredom. Alvin wondered if he should text his sister and tell her their father was in town. It was less that he thought it would be a good idea for Ursula to see him, and more that she would feel betrayed later if she found out he had kept that from her.

Alvin reflected on the past two years. Things had been hard for him. Ursula didn't understand, because unlike Alvin, she passed as white. Every time Alvin noticed an errant stare, or a skeptical glance, he wondered if people suspected he was Vietnamese, or if it was all in his head. But when he thought about how terrible this sensation was, he reminded himself that he was one of the lucky ones—that he shouldn't feel self-pity when so many people had been detained. In this world, there was no place for how Alvin was feeling.

When he finally reached the teller window, he asked if he could withdraw everything from his savings account. At this point, it was nearly ten thousand dollars.

"For withdrawals of this amount, I'm going to need to talk to my manager."

"That's okay," Alvin said. "Let's get the manager."

Even denominated into hundreds, the envelope of cash felt thick. Alvin gripped it in his jacket pocket for the entire walk home, holding it so tightly that his palm began to sweat, and when he revealed the envelope to his father, he was embarrassed that the bills had gotten slightly damp.

They'd met at Dan's car, where he appeared ready to leave—anxious, even.

He finally turned the key. The engine coughed and rumbled. "It was good to see you, Alvin. And thank you for this." He raised the envelope, shook it around with delight, to show what he was grateful for. Then he drove off.

Alvin had always been motivated—to get strong grades, to get into a great school, to get the kind of job that made people softly nod with approval when you told them what you did for a living. Somewhere in that string of logic Alvin believed that these things would make him a good person, a valuable one, someone who others wanted to be around. Maybe his dad would even want to be around.

It was only now clear to Alvin now how foolish this idea was. Growing up, it was hard not to feel like Dan's absence was Alvin's fault—if he'd been better, maybe his dad would have been more present in his life. But that was the self-centered thinking of a child. Why did Alvin think that his father would care about his son attaining all the things that he had rejected?

After Dan left with the money, Alvin understood that it had nothing to do with him at all. This had always been someone who ran, who left people behind. Someone who could constantly justify this behavior to himself. Alvin could imagine his father's failures as someone else's, rather than his own.

Though the more important realizations would come to Alvin later, some of the lessons were already starting to sink in. In just the time since he'd been at Google, he was coming to terms with the fact that maybe he hadn't earned all the conveniences of his life. Sure, he'd worked hard—whatever that meant. But many forms of privilege had also set him in that direction. It had even kept him out of camp. No one deserved to be in detention. But also, who deserved not to be?

Throughout his life Alvin had coasted. The ugly truth was that good SAT scores, a college diploma, and gainful employment had only finally meant something when Dan came around asking for money. Because only then did Alvin feel needed.

DENNIS

—

"You're selfish, you know that?"

Jen scoffed. She tried moving her arms. They were tied behind her, pinning her to the chair. Her legs were bound together.

"No, really," Dennis said. "Think about all the harm you caused. Thanks to you and your hack journalist sister, no more El Paquete. Food and supplies, all the medication people rely on—gone. TV shows? Music? Gone, gone, gone!"

She attempted to squirm a bit, and even tried to stand up, but Dennis pushed her back down into the chair, hard.

"There were so few freedoms in camp, and you robbed everyone of even the small joys they had."

Jen realized she was in the mess hall where poker night was held. Now it was vacant. The evening she'd visited, the room had been lively, a celebratory air as men packed in to lose what little of what they had left. Now it just looked like any other interior in camp: empty and dark and purposeless.

"I didn't know she would get El Paquete shut down," she said, weakly, not making eye contact.

Dennis knelt down in front of her. "What did you think would happen?"

Jen didn't really know. What *had* she expected? She'd assumed—really, hoped—that giving Ursula tips was simply doing what was right. Getting stories out from camp, telling people the truth of what was happening. You weren't supposed to be punished for doing the right thing.

———

DUNCAN HAD NO idea where to start. Brandon had found him, told him his sister was in danger and little else. So Duncan took off searching camp for Jen, not caring about the risks, knowing that he would be in serious shit if a guard caught him out after dark.

He hadn't spoken to Dennis since he'd turned him down. Jen said that Dennis was spreading harmful misinformation and clearly wanted to expand his footprint. What was he hoping to accomplish? What did he have to gain by lying to so many people?

None of that mattered. Right now, he just had to find his sister.

DENNIS WOUND UP for a punch, his fist circling in the air in an exaggerated, comical fashion. But it wasn't funny. It loomed there, the anticipation of violence more painful than the strike itself.

His hand struck across Jen's face. She held in a scream. Okay, maybe the actual pain was worse. She gazed down at her feet. She could see blood dripping onto her sneakers.

Dennis hovered in front of Jen. She wouldn't look at him, but she could smell his sour sweat, feel his breath.

"You know, I feel sorry for you," Jen said.

That shifted Dennis's mood from anger to amusement. "You feel sorry for *me*?"

"You're pathetic. You act like you're magnanimous, but that's bullshit. All you do is serve yourself. And it doesn't matter to you that you spread lies around camp, as long as it makes people listen to you. Pay attention to you. You're a sad little man that just wants to feel powerful."

"This isn't about power. It's about doing something good."

He leaned in, spoke right into Jen's ear.

"People need what I am giving them."

He pulled away.

"Everyone has questions, and I'm giving them the comfort of answers—of understanding."

"It's not the truth."

"It's a kind of truth they can believe in."

"You're lying, even to yourself—"

This time, the strike was sudden—no windup, just the callous impact of knuckles to Jen's cheek.

She shrieked.

Dennis squatted down so that he was looking up at her. He stared at her with anger, with contempt. And yet, in the light, something about Dennis seemed boyish. There was a softness to him.

"You don't understand how close I was. *Nhật Báo* was going to reach other camps, help people elsewhere. But you had to be so selfish. So fucking selfish, Jen."

Whether from pain or from fear, the tears were coming now. She didn't have control. Her breaths were shortening, and any air that came into her lungs seemed to need to escape more quickly now.

"I'm going to hand you over to the guards. They sent Allegra away discreetly. I think they'll do the same with you."

Suddenly, Jen felt only rage, its heat intensifying. The anger gave her the strength to make eye contact with Dennis.

"I see it now. I see what it is about you," she said with newfound clarity. "Dennis, you love it here. Because outside of camp, you're nothing. You're scared of going back there, back to a world where you are powerless. Here, among the miserable and the suffering, you finally mean something. Little Dennis has finally found the place in the world where he is a big man—"

He struck again.

DUNCAN HEARD THE CRY—a sharp, piercing scream. It came from down the block. Another screech, and Duncan noticed the building it was coming from. A few detainees had crowded around but didn't dare approach. He rushed toward it.

A large figure was guarding the door. It was dark, and he never even saw it coming. Duncan lowered his shoulder, and before the man could look up, 220 pounds of Duncan had made contact with his head, slamming him back against the building. As the man's body slumped to the ground, Duncan recognized him: it was his teammate Phúc. He'd have to apologize later.

Immediately, through the door, Duncan couldn't believe what he saw. His sister, tied to a chair, covered in blood, passed out. Her hair was drooped over her face. Duncan moved closer and knelt in front of her.

"Sis! Jen! Are you okay?"

He shook her.

"JEN!"

Suddenly she was alert.

"Duncan . . ."

"What the fuck happened? Who did this to you?"

She mumbled something, disoriented and barely conscious. She lifted her head and met Duncan's eyes. And then looked past him before screaming.

He'd never have a moment to process everything, never realize that what happened next was complete luck. So many things had had to fall into place, but the most fortunate was turning around at the exact right moment for his elbow to connect with Dennis's head, immediately knocking him off a trajectory that would have otherwise ended with a knife in Duncan's back. It was just enough to destabilize him, giving Duncan time to lunge. Dennis dropped his knife on contact, and Duncan took him to the ground.

Duncan experienced the next moments as sensations: the sound of Dennis's nose as it cracked. The smell of Dennis's blood, the tang of iron as it gurgled out of his mouth. And when Duncan was finished landing all of his blows across Dennis's face, leaving a mess of red and swollen tissue, Duncan finally felt the pain in his throbbing fists, the knuckles he'd shredded somewhere in the process of trying to kill the man who had done this to his sister.

SENSATIONS

—

URSULA'S INSTINCT WAS TO OFFER HIM SOMETHING. THERE WERE SOME leftovers she could heat up, although Alvin didn't appear particularly hungry. Maybe a drink? Actually, he probably needed to hydrate more than anything, since he already reeked of booze. She found a LaCroix in the fridge for her brother, who had only just arrived and had immediately slumped over on the couch.

"Everything okay?" she asked, handing him the can.

"Seltzer? Who drinks this stuff? Whatever happened to regular water?" Alvin complained.

"I can get you tap water."

"No, no, this is fine. Thank you." He snapped the tab. "What the hell flavor is pamplemousse?"

"It's the French word for grapefruit, I think."

"Didn't you take four years of French? Shouldn't you know that?"

"Do you want something else or not?"

"French, the language of the colonizer," Alvin joked, somewhat smugly, very drunkenly.

"Colonizer languages were our only options. You seriously have become so obnoxious since you discovered the library."

Ursula was proud of all the history that her brother had been cracking. But a side effect of education was becoming insufferable. Alvin nodded, to concede that she was making a fair point, and finally sipped his seltzer.

She seated herself across from him.

"So, what's up? You show up here, in the middle of the night. Clearly, you've been drinking. You don't even text me to say you're coming."

They finally made eye contact. Ursula had never seen her brother like this. Yeah, he was a bit of a dope at times, but he always had it together. Every problem seemed to roll off him; every conflict he managed to charm his way out of. Even when he'd been fired from Google, he had delivered the news to her like he had it under control.

Right now, on her couch, he seemed lost. Something had slipped away. Ursula could see it on his face. His eyes were red—maybe he'd been crying, but it could also just be the alcohol.

"It seems like you've had enough to drink, but"—Ursula walked back over to the kitchen—"do you want another? I'm gonna have a scotch."

"Since when do you drink scotch?"

"We have this ethics policy in the newsroom—you can't accept any gifts. No one sends me shit, of course. There aren't, like, cool PR gifts for the Vietnamese detention reporter. But some of the other journalists get things in the mail all the time. The food writers are always getting free bottles of booze sent to them but can't keep them, so this restaurant reviewer, Claire, gave me a fancy bottle of something and I've been saving it for a special occasion."

Alvin was lying down now. "What's the special occasion? Dumbshit brother shows up at an odd hour of the morning and won't say what's wrong?"

Ursula returned with two wineglasses, since she had nothing more suitable, and poured a pair of healthy servings of scotch.

"The special occasion is not drinking alone."

The siblings clinked glasses and took a sip.

"Wow, that is . . . a lot," Ursula said. She'd only had scotch once or twice before. She had no idea why she'd thought she would enjoy it this time. Alvin seemed to like it, though. Or maybe he could just put it back.

"Do you want to watch TV or something?" Ursula offered.

Alvin shrugged noncommittally. She still didn't have an actual TV, so she went to fetch her laptop. When she returned, Ursula planted the computer on the coffee table, then tapped the trackpad to wake it up. Somehow, she'd forgotten what she was doing right before Alvin showed up unannounced—

Ursula scrambled to close the browser window she had open. Frazzled, she only managed to maximize the window instead of minimizing it. Why was she even bothering to hide it? Alvin had already seen it.

"Listen, I was getting ready for bed, and you showed up without any warning," Ursula explained.

"I would've texted you, but"—Alvin made an exaggerated motion toward his pockets—"I left my phone at the bar."

"For the record, it is extremely normal for women to watch porn."

"I wasn't judging." Another long sip of scotch.

Ursula thought about telling her brother to slow down, but at this point, what did it matter? Maybe it would be better if he passed out on the couch sooner than later. In fact, it was already later.

"So what are you into?"

"Oh my god, Alvin."

"Who's judging now? I am just asking, like . . . what am I looking at?"

Why not tell him? Ursula had felt bad about how quickly they were growing apart in the mere weeks since he'd moved out—and anyway, she was beyond caring.

"It's this production company called Sensations. It's all women-run, and the directors are women. So it's porn you can feel good about watching." She would never admit that she learned it from a Top Story Entertainment article, but Ursula felt compelled to add: "Less exploitation, and all."

Alvin was sipping his pamplemousse LaCroix again, nodding, eyes fixated on the laptop screen, which was a video paused on a woman who had a penis in her mouth and another one in her vagina.

"Okay, I'm closing this now."

"No, no, play it," Alvin insisted.

"We are not watching porn together."

"God, Urs, we're not gonna jerk off or anything. I just want to see it."

This was getting pretty weird, but clearly Alvin was in some kind of state. And maybe it was the older-sister thing kicking in, since her only impulse was doing whatever might bring him some comfort during what appeared to be a crisis.

So she hit play.

Suddenly, the dicks were in motion again, on both ends of the woman on the screen. Alvin looked on. Ursula no longer regretted pouring such a large scotch.

They didn't watch for very long before Alvin said to turn it off. In Ursula's memory of that night, most of which would remain vivid for a long time, the details of what they watched would evaporate. But she would remember the vague facts about what had shaken him up so much.

He'd had a strange visit that day, an unexpected one. Ursula assumed it must be some girl who she'd never heard about. Maybe her poor brother was capable of having his heart broken.

"But I think I realized something today, Urs," Alvin said, his eyes trained on the laptop. "I might never see them again, and I think I'm finally okay with that."

She still didn't understand why it was all such a big secret. Who was he talking about, and why couldn't he tell her? Clearly there was not much left to hide between them.

Ursula overestimated how quickly he would fall asleep, and the two of them watched TV until it was beginning to get light out. When Alvin finally nodded off, Ursula tucked a blanket over him and brought the wineglasses of scotch to the sink. Then she retrieved her laptop and went to her bedroom. Suddenly she was exhausted, too, but Ursula needed to do one thing.

Once she finished, she tabbed over to her email and wrote a message to Rosco, explaining that she needed to take a personal day. The draft she had due—she would need another day on that, the first time she'd ever asked to push a deadline.

Something came up that was more important, Ursula admitted in her email, which wasn't something she needed to write for her boss, but for herself.

The recollections of that night would stay with Ursula. She'd realize something then: that it mattered less what you said to a person in their moment of need, and more that you were present and willing to sit beside them. That her own need to know and understand the problem was selfish. That often, the best way to support someone was just to be there and do nothing else.

WEATHER SYSTEMS

—

JEN CAME TO, BARELY. SHE COULD SMELL THE SWEAT ON HER brother—familiar. Where was Duncan taking her? Why was he carrying her?

Then she noticed the blood. Hers. It was everywhere, but starting to dry. It had seeped through her T-shirt, her favorite—the Federal Boob Inspector one. Well, Má would be happy about that at least.

Then there was the acute pain. She was doubled over by the throb of the worst headache she'd ever had. As soon as she was aware of her wounds, she could think of nothing else. Not the stink of her brother. Not being covered in blood, or the sudden chill she felt throughout her body. Not the wet feeling of her clothes, thick and sticky. Just the tremendous sting coming from the back of her brain.

She looked up. Her brother was shirtless, her head pressed against his stomach, his flabby pecs, the sweat coming off his big head, dripping into her hair.

Duncan was shouting. Jen could barely make it out at first, but it was obvious after a moment. The repeated scream of "help," desperate and searching for anyone who might provide it. His voice was raspy.

Her vision was blurry. Probably lost too much blood from her head. But her senses were slowly returning. She was gaining strength, consciousness, awareness.

"You can put me down," Jen whispered.

Duncan didn't hear her.

"You can put me down," Jen said again.

His eyes were still darting around, looking for someone else.

"You can put me down."

He finally noticed. "Oh my god, you're awake. You're *awake*." She recognized a moment of joy in Duncan's face. She could see it. He pressed his head against hers. She used to do this to him when they were much younger. Just touch foreheads, usually when something bad had happened, to show they were there for each other. Like when Dad left. Or like when Dad left. Or like when Dad left. Or like—

"Duncan! What the fuck happened?"

"I need to get her to the infirmary."

"At the ODC building?"

"Yeah, help me carry her."

"It's fucking crazy over there right now. People have lost it."

"What do you mean?"

"The Tower. People are attacking the Tower. They think it's the reason El Paquete shut down."

Jen turned. It was Brandon. Even while she was being cradled by Duncan, Brandon looked so small, so concerned, panicked.

"Can she walk?" Brandon asked.

"I'm not sure. Dennis had her tied up."

"Dennis did this?"

"It's okay. I worked him over pretty good."

"Where is he now?"

"One of the mess halls. I don't think we have to worry about him for a minute."

"Are you sure? Because I think that's him."

Brandon pointed to a figure running in the distance. Duncan spun around quickly to look, dropping Jen in the process.

"Goddamnit, Duncan," Jen said.

Brandon knelt by her. "Can you stand?"

"Yeah, I'm okay."

Duncan had taken off.

"Where are you going?" she shouted after him.

It was stupid to ask. He was going after Dennis.

—

DUNCAN WAS SURPRISED how quick Dennis was. But it didn't matter. There was no way that he wouldn't catch up. He'd practiced it so many times before.

"Get back here!"

The man ahead turned for just a second—his eyes briefly making contact with Duncan's—before spinning back around and taking off even faster. It was enough of a glimpse to confirm that it was the bastard.

"Keep running! It won't make a difference!"

The only thing that would satiate Duncan's anger was to instill fear in Dennis, to make Dennis understand that he was weak, that fleeing would just delay the additional pain that he was entitled to. Running was cowardly, and it was fruitless. The helplessness of this small, sadistic man gave Duncan some satisfaction, a smirk crossing his face as he, too, picked up the pace.

As they raced past the rows of bunks, Duncan could hear a commotion in the distance. Something unusual was happening, something big. But he could figure out what later. Instead, he chose to imagine it as the roar of a crowd, cheering for him as he chased down his man.

THE TEMPERATURE ALWAYS dropped in the evening, but it felt especially cold tonight, frigid. Jen looked up at the sky. It was black, but in the brief glimpses of light, she knew that she was not mistaken.

"It's snowing?" Brandon said, in a moment of awe.

"Something is wrong with this place," Jen said.

They tried to follow Duncan, but they weren't nearly fast enough and quickly lost track of him.

"Duncan is chasing Dennis. So where do we think Dennis is headed?" Jen asked.

"Maybe the ODC building? That's where the infirmary is, and he's hurt."

It seemed as good a guess as any.

Suddenly, in the distance, they could hear shouting. It sounded like a mob. As they neared the ODC building, they saw the crowd. Dozens of detainees had surrounded the Tower. People were screaming in English and in Vietnamese. Someone was shouting about how the Tower was making them infertile, that it was killing their sperm count.

"They can't be serious, right?" Jen asked. "This is what they're mad about?"

Brandon suggested they avoid whatever was happening.

Jen could see that the detainees were growing in number, surrounding a handful of ODC guards anxiously trying to keep the crowd from pushing in on them. They were defending the Tower.

"Stay back!"

"Get the fuck away or we'll shoot!"

If the mob took the threat seriously, it didn't appear intimidated. Someone threw a bottle at one of the guards.

"Please step back. Please step back."

Jen recognized the voice. It was Hugo. He had a pistol drawn and looked terrified that he might have to use it.

"This is Dennis's doing. He stirred up all this shit, spreading lies about the Tower," Brandon said.

"Didn't you let him?" Jen said.

The ODC building was well lit. Usually, it was heavily fortified, but the guards, armed with their assault rifles, were rushing from their posts to help their colleagues nearby defending the Tower.

A voice crackled through a megaphone. "Do *not* come closer. This area is off limits after curfew."

"We have someone that needs medical attention," Brandon shouted back, squinting into the light, unsure of who he was addressing. "Please, she's badly hurt."

It took a moment for Jen to realize he was talking about her.

"Shut up, I'm fine."

"There they are!" Brandon pointed at two figures—a small one, with a larger one closing in from behind. Jen couldn't make out their faces, but she had no doubt who they were. They were sprinting toward the ODC building.

Jen had heard so many men die right at this entrance.

"Duncan!" she screamed. "Duncan, don't!"

EVER SINCE ARRIVING in camp, Duncan had nosebleeds often and at random: in the shower; during practice; sometimes they even woke him up in his sleep, sending Duncan scrambling for his towel so as not to stain his bedsheets. At first, he thought his body was just adjusting to the dry air of the desert. But two years later, they came with the same frequency. It was just part of his life.

Despite the warnings of an ODC guard not to approach, Dennis proceeded toward the building. For a moment, he hesitated, like he was deciding between turning around and facing Duncan or taking his chances forward. He kept going.

Dennis was shouting in the direction of the building. "You have to help me!"

Duncan could have processed why Dennis was pleading to the ODC guards. But when he was in pursuit, he couldn't think about anything else. The only way to achieve excellence was to focus, to put every other thought out of your mind. This discipline was what made Duncan special on the field. It was what allowed him to channel every violent urge and resentment—about his father, his family, his frustrated life— into something productive.

And if Dennis wasn't going to stop running, neither was he. Even when the floodlight of the ODC building beamed in his face so brightly that he had to shield his eyes with his arm. Even as he heard a loud crack and watched Dennis stumble forward, fall to his knees, and his face plant in the ground. Even when a second crack echoed across the desert, followed by the sound of a scream—not his own but one that sounded like Jen's, coming from somewhere in the distance.

Duncan noticed blood on his shirt, pooling around his chest. *Great, another nosebleed,* he thought.

THE FALL OF THE TOWER
—

In reporting on Vietnamese detention camps over the course of three years, the greatest challenge was keeping it relevant to the newsroom. When the detention first occurred and stories of the camp conditions were trickling out, it was easy to make the case that we should report on it, write about it, and most importantly, publish it.

But as months, then years, went by, very little changed within the detention centers—at least in what could be perceived by journalists on the outside. That made it difficult to push stories about camp through my editors. The civil and human rights violations were still happening to Vietnamese Americans. But that was already out there, which meant that even though it continued to happen, it wasn't a story anymore.

When the Tower in Camp Tacoma fell, it returned Viet detention to the news cycle. Though the Tower—which blocked all cell and wireless signals within each camp—was repaired and restored within a couple days, that roughly forty-eight-hour window was enough for a flood of new material to escape camp. It turns out that many detainees had phones, despite the Tower crippling them with its electric fog. So when the Viets suddenly had bars of service, they began sending messages to loved ones—people who they hadn't been able to contact in over two years.

What happened in Camp Tacoma that night would set in motion the end of Vietnamese American detention. The videos from detainees showed chaos and violence. The sound of gunfire and screaming. The explosion—ultimately what would bring down the Tower—was captured at many different angles, and broadcast on every single news outlet in some form or another.

Will anyone forget the footage of the Tower looming in the distance, its figure emerging through a blizzard, crumbling to the ground, and the metal screech that followed? If Americans had forgotten or suppressed the reality of Vietnamese detention, then here was an image that became a stark and constant reminder.

But more than anything that happened that evening, it was newswor-thy. It would spur more investigations into what was really going on in detention centers—by journalists, by senators, by DHS itself.

In that two-day window, enough evidence leaked out of Camp Tacoma that even the powers that had a vested interest—political or capital—in maintaining the current conditions of detention had to concede.

Those two days allowed the terror to be too legible.

V
—

ONE YEAR LATER

REPRESENTATION

—

URSULA WAS MEETING WITH AGENTS. THERE WERE MANY KINDS, IT turned out. A book agent, obviously, to get her a deal with a publishing house. A film and TV agent, in case there was interest in adapting her reporting for the screen—that was where the real money was, Ursula was told. And then there was a representative for all of her speaking gigs, who wasn't technically an agent but, in many ways, was the person who acted the most how Ursula had imagined, always shouting and cursing like, well, agents. It occurred to Ursula that maybe she had based her entire assumptions about how they acted on *Entourage*, which she binged in the background to stay awake on those late nights when she really had to push herself. She'd borrowed Rosco's HBO login to watch it.

Speaking of Rosco, most of the agent meetings came through him. She was still frustrated, despite this help—as a boss, he was mediocre on so many levels. But maybe the best thing he could do was connect her to more influential people.

Ursula knew she couldn't hold it against him. At one point, she was a nobody. Not a single person cared about her or who she was or what she could do, including Rosco, until he saw how she was useful. Now, after three years of reporting on Vietnamese internment, she'd surpassed him in terms of relevance and power—at the company, in the industry, culturally. She had to give credit to Rosco for seeing that. Maybe he was just thinking about how she could be exploited. Whether she was or not was beside the point. She was here now, talking to agents—a TV agent. Or, wait, was this a book agent? Turned out it was neither.

"We are going to put you on the circuit," the tiny white woman said. "All the major cities. Some of the Ivies, if they can afford it."

She was a little older, with a short, severe haircut, graying on the sides. She looked very cool. Also very serious.

"You know, they're ridiculous," she said.

"Who?" Ursula asked.

"The Ivies."

"Okay," Ursula responded, enthusiastically, not knowing how to answer.

There was the promise of a TED Talk, which was an ungodly amount of money for only a few days of work, if Ursula could stomach the idea of wearing a weird skin-colored mic headset thing and being streamed on YouTube.

There were many more meetings for the other two kinds of agents. The literary agent assured her that a book would go for the high six figures, if not seven, based on just a few thousand words' worth of a proposal. Soon after, Ursula sold a book connecting all of her previous reporting, pitched as the definitive history of Vietnamese internment. The money was great. Even if it would be paid out over five installments, over the course of several years, that was more than she had ever made from her job. The publisher insisted that the book have a title that would feel comprehensive, authoritative, and human. She would call it *The Viets*.

The rights to the book were sold as an eight-part documentary series, even before a draft was done. At her Netflix meeting in L.A., a producer assured her that it did not matter if her book had been written yet. History had been. The money from the film deal was more than she ever dreamed.

Yet Ursula carried a strange feeling in her stomach. Sure, she'd done the most impactful reporting about Vietnamese detention. She'd broken huge stories, changed the focus of the national conversation, possibly resulting in the detained Viets getting a form of reparations. But she had not been there. In fact, her life had been extremely privileged throughout those horrible years when people suffered—people she knew, her own family.

Still, she had done the work. A lot of work. It had been well received. What else was there to ask for? At what point would she actually believe that the work she did was worthwhile, let alone valuable, let alone excellent?

It seemed to make sense to put all her agents in the same room. Well, on the same conference call. So she did that, and they bickered and argued about what seemed like every line of every contract. Ursula barely talked. But the one thing they could all agree on: no one was better suited to tell this story than her.

IT WAS A Tuesday afternoon and Ursula had never been more relaxed. She could feel the sun on her skin, smell the chlorine off the pool and, in the distance, the saline of the ocean. The lounge chair was at once stiff and extremely agreeable to her back. She would order another drink—an endless series of generously poured servings of wine that she could put on her room tab.

She had never been to Miami, and even after an entire week there, Ursula would leave feeling like she still hadn't been. She'd planned to explore the city but instead mostly hung out at the pool of her beachfront hotel.

As the deadline for the manuscript approached, her agent—the book agent—had suggested going somewhere to focus on her pages. Somewhere comfortable, with few distractions. The agency had a special rate at a Miami resort.

When she arrived, Ursula found that the accommodations were far nicer than any place she'd ever stayed; the weather ideal—just warm enough to make her sweat, but with a salty breeze coming off the ocean often enough to cool her down. The room was small but clean and cozy, a big bed with fresh sheets. A New American restaurant and bar open at all hours of the day, waiting to cater to her every hunger. The trip immediately felt like a mistake. How could one be expected to produce a book in conditions that were so . . . forgiving?

But it turned out that a beautiful, tropical prison was exactly what Ursula needed. She quickly figured out a schedule for her most productive self: wake up early, drink some coffee, and write for an hour. Then go lounge and read by the pool for two hours. Eat a light lunch at the bar, munching on a salad while listening to a podcast. Then back to her room to write some more—as much as she could, before she was tired. Some days she could go for as long as four hours before the computer screen began to hurt her eyes. Then grab a glass of wine and head back to the pool, and if she wasn't feeling too tipsy, read a bit more. Then eat a big solo dinner, with dessert, with many more wines, and then take a dip in the hot tub. When she was good and pruny, she would go back to her room and wash off in the shower. Feeling clean and refreshed and exhausted by all that time in the sun, Ursula would stream a shitty movie on her laptop, touch herself, and eventually slip into a deep and fulfilling slumber.

The last time she'd booked accommodations, it was a shitty motel in Independence, California. Even though that reporting had been the breakthrough that had made her career, she'd still never told anyone what had happened with Tyler. Why did it matter? She'd gotten the story. And now this experience, she supposed, was what she deserved for enduring the violent encounter of that trip: long, perfect days of productivity and relaxation.

REUNION

—

"IT'S A SHOEBOX, BUT IT'S SO HARD TO FIND AN AFFORDABLE ONE-bedroom in this city." And almost immediately: "I'm sorry, that was insensitive of me," Ursula said, her apology sincere. "This probably seems like a lot of space to you."

It didn't, actually. Camp bunks were crowded, but there was a lot of space—the desert offered miles and miles of it. The experience was like inverse claustrophobia, the vastness its own kind of confinement. But Jen didn't want to talk about that right now. She just nodded as Ursula explained that she was still putting the place together, and that most of the furnishings were "pieces of shit" from West Elm.

Everything in her apartment felt so neat. All the furniture matched, a tasteful mix of midcentury modern with a splash of kitsch. The art on the walls was pleasant and noncommittal. A fuzzy multicolor throw was draped over the back of a gray sectional. It was very attractive, very adult, though not particularly lived-in.

The only signal that Ursula spent time here was the already-open bottle of wine she pulled out from the fridge, and the two stemless glasses she rinsed in the sink.

"Cheers," Ursula said, and they clinked.

"Your place is so cool," Jen said. "It's what I imagined when I thought about you on the outside."

Ursula blushed. "I'm glad you didn't see the apartment I used to live in." She took a sip. "It was the *worst*."

To Jen, Ursula appeared more beautiful, more mature. Her hair was freshly cut into a tidy, angular bob. And her outfit—a mustard top, high-waisted jeans, a blazer with the sleeves artfully rolled back to the elbows—looked casual but deliberate, styled not unlike the apartment. Ursula was all made up.

"You look . . . so skinny. God, did they feed you in there?" Ursula asked. "Stand up," she commanded, and Jen obeyed. Ursula gestured toward the mirror. "Let's have a look at you." An invitation to self-inspection.

Ursula stood behind her, as if examining what had happened to her poor cousin after three years of detention. Jen checked herself in the full-length mirror, meticulously propped up at a flattering ten-degree angle. The glass was so clear, so clean. Everything in camp was dirty and covered in a layer of dust. Looking at herself, Jen certainly didn't feel any thinner, though she hadn't really seen herself over the past three years.

Ursula wanted a closer look, to catalog the changes, take stock of the damage. It was unclear to Jen whether Ursula was still collecting notes for a story.

AFTER THEIR RELEASE from Camp Tacoma, Jen and her mother spent two weeks in temporary housing, provided by the government. It was basically like being at the detention site, only now there weren't three hot meals provided. But being more or less free still felt great. The government was kind enough to give everyone a small stipend—a lump sum of four thousand dollars, which was to last several months while they got back on their feet. Her mother put her money immediately toward ordering all the foods they'd missed.

Because their home in Indiana had been seized by the government three years ago, it was unclear if they would get it back. Worse, it would likely take months for them to even know if the house still belonged to them, since the newly formed Department of Detainee Relocation, made up mostly of the former Office of Detention Culture, was backed up with tens of thousands of cases like theirs. And in the meantime, there was no way to see what condition the house was in. It was entirely possible that it was sitting there empty, waiting for Jen and her mother's return. It was just as likely that it had been sold, and another family had taken up residency. The only tangible thing was the paperwork, which Jen took to filling out on her mother's behalf. The forms were hard to read, and it strained Má's already bad eyesight. Add that to the list, Jen thought, new glasses for Má.

They were also given travel vouchers, good for a one-way flight anywhere domestically. Despite the uncertainty about their housing, Má wanted to return to Indiana anyway. Jen said she would go with her, but to her surprise, Má suggested she take the opportunity to live with Ursula in New York.

"How did you know Urs offered?"

The two cousins had had such little communication before they agreed. Ursula explained that she just had a couch, but Alvin had slept comfortably on it for nearly two months. And actually, she'd be happy to purchase an air mattress if that would make the arrangement more appealing.

"You took care of me in camp," Má said, "and now you should think about yourself."

They'd gotten closer in the last year. Jen focused on her duties at the *Loyalty*. She stopped working on *Korematsu*. Instead, she spent as much time with Má as possible. Painful as it was, she even went to church services. Her priority had become her mom's well-being, the only thing that felt important anymore. They always talked around what had happened, but each could see in the other that it was never far from their mind.

Jen used her travel voucher for a ticket to LaGuardia. She'd never thought of her mother as an intuitive person, but it seemed that Má had understood what Jen wanted before she did: to be with Ursula.

THAT FIRST DAY when Jen got settled in Ursula's apartment—Ursula bought an air mattress after all, though it was still sealed in the box—they left to get something to eat. Ursula chose a small Italian restaurant in the neighborhood, where Jen ordered a chicken parm sandwich, which she immediately declared was the best thing she'd ever eaten in her fucking life. Every meal since she'd left Camp Tacoma was the best meal of her life, and if there was at least one upside to having three years robbed from her, it was having a series of ecstatic dining experiences. Would the joy ever end? Midway through her sandwich, which she was wolfing down with alarming velocity, it seemed the answer would be a resounding "no."

Ursula licked the tip of a napkin and offered to dab red sauce off Jen's chin, like a mother tending to her infant. Jen didn't exactly stop her.

They walked to the movie theater, the neighborhood one that played older films for two-dollar tickets.

"You like superhero movies, right?" Ursula said. "You missed some good ones."

"I don't like them. But I've seen them all."

"A bunch came out while you were gone, though."

"We got them in camp, through El Paquete," Jen said, and then elaborated, "I guess we missed all the stuff that came out in the past year, since it shut down."

The final year in camp was its own kind of hell. After the Tower fell, the ODC cracked down, and all the leniency that existed before was suddenly gone. Quickly, a new Tower was erected, El Paquete gone. Detainees were even more miserable than they had been before. No one got to see the ending of *Game of Thrones*.

"Of course." Ursula nodded. Jen could see the guilt washing over her cousin.

"But it's been forever since I've been to a movie theater."

Jen insisted that she pay. So they saw the new *Avengers* for four dollars, and Jen took mental stock that the ticket had cost her one thousandth of all the money she had in the world.

JEN HAD SPENT so much time in camp thinking about getting out of camp, but she'd seldom imagined what her life would be like after she left. It was stupid, but she'd assumed that everything would just pick up where she left off. She could still return to NYU—though she'd been informed that because she was arriving midsemester, she'd have to wait until the end of the term, and that also her previous financial aid package was no longer valid. But even if money weren't a concern (which, to be clear, it was), the thought of being a freshman at age twenty-one, and seeing all of her old friends, now seniors, was too much to bear.

"You're welcome to stay with me as long as you need," Ursula said. They'd dropped into a bar around the corner after the movie.

"That's generous. Hopefully I won't need to stay too long."

"Just promise me you won't go back to Indiana." Ursula was dead serious. "You can move to some other city, but don't go back home. There's nothing for you there."

Jen hadn't told her that the house she grew up in no longer belonged to her mother, that she'd just learned the government had seized it, and then sold it. That Má was now living in some kind of subsidized housing that the church had provided her out of biblical compassion. Ursula talked about Jen's future like there were options, possibilities. Maybe there were choices she could make. But she was only getting as far as $3,996 would take her.

Jen could tell what Ursula really wanted to talk about: What was it like watching your kid brother get shot in front of you? What kind of funeral service do detainees get in camp? How does it feel knowing that if you ever want to see his grave, you'll have to revisit the place you were held captive for three years?

Instead, draining her Malbec, teeth stained red, Ursula asked Jen what she wanted to do next.

"Is it too soon to eat again?"

CHARLIE IN SPACE

—

ALVIN DIDN'T KNOW WHAT TO EXPECT. NOBODY IN THE FAMILY DID. But at least everyone was here. The extended family, aunts and uncles and cousins, had mostly flown into New York from California, where they were slowly trying to rebuild their lives. Even though everyone had grown—aged, hardened—there was still a comforting familiarity in it. The closest thing to a family reunion in nearly four years. Despite the expense, nearly everyone had shown up.

Surprisingly, Jen's mom, Aunt Ai, didn't make it. But in her place, just as surprising, was Alvin's mother—the one white person in the family. Pam had driven up from Massachusetts and was staying with him. (Ursula insisted that her place was not an option, given how busy she was.) Through much insistence, Alvin convinced his mother to take the bedroom while he slept on the couch.

Tom had described the event as a preview, meaning that his production was nearly ready for an audience. The theater was off-Broadway, but according to Tom, "*barely* off-Broadway." Nothing could take away how impressive Tom's accomplishments were. He wasn't even twenty—still in his teens—and he'd written and directed an entire play, one that people would pay to come and see and review, in the theater capital of the world. Sure, Tom had always been a pretentious little shit. But now it was paying off.

The family had gathered at a mediocre barbecue restaurant. There had been reported instances of violence against Vietnamese since they were let out of camp, though Alvin hadn't experienced or witnessed any of it himself. But he imagined this dinner party of over twenty Vietnamese people was probably pushing the limits of what customers could handle. He caught glimpses of sneers, incredulous looks, whispering among tables. Strangely, he seemed more sensitive to it than the rest of his family. Everyone had strolled in loudly and paid no mind to the people around them.

The waiter was a little rude, though that could be because he was serving a table full of people who were also rude. Alvin imagined that the chefs in the kitchen were spitting into all of the food. He wished they'd spat more, really. Maybe then his brisket wouldn't have been so dry.

Tom was, understandably, absent from the meal. He had to prepare for the show. But he was the topic of conversation as everyone chowed down, barbecue sauce dotting their chins as they ate.

The family had a vague idea of how Tom had been empowered to stage a production at his age. His parents—Uncle Minh and Aunt Lan—had proudly laid it out. After returning home, the videos that Tom had shot in camp had done the gallery circuit as a multimedia installation. From the renown he'd gained in art circles, he had new mentors and patrons who encouraged him to apply for a special Guggenheim Fellowship. He vowed to make complicated, sophisticated art based on his experience in camp—the horrors, the joys, the aching, longing stretches of boredom.

"How much was the fellowship for?" Aunt Nga asked, midchew of cornbread.

Uncle Minh announced proudly: "Forty-five thousand dollars."

That figure silenced the table.

Ursula nudged Alvin and whispered, "That's not nearly enough to stage a play in New York." And she went back to mangling a beef rib.

ALVIN DIDN'T KNOW what to expect. But the title, *Charlie in Space,* was more provocative than he'd expected. Up until this point, since Jen had organized everything about this reunion—everyone's flights, coordinating schedules, even booking that mediocre barbecue meal—it had never occurred to Alvin to wonder what the play was called. In his head, he'd just kept thinking of it as "Tom's play."

At the theater, Alvin was seated next to Jen and could hear her stomach grumbling. She'd explained that, after camp, her body was still getting used to eating so many rich foods, and especially that much meat in a single sitting. He didn't expect to hear there wasn't much meat served in camp. Jen explained that calling what they ate "meat" would be generous.

Tom got up on stage to address the audience. Some of the cousins whooped. One of the aunts clapped.

"Thank you, everyone, for coming." Tom bowed, which was odd for the beginning of a show. "As you know, tonight's production is just a preview, so while we feel very sure that you guys are going to love what you see, we are still working out some of the kinks."

Tom took a step forward, now perched nearly at the edge of the stage. "I was incarcerated at Camp Tacoma for three years. During my time there, me and my family endured so much punishment. If it wasn't the dust in our lungs, it was the constant threat of the ODC guards, who might get bored and decide to hurt us, just to see how we'd react."

Now people were silent. Alvin turned around and saw a handful of audience members in the back ferociously jotting notes. Critics, probably.

"But in writing this play, I wanted to tell an unconventional story of Vietnamese detention. I wanted to capture the feeling of losing time, losing your life. Things weren't always so bad. But we had no idea how long we would be there. We couldn't see the end of it, and the existential trauma weighing on us every day." Tom paused, to really ham it up. "I'm not sure there's a way you can ever recover from that."

THE PLAY TOOK place at a high school, sometime in the future. Tom's two main characters were girls, Charlie and Audrey. They navigate classes, crushes, and bullies. But quickly, it's clear this is no ordinary high school. The students are recruited for the military. In a distant galaxy, vicious space bugs pose the greatest threat to Earth, and so the Intergalactic Combat Force is tasked with proactively eradicating an infestation of extraterrestrial insects.

Alvin found it an odd choice that for a show supposedly about Vietnamese people, Charlie and Audrey were played by two nearly identical, thin white women, one with pink hair and the other a brunette. Everyone else in the class is an archetype—a jock, a nerd, a goth, a cheerleader—bragging about why they'll be chosen to be sent to space to fight the good war.

Pam turned to Alvin and said she didn't understand a lick of what was going on. Alvin admitted that he only followed a couple licks more than her. It was the kind of joke that Pam would laugh at a little too long and a little too loudly, and eventually she was hushed by one of the notebook-wielding critics in the back.

Considering the only theater he'd ever sat through was written by Shakespeare or featured the music of ABBA, Alvin was surprised and at times bewildered by what he was seeing. Charlie and all her friends are selected by the ICF—except Audrey. The two have a tearful goodbye, pledging that they'll still be best friends when Charlie returns from her mission. That's the rub: because the alien planet is so far away, the teenage soldiers have to be cryogenically frozen for the journey. They are thawed for combat, and then frozen again for the return trip. This means that the tour will only age Charlie a couple months, but everyone on Earth will be three years older by the time she comes back.

The first act ends with Charlie shipping off, dressed in a Technicolor jumpsuit that really highlights the size of her breasts. (Apparently Tom was inspired by anime.) She says goodbye to Audrey, puts on her helmet, and heads to exit off the right side of the stage. The scene is moving, especially when contrasted with the pastiche of the costumes and set. Here are two friends who don't know if they'll ever see each other again. And even in the best-case scenario, when they meet again, they will be two entirely different people.

The last thing Audrey says to Charlie: "Kick the shit out of some space bugs."

The set does a clever thing between acts. One half of the stage shows

Charlie, strapped into the cockpit in her mecha suit. Lots of flashing lights, the sound of explosions, some smoke. Her face is colored with cuts and bruises, tormented by the horrors of war. On the other half of the stage, we get scenes of Audrey's life moving quickly. She's studying in college. It goes black, and when the lights come back on, she's unpacking boxes in what appears to be her new apartment. Another fadeout and -in and Audrey is at the office, working late, visibly frustrated.

They let out a primal scream in unison.

ANOTHER THING ALVIN did not expect: a full-on Q and A after the performance. The actors had bowed and left the stage. The lights came on, and Tom, standing by himself at the front, fielded questions from the critics in the back. They had concerns. A *lot* of concerns. About the characters, about the themes, about whether this was really the best way to stage a story explicitly promised to be about Vietnamese detention.

The judgments were surprising to Alvin. He turned to Ursula. "I can't believe these critics are giving Tom notes."

"I don't think they're critics. They're the people that helped Tom fund the play." She clarified. "From the Guggenheim Foundation."

It became clearer what was happening as Tom defended himself, handling the criticisms eloquently, but slowly wearing down under the pressure of their expectations. Finally, one of the older bespectacled white men stood up, tired of all of Tom's deflections about his artistic intention. He waved his notepad around as he talked.

"You promised us a story about the suffering of Vietnamese people, and you instead wrote this horned-up science fiction garbage!"

"Is that a question?" Tom replied.

Later, at the bar, both Alvin and Ursula danced around saying anything critical about Tom's play until they couldn't keep it inside anymore, about three sips into their first drinks.

Alvin admitted it was heartbreaking to watch two friends grow apart—literally—and struggle to find ways to understand one another. They both seem keenly aware of what they have lost. And in some ways,

Charlie and Audrey envy each other. Charlie looks at Audrey's life, its domestic arc, and wonders if she'll be capable of having that, given how much the interstellar combat with space bugs has damaged her mental health, the PTSD it's left her with. On the other side, Audrey is happy to have raised a family, but wonders what her life would be like if she was still young and ambitious and doing something noble and selfless. Domestic life is not all it's cracked up to be.

During the fifth return, Charlie and Audrey can't find any common ground, and begin to fight, taking petty snipes at one another. By this point, they're fifteen years apart in age. The argument escalates—their resentments revealing themselves—until Audrey finally apologizes. She's just been diagnosed with breast cancer. It's treatable, but it's scary. Stunned, and terrified for her friend, Charlie says she will quit the Intergalactic Combat Force to take care of her. Audrey assures her that it's not necessary, that her best friend has more important things to do, out there in space. They embrace, knowing it may be the last time they ever see each other. It is.

"So are Vietnamese people supposed to be represented by Charlie or by Audrey?" Ursula asked.

Finally, Alvin had an answer. "I'm pretty sure it's Charlie."

"What makes you say that?"

"Charlie is in a state of arrested development, watching the people from her former life grow and have experiences and mature. And then she comes back and witnesses just how much is changing without her," Alvin said, suddenly impressed with his own explanation. "Also, Charlie was a derogatory term for Vietnamese people."

"Really? It's not"—Ursula lowered her voice to a whisper—"'chink'?"

"'Charlie' is what American soldiers said when they wanted to refer to the Vietcong."

"Right, I knew that."

"Clearly, you've never watched a single war movie set in Vietnam," Alvin said. And because Ursula was on her back foot for once, he couldn't help himself: "Guess you're too busy watching—"

"We do *not* have to bring that up again," Ursula shrieked, playfully jabbing her brother in the rib.

Right after they ordered their third round of drinks, Ursula's phone buzzed. She looked at it, concerned.

"It's Jen. We'll be here for a little while longer, right?"

Soon after, Jen materialized behind them, waved down the bartender, and asked if it would be okay to drag another barstool over so she could sit with her cousins. The bartender seemed confused as to why she was asking. It was a bar, you could do whatever you want, people were drunk here, what did you want to drink? Jen secured a seat for herself.

"Did you guys like Tom's play?" she asked. She'd ordered a beer, though it seemed like she'd only gotten it out of etiquette and appeared largely uninterested in drinking.

"I did," Alvin said.

"I was lukewarm on it," Ursula said, maybe too honest. "Alvin and I have been talking about it for the past hour or so. We just don't really understand what it says about"—and here Ursula wanted to tiptoe, to choose the right wording, so as to not offend Jen—"the experience of camp. You know?"

Jen was taking polite sips of her beer and nodding.

"It was gripping to see that experience in a story that was so removed from what actually happened," Jen said. "It felt true."

At first, Alvin had expected her to argue more forcefully with Ursula. That was their old dynamic, one of constantly butting heads. But Jen was different since she returned from camp. Quieter, more pensive. There were moments when she seemed to drift off, like she was being haunted. Maybe she was just grieving the loss of her brother. Sometimes, Jen just appeared aloof.

But she was onto something. After being ignorant of his family history for so long, Alvin had done the work and tried to learn as much of it as possible. Yet he felt a remove, a distance from what anyone had actually gone through. The books provided an exhaustive record, and yet, for all their thickness, they didn't bring Alvin any closer to understanding the people he was closest to. Even Ursula's reporting, borne out of Jen's experiences, read as cold and remote. Alvin didn't recognize what Jen felt in anything Ursula had written. He still couldn't fathom the behavior of his father. Nothing explained why his cousin was missing from their lives.

If what Jen said about a felt truth, as opposed to a factual truth, had made Alvin more reflective, Ursula's response was immediately defensive. Journalism was about an objective reality, she explained, somewhat patronizingly. Alvin sat back and watched the conversation between them rapidly devolve into something more personal, more petty. Jen was activated now, ready to argue back. Maybe things hadn't changed that much after all. Still, the three years had turned Ursula from a nobody into an extraordinarily successful somebody. Earlier that evening, she'd told Alvin that she was now negotiating a big offer from *The New York Times*. He was proud of her.

Jen had remained mostly herself, even if she quickly lost the thread of a conversation. But the thing that had always set her off was Ursula's unwavering confidence. That still, without fail, inspired Jen to try to undercut her cousin's cloying sense of self-importance.

It was like watching act V of *Charlie in Space* again. Except, unlike in Tom's play, there was no turn, no resolution. They just kept going.

Alvin just leaned over on his barstool. Sometimes, on nights when he wasn't feeling great, he'd pull up his old text messages with Duncan, the record of his communications with his lost half brother, and smile. Not everything had broken.

WHO WILL SURVIVE IN AMERICA?
WHO WILL SURVIVE IN AMERICA?
WHO WILL SURVIVE IN AMERICA?
WHO WILL SURVIVE IN AMERICA?
WHO WILL SURVIVE IN AMERICA?
WHO WILL SURVIVE IN AMERICA?
WHO WILL SURVIVE IN AMERICA?
WHO WILL SURVIVE IN AMERICA?
WHO WILL SURVIVE IN AMERICA?

HUMAN INTEREST

—

Everyone was writing about the same thing: the American Advanced Protections Initiative had separated Vietnamese fathers from their families, and now that detention was over, they were being reunited for the first time in three years.

Ursula understood why. It was perfect stuff for nightly news programs—a setup, obvious characters, with the promise of a big cathartic moment. To Ursula, local TV segments were not all that different from watching daytime talk shows. The journalism was always dumbed down, the volume turned up.

That said, Ursula understood why Rosco was asking for the reunification story. Tens of thousands of fathers, locked up separately, put in even worse conditions than the other detention camps and interrogated day in and day out, were finally free. She'd watched a few of these stories on YouTube. The clips were unavoidable.

"It's like you always say," Ursula said, trying to stave off the assignment, "this is a thing that's happening, not a story."

"You're going to throw my advice for college undergrads back in my face?" Rosco said. "We're looking at a couple afternoons of reporting and an easy traffic win—your name at the top of the pageview leaderboard."

Rosco was right. Something was up. It was time for Ursula to tell Rosco that she'd gotten an offer from *The New York Times*. And *The Atlantic*. Also pretty far along at *The Washington Post,* and would likely get that job, too. She was leaving.

But before she could say anything, he preempted her.

"So, you got that job, I imagine?"

How did he know?

"Dara mentioned she'd put you up for it," Rosco said. "And I was happy to put in a good word with some other friends I have there, not that you needed it."

Ursula didn't know what to say, so she apologized.

"I'm sorry, I should've told you."

"No, you shouldn't have. That's not how jobs work." Rosco extended a hand to her. "Congratulations, Ursula. I'm proud of you."

ONCE ALL THE PAPERWORK was signed, Ursula felt compelled to celebrate. There was the new job, and also the upcoming book, which she was rushing to finish. Who would want to get a drink?

Also, she needed a break from Jen, whose moods were strange and unpredictable. Alvin seemed to talk only about the incredibly long history books he was reading these days. As soon as she'd put in notice, Rosco started texting her about hanging out, but he'd also made several references to how he and his girlfriend of three years were probably finished. Ursula didn't know how to navigate that. There was the handful of other journalists who Ursula knew—her peers—who always wanted to drink. But she could never escape the feeling that they were angling for their career, and now people were going to be extra nice to her, since she'd made it to *The New York Times*.

It suddenly depressed Ursula. If you couldn't figure out who to drink with in this city, did you really have friends?

Then, from nowhere, a text from Susie.

heard you on NPR. how've you been, you gorgeous bitch?

URSULA HADN'T HUNG out with Susie in years, but drinking with her felt like old times.

"What was Terry Gross like?" Susie asked.

"Oh, I didn't really get to meet her," Ursula explained.

With many radio interviews, you were invited to a satellite recording studio. An engineer would set you up with a mic and headphones, and a remote producer on the other end would cue you up. Then you'd get put on with a host, like Terry Gross, and the interview would be over faster than you realized. And then you were shuttled out of the studio with little fanfare. You could talk to someone for radio and never meet them.

"That's disappointing," Susie said.

"You know, it *was* a little disappointing."

Susie offered her wineglass up, and Ursula clinked it.

Susie's life had changed significantly. The priorities of her academic field, Asian American Studies, had changed quickly after AAPI had passed. The ivory tower was supposed to be shielded from the whims of current politics, and yet, it also became strangely reactive to what was happening outside the campus.

"There was suddenly a lot of interest in really mediocre Vietnamese PhDs," she said. Then, realizing that might be too frank, she followed up with "Sorry."

Ursula told her not to worry about it. No offense taken.

So Susie bailed. Now she was working in marketing for a bank, which was a job that paid well and used zero of Susie's intelligence or creativity.

"I feel guilty about it because, honestly, I am so much happier than I was before." Even her therapist had noticed, she said.

"Isn't she paid to notice?"

Maybe it was the third or fourth glass of Lambrusco—or the fact that Ursula was often around other journalists, who she was constantly competing with and feeling judged by—but she felt like she could be honest with Susie.

And it all came out: Ursula's kindness toward Jen, letting her live at the apartment, spending all this energy and social capital trying to get her cousin set up with a job, a project, a life of any kind. And all it seemed to do was create resentment.

"I get that she's, like, *traumatized* or whatever," Ursula said. "But would it kill her to say 'thank you' once?"

Susie was understanding but saw Jen's side. "She was in camp for three years. I imagine acclimatizing to real life must be daunting."

"I know, I know, I'm just being a bitch."

"I don't think you're being a bitch—"

"No, I am. It's okay. I understand what Jen is going through, and I recognize, rationally, that all of this must be intense and difficult and embarrassing for her. I'm sympathetic, I really am. It's just that some days I want someone to see that this is also hard for me. I'm doing as much as I can, you know?"

Susie put a hand on Ursula's shoulder. A comfort.

"You know what the shittiest feeling is? It's that I can't even tell if I am doing all these things for Jen because I actually care. Like, I love my cousin a lot. She means the world to me. But am I helping her because I'm a good person, or because I just feel tremendous guilt?"

Like a dependable friend, Susie leapt into action, telling Ursula, no, she was a good person, that she shouldn't blame herself that a million Vietnamese people were detained by racist, unconstitutional policy, to remember that she had spent that time doing brave and impressive work trying to undo that damage through her reporting, that at every step of the way, Ursula had done her best.

THE PERPETRATORS

—

The initial six attacks were coordinated, the seventh was cruel: the explosion at Rockefeller Center on Christmas. The seventy people killed, and the additional forty who were injured, was a higher number of casualties than the six airport bombings combined. The lingering image of the tree falling, recorded and replayed endlessly for the next month.

The captured perpetrator, Calvin Le, claimed the target was chosen for its symbolism—that it stood for capitalism, a holiday that signified consumerism. Of course, no one accepted this as a realistic motive. To be moved to such violence over Christmas? Absurd.

Violence demands an explanation, and it usually comes in the form of one of several answers: anger, greed, stupidity. Years later, though, we now know who the perpetrators were. We know how they planned it, recognize the ruthless efficiency with which they executed it, and now we reckon with the legacy that it wrought: America's overreaction, and how it, for the umpteenth time in the country's nearly two-and-a-half-century history, was a national loss of innocence.

But even with the full resources of the government—its bodies of surveillance, legal maneuvering, abuse—we are still no closer to understanding why seven middle-aged Vietnamese men committed the worst domestic terrorist attacks to ever happen on U.S. soil. We know that they were heavily influenced by forms of misinformation. We know they were active on forums and Facebook. We know they were confused but organized. But we still don't know: *Why?*

That was the question that had pushed the country into one of its darkest moments. In the absence of real information, conspiracy theories bloomed, went viral, infected anyone who wanted to believe in something. That encouraged brutality against all Asian Americans, and, of course, the detention of nearly every Vietnamese American, which I believe will be remembered as one of the great shames of our nation, a violation of the Constitution that is so flagrant that we may never rid ourselves of its stench.

At this point, I don't believe we will ever understand the motives of those seven awful men. I also think that is no longer the point, nor is it a pursuit we should even bother with. I once thought that, in the face of needless cruelty, the bravest thing you could do was ask questions, do the audacious thing, turn to your persecutor and ask them point blank: *Why?*

But I don't feel that way anymore. From years of reporting on Vietnamese detention, I now understand that *Why?* was the question we used to justify detention, because we knew no answer would be satisfactory. In my study of this short but tragic time in American history, I've revised the notion I set out with. Violence doesn't demand an explanation. No, violence just creates excuses for itself.

THE COMPLETE KNOCK
—

IT WAS UNCLEAR TO THE FAMILY HOW MUCH URSULA HAD GOTTEN FOR her book advance, which was odd, considering how often the family talked openly about money—as a matter of transparency, but also, pride. Everyone assumed it was a lot. It must have been, since Ursula was being so generous.

She sent money to Jen's mom, enough for her to get out of the housing that the church had provided, even though, as far as Jen knew, her mother was happy with her arrangements.

Ursula vowed to get her cousin set up with opportunities to meet people, talk about jobs. If Jen wasn't going back to NYU, she would have to do something.

Even after leaving camp, Jen still wore her flash drive around her neck. She'd gotten used to it—the feeling of a piece of chunky plastic resting against her chest. She clutched it in moments when she felt anxious or overwhelmed, when it seemed like people were staring her down on the subway. She worried sometimes about how tightly she gripped it, about how the sweat of her palms would corrode the memory stick, about how all of her lingering fears could erase everything she'd saved.

JEN STARTED SLOW. The first person she looked up was not a detainee but Hugo Perez. The search took an afternoon because there were so many Hugo Perezes on Facebook, but eventually she found him. He still worked for DHS, though it was unclear in what capacity. Despite his employment by an oppressive institution, she wished him well and hoped he was okay. Hugo accepted her friend request immediately.

Next, she looked up the people who'd lived in her bunk. But a great challenge of tracking down Vietnamese people was that many of them shared the same name. Often it was one of four popular surnames, plus extremely popular Anglo first names. Mike Le. Alice Tran. Andrew Pham. Kevin Nguyen. It was even harder now, because Jen couldn't even filter by where they lived, or what they were doing. She had no idea who they were in real life.

URSULA HAD SET Jen up with publisher meetings. Well, Ursula's agent had. There was some early interest in Jen's writing from camp. In her mind, she imagined a book that collected all the issues of *Korematsu*, "a chronicle of culture and resilience from Camp Tacoma," as she phrased it.

Editors seemed interested. But they all had the same issue with the project: that Jen's book idea circled around the idea of joy in camp, when the real story—to them—was the savage reality of it.

Jen defended her idea. Camp was cruel, yes. She should know, she'd lost her brother there. She'd suffered. But to only show those horrors was to dehumanize Vietnamese people. To illustrate only the misery was to ignore the rich textures of their lives, that even in austere conditions, this was a population that survived by adapting and creating meaningful and fulfilling days. Each morning was the same as the last, and yet the detainees who Jen was around kept trying to make the best of it. After all, what was survival if not trying to make the best of every minute, every hour, every day?

One editor showed enough interest to meet with Jen. She was an older editor whose parents had been interned at Manzanar.

"I have to ask, why did you name it *Korematsu?*"

She felt stupid—she'd been unable to learn the Japanese history behind the name "Korematsu" while in camp. But in the months since Jen had been out, she'd forgotten to look up the Wikipedia entry for it. The name was, and had always been, an abstraction to her.

"Oh, I didn't name it *Korematsu*," Jen replied, scrambling. "Allegra did."

The editor asked who Allegra was.

Later, she would get a polite rejection from that editor, forwarded on by email from Ursula's agent. It was kinder and more thoughtful than the other feedback she'd gotten, but it was still a no.

JEN DID FIND BRANDON, though. After her friend request had been accepted, they messaged a little. It appeared that he was doing well. He was finishing up school at Northwestern, engineering. Google had set up a special program where it would hire former Vietnamese detainees, and he had been selected for a class of pitied recruits. Jen teased him about it, that he might be better off after camp than before, and he stopped responding.

Jen internet-stalked Brandon like an ex, even though he technically wasn't one. He was posting a lot—photos of friends, of food, of his life returning to a blissful normalcy. She was happy for him. Happy for his social college days in Evanston. Happy for the way he was able to project all of it. Happy that her friend could be successful and fulfilled and seemingly okay. She just wasn't sure she believed it.

URSULA WAS DETERMINED not to give up on Jen, which only made it more difficult for Jen to acknowledge that things weren't working for her, that she couldn't find her footing. She threatened to leave New York, and Ursula promised it would get better. She would keep paying Jen's rent.

Jen's next project was collecting the photos that she'd taken in camp. She had a flash drive full of them. It would be the most honest look into camp yet. Surely, someone would want these pictures. (Always more meetings.) A few galleries got in touch. Jen would sit down with curators, bringing samples of her work. They seemed largely unimpressed. Sometimes they were frank and critiqued the composition of photos. Others wondered why Jen's work was so sunny.

"Sunny?"

"Detention was hard, no?"

"Of course."

"Then why don't I see that in these pictures? Where is the real struggle?"

ALLEGRA WAS NOT a very common name among Vietnamese Americans, or at least the ones on Facebook. Jen scrolled through a couple profiles, but both were clearly not the Allegra she knew from camp. In her heart, Jen knew Allegra was too cool to have ever been on Facebook.

Jen expanded her search—other social media platforms, even LinkedIn—and turned up nothing. Several late nights and still no dice. Her imagination told her that Allegra was fine, she was living a good life, somewhere far enough away that she didn't have to deal with any of this bullshit.

THE EARLY REVIEWS of Ursula's book were glowing. She had a spate of media appearances: TV, radio, podcasts. But the thing Ursula was most nervous for was her TED Talk. It was a big one, hosted at Lincoln Center. Jen had helped her prepare, hours of listening to a presentation that, on the whole, had bored her—she had lived it after all—but that she knew others would eat up.

Backstage, Jen sat with Ursula while she was getting ready. The stylist didn't do much in the way of makeup, but spent most of her energy with Ursula's hair, making it big. There was a lot of hair spray, and Jen caught whiffs of it in her mouth. Eventually, a technician came in to affix a microphone to the side of Ursula's face—one of those skin-colored mics that keeps the speaker's hands free.

Finally, Ursula took the stage. Rapturous applause, as she deserved. Jen watched from behind a curtain offstage, wishing her cousin all the best. And she meant it. This was Ursula's moment, and Jen couldn't have been more proud. She was nailing every beat, and, looking at the crowd, Jen could tell that the presentation was going over well. Ursula was smart about taking pauses to let the audience clap, to allow her deeper condemnations of the U.S. and capitalism and racism room to settle in. And then, the close.

"We all lost something because of Vietnamese detention," Ursula said. "America lost its innocence. Families lost loved ones. So many Vietnamese lost their lives."

Jen had heard this all before in practice. But now, Ursula was really delivering.

"I personally lost someone. And I think about him every day."

Wait, this wasn't on script. What was she tal—

"He was the best person I ever knew. So truly kindhearted, and I have to live with the fact that the racist legacy of America has taken away someone I truly loved."

You've got to be kidding.

"My brother Duncan. He died in Camp Tacoma. And no matter how much we learn, how much we try to rectify the mistake of Vietnamese detention, nothing will bring him back."

Jen screamed. But no one could hear her, not over the applause.

ACCORD

—

It was supposed to be Ursula's night, and somehow, Jen was making it all about herself.

Everyone had shown up. Friends had come out of the woodwork. A surprising number of her new colleagues from the *Times* were there, Rosco and a few others from her old job had made it, even her old boss Amelia on the Entertainment side of Top Story popped by to congratulate her. Plenty of family had shown up, too, enough that it didn't even bother Ursula that it was fewer than had come out for Tom's weird play. Book events were not as exciting as plays, even if they were off-Broadway. Ursula understood.

It took a surprising amount of time for Ursula to finish her book signing, but when she entered the bar, she was met with applause. All of the most important people in her life, personally and professionally, were here.

Everyone was cheering. Everyone except Jen. Because Jen didn't have congratulations. She had news.

She was doing that annoying thing where she hung out in the corner and didn't talk to anyone, aside from some small chitchat with Alvin. Her brother seemed to be socializing, and Ursula appreciated that he was checking in on their cousin every once in a while.

"Does she seem okay?" Ursula asked.

Alvin shrugged and inquired if Susie was single. The party was a collision of worlds.

"She's wearing an engagement ring," Ursula said, never underestimating how dense her kid brother could be on some days.

"I had to ask," Alvin said, convinced that he did.

Tracy from Vietnamese lessons had shown up, even though Ursula hadn't talked to her in years. They'd kept in touch ambiently by liking one another's posts on Instagram, and occasionally messaging. She was excited to introduce her to Susie.

Out of the corner of her eye, she could see her old roommate Genevieve chatting with Dara, and she made a mental note to say hi later—it'd been too long.

And then Ursula got to introduce her mother to Rosco.

"Pam, this is Rosco, my old boss at Top Story News."

"Are you excited to have my daughter out of your hair?" Pam asked.

"We're always sad to lose a generational talent like Urs," Rosco said, ever the charmer. "But I won't miss all the late-night emails."

Pam laughed a little too hard. Ursula rolled her eyes. No one else knew, but since she'd left her old job at Top Story, she and Rosco had started seeing each other. It wasn't very serious—nor could it be, with the optics of it—but it was the most consistent sex she'd had since college. And Rosco getting along with Pam seemed to be a good sign.

She could unpack all those feelings later, after she was done celebrating. *The Viets* represented a culmination of all her hard work: the long hours, the social life put on hold for the sake of reporting. She'd put her heart and soul into this book, and she knew it had been worth it once she held the hardcover in her hands.

"OKAY, WHAT'S UP? Why are you moping in the corner?"

Jen was immediately defensive. Of course she was. Nobody likes being accused of being a party pooper.

"I have something to tell you," Jen said. "And you're not going to like it."

That's rich, Ursula thought to herself, as if there was anything to like about Jen's attitude as of late. Their relationship had gotten significantly worse after Ursula's TED Talk, when Jen had reamed her out for what she'd said about Duncan. She'd disagreed with the use of her dead brother as some kind of prop, as a gross way for Ursula to up her credibility as someone who understood the pain of Vietnamese detention. Ursula had, in the moment, objected to these accusations. For one, she didn't need credibility. Three years of investigative reporting about camp gave her the authority to talk about detention. Jen asked where all her stories came from, and that really set Ursula off.

That night they had fought backstage for so long that neither of them was really making coherent arguments by the end. Jen had gone home to their apartment instead of joining the family with Ursula after. Despite them living together, it took two weeks before Jen had uttered a full sentence directed Ursula's way.

A month went by, and Ursula started to wonder if she should apologize. But it was Jen who would say she was sorry first, that even though over a year had passed, she was mourning the loss of Duncan, and that she was, perhaps, taking out that pain on Ursula. In reciprocation, Ursula said she was sorry, too, that she should have asked Jen first if mentioning Duncan was okay.

Things still weren't back to normal, though. Ursula and Jen continued cohabitating, with the remove one would expect from roommates, not cousins, not sisters.

"I'm leaving," Jen announced.

Ursula felt relief, but then felt compelled to feign disappointment. "Oh no, you don't have to move out."

"Really, I should. I can't be here anymore."

"Let me help you look for apartments. I have a broker who can find you a good deal. And he always has the cutest places."

"I don't need your help."

"It's really no trouble."

"I'm not staying in Brooklyn. I'm *leaving*."

At first, Ursula thought she misheard Jen. The bar was loud, rowdy with Ursula's closest friends, here for a good time. But Jen repeated herself, explaining that she was going to buy a car and head somewhere else.

"Where?"

Jen didn't know yet.

"Do you have a plan?"

She did not.

"What are you going to do for work?"

She didn't know.

"Why are you doing this?"

Vaguely, because she felt she had to.

"Okay, then, what kind of car?"

She'd found an old, used compact sedan. A Honda.

"What *kind* of Honda?" Ursula knew she was yelling and couldn't help it.

URSULA SPENT THE NEXT week trying to convince Jen this plan—this idea, really, there was no plan—was foolish. But her cousin remained unmoved. She wouldn't listen to reason.

Hoping someone else might know how to talk sense into her cousin, Ursula called Jen's mother. Aunt Ai appreciated the call. When it became clear she didn't have any answers about Jen's behavior, Ursula just resorted to complaining to a sympathetic ear.

Then a surprise: Ursula's aunt launched into a long story about how she'd been crushing on someone at her church. This was so scandalous for Aunt Ai. The man was married, so nothing could ever happen. But they played tennis together twice a week. And the conversations they had—they felt illicit, exciting. Ai knew this was a little wrong, but she wasn't breaking any actual rules. She joked that this was what she liked about being devout: the church made the rules explicit, which meant you knew how to walk right up to the line without crossing. For how tame the promiscuity was, Ursula found Aunt Ai's recounting of it thrilling.

The conversation eventually worked its way back around to Jen, and Ursula's frustrations with her. Her aunt understood.

"Children reach an age where they realize they're smarter than their parents," Aunt Ai said.

"I think that's the definition of adulthood."

"When that happens, your kids don't suddenly think of you as a person. They can't imagine you as a person with needs or desires," she continued. "They just see you as old."

Ursula agreed on the phone, but she knew she had been guilty of the same thing. Had she ever considered what Pam wanted? What she desired?

"Have you told Jen how you feel?" Ursula asked. It was the kind of follow-up question a journalist would probe with. "Have you asked her if she's able to see you as a person?"

There was a brief silence on the other end. Then a sigh. Then a response, one of total generosity, the kind that could only come from a loving mother who wanted the best for her daughter.

"That's a lot to ask of someone who is still figuring herself out."

MONTHS LATER, LONG after Jen had bought her mysterious car with her remaining money and hit the open road, with a promise to check in every once in a while, Ursula would reflect on how she felt that night. At first, she thought her anger had come from a place of concern, of caring. But when she was really honest with herself, Ursula realized the truth: she was mad that Jen wasn't listening to her.

In that moment, though, Ursula felt out of sorts. After months of supporting her sister, Jen had the audacity to just leave? Had Ursula ever been this furious at another human being? Had Jen ever acted so stupid? Why was Jen doing this to her?

DEATH OF AN AMERICAN HERO

—

The Senator died of brain cancer in August just before the detainees were released, having been diagnosed the winter previous and received intense treatment since. His obituaries hailed him as a Republican war hero, recounting his time as a prisoner during the Vietnam War. Out of respect, I will do the same.

In 1967, on this twenty-third bombing run, The Senator's fighter jet was shot down over Hanoi. After a successful ejection that left him with two broken arms and a shattered leg, he landed in Trúc Bạch Lake, where he was pulled ashore by North Vietnamese soldiers and beaten. The Senator was then taken to Hỏa Lò Prison, a site where French colonists had previously held political prisoners. Americans nicknamed it "the Hanoi Hilton." In Vietnamese, Hỏa Lò translates to "hellhole."

For the first few days, the War Hero Senator (who was not yet a war hero, nor a senator) was interrogated. The soldiers said he wouldn't receive medical attention for his injuries until he surrendered military information. He refused to say anything besides his name, rank, and date of birth.

In his own words, in an account he wrote for *U.S. News & World Report:*

After I had been there about 10 days, a "gook"—which is what we called the North Vietnamese—came in one morning. This man spoke English very well. He asked me how I was, and said, "We have a Frenchman who is here in Hanoi visiting, and would like to take a message back to your family." Being a little naive at the

time—you get smarter as you go along with these people—I figured this wasn't a bad deal at all, if this guy would come to see me
and go back and tell my family that I was alive.

The Frenchman recorded the message and delivered it to his wife. Later,
that video would be broadcast on CBS.

He became the most famous prisoner of war. From those articles, the
North Vietnamese learned that The Senator was the son of an admiral,
which led to him being tortured under the assumption that he might have
tactical information. His name would be released, and publicized, in North
Vietnamese propaganda.

He was held captive for five and a half years. He was beaten and
starved. His weight dropped to 105 pounds, and he attempted suicide
twice. Much of his imprisonment was spent in solitary confinement.

To fend off despair, The Senator imagined stories for himself. "It was
easy to lapse into fantasies," he wrote. "I used to write books and plays in
my mind, but I doubt that any of them would have been above the level of
the cheapest dime novel."

The approval ratings for the American Advanced Protections Initiative
were mixed by the end. But initially, the huge funding increase to the Department of Homeland Security had been popular across both parties.

AAPI had promised two things: to keep America safe, and to create
jobs. History will judge its success on these two dimensions. You could
argue, because there were no other major instances of domestic terrorism, that AAPI prevented another attack on American soil. But would they
have happened anyway? It is hard to measure the success of something
preventative, especially in the case of the Seven Attacks, which even to
this day cannot be explained with any satisfaction.

Though The Senator wouldn't live to see his next election, the early
polling about his chances at another term appeared unlikely. It was less
important to Americans that AAPI, the legislation he'd championed, was
preventing instances of terrorism than that it might stimulate local econo-
mies with new DHS jobs. And, though the early days of Viet detention had

been a boon, those fortunes slowly flattened out, and eventually dipped. Many of the detention sites had become sources of cheap, low-skilled labor, undercutting what remained of manufacturing roles in the U.S.

Through my reporting, I heard many rumors from sources at all levels of the Republican party. More often than not, they had opinions rather than facts. Once you got through the reverence for a fallen American hero, the prevailing sentiment after The Senator's death was relief. The man had accomplished a tremendous amount in his life, but more than anything, he had survived so much.

As one Republican aide put it, "But no one, not even the War Hero Senator, could survive job numbers falling that much."

MAKING GOOD TIME

—

The dealer walked Jen around the Honda Accord. It was in good shape, a nice polish on the car's inoffensive metallic-beige body. There was some wear on the interior seats, but Jen hardly noticed or cared. "It runs like a dream," the dealer said, "especially for having over two hundred thousand miles on it." The important thing was that it was a vehicle that worked—and was in her price range. So Jen forked over what was most of her remaining cash, signed the paperwork, and drove it off the lot that day.

She made her way back to the apartment to pick up her things. There wasn't much, really, just a suitcase of clothes, most of which Ursula had bought her and that she had never worn. Everything fit in the trunk, with plenty of room to spare.

In the weeks leading up to Jen's departure, Ursula took every opportunity to tell her how irresponsible she was being: to leave with no plan, no job, no clear way to live. Ursula was spending more time at her boyfriend's, but when she was around, she was constantly scolding Jen. This was irresponsible, shortsighted. How would she even make money?

"It's not about money," Jen said.

"That's what people say when someone else worries about money for them," Ursula protested.

Finally, in the days before the move, Ursula relented, accepting that there was nothing she could do to sway Jen from leaving. As a last gesture, she said, if Jen ever got in a bind financially, to please call and ask for help. It seemed very clear to Jen that for Ursula it was only ever about the money.

—

JEN USED TO wait in line for meals. She used to wait in line for the bathroom. She used to piss and shit in front of other people. She used to have a curfew. She used to have dreamless sleep. She used to be disconnected from the world. She used to be bored. She used to have nothing. Well, that wasn't totally true. She used to have a brother.

AFTER LOADING THE CAR, Jen went back into the apartment to tidy the kitchen and to wipe things down thoroughly. She wanted to leave things as if she'd never been there.

A sound at the door. Ursula appeared in the kitchen. "Oh good, I thought I missed you," she said. "You don't need to clean."

Jen said she was just making sure things were neat.

"No one in New York cleans up when they move out," Ursula said.

"You just make it someone else's problem?"

"It *is* someone else's problem."

This had been the tenor of their conversations for the past month: a dance of short snipes and eye rolls.

"I didn't come here to argue with you," Ursula said. "Do you want help?"

Jen grabbed a bag of trash and pointed Ursula to a bag of recycling, which they took down to the street together. It was a warm day, rich with the aroma of garbage baking under the summer sun.

She thought the two of them must've looked like an odd pair: Ursula, dressed professionally, Jen like she'd been on her knees scrubbing the floor. Still, on that day, Ursula must've been hot in that blazer, and the breeze felt cool against Jen's oversized Big Dog tee.

"This is the car, huh?" Ursula said, unimpressed by the old Honda.

Jen ignored the comment and popped the trunk to place her last few remaining items. She slammed it shut, a satisfactory thunk, and with that, she was ready to go.

"How long are you going to do this?" Ursula asked.

"I don't know, Urs." She clarified. "I think part of the point is not knowing."

"Just stay safe. And have fun. And promise that you'll come back when you're ready."

Jen didn't promise, but she did accept Ursula's embrace. Her cousin sniffled and squeezed hard. As Jen let go, Ursula placed something in her hand: a credit card.

"For emergencies," she said.

JEN WOULDN'T LIVE anywhere specific. She wouldn't be tied to anything. She wouldn't work. She wouldn't pay taxes. She wouldn't date, wouldn't have a family. She wouldn't do the things she'd been told to do, avoid all the expectations of what people said constituted "living." She wouldn't be doing any of that. But what *would* she do now? Jen would be as unproductive as possible. She would resist. She would slouch. She would drive.

JEN HAD NEVER liked driving. In high school, she was the only one of her friends who wasn't thrilled by the prospect of getting a learner's permit. But she didn't have an option. Má made her take the driving classes and taught her how to parallel park. Jen's mother needed someone else to help lug Duncan to and from football practice.

She let Má know her plans—or, really, her nonplan. Eventually she would roll through Indiana, she just wasn't sure when. Jen expected her mother to try to talk her out of it. But she approved, or at least she didn't put up a fight. She just wanted Jen to call every so often, a reasonable expectation.

"Will you visit your brother?" Má asked.

The question caught Jen off guard. That would mean going back to Camp Tacoma, where he was buried. Jen didn't think she had it in her. Not yet.

"When I think about what your brother did, I have to imagine him doing it out of compassion. He wanted to take care of us. He died trying to protect you." This was the most directly Má had talked about Duncan since. Her voice remained resolute. "And maybe if he'd thought about himself more, he might still be with us."

"You believe that?"

After a moment, Má admitted: "I have to."

Then they were silent.

"You were never a great driver," Má said, "but you'll get better."

Jen thought about how she used to drive: frenzied, hurried, always trying to "make good time." Today, with no destination in mind, she began to drive and for the very first time, free of purpose, she loved the feeling of being behind the wheel. It didn't even matter that leaving New York City meant a crawl of stop-and-go traffic. Jen was unburdened by responsibility. She craved a sense of place, without needing a place to be. Jen decided, arbitrarily, to head south.

After being on the road for a couple hours, Jen's seatbelt started to feel uncomfortable. It was pressing on the flash drive that she'd had from camp, still slung around her neck. Jen had imagined that at some point she would toss the USB drive into the ocean, or burn it in ceremonious fashion, as a means of letting go of everything that had happened at Camp Tacoma. A cathartic final act. A symbol of progress.

Instead, Jen undid the lanyard. She looked around the car and decided the only place for it that made sense was snuggled inside the glove compartment atop the envelope with her title and registration, the only documented proof that anything in this world belonged to her.

THE LAST YEAR

—

When Dan drove away from Alvin's apartment, he felt unsatisfied. He'd gotten what he needed—just a bit of cash, enough for him to go another year, maybe longer if he could stretch it, all collected in a neat envelope that lay on the passenger seat. But as his Land Cruiser exited the city and onto the highway, Dan found himself eyeing the money. He'd spent two years driving this car alone. For the first time, it felt like there was another presence with him.

To survive, you had to be selfish. This was what Dan's mother had told him from a young age. It was what she'd whispered in his ear the night they fled Saigon. It was what she repeated during the long, hot days in the refugee camp. It came up as a refrain throughout his life, a phrase that had guided many of the decisions that Dan had made to this day. There was always the option to leave. And if people judged you for running away, it was because they had the privilege to stay.

Still, something about his last interaction with Alvin was different. As the Land Cruiser had pulled away, when Dan glimpsed his son in the rearview mirror, Alvin had had an expression that could be read as disappointment. That didn't really bother him, though. But as the long road gave Dan time to think about his son's face, a new idea possessed him: that Alvin might have just seen their time together as a chore, an obligation, some annoying responsibility, *work*.

The thought was crushing.

—

DAYS AFTER LEAVING his son in New York, Dan did the unthinkable: he turned himself in. He stashed the Land Cruiser, and the cash—none of which he'd spent yet, except on some gas and a last shot of whiskey—and approached a police station in a small town upstate. As in his most recent interaction with the cops, they wanted nothing to do with him. This simply wasn't their problem. But Dan persisted enough that they could not ignore his request. Send me to camp, Dan said. Send me now.

The police had no choice but to contact Homeland Security.

THOUGH HE'D SPENT very little time with his children, Dan did think about them a lot. Mostly, just how different they were from him. Every time he called, they wanted to tell him how much they were doing. These kids seemed to always be doing something, and aspired to do more.

Dan found these conversations exhausting. How did every single one of his offspring have such a conflicting approach to life to his? Maybe if he'd been around more, they would understand that there were no rewards for the tenacious hard worker. It was all a lie. That living—*truly* living—required the bravery to think about the things that you really wanted, not what others expected of you.

Instead, he stopped calling.

FOR AS MUCH as Dan had read about camp, the circumstances confounded him. He'd expected to be assigned to a detention site with family. When the ODC officer told him where he was going, Dan joked with him that he was bound to have some kids there—you know, because he'd had so many. Not a laugh, not even a smile. Homeland Security did not find him charming.

Perhaps it was because Dan had so many families that they didn't know where to place him. He ended up at Camp Iñupiat. He could tell from the flight, its landing, and the mountains that surrounded him that he had been sent to Alaska. It was a gorgeous place that seemed uninterested in obeying the laws of nature. The sun was either out too much or not enough; the topography looked like it was carved out by a drunk; the trees were lush, the water a rich, glacial hue. It was a kind of paradise that existed outside of any place Dan had ever been.

In his two years of nomadic travel, he'd been to every state in the contiguous U.S. He was finally in Alaska.

THERE WOULD BE only a year left of Vietnamese detention, though he didn't know it yet. Each day felt so long that Dan imagined his incarceration going on forever.

The experience of camp was not as bad as Dan had expected. In many ways, it was better than driving down back roads, trying to avoid detection. He didn't have to be paranoid about what people thought of him. In this place, he felt safer than he had before. How messed up, he thought, trying to get some shut-eye during the months when the sun refused to end.

THE ODC BROUGHT him in frequently for interviews, often enough that the line of questioning followed familiar rhythms. There were the establishing queries—ones to warm Dan up, or just calibrate the lie detector. And after that, the tough ones. An ODC interrogator was always asking about his time in Vietnam, and fleeing it. Whenever Dan described the experience, which he often qualified with the fact that he had barely been old enough to remember anything, the interviewer would ask him how it all made him feel.

Made me feel?

"How would you describe that trauma?"

Dan was reluctant to call anything he'd experienced trauma. And yet the word kept resurfacing, in every interview, which became daily. Dan kept denying he was traumatized by the war and everything that came after. He suspected the ODC was trying to find motive. For someone whose entire life was without, he thought, *Good luck!*

—

EVENTUALLY, CAMP ENDED. It was much sooner than Dan had expected. Released and free, he returned to the life he'd had before. He recovered his old Land Cruiser, which was, remarkably, exactly where he left it, hidden in the back roads, somewhere in upstate New York. The money that Alvin had given him was still there in the glove compartment.

The car, of course, didn't start. He'd need a jump, though Dan always felt if someone ever needed evidence of humankind's compassion and generosity, roll a dead vehicle to the street and wait for someone to come by. Eventually, some wiry teenagers pulled over to help, excited because they'd never jumped a car battery before. To Dan, it was a perfect interaction.

Afterward, in a great mood, he began driving, unsure of where he was headed. There was no destination, and everything ahead of him seemed like a possibility.

Dan's mother was wrong. Survival was not a selfish act. Living was. Behind the wheel of his beloved vehicle, Dan realized that he had already been in that place, and been there a very long time.

To HIS SURPRISE, months after release, Dan got a phone call from one of his daughters. She just wanted to give him a quick update and explain that she was going to live out of her car for a while. She knew that he'd spent the better part of two years doing that, while somehow avoiding Homeland Security. Did he have any tips for her, for how to achieve a nomadic life?

He sure did! And he was touched that she'd thought to ask. They talked for a couple hours on that call, and Dan spilled everything he'd learned. It was about discipline—settling into a daily rhythm, staying frugal, and being diligent about car maintenance. A camping stove was cheap and crucial. You could never have too many blankets. Try to shower once a month, and never forget to turn off the radio before you fall asleep. You didn't need to avoid highways anymore, but surface roads, he found, were always more gratifying. He was excited for her.

She was about to see so much. He hung up prouder than he had been in a long time.

Maybe one day they would be headed the same way. It would be nice to run into her. She told him she was driving south. It wasn't much to go on, but he headed that direction, too.

ACKNOWLEDGMENTS

—

Though this is a work of fiction, I wanted to recognize two nonfiction titles that helped give this book a strong historical footing: *Desert Exile* by Yoshiko Uchida and *Bring the War Home* by Kathleen Belew.

This project would have never become more than a bad draft without the vision and guidance of my agent, Sarah Bowlin, and her willingness to answer all my annoying text messages. I'm grateful to Sun Robinson-Smith and Chris Jackson for their creativity and editorial precision, as well as the rest of the One World team for their remarkable approach to publishing.

Special thanks to early readers Robyn Kanner, Brendan Klinkenberg, Tamiko Nimura, and Corey Sobel.

I'm grateful to my family—even the cousins—and thanks especially to my dad, who put together a helpful oral history of his siblings' experiences growing up in Vietnam.

And to Naomi: I know we're always saying how much we enjoy and appreciate the life we've built together. But sometimes it's fun to put that appreciation in a book, too.

ABOUT THE AUTHOR

—

KEVIN NGUYEN is the author of *New Waves*. He is the features editor at *The Verge* and was previously a senior editor at *GQ*. He lives in Brooklyn.

ABOUT THE TYPE

—

This book was set in Caslon, a typeface first designed in 1722 by William Caslon (1692–1766). Its widespread use by most English printers in the early eighteenth century soon supplanted the Dutch typefaces that had formerly prevailed. The roman is considered a "workhorse" typeface due to its pleasant, open appearance, while the italic is exceedingly decorative.